PENGUIN BOOKS

CHILDREN OF THE SAVAGE CITY

Elizabeth Heider is the author of *May the Wolf Die*, named a *New York Times* Best Crime Novel, a *Washington Post* Best Mystery, and one of *Publishers Weekly*'s best books of the year. Her short fiction has been recognized by the Santa Fe Writers Project and New Century Writer Awards.

She holds a PhD in physics and most recently worked as a program manager for Microsoft's AI4Science and as a scientist in the European Space Agency's human spaceflight program. She's authored original scientific research, a patent, analytical reports for the US government and military, and coauthored a journal article with astronaut Thomas Pesquet. She lived and worked in Naples, Italy, as a civilian analyst embedded with the US Navy's mission in Africa, where she deployed aboard US and European naval ships. Originally from Utah, she now lives in The Hague, where she's working on the next Nikki Serafino novel.

ALSO BY THE AUTHOR

May the Wolf Die

CHILDREN OF THE SAVAGE CITY

ELIZABETH HEIDER

PENGUIN BOOKS

PENGUIN BOOKS
An imprint of Penguin Random House LLC
1745 Broadway, New York, NY 10019
penguinrandomhouse.com

Set in Photina MT Pro
Designed by Sabrina Bowers

LIBRARY OF CONGRESS CONTROL NUMBER: 2025034633
ISBN 9780143138198 (paperback)
ISBN 9780593512333 (ebook)

Printed in the United States of America
1st Printing

The authorized representative in the EU for product safety and compliance is Penguin Random House Ireland, Morrison Chambers, 32 Nassau Street, Dublin D02 YH68, Ireland, https://eu-contact.penguin.ie.

FOR LOFTIN HARVEY,
who shared creative writing, compassion,
and a safe harbor.

CHILDREN OF THE SAVAGE CITY

ONE

The rain was letting up.

The studio door was propped open and, through the gap, Nikki could see the deluge giving way to a mild patter. Wet cobblestones and asphalt glistened, reflecting the flash of headlamps and the red glow of brake lights. She turned back to the room and clapped her hands.

"Alright," she shouted. "Ten minutes to go. Keep it up! Switch sides."

The students were sweating. She was sweating. The ventilation in this place was shit.

Five groups of students were taking turns with yellow plastic prop knives, practicing disarming techniques. One woman had given up and, blonde hair plastered to her face, was sitting on the floor, back against the cinder-block wall, sucking air.

This was the fifth Krav Maga self-defense class Nikki had taught in the city center this fall. The turnout was good tonight—a mix of Americans from the nearby US military base and local kids from the Naples neighborhoods. Most were curious and eager to learn, and Nikki usually enjoyed teaching. But language and cultural differences meant the two groups didn't mingle well and, after two hours, Nikki was worn out from swapping between English and Italian.

Despite the extra effort, these lessons were a welcome distraction. In this classroom, she was in control. She was in her body, nerves and heartbeat and breath—and these students relied on her. She scanned the assorted collection of teenagers and military wives in jeans or gym gear—the slow, awkward movements, the way they spoke the instructions aloud, executed the sequences, the way they fumbled and dropped the plastic weapons. It was unlikely that any one of them would become a martial arts expert. But that wasn't the point, was it? She needed to give them just a little more awareness, a rehearsal of the shock you felt to have someone stick a knife or a gun in your face, and a sense of being able to move, to help yourself if god forbid that moment ever came.

She was preparing to start the cooldown sequence when the door opened fully, letting in the street noises. Two men strode through. They wore puffer jackets, slick with the rain. A damp breeze wafted in as the door shut behind them, breathing diesel fumes and ozone.

"Motherfucker," exclaimed the first man, the word reverberating in the small space.

He was muscular with a thick neck and short haircut. He leaned over to slap the water off his head, spackling the floor.

"Keep going," Nikki shouted to the students, who were slowing, turning to look. She moved to meet the men.

"Can I help you?"

"Buona sera, signora," said the second man. "What a lovely night for . . . what is this? Aerobics?"

He was tall and rangy, with wide, bulging eyes and thick eyebrows. His smile was unpleasant.

"Self-defense. I'd invite you to join but we're nearly finished. We have other classes on the schedule if you'd like to come then. There are flyers by the door."

She spoke the words in an efficient, clipped manner, hoping it would urge them to leave. But something about them told her that this was more than an innocent escape from the rain.

Close to them now, Nikki became keenly aware of the height difference. She was accustomed to being the shortest person in the room, and relied on a muscular physique and confident bearing to make up the difference. But these men were significantly larger than she, and they drew in, looming over her, a challenge in their posture.

Nikki recognized the type from her years as a bouncer: pack animals, puffing their chests, slamming their heads to assert dominance.

"Self-defense?" snorted the muscular one. "Very important. This isn't a safe neighborhood, you know?"

"Indeed," said Nikki, squaring herself to him. "Which is why I need to get back to teaching. The rain has stopped. You should leave now."

The man with the bulging eyes looked over her head and called out to the group. "We're in the same business, you know? Self-protection. How much are you paying for these lessons? Sixty? Seventy? We can protect you all for much less."

His words jarred Nikki, the metallic flavor of adrenaline suddenly in her mouth, pulse accelerating.

"Are you fucking kidding me?"

"Listen," said the muscular man, pressing in closer and adopting a reasonable, brotherly tone. "We only want to help you stay safe. These are dangerous times."

"Fifty euros," said the other one in English, once again to the class. "It's a good price."

Rage surged in Nikki's gut, in her throat, behind her eyes—hot and electric.

"Or what? You'll do something stupid in front of seventeen witnesses, everyone taking pictures? Get the fuck out of my class."

She stared unblinking at them, a sort of mania in her fury that she held back with effort.

The muscular man met her gaze for a few beats, then laughed. "Aren't you adorable? No offense, signora. No offense at all. We're just here to help."

"I don't need your kind of help."

The rangy man began laughing, too. "We'll give you some time to think about it," he said.

They left, and Nikki watched the door swing shut behind them. She fought an instinct to rush forward and turn the bolt; it would only signal fear to those assholes.

Slowly, she turned back to the class.

"Good work," she said. "Let's cool down and do some stretching."

Afterwards, as the students left by twos and threes, Nikki gathered her gear, shoved it in a duffel bag, and swung this across her body. She was drained, and ready for bed.

The past few months had been unexpectedly difficult—and Nikki often felt as if she were wading knee-deep through sludge. She prided herself on her resilience, an ability to pick herself up off the mat and come back swinging. But the events this past summer had cost her more than she wanted to admit. She hated the vulnerability, the sense of weakness in body and mind. She wanted something solid to slam with her fists. But there were only shadows, rumors in the dark. She moved ever onward to the next thing, and the next, but couldn't shake the sense that some terror was breathing down her neck, scraping at her heels. She steadfastly refused to give it attention, yet this only seemed to intensify the dread.

She checked the toilet, switched off the lights, locked the door to the storefront studio, pulled down the graffiti-tagged metal grate, and locked that, too. Rent for this place was inexpensive—an arrangement made through a friend of a friend. It had seemed like a good deal at the time, and she liked that it was accessible to the metro so that her students could come from across the city. She'd spent a few evenings tidying it up, scrubbing away some of the grime, and getting a plumber in so that the toilet flushed properly. But Nikki didn't know the neighborhood well. More important, she didn't know the neighbors—so there was nobody to keep an eye out, to whisper in the right ears that she was one of them, someone who could slide by without excuse or toll. Being an outsider put her and her students at risk, and she didn't like it.

She didn't know exactly what had prompted this impractical urge to start teaching again. She'd instructed the occasional course on the US military base, but that had been easier—requested by the base commander and readily supported by her supervisor, Angelo. This, by contrast, was her own initiative, and it had been difficult to work out with her schedule and duties as a Phoenix Seven liaison officer. Phoenix Seven was staffed by Italian security investigators and served as an interface between the US military and local law enforcement. They worked on shift schedules, and Angelo had seemed particularly unwilling to accommodate Nikki's new teaching duties.

"Your work should come first," he told her. "What you decide to do on your own time, and how you manage it is *your* responsibility."

He seemed to deliberately plan her shifts during the times she was scheduled to teach. So, she stopped sharing her schedule requests with him. She bartered with the other members of the unit, trading shifts when necessary—more often than not taking the night shifts. She could have predicted Angelo's obstinacy, but watching it play out, maneuvering around it, was exhausting.

The sounds of the city echoed on the stones and storefronts around her, the traffic noises somehow altered and amplified by the clarity of the rain. Rain spattered her face, dripped down her neck.

Nikki was almost to her Honda Hornet when the attack came—a rapid slap of sprinting feet. Before she had time to turn or brace, thick arms lashed suddenly around her from behind, gripping her in a bear hug. His body stank of sweat and cologne, his breath the stale acrid odor of coffee, beer, and cigarettes. He was taller than she, and stronger, and she felt almost like a child, upper arms pinned at her sides. He shook her like a rag doll, lifting her once, twice. Her feet came off the ground. She hammered down a fist, aiming for his groin. Then, gripping his hands with both of hers, secured them away from her chin so he couldn't maneuver her into a headlock. But he was lifting, dragging her backwards and into the shadows of an alleyway.

No way. No fucking way.

She counted, waited until her feet were both on the ground again. Then, tucking her head to her left shoulder, she shoved her right hip out and, with the same motion, raised her right elbow, creating just enough space to pull herself out of his hold. She'd practiced the maneuver plenty of times in training, but this was different. Her attacker was motivated, and gripped harder, swearing and grunting, as she slithered from his grasp. She'd just gotten free when he caught hold of her bag strap and yanked her inward. The sudden impulse jolted her and she raised her elbow as he brought her into him, aimed it for his throat. But he was tall, and the strike glanced off his chest. And now he grabbed her wrist. She was off-balance. Leaning, she struggled to regain her center as she brought her knee up again and again.

Suddenly, without warning, he released her. She didn't wait to find out why. She lashed out hard with elbows and knees, then danced backwards, putting distance between them. To her surprise, he didn't pursue.

Her attacker was frozen, breathing hard, hands raised. He stared at her with bulging eyes, and she recognized him: the rangy man who'd come into the studio tonight. She scanned the street for his companion. He was nowhere to be seen.

For a wild moment, Nikki thought he was surrendering to her. But the truth became evident when she saw the dark shape of a gun pressed to his head, and a low voice growled, "On your knees."

The bulging-eyed man descended slowly to the hard wet stone, and behind him, Nikki saw the man with the gun more clearly.

He was short and compact, with a neatly trimmed beard and arched nose, his lips in the delicate shape of a crooked cupid's bow. He held the Beretta with practiced ease, as if it were merely an extension of him. She had seen him only twice before, but knew him immediately.

"Signor De Rosa."

He didn't respond, only kept his attention, his gun turned on her attacker. He stepped around the man, facing him.

"You've made a poor decision," said De Rosa to the kneeling man. "Do you know who I am?"

The man nodded, but De Rosa said with slow emphasis, "Use your words. Say who I am."

"You're Tito Calandra's man."

"Good boy. And do you know who this is?"

He lifted his chin towards Nikki. The man shook his head.

"You are not to touch her," said De Rosa. "Tell your friends. Tell your friends to tell their friends. Do you understand?"

He nodded again.

"Say you understand," said De Rosa.

"I understand."

De Rosa gestured with his gun. "On your feet, and out of my sight."

And just as rapidly as he had attacked moments ago, the man retreated into the darkness.

Nikki felt numb as the rain came down on her, as De Rosa's eyes fixed on her.

"Did he hurt you?"

"I'm fine."

She wasn't sure if it was true. The adrenaline was draining away, leaving her sick and trembling. She wanted to scream at De Rosa, to tell him to leave her alone, to tell him that she could fight her own battles. But a hollow space had opened inside, and she stood paralyzed, as if any movement would tip her headlong into it.

Benedetto De Rosa was Tito's man, a refined contrast to Calandra's brutal reputation.

"Were you following me?" she demanded.

He stared back for a beat without expression.

"Shall I walk you to your motorcycle?" he said.

It wasn't a question.

Nikki forced her body to move. He kept pace beside her, gun vanishing into his jacket.

At her bike, Nikki shoved her hands into her pockets. They were shaking and she didn't want to fumble the key—not while De Rosa was looking.

"I'd prefer you not follow me," she said.

"I understand," said De Rosa. "There's something I'd like you to see."

She inhaled deeply and looked at him. He took a phone from his pocket, scrolled through the pictures, and held it out. Raindrops beaded on the screen, distorting the image.

"Do you recognize this man?" he asked.

Nikki didn't look at the screen or take the phone as he so clearly intended. If she cooperated, she would be complicit in whatever Tito was up to. Instead, she stared back at De Rosa.

"Who is he?" she asked.

"If you meet him, or learn anything about him during your investigations," said De Rosa, "we would consider it a favor if you tell us."

"By 'us' you mean Tito."

"Yes."

"I don't trade in favors," she said.

He studied her for a beat, then retracted the phone, wiped the rain from the screen with a handkerchief, and pocketed it.

"Not a favor, then," he said. "Consider it . . . a civic duty."

Nikki raised an eyebrow. "You want me to report on a police investigation, and consider this a civic service?"

De Rosa's expression remained unperturbed. "It's unlikely the police understand how dangerous he is. They won't know how to deal with him appropriately. What I'm asking from you . . . to look . . . to let me know . . . it isn't illegal."

Nikki clenched her teeth. She didn't like this burden, this sense of Tito pushing his way into her life. If she agreed to this, if she let him take any portion of her integrity, no matter how small, she risked slipping into his gravity.

She resisted. "No. I can't do that."

He seemed to consider. "You live in a battlefield. Can you really think your ignorance protects you?"

"Whatever it is," Nikki said, "keep me out of it. I don't want to be involved."

He turned and began walking away.

Nikki pulled her key from her pocket. Her hands were still shaking as she put it in the ignition. She took her helmet from the duffel and was about to pull it on when she heard him speak her name.

Benedetto De Rosa had paused in the yellow light of a window.

"You should stop lying to yourself," he said. "You are involved."

TWO

Valerio wished he hadn't worn his good shoes.

It had been pissing rain all afternoon, but as he left work the clouds dissipated and he saw patches of blue. The streets were dry as he walked to his apartment to shower and change. Unfortunately, the pause in the rain had only been the weather god taking a deep breath before a howling tantrum. Valerio was midway across the city when the skies unleashed a biblical flood. Gutters overflowed and cars, maneuvering in the heavy traffic, sluiced walls of water onto pedestrians.

Valerio jogged through the deluge and ducked under the awning of a nearby gelateria, his best shoes ruined. He was joined by three tourists wearing backpacks and sneakers, then a bedraggled woman in heeled boots, and finally, a muttering vagrant hauling his stinking bags.

Valerio opened the dating app and texted an apology for the necessary lateness. Then, while he waited, he scrolled again through the profile. Her name was Maria. Photos showed a lovely face, luminous skin, beautiful eyes with thick lashes, full lips, and long dark hair. He particularly liked one full-body shot displaying a very nice figure in a tightly fitting black dress.

The past few months had been the thirstiest of Valerio's life. He'd always found it easy to attract women—but something had been off since the summer, after the end of his last relationship. He'd met a few women, but some fundamental spark had been missing, and the experiences were forgettable.

Work had kept him busy enough, distracted so he couldn't brood over the lack in his life. He and his partner, Maurizio, had been working an extortion case for the past few weeks, and they were close to making an arrest. But he was tired of eating alone, watching TV alone, going to bed alone.

The dating app had been his daughter Gemma's suggestion. At work, when he brought it up, Maurizio scoffed at the idea.

"Dating apps are a scam," he warned. "There are podcasts about it: Only the top ten percent of men see any action at all—the rich ones and the gym rats."

"I go to the gym," protested Valerio, who had been making a particular effort lately and proud of it.

"You know what I mean," said Maurizio. "The twenty-five-year-old gods."

Valerio conveyed Maurizio's arguments to Gemma. She rolled her eyes.

"It's how everybody does it," she told him with an emphasis bordering on exasperation. "*Everybody!*"

For his profile, he snapped a picture of himself in the bathroom mirror. He also posted a photo aboard his sailboat, *Calypso*, and one at the gym. Then he posted another from his cousin's wedding last year, where he was wearing a suit and looking quite dapper. Within hours, Maria had reached out with a wink emoji.

Her beauty and obvious interest in him did plenty to ease his reservations. After nearly two weeks of increasingly tantalizing texts, he was eager to meet her.

"She's clearly too good for you," Maurizio teased. "Wait and see . . . she's probably a catfish."

By the time Valerio pushed through the glass doors of the restaurant, his slacks were sopping, toes like cold pebbles inside wet shoes. Despite a last-minute purchase of a flimsy umbrella from a street vendor, rain had invaded his jacket and run down the collar of his shirt. The maître handed him a cloth napkin, and Valerio mopped his face and neck as he followed the server back into the space.

Maria had chosen the location, a restaurant called Cigno, in a good neighborhood. This turned out to be far more elegant than the places he'd suggested—local haunts where he could get good pizza and good wine at a good price. The room was dimly lit, the walls black. White-topped tables stood out in individual spotlights—bright flowers on a dark sea. The back wall was uneven slate and hanging plants, with a ceiling-to-floor waterfall. The icy breeze from the waterfall chilled his already wet shirt and he shivered.

But Valerio's tribulations were forgotten as he approached the bar, where a vision of beauty perched, sipping a glass of wine. She wore a pair of high-waisted silk slacks, a blouse in shimmering gold, and a delicate gold chain. She set down her glass and rose to her feet as he came near.

"Valerio?" she said, tilting her head.

"Piacere, bella, a pleasure to meet you in person!"

He leaned in to kiss her cheeks, and his face plunged into the fragrant fall of her hair. She smelled sweet, like candied apples.

"It's my favorite raw vegan place," she told him as they followed the waiter to a table beside the wall of water. "Healthy—and ethically sourced."

The menu was singed into the surfaces of polished wooden boards. Valerio ordered a glass of red, and eagerly perused the list. The prices nearly made him spit, but the cold weather had primed his appetite. He just wanted to eat. Besides, he was proud to be with this stunning woman. The eyes of other men were on them, jealous of his good fortune.

"What do you recommend?" he asked Maria.

"Oh, it's all nice!"

At her encouragement, Valerio ordered the lasagne, and Maria, pesto spaghetti.

He reminded the waiter that he'd forgotten to bring the bread.

"Oh, we don't serve bread," came the reply.

"It's a raw vegan restaurant," Maria gently reminded.

"Bread is vegan," he said.

"But it isn't raw," said the waiter. "Can I perhaps interest you in an appetizer? A house favorite is our zattera di verdure—tartare of shredded radicchio, mango, pine nuts, and paprika served in charming avocado boats."

"That sounds delicious," said Maria.

"Okay," agreed Valerio, who hadn't moved past the disconcerting news that bread wasn't served. His stomach made an uncouth grumble.

"Tell me about yourself," Maria encouraged when the waiter retreated. "You seem like a very successful man. What do you do?"

Valerio shrugged, trying to remember what he'd put in his profile. Certainly nothing about his police career. He worked for the anti-corruption unit, Sezione Falchi Squadra Mobile, and this was something you just didn't advertise.

"I work for the city," he said.

She leaned forward, eyes glimmering with candlelight. "I'd love to hear about it."

He wished he could tell her, impress her with his clever investigations, his stakeouts and strategies, the criminals he'd gotten to confess. But that would have to come later, when he knew her better.

"I do my part," he said. "Some of it's dull. But it can be satisfying."

The wine came, and Valerio was grateful for the familiar flavors, and the heat in his empty belly.

He redirected the conversation to Maria, and was surprised to learn she was younger than the twenty-seven years she'd claimed on her profile.

"I say that to weed out the creeps," she told him. "I'm actually twenty-one."

"That's very young!" he realized.

Gemma had just turned sixteen in October.

She laughed. "I'm legal, if that's what you're worried about!"

His neck flushed with sudden heat. That particular concern hadn't occured to him. He did the math: He was old enough to be her father. The uncomfortable thought lodged like a sliver into his mind.

The appetizers did little to take the edge off Valerio's hunger, and by the time his meal arrived, he was disappointed that the lasagne serving was little larger than a deck of cards. But the real insult came when he took a bite.

"It's cold!" he exclaimed. It tasted awful, too. Where was the crust of cheese, the hot noodles and tomato sauce, the creamy ricotta, the hearty chunks of meat? He wanted to spit it out, scrape it off his tongue. "What is this?"

The waiter hurried back to the table. "Is there a problem, signore?"

"This isn't lasagne. What is it?"

"This is a raw vegan restaurant, signore. The noodles are comprised of thinly sliced zucchini, with a delicate sauce of crushed tomatoes, garlic, and cold-pressed olive oil. The cheese is homemade from cashews . . ."

Valerio struggled to chew and swallow. The gritty white paste masquerading as cheese coated his mouth.

"Cashews?"

"Sì, signore."

He glanced at Maria, who showed signs of embarrassment. He felt suddenly very old and very tired. He didn't belong in a place like this, where people ate air. What he really wanted right now was a big slab of steak, and butter, and a whole loaf of bread to sop up the juices.

"Very well," he said.

He drank wine, ordered another, and did his best to choke down the cold vegetables. What he couldn't eat, he pushed around on his plate. Maria showed every sign of enjoying a pasta made from raw squash and pesto. He led her to talk about her work as a model, and her blossoming career as a social media influencer. She seemed intelligent and engaged, and mature for her age.

"It doesn't bother you that I'm so much older than you?" he asked.

"I've always been attracted to older men," she told him.

Learning how young she was had unsettled him at first. He'd hoped to find a girlfriend closer to his own age—someone who had seen enough of the world to understand him and his work. Now it occurred to Valerio that being with a younger woman might be its own sort of adventure. She was so full of life and enthusiasm. He could introduce her to new experiences and ideas. The idea had a certain appeal.

"This is the first time I've tried internet dating," he confessed when the meal was nearly complete.

Her smile was friendly. "I can tell. You're so sweet."

"How long have you been doing it?" he asked.

"Not long," she said. "My last relationship just ended."

"I'm sorry to hear that."

"Grazie." She reached out, brushed his hand with her fingertips. "But I'm glad I met you. I like you, Valerio."

This warmed him. He took her hand. "I like you, too. Shall we get out of here? Head back to my place?"

Maria nodded and he signaled for the waiter.

He would take a taxi to keep Maria out of the rain. He mentally plotted their route, and thought about the storefront kebab shops he'd passed on his way here. He would ask the driver to stop by one of those, and get a big greasy meat wrap.

Maria said, "My last daddy was such a sweetheart. I've been so lonely since he moved back to Brussels. But you're a sweetheart, too. I can tell."

Some heavy gear clunked in Valerio's mind, and everything ground to a stop.

"Your last daddy?"

She nodded. "If it's okay with you, it's probably best to set the ground rules about this relationship before we move on to the next stage. I'll need twenty-four hundred a month for basic living expenses, and a monthly spending allowance of twelve hundred."

It took a moment for Valerio to process what she was saying, and by then, the waiter had arrived with the bill.

He stared. "You're a prostitute?"

He hadn't meant to speak so loudly. The words just fell out.

"No!" Maria gasped, face flushing.

The waiter set down the bill and hurried away.

Valerio leaned in, and spoke more quietly this time. "Then why are you asking for money?"

Her body was tense, expression taut. For a moment, he thought she would bolt out of the restaurant. But she seemed to make a deliberate effort to calm herself. She breathed deeply, gave a Mona Lisa smile, and leaned forward.

"Every relationship is a transaction," she said. "I just prefer to keep my relationships well defined. I prefer dating mature men. They're more practical about this, they appreciate what I can offer, and they can afford to keep me happy. If you keep me happy, I'll keep you very happy."

"You've done this before?"

"Like I said, my last relationship just ended. He was a NATO officer and he's moved back to Brussels."

Valerio took out his wallet, placed on the table every euro he had with him. It was barely enough to cover the bill.

"You're a very beautiful woman," he told Maria. "But you're also young—and this is a dangerous game you're playing. The men who do this . . . they may think you owe them more than you want to offer. You could get hurt."

Now she really did get angry. Patches of red rose in her cheeks. She stood, and spoke in a clipped tone.

"You don't know the first thing about me. I'm not some naive, stupid girl. I don't need your lectures."

Valerio watched as she strode away, smelling the last tones of her sweet perfume. His phone rang.

It was his mother.

He picked up. "Ciao, Mamma."

His words were answered by a panicked wail.

Valerio stood from the table and strode to the restaurant entrance. Through the glass doors, the rain came down in sheets.

"Mamma," he begged. "Please, Mamma! Talk to me! What's happened?"

The screaming stopped, and Valerio listened to his mother's labored breathing, then a grunting sob.

"So terrible," she moaned. "So much blood!"

"Where are you?" he shouted. "Tell me where you are!"

Without thinking, without waiting to shrug his jacket across his shoulders, he pushed through the glass doors and stepped into the street. Rain battered Valerio's body, and poured in icy rivulets down his shirt as he ran.

THREE

The crowd clustered like ants under the protection of the elaborate Baroque entryway of the massive cathedral.

Only one person stood in the piazza.

Arms outstretched, Leonora Alfieri looked like a statue of the Madonna—palms up to receive the rain. It was only as Valerio drew closer to his mother that he saw the reason: She was trying to wash the blood from her hands.

"Mamma, are you hurt?" he called, words drowned in the storm.

She stared, blinking, seeming not to recognize him. The hood of her clear plastic rain shield had fallen back, and her hair was slicked to her head. Valerio took her hands and turned them over, searching for injury. To his relief, the blood didn't seem to be hers.

Wrapping an arm around her waist, he ushered her up the stairs and into the shelter.

He held his badge to the small crowd as he approached, and they parted to make way.

"What's happened here?" he demanded.

Voices overlapped, everyone speaking at once.

"Silence!" Valerio shouted.

He pointed at a short, heavyset man in an expensive-looking rain jacket. "You!"

The man answered, "There's a woman dead."

"Dead? Are you sure she's dead?"

"Murdered!" came a cry from the back. "Poor girl was stabbed to death."

"Did you see the attack?"

"No—but it happened right there. In front of everyone . . . and during mass. She's dead!"

This voice was joined by others, a cacophony amplified by the stone.

"Quiet!" bellowed Valerio.

If there was a chance the victim was still alive, he needed to get to her quickly.

"Is the attacker still inside?" he asked.

When nobody had a clear response, Valerio suspected the answer was no. Comfortable voyeurism was only possible when the threat was gone. But he didn't want to take chances.

Beside him, Leonora was pale and shivering, eyes squeezed shut.

"Fuck," he muttered. He couldn't wait any longer to make a decision. He pulled his mother close, and rubbed her shoulder. "Come, Mamma. Let's get you warm."

To the crowd he yelled: "You're witnesses. Don't leave until you give police statements. Do you understand?"

Then he pushed through them, and pulled his mother into the church.

The voices suddenly faded as the heavy wooden door shut behind them.

Out of habit, and because his mother was with him, Valerio crossed himself.

Valerio knew Chiesa del Gesù Nuovo just as he knew every church, chapel, and shrine in the city. In childhood, he'd spent minutes . . . hours . . . days in such places. Leonora visited God with the same regularity that other people visited shops or the neighbors. If a walk through the city took them past a church, she would stop and pray. She treated it like fueling the tank: necessary, and any station would do. Her personal conversations with Mary were desperately embarrassing to the young Valerio.

"I'm sorry to bother you again, Signora," she would say, as if asking to borrow some milk, or an egg. "But Orlanda has been sick with fever and won't keep food down! I've tried everything. Salt! You're right—I should try salt. And I'm ashamed to tell you that Valerio is getting into fights at school. What can I do with such a son? I'm only one woman . . . and a widow. You know I don't blame you for that—but I need special help, you understand."

Of all the cathedrals in the city, the colossal and ornate structure of Chiesa del Gesù Nuovo had always overwhelmed Valerio. Something about the scale, the elaborate decorations, gave him a sense of an alien, impersonal god. Never more so than now, as he and his mother stood dripping onto the intricate inlaid marble floors. Dozens of Corinthian columns in pink marble and alabaster stretched into arches high above, where detailed murals and sculptures gave the impression of gold extending into the domed roof. Far ahead, nearly the distance of a football pitch, was the apse, where an enormous statue of the immaculate Madonna stood on a blue lapis globe, surrounded by a collection of fat marble cherubs.

"Buona sera," Valerio called, his voice swallowed by the cavernous space.

He had hoped to find someone here—a priest, perhaps. But they seemed to be alone. He considered what to do next. He turned to his mother and was about to speak when she shook him off.

"How could you let this happen?" she said in a harsh whisper. "In your house!"

At first, Valerio thought she was talking to him, but her attention was on the altar. She moved towards it unsteadily, like a sleepwalker—slow at first, then with more surety.

"Are we not in your arms? How could you allow this?" She gestured, taking in the whole building, then reached towards the Madonna—a plea and a rebuke.

She shouted, "Are you there? Do you hear me?"

From across the nave, a steely-haired priest hurried towards them, footsteps clipping on the polished floor.

"Signora, please! The church is closed."

Valerio jogged to intercept.

"Padre," he said, holding up his wallet and identification. "I'm Capo Valerio Alfieri."

The man paused, posture suddenly rigid. Only then did Valerio notice the blood on the white of his robes.

"You're with the police—for the dead woman."

"You're sure she's dead?" Valerio asked.

The priest nodded.

"Did you call one-one-two?"

"Sì."

"Good. I need you to show me the body. And my mother's in shock. Is there someplace warm she can rest?"

They followed the priest clockwise through the dimly lit church, the stone floor hard and radiantly cold beneath them. They passed rows of empty wooden pews, the confessional boxes carved of dark wood, and the shadowed recesses of the side chapels. At the third chapel, the priest stopped and pointed.

"The sacristy is through those doors. It's warmer there."

It was then Valerio saw the bloody footprints. Everywhere. An overlapping, chaotic mess on the inlaid marble.

"Please take my mother," he told the priest.

Using the light from his phone to examine the floor, he carefully stepped outside the range of bloody footprints and scuffs, and followed them to their inevitable, terrible destination.

The body was at the far end of the church—in the Chapel of the Crucifix, the area lit by a bank of electric candles.

She was young. Not much older than Valerio's daughter, Gemma. Early twenties, perhaps, like Maria at the restaurant. Her clothing was soaked, spattered, and smeared in crimson. Blood pooled around her, dark and glistening. A cloying, metallic smell hung in the air. Her pale brown skin was unblemished, and her cheeks were full. Her mouth was open, as if in a last gasp of surprise. Blood on her eyelids indicated that someone had closed them posthumously. Similarly, her posture had clearly been arranged—hands folded across her chest. Her clothes were stylish and tidy: jeans, boots, and a powder-blue puffer jacket, unzipped to reveal a soft grey sweater. Feathers, burst from slashes in the jacket, had settled onto everything.

A priest in a black suit knelt at a nearby chapel pew, hands clasped around the rosary, eyes shut.

"Padre," said Valerio, "I'm with the police."

The man opened his eyes and stood. Valerio stopped him with a shout.

"Please stay where you are!"

The priest nodded, and slowly sat.

"Did you see what happened?" Valerio asked.

He bowed his head. "I was too late to give her last rites."

"Can you tell me what you saw?"

"I was in the sacristy—I heard screaming. Three women were with her. I think they were trying to help . . . but she was already gone."

"Did you see anyone else?"

He shook his head.

From far away came the sound of sirens—muted at first, then suddenly loud as the cathedral doors slammed open. The noise of pounding footsteps and shouts was a relief.

He shouted, "Back here!" and ran to join them.

Uniformed policemen had entered the cathedral, along with two ambulance soccorritori and Sonia Dieng, a plainclothes detective from the homicide unit. Valerio hadn't expected Homicide to respond so quickly—but was glad she was here. He greeted her, ready to transfer the burden to competent shoulders.

"What do we have?" she asked.

They walked and talked.

"Female. Early twenties. Stab wounds in the chest and abdomen."

"Witnesses?" Sonia asked.

"There's a priest with the body. He says there were three women with her when she died. One of them was likely my mother."

Sonia paused, turning to face him. "Your mother? Is she alright?"

"I don't know," Valerio said honestly.

"What did she say happened?"

"We haven't spoken. She's in the sacristy."

Sonia nodded and they started walking again.

"Take the medics and check on her," she said. "I'll join in a few minutes."

Valerio was wringing wet and numb as he opened the door to the sacristy, warmth leeched from his body. It was a surprisingly spartan space—with plain wooden cupboards and frosted 1970s glasswork.

Leading the ambulance workers, Valerio followed bloody footprints and drips to a door on the far end, where he knocked and, not waiting for a response, entered.

This room was small, informal, warm—a rug on the floor, and an ancient space heater, gunmetal grey, with red glowing elements.

Two young women huddled by the heater. They were roughly the same age as the murdered girl. One with dark skin—only slightly lighter than Sonia's; the other with pink cheeks and long white-blonde hair, dipped in red. Blood painted the hems of their coat sleeves, the front of their pants, and their shoes. The dark-skinned woman sat with her head in her hands. She gazed at Valerio, eyes hollow—a resonant aftershock of horror.

Leonora's hands had been cleaned, the wet rain shield removed. A rough woolen blanket wrapped around her shoulders. The grey-haired priest was praying with her.

Valerio crossed to them.

Leonora tried to stand. He pushed her gently down, and signaled for the emergency workers.

"Rest, rest, Mamma," he said. "Let the soccorritori do their work."

To the young women, he held up his identification, and introduced himself.

"I'm with the police. What are your names?"

The women exchanged looks.

"We don't speak Italian," the dark-skinned girl said in English.

"Okay," Valerio said.

He could understand and speak some English, but he didn't like it. He'd never taken classes—just learned from American movies and YouTube. This would have to wait for Sonia, whose English was better.

"We're American," the blonde girl articulated slowly. "My father is Paul Lissom—the United States ambassador. Do you understand? The ambassador."

Valerio nodded. "Capisco. I understand."

She held out her phone, pointing at the screen.

Valerio took it and read the bubble text message she indicated.

Tell the police to call Phoenix Seven. Tell them to get Nikki Serafino.

FOUR

It was 01:30 and Nikki was awake. There was no good reason for it. The day had been exhausting—starting with a 07:30 work shift. Afterwards, she'd had a workout, grabbed dinner, then powered through the Krav Maga class. Between the intense schedule and the cold rain sapping her warmth, she should have been ready for an early sleep. But the attack on the street outside the studio had shot her through with adrenaline.

Again and again, her mind dragged her back to those furious moments of the assault, replaying the fear and rage—the way he'd used his size and strength to clamp her arms to her sides, hoisting her off the ground. She wished De Rosa hadn't interfered. She was relieved when the attack stopped—of course she was! But the abrupt end left her with an unsettled sensation—like a half-finished melody. She needed to know for certain that she could have fended off the bastard on her own. That was simply unknowable now.

At home, she punched and kicked the bag until she was dripping with sweat, too tired to continue. It was nearly midnight when she showered and collapsed into bed. She awoke too soon with a churning fear, and a dread of reentering her dreams. She got up, switched on the lights, and went to the kitchen.

There was a time long ago when nightmares like this had been persistent—in the months after Adriano's death. Awake, the knowledge of his loss wrapped around her like a blanket, an inescapable smothering reality. But in sleep, she sometimes forgot her brother was gone, and her mind would work out a thousand ways to rescue him from the bullet. It always found him, and she woke herself screaming.

For a while, she'd stayed with Aunt Izzy and Uncle Preston in their small London flat, and was mortified on the nights she woke them, too. They were always kind about it—turning on the lights, and Izzy would heat water for tea and play a cassette tape, some soothing melody of Brahms or Elgar.

"There," she'd say, handing Nikki a mug of hot chamomile. "Therapy in a cup."

For his part, Preston would eat chocolates from a box, and discuss some passage he was teaching in class that week, excavating Shakespeare for advice.

"'Give sorrow words,'" he told her. "'The grief that does not speak knits up the o-er wrought heart and bids it break.'"

But Nikki wasn't good with words and couldn't ever describe the feeling of wrongness. The brightness of her brother had left the world. Her love for him had lost its place to rest.

Nikki heated water. The soft floral notes of the chamomile comforted her, and the ugly feelings that had surged like the tide over a seawall began, gradually, to recede. She was growing tired again, the stark clarity and terror of her dreams dipping below waves of fatigue. Finishing the tea, she was returning to bed when the phone rang: a call from the Phoenix Seven duty line.

She answered, recognizing the nasal tone of Romano, the youngest investigator in Phoenix Seven: "Angelo needs you to come to police HQ."

"It's the middle of the night," she protested. "I'm not on duty."

"You have to," he insisted. "The police say it has to be you."

"Can it wait till morning?"

"They need you now."

Police HQ was brightly lit, giving the illusion of daytime in those windowless, high-ceilinged corridors. Nikki showed her Phoenix Seven ID card to the night guard, who called for an escort.

The plainclothes officer who came to meet her was Emilio, a nice-looking man with a fit body, thick hair, and a neatly trimmed beard.

"Ciao, Nikki."

"Emilio! I didn't expect you!"

The words sounded more severe than she'd intended.

Emilio was a homicide detective she had met last summer while working the Markham case. That he was here meant the situation wasn't the usual drunk American sailor making a scene in a downtown bar, or a traffic incident. A knot of dread coalesced in Nikki's stomach. She wanted to run . . . to get far away. She'd had enough of death.

Emilio moved in with a handshake and apologetic smile. "Sorry to drag you out of bed."

"No problem," she said, then urged her feet to follow. They walked together down a long corridor with chipped tile and yellowed paint. Bright lights buzzed overhead.

Absent the usual bustle, the place felt desolate.

"Stabbing death in Chiesa del Gesù Nuovo just after the eight o'clock mass," he told her. "Victim was a twentysomething woman. Nobody saw the stabbing, but three bystanders tried to administer first aid. They fucked up the crime scene. The only prints we could pull off the knife were from our good Samaritan."

"Was the victim American?" Nikki asked. The police only called Phoenix Seven in situations involving personnel associated with the US military.

"Don't know yet," he said. "She didn't have ID, and none of the witnesses recognized her. But one of the helpers—the one with the prints—is Monica Lissom. She's got an important father: Paul Lissom is the United States ambassador to Italy. He and his wife are in the US right now, but he's sent his defense attaché down from Rome, and told Monica not to cooperate with us unless you're involved."

Nikki's thoughts seemed to tangle in heavy clumps.

"How does the United States ambassador know who I am?" she asked.

Emilio shrugged. "They didn't say. Anyway, we called Phoenix Seven and asked for you. But two of your guys came instead. They've stepped in this one pretty bad, and our witnesses won't talk."

They'd reached the end of a corridor. Emilio pushed the door wide and they were drowned in a torrent of competing conversations.

Carving a path with Emilio through the clusters of uniformed men and women, Nikki spotted the tall and sober detective Sonia Dieng.

She was speaking with a man in a dark blue uniform whom Nikki guessed was the US attaché.

His posture was rigid, his jaw set, and he spoke English with a harsh American accent: "The ambassador isn't asking for special treatment. He's asking for respect."

"Unfortunately, we can't release Ms. Lissom or Ms. Washington yet," Sonia responded in a firm, even voice. "There's a murderer on the streets tonight—someone bold enough to kill in a church, during mass. We need information as soon as possible."

After the Markham case last summer, Nikki and Sonia had become friends. Outside work, the detective had an easy manner and biting sense of the absurd. Inside the office, however, Sonia was professional and humorless, a personality shift that jarred Nikki once she'd experienced the other side.

"It's the middle of the night," the attaché protested. "Are they under arrest?"

Sonia didn't have a chance to reply.

The door crashed open and a voice bellowed in Italian: "What the fuck were you thinking?"

Conversations stopped as everyone turned to look.

Nikki almost didn't recognize her friend, undercover police officer Capo Valerio Alfieri. He wore a nice shirt, slacks, and stylish leather shoes—a departure from his usual scuffed trainers and slouchy sweatshirts. But these clothes were wet and disheveled, the right sleeve of his shirt smeared with blood.

He was upset, breathing hard. Seeming not to notice anyone else, he bore down on a balding man in a polo shirt: Angelo Figliomeni, Nikki's boss and the supervisor of Phoenix Seven.

"You're supposed to liaise, to translate . . . you're supposed to *assist*," Valerio yelled. "Instead, you played cop and threw your weight around!"

Angelo grimaced. He glanced around as if looking for support. "The girl is lying. Anyone can see that she's lying."

"Are you really that stupid? They're witnesses, not suspects! They're in shock!"

"You don't know Americans." Angelo emphasized the words with both hands. "I have a cultural understanding you're blind to. You should trust my judgment."

"Your judgment?" Valerio scoffed. "Your judgment means that the witnesses aren't talking now—that we're further behind than when we started. It means that the Americans have a legitimate complaint against the police."

Angelo was unrepentant. "Let me deal with the Americans."

"Oh, I think you've done quite enough!"

Navigating the crowd, Sonia stepped between the two men.

"Thank you for your assistance," she told Angelo. "We'll take it from here."

Angelo seemed to hesitate, glancing between Sonia and Valerio.

Valerio stalked away, slamming back out through the door.

Nikki had never known Valerio to burn hot. In their years of friendship, she'd relied on him to be calm and reasonable. She took a step to follow, but the movement caught Angelo's attention.

He pointed at her. "There you are!"

Then he gestured to Romano at his side. "You. Go get the car."

Then, back at Nikki: "Where the hell have you been?"

"I'm here now," Nikki said evenly.

"Alright!" He straightened his shirt, squared his shoulders. "I'm leaving. I'll see you on the morning shift."

Nikki pushed back. "I can't work the morning shift now. I haven't slept."

"You need to take your work responsibilities seriously!" he barked. He seemed to vibrate with fury.

Sonia's calm voice broke across them. "I expect we'll need Investigator Serafino for the next few hours. I'd appreciate it if you adjust your schedule."

Like an attack dog changing targets, he turned on the detective, eyes bright and feral.

"I manage my teams!" he bellowed. "I'm the supervisor. Not you!"

Sonia's expression, always unreadable, hardened.

"Reconsider your approach, Investigator Figliomeni," she said. The words were quiet and clipped. "The Polizia di Stato have a good working relationship with Phoenix Seven. Do not harm it now."

Angelo stared back at Sonia, breathing heavily through his nose. She met his gaze.

"Your witness is lying," he grumbled. "Know that your witness is lying."

In the awkward silence after Angelo's departure, Sonia greeted Nikki with her typical professionalism.

"Our witnesses are tired—but we need them to tell us what happened. The longer we wait, the less likely we are to catch our killer. Would you translate?"

The interview room wasn't designed to be comfortable, but the police had clearly done what they could for Monica Lissom. She was wrapped in a blanket, and clasped a steaming cup.

"I want to apologize to you for the behavior of Investigator Figliomeni," Sonia said. "It was inexcusable. We'd like to start over. Can we do that?"

The young woman was thin and pale, with long, stringy blonde hair streaked with blood. Her eyes were a translucent grey, with brows so light as to be nearly invisible—giving the impression of perpetual astonishment. She was puffy with crying, forehead and cheeks patchy. A small downy feather had settled on her shirt.

She stared at Nikki.

"Are you Nikki Serafino?"

She had a gently twanging American accent.

Nikki handed over her Phoenix Seven identification card, and Monica examined it, fingers trembling. She took a deep breath, and the tears started.

"I was supposed to wait for you," she said.

"Tell us about yourself," said Sonia. "What are you doing in Naples?"

"Um . . . Kami and I just graduated from college . . . Texas A&M. We're doing a Europe trip. Paris first, then Florence. Then Rome to see my dad, then we came here."

"When did you arrive in Naples?"

"Sunday."

"What have you been doing?"

"We went to Capri . . . and Pompeii. This morning, we visited the archaeological museum . . . and . . . Christmas Alley."

"And what were you doing in Chiesa del Gesù Nuovo?"

"What?"

"The church."

"Oh . . ." Monica reddened. "There was a service."

"You attended mass?"

The flush deepened, a distracting contrast to her white hair and eyebrows—an extreme physiological response to stress. Nikki wondered if this was the reason Angelo had thought she was lying.

"We weren't really planning to stick around for the service. Just walking around with the other tourists."

"How many tourists would you say were in the cathedral?"

"Twenty? Maybe more."

"Okay, then what happened?"

"Kami and I heard something. We went to take a look. And we found her."

"What sound did you hear?"

"Like a grunting sound . . ."

"Can you please describe what you saw?"

Monica flinched. "Well . . . she was on the ground . . . flopping around. I thought she was having a seizure. But there was blood everywhere."

"What did you do?" Sonia asked.

"We wanted to help. Kami knows first aid. We put pressure on the wounds, tried to stop the bleeding."

"Did she say anything to you?"

Monica shook her head. "I think . . . she couldn't breathe."

"Then what happened?"

"We were calling for help. An old lady came. She held her hand and talked to her. Then the girl stopped breathing . . . stopped moving."

"Did you try to resuscitate her?"

Monica's gaze tracked up to the ceiling. She grimaced, then squeezed her eyes shut.

"I don't know CPR," she said, "and Kami was—well, she was just freaking out. We both were. There was so much blood. I don't think . . . well, I don't think CPR would have helped."

"Then what happened?"

"Then there were a lot of people. Screaming. A priest came. He said a prayer. They called the police . . . and then they came. That's it." She exhaled shakily.

"When you arrived in the chapel where the woman was stabbed," Sonia said, "did you see anyone else?"

She shook her head, face turning pink again. "No."

"We didn't find any identification," Sonia pressed. "No wallet or purse. No phone. Did you happen to notice a phone on or around the woman?"

"No . . . nothing like that."

"Did you recognize the victim?"

Monica shook her head. "No."

Sonia said, "Is it alright if I show you a picture?"

She opened an electronic tablet and flicked through the photographs before setting it on the table between them.

Nikki hesitated.

She disliked seeing accidents or violent crime scenes. Death stripped away a person's depths and nuances. Relationships, experiences, desires—all reduced to the crudest dimensions: meat, bone, blood. In death, a person was at their most vulnerable; to witness it an intimate invasion.

At last, she turned to the image.

The woman was young—brown cheeks full, soft lips parted as if in surprise. There was blood on her face, and small soft white feathers, like a wounded bird.

"Do you recognize this woman?" Sonia asked.

Monica's already pink face reddened.

"No," she said, and squeezed her eyes shut.

Sonia nodded and leaned forward on the table. "The knife," she said. "Did you happen to see the knife?"

"I don't know," said Monica. She passed a hand across her face.

"We found the knife," Sonia continued. "It was by the altar in the chapel—far from the body. There were marks on the floor. We think somebody threw it. Was it you?"

"I don't remember," Monica said. She seemed dazed, eyes focused on some distant point.

"You didn't throw it?"

"I don't know."

"Your prints were on the knife," said Sonia. "So, we know you held it."

Some light seemed to blink out behind those clear eyes. Monica rested her head in her hands and spoke to the ground. "I don't know."

They stayed in the interview room for another hour, but Monica provided nothing else.

Monica's friend and travel companion, Kami Washington, was more expressive. Despite the hours alone in an interview room, she was alert. Anger seemed to assert and sort her thoughts, a fuel of injured justice.

"We were the good guys!" she shouted. "You can't treat us like suspects. We were the fucking heroes. You need to catch the motherfucker who did this. You hear? You need to fucking catch that guy."

"Was it a man?" asked Sonia. "Did you see the person who stabbed her?"

Kami was emphatic. "He was long gone by the time we got there. It was a figure of speech, you know? *The guy?*"

She told the same story as Monica—about hearing a noise and investigating, about finding the stabbed woman, and administering first aid. But there were places where the story diverged.

"She definitely said something. It was like *Gerd* or *Greed*, or something. You'll have to ask Monica."

She also remembered the knife.

"Oh yeah," she said. "Monica threw it really hard."

Afterwards, Emilio and Sonia and Nikki talked it over.

"Do you think she really doesn't remember picking up the knife?" Emilio asked.

Sonia shrugged. "It was an intense and traumatizing moment. Sometimes people forget."

"I hate to admit it," said Emilio, "but I'm inclined to agree with Angelo. They're lying. We should keep them in custody."

Sonia turned to Nikki. "What do you think?"

"Not lying," she answered. "Or, at least, not exactly. I don't get the sense that they're a threat—but they aren't telling us everything."

Sonia pressed fingers to her lips. "So, you don't think we should keep them?"

"I'd prefer you didn't," Nikki said. "The ambassador is on his way back to Italy and this could become a political headache if you put them in jail. I think it would be a gesture of goodwill if you let the American attaché take charge of them."

Sonia nodded. "I don't think they were directly responsible for the assault. But we need to push on their stories. Once they surrender their passports, they're free to go—but tell them not to go far."

The sun was rising over the city, the air chilly and damp as Nikki rode her Hornet the short distance to her flat. Hours ago, the empty nighttime streets had given her a clear path to the station. Now, under the grey glow of a cloudy sky, the roads were chaotic and crowded. She maneuvered around it all, brain sluggish, the residual thrumming energy from the nighttime coffee insufficient to focus her.

The interviews seemed to have recorded badly in her tired mind.

Memories juddered and stalled, replaying unimportant details: mascara smudged beneath Kami Washington's eyes, and Monica Lissom's hands, nails bitten to the quick.

Nikki kept her bike in a tiny spot in the alley behind a nearby jewelry store, the privilege for which she paid a monthly fee to the owner. Carefully, she maneuvered the Hornet into its place, then walked the few blocks home.

The door in the large metal gate wasn't secured. It creaked wide open and she stomped into the bare space, glancing briefly at the old chapel in the courtyard with its chipped stone cherubs before heading up the steep concrete stairs.

Arriving on the landing, she heard the shuffle of steps, the muttering, the dull scratch of metal. A figure stood at her door, trying a key in the lock. Nikki paused, heart suddenly loud in her ears, watching someone try to break into her house.

A moment later, she realized the truth.

"Massimo?" she called.

The old man's back was to her—the peculiar erectness of his posture a contrast to the disheveled appearance: white hair mussed, a flattened tangle at the back of his head. He wore a threadbare cardigan, wrinkled slacks, and leather loafers tight on swollen feet.

Nikki cleared her throat, and called his name again. But still he startled when he turned and stared, rheumy eyes drooping and tired. "The key doesn't work," he said.

In the decades before Nikki inherited the flat from her mother, Massimo had managed the property. He'd been a fixture in her childhood, and memory showed him as a stylish playboy, a fashionable woman always on his arm. That memory seemed cruel now—a contrast to this quavering form.

Massimo's face was pale and sweating. His hands had lost their elegant definition and strength. They were gnarled, spotted, gripping the jangling key ring.

"Massimo?" Nikki said again.

At her voice, he seemed to relax.

"Oh, Beatrice," he said. "I'm glad you came. I got the signal. Last-minute visitors and the place isn't ready."

"It's Nikki, not Beatrice," she said gently. "That key won't work. I changed the lock. What are you doing here?"

Massimo returned to his task, fumbling through the keys.

"It's here somewhere," he muttered.

"I've got it," said Nikki. She unlocked the door, and guided Massimo through to the living room, settling him on the sofa.

"I'll get you water," she said.

In the kitchen, standing at the tap, she checked her watch: 06:49.

She badly wanted sleep, but she couldn't abandon Massimo. She'd never seen him in this condition. He was usually sharp—ready with a quip or a compliment.

She dialed her father's number.

Raoul Serafino was an early bird—a habit left over from his military career. He answered on the second ring, voice clear and resonant. She imagined him on the porch in Benevento, sipping coffee.

"Ciao, bella."

That voice, frigid and formal, had softened with age.

"Massimo Fattore's at my house," she told him. "He was trying to use his old key to get in. He's confused; I think he's sick . . . he thought I was Mom."

Raoul made a low noise. "Where is he now?"

"In the living room. I think he needs to go to hospital. Do you have a number for his family?"

"I have the number for Stefania, his niece. Tell me more. What did he say?"

"He looks awful. He's shaking. He said something about a signal."

Raoul grunted again. "Sounds like low blood sugar from his diabetes. Give him juice—and I'll call Stefania."

Nikki poured orange juice.

Carrying the cold glass to the living room, she stopped, taking in the unexpected disorder.

During her short time away, chaos had erupted.

The coffee table was upended, papers strewn across the floor. Massimo was pushing on the sofa, the rug beneath rippling and bunching.

"Hey! Hey! What are you doing? Massimo!"

His arm was slick with sweat as she tugged him away and helped him sit. His movements were sloppy, uncoordinated.

"We have to warn Adriano!" he pleaded. "We have to warn him!"

At the name, Nikki froze. She remembered her nightmares in the early hours of the morning, the anguished sense of missing her brother. Today was the bitter anniversary of Adriano's death, and the world was that much darker.

"Adriano's gone," she said.

She pressed the glass into his trembling hands. "Drink this."

Childlike, he complied, a shudder across his fragile shoulders.

Gradually, Massimo's breathing became less labored, color returned to his cheeks, and his hands stopped shaking. His face lost its sheen of sweat.

"Grazie, bella," he said. "Grazie."

FIVE

Valerio's sisters were awake and in the kitchen of their mother's apartment when he let himself in at nearly three a.m.

He found Orlanda at the stove, scrambling eggs. She wore an old T-shirt and pajama pants, long hair tied in a sloppy bun. The burnt remnants of an unsuccessful earlier attempt were blackened and wet in the kitchen sink. The stink still hung in the air.

"Oh good," she said, glancing up at him. "There you are. Penny wouldn't let us go to bed until you got here."

"Did you catch the bastard?" asked Penelope from her seat at the table.

His older sister had their mother's way of stacking and sorting. The pile of detritus on the stiff plastic tablecloth was organized into rows: little battalions of teaspoons, sugar packets, chocolate wrappers, and breadcrumbs.

"Working on it," said Valerio. He crossed to the sink for a glass of water. "How's she doing?"

"The doctor gave her a pill to calm down," Penelope said. "You know her heart isn't good. You know that, Valerio! This sort of thing is dangerous for her."

Her glare was accusing.

"Did she say anything about what happened?" he asked.

"She says it's in God's hands," said Orlanda. "She prayed all night. You want eggs?"

His stomach, achingly empty for hours, lurched.

"Yeah," he said. "Thanks."

Valerio felt a wave of gratitude for his younger sister. As children and teenagers, Orlanda never offered anything without a jab to follow. But they'd grown closer in the past decade. She seemed less inclined to tease and fight, more eager to help.

"You can have mine," she said, spooning the steaming eggs onto a plate. "I'll make more."

Valerio took the offer without grace, scraping the eggs from the plate directly into his mouth. They were overdone—thick and rubbery—but hunger kept him from caring.

Penelope gestured imperiously.

"Sit down!" she commanded. "Eat at the table like a civilized person! I swear, you're like one of my heathen sons. Is your shirt wet?"

Valerio rummaged in the bread box before taking a seat at the table. The rickety chair creaked and wobbled under his weight.

"Maybe we should call the priest," suggested Orlanda.

"The priest can wait," said Valerio, mouth full. "Mamma's got to talk to the police when she wakes up."

His older sister stared at him as he ate, eyes wide and hawkish. He tried to ignore it, but he had the unreasonable feeling of being a child again.

Penelope adhered to the same style she'd developed as a teenager, even as age thickened her face and waist and eyelids, softened her neck and arms. She dyed and styled her hair the same, hair spray molding her bangs into a solid shell. He'd never known her to be without bright colors and long, painted nails, red lipstick, and huge earrings. With her adornments missing tonight, there was something strangely vulnerable about the pale, naked skin. Her hair was soft and thinning. It draped against her skull, grey at the roots.

"Well," she said, watching him for a few more beats, "are you going to tell us what happened?"

At the stove, cracking eggs into the pan, Orlanda swiveled around to look.

"I told you: She was a witness to a crime," Valerio said, sopping up the greasy remnants of the egg from his plate with a piece of spongy bread. "I can't discuss it!"

Orlanda gave a frustrated groan. "Give us something! What was the crime?"

"A woman was murdered," said Valerio.

Both sisters started talking at once.

"I really can't say more," he said again. "I mean it. No! Stop. Are you two staying over tonight?"

"I've got to get back before lunchtime tomorrow," said Penelope. "I can miss breakfast, but they'll be howling by noon. Nobody can feed themselves without me."

She brushed her palms on the table for a few beats before pushing to her feet.

They slept in their childhood places. Penny and Orlanda shared their old room next to the bathroom. This was where Valerio's children, Davide and Gemma, slept whenever they stayed with their grandmother—so it was kept clean with fresh linens. Valerio's narrow childhood bed was in a closet-size room at the end of the hall. He opened the door to find the space full—bed and floor stacked high with teetering plastic and cardboard boxes, pallets of canned food, bolts of fabric, and folded tablecloths and towels. It took fifteen minutes to empty it, piling everything into the hall.

He worked numbly, automatically, body on the edge of collapse. His mind returned to the gruesome scene in the church—the wrecked young woman, tiny white feathers settled onto crimson pools; hundreds of bloody footprints; clumsy helpers who obscured any useful evidence the murderer had left behind. He thought of his mother's hands dripping with blood and rain. And the shock that had numbed her into silence. No, not silence. She had shouted—and at the Madonna! His mother, who had always been so respectful, who had rapped his knuckles when he didn't display the correct piety—she had screamed at the Immacolata!

In a cardboard box he found one of his old T-shirts—mustard brown. It was folded and smelled clean, if a bit stale. He stripped off his wet clothes and put it on. Then, wrapping up in his old childhood quilt, he was asleep almost as soon as his body hit the mattress.

Sun glinted through the window when Orlanda woke him with a knock on the door.

"There's someone here to see you."

"Thanks. Is Mamma awake?"

"Not yet."

His trousers, when he pulled them on, were wrinkled and a little damp.

He'd expected Sonia and Emilio. They were supposed to come by and interview Leonora first thing this morning—so he was surprised to see a tall, birdlike man standing on the rug in his mother's small living room. He wore thick-soled white sneakers with Velcro straps, and black-rimmed glasses perched on wide ears nestled in a rim of grey hair. Narrow shoulders jutted from his collared shirt, and large bony hands kneaded against each other, fingers flexing.

"Federico!" Valerio exclaimed. "What are you doing here?"

This was Federico Errichiello, proprietor of a local salumeria, and the last person he'd expected to find in his mother's house.

"I gotta talk," Federico said, staring over Valerio's shoulder to where Orlanda stood.

Valerio gave Orlanda a look. She took the hint and retreated.

"Come to the kitchen," said Valerio, yawning. "I'll make us coffee."

His mind worked as he dolloped coffee grounds into the Moka percolator and sliced bread.

Valerio had met the old man about a decade ago; Federico had been an addict desperate to get clean and excise himself from the criminal network run by his brother, Luca. Impressed by the man's determination and grit, Valerio had helped where he could. And Federico had done the miraculous impossible: carved out an honest life for himself, an island above the eddies of corruption and criminality surging around him.

Months had passed since Valerio had visited Federico's shop. The last time had been in the summer—when Valerio had begged for help. The memory stabbed him with guilt. He should have poured out his gratitude or, at the very least, checked in.

His mouth was dry as he put coffee on the table. He wanted to apologize, but couldn't find the words. Instead, he said, "How did you know where to find me?"

Federico shrugged. "You weren't answering your phone. You weren't at home, or at the station. I asked around."

"So, you know what happened last night? At Chiesa del Gesù Nuovo?"

Federico nodded, scooped sugar into his coffee, and stirred. He drank it down hot.

"Everybody knows what happened."

"What have you heard?" Valerio prodded, suddenly hopeful for a lead on this messy case. But a tremor seemed to run through the old man. He shook his head.

"That's not why I'm here. Luca wants to call in his favor."

The coffee in Valerio's mouth turned to tar.

Suddenly, he knew why he hadn't visited.

Valerio owed Federico the deepest appreciation for helping him and, in so doing, crossing lines he'd sworn he'd never breach. Valerio had been desperate to find his daughter, and Federico had arranged a meeting with his brother, Luca Errichiello—a Camorra capo, and the vilest man Valerio had ever met.

In his elation at finding Gemma alive, and the renewed closeness this had brought with his children these past few months, Valerio had tried to erase that ugly, shameful part of the story. This was why he'd never visited, never thanked Federico. He hadn't wanted to remember.

Federico spoke his name and Valerio realized he'd been silent in these thoughts. He shook himself.

"What's the favor?"

"Don't know. He wants you to see him. Today. Now."

"I can't just drop everything. Detectives are coming to interview my mother any minute now."

Federico's shoulders rose, head dropping down. He pushed away from the table.

His voice was low and rasping. "Luca doesn't take nos."

"Can you tell him . . ."

But Valerio couldn't get the words out. Federico's head jerked up, eyes full of fire.

"I did my part," he snarled. "I gave the message. I'm not his errand boy. I'm out. Do you hear? I'm never going back. This is yours now. You made the bargain with the devil. You!"

He stood and teetered unsteadily for a moment before striding out of the kitchen.

Valerio followed.

"Federico. I'm sorry."

But Federico didn't answer. He was through the front door. It slammed behind him.

Valerio's phone was dead. He plugged it into the wall, but it still wouldn't start. He hoped it hadn't shorted out in the rain last night.

He showered in the old tub, the water coming in too hot and then too cold, the pipes moaning all the while. He squeezed toothpaste onto his finger and used this to brush the foul taste from his teeth and tongue.

His clothing from last night was drier, if worse for the wear. His shirt sleeve had a bloodstain, and he scrubbed at it in the kitchen sink for several minutes before Penny saw what he was doing.

"Is that blood?" she said, nudging him aside. "Give that to me!"

When she returned it to him, the blood was mostly gone, but the shirt was dripping. He wrung it out, then hung it on the bathroom heater, and wore the mustard-colored T-shirt instead. He'd just pulled it back over his head when the knock came at the door.

"Please tell me you have coffee," Emilio said when Valerio opened the door.

"You two look like shit," Valerio observed, stepping aside for the detectives to pass. Sonia gave him a cold stare and Emilio yawned.

Orlanda, who had trailed behind Valerio, extended her hand. "I'm Valerio's sister. Orlanda."

Sonia introduced herself and Emilio, then asked, "Is your mother at home?"

Orlanda turned and shouted, "Penny! The detectives are here! Bring Mamma, will you?"

She herded the group into the small living room and seemed ready to join them on the shabby brown sofa when Valerio shooed her away. "Coffee, Orlanda!"

His irritation with his sister was some warped residue of their combative childhood and teenage years. He felt the steady, predictable climb to the top of a familiar roller coaster ride, knew the wild descents and loops that would follow, and for a moment, felt powerless to alter them. He braced for the fight. Then he caught the wounded expression in her eyes, and a memory shoved into his mind: three years ago, late at night, and he'd answered the door to find his sister's bloodied face, lip split and swollen, a black bruise blossoming on her cheek. The sight had shocked him. More than this, he'd been shaken by that look in her eyes—raw and pleading, the doors of her soul flung wide.

"I'm sorry," he said. "Hey, I'm sorry. Would you mind making more coffee? I think everyone's tired."

Leonora, when she came into the room with Penny, was dressed in her best maroon pantsuit, white hair brushed and shaped into hard curls, retaining the form of the curling iron. Tan makeup coated his mother's wrinkled face, rouge on her cheeks and dark lipstick on thin lips. She had the same cross around her neck that she always wore, large pearl clip-on earrings, and a gold brooch on her lapel in the shape of a honeybee.

Penny carried two wobbly wooden chairs from the kitchen into the living room for herself and Orlanda, and Valerio helped his mother into her favorite armchair, facing the detectives. Orlanda served the coffee.

"Thank you for meeting with us, Signora Alfieri," said Sonia. "I hope you got some rest. How are you feeling?"

"I've been praying," she said. "I've asked God why he would allow such a thing. Why he would show it to me . . . to see that poor woman—hold her head in my hands. Why, God? What is your meaning?"

She gestured towards the ceiling as if Jesus himself were hovering there.

"I can't imagine how it must have felt, Signora Alfieri," said Sonia.

"It's understandable that you would want to find meaning in such a terrible act of violence."

"God gave me an answer," Leonora said. "He gave me a sign. He sent his messenger."

"Mamma," breathed Orlanda, her head ducked, shoulders raised.

Valerio shifted, feeling his sister's posture reflected in his own. A primitive shame crawled across his skin, hot and itchy.

"An angel came to me," his mother said with firm certainty, staring at each of her children in turn, eyes wide, as if they had openly contradicted her. "It *did*. An angel—in the form of a spider coming from beneath the picture frame on its fine web."

Then, turning to Sonia and Emilio, her gaze softened.

"You see, the picture was of my dead husband, Costanzo. And I know that Costanzo was the angel, and that he'd come to tell me what I should do."

Sonia seemed unaware of the embarrassment gathering like sticky threads between Leonora's children. She looked calmly at the old woman. "And what do you think you should do?"

"I must help your investigation," said Leonora. "I've asked God to preserve my memories—to tell you everything that happened, so you can find the man who did this."

Valerio exhaled.

"Good," said Emilio. "That's very good. Last night, when we spoke, you said that you often attend mass at Chiesa del Gesù Nuovo?"

"Sì."

"Did you recognize any of the congregation?"

"Sì."

She patted her pockets, then pulled out a folded sheet of paper and extended it to Emilio. He opened it carefully.

"Those are all the people I remember in the congregation," she said.

Valerio leaned over to read his mother's painstaking looping writing. It looked like one of her meticulous shopping lists.

"The sister-in-law of Graziano the mechanic," Sonia read aloud. "Do you have a last name for Graziano?"

Leonora shook her head. “I don’t know. But his repair shop is near Garibaldi.”

“You wrote here: *The woman whose son was in the hospital for mumps last year.* Do you have a name for this woman?”

“She’s a very nice lady,” said Leonora. “She’s fat because of a thyroid sickness. She says her husband left her because she became too fat.”

“Okay,” said Sonia. “This is very helpful. We may need to ask more questions about each of these people—especially the ones without names. Was there anybody in the congregation you didn’t recognize?”

“Before the service started, there were tourists. There are always many tourists. That was where I saw the girl.”

“You saw the victim?” Emilio asked, leaning forward.

“Sì.”

“Where was she?”

“Near the Chapel of the Holy Martyrs.”

“Did you see what she was doing?”

“She was kneeling on the floor . . . looking for something in her bag.”

Sonia raised an eyebrow. “She had a bag?”

“Sì.”

“Can you describe it?”

“It was a backpack. Black.”

“We didn’t see the backpack. Did you notice it with her afterwards . . . close to the body?”

“No. It was not with her when she died.”

“So, you saw her looking in her bag,” said Sonia. “Was she with anyone else?”

“No. She was alone. But the Chapel of the Holy Martyrs is near the church entrance—and she was looking at the people coming into the church. I thought she was waiting for someone.”

“You didn’t see who she was waiting for?”

“No. I went into the church to pray.”

“Did you see the woman at any other time?”

“No . . . not until later. . . .”

Interlacing her fingers, she bowed her head and pressed her knuckles into her lips.

A few moments passed, then Sonia said gently, "We'd like to talk to you about that, if you're able."

Leonora's head lifted.

"I never leave mass. Never! I always stay until the end. But yesterday, something happened. I felt Costanzo with me . . . my angel . . . holding my hand, so I left to talk with him in private. I was not with the congregation. I was not with the priest, accepting the holy Eucharist. Instead, I was praying in the chapel next to the sacristy when I saw the murderer."

Valerio stared at his mother. "You saw him?"

She lifted her chin defiantly. "I saw him. Like the devil rushing past me. Then I heard screaming." She crossed herself.

"Can you describe him?" Emilio asked.

"He was dressed in a black robe with a black hood. A messenger of Satan. I could feel the evil coming from him. How could God allow such an evil creature in his house?"

"Did you see his face?"

She shook her head. "I try to remember. I ask God to tell me. But it was covered by the hood. I did not see his demon face."

"Was he carrying anything?"

She shook her head. "I don't remember."

"So, he didn't have the backpack?"

"Maybe . . . I don't remember."

"But you're certain it was a man?"

"Sì."

Emilio spent several minutes prodding, but the only details this revealed were increasingly supernatural—a whiff of sulfur . . . the snorting breath of a demon . . . a cold chill. Sonia made a small gesture and he stopped the line of questioning.

"So, you saw this person in a dark hood rushing by," she said. "Can you remember how much time passed before you heard the screaming?"

"No time at all," said Leonora. "The screaming started when I saw him."

"What did you do then?"

"I ran towards the screaming," she said. "There was so much blood. Two girls were trying to help. I wanted to help. . . . I wanted . . . I hoped . . ."

Her voice trailed off. She breathed rapidly, chest heaving.

Valerio reached out a hand and she clutched it. Her fingers were cold and damp. She turned her face to him. Valerio read the anguish in her eyes, and didn't know how to take it away.

SIX

The afternoon sky was blue, a clear view to the double peaks of Vesuvius on the horizon as Nikki rode her Hornet to the US military base at Capodichino. She'd slept fitfully through the bright morning hours, city noises echoing up through her bedroom. Now she was strangely disconnected, as if pieces had shaken loose inside. She wanted to hit something hard enough to knock everything back into place.

Entering the gate lent her a sense of normalcy, the uniformed guard checking her through with a friendly "Have a nice day, ma'am." Less reassuring was what met her at the office. Her on-duty partner for the afternoon shift was Mario. He skulked in his cubicle, the fluorescent overhead lights seeming to paint the frown onto his heavy jowls, vertical lines slashing the edges of his mouth like a ventriloquist dummy. He didn't look up or acknowledge when she entered, removed her rucksack and jacket, and started her computer.

Angelo usually made it a point to keep Nikki and Mario separated on the duty roster. It had been months since they'd spent time together. But the last-minute schedule change forced an unwelcome overlap.

Nikki's biggest problem with Mario wasn't the relentless bullying, the physical aggression, or his casual sexism. Obnoxious as those traits were, Nikki could tolerate them as long as they didn't interfere with the job. But he'd failed to help her when she called for backup last summer during the search for the kidnapped base commander, Admiral Redford. Mario had allowed his personal dislike of Nikki to eclipse any remnant of professionalism, and it had nearly gotten her killed.

Afterwards, during the investigation, Mario refuted Nikki's testimony—that he'd rejected her call for support. He claimed a poor connection, that he hadn't heard her request, that the line had disconnected.

"It was a stressful time," he said. "Investigator Serafino was clearly emotional . . . it must have affected her judgment. She might not remember what *actually* happened."

Without recordings or witnesses to prove otherwise, Mario had suffered no consequences to his career in Phoenix Seven. But the lie and its implications hung off him like a noxious stink. The annoyance Nikki usually felt for him solidified into contempt.

Doing her best not to look at or think about Mario, Nikki tended to her work, tidying leftover paperwork and checking emails.

Then she scrolled through the texts on her phone, hoping to find something from Valerio. Nothing.

She called. No answer.

She hung up and texted, **You okay?**

No reply.

Valerio's outburst at Angelo last night was so unlike him. It worried her. She hadn't talked to him for a while; they'd both been too preoccupied with work, and besides, the weather had been too shit to take their sailboat, *Calypso*, to sea.

At the station, there had been blood on Valerio's sleeve. The same blood streaked through Monica's hair—from the woman at the church.

Nikki exhaled.

She didn't want to be part of another murder investigation. Even brushing up against this case knotted a cord of dread around her throat. But she also didn't want to walk away. How could you see something like that—know that it had happened—and not help?

When she closed her eyes, Nikki saw the childlike face, the pooling blood, and the fine layer of feathers. Everything arranged beneath the altar as if a young angel had fallen violently to Earth.

Had she come into Chiesa del Gesù Nuovo seeking refuge? If so, there'd been none. The beasts of Naples hunted even here.

There it was: That constricting grip. Helplessness. Fear. Nikki hated it.

Well, at the very least, she could do some due diligence for the case and look into the witnesses: Monica Lissom and Kami Washington.

Both women had a robust presence on social media, their European holiday thoroughly documented. Dancing in heels and slinky dresses at the Louvre, sipping espresso in the Vatican's courtyard café, shopping on the Ponte Vecchio. Ideal, effortless fun that was clearly carefully staged.

Nikki scanned these profiles, then traced both women backwards in time to graduation pictures and photos of student and sorority life at Texas A&M University: hundreds of images of parties, football games, tailgating, drinking, dancing, and more parties. Turning next to news and public records, Nikki assembled biographies.

Monica Lissom was the only child of an ambassador father and socialite mother. From an early age, she appeared in photographs at galas and philanthropic events. She'd studied economics in college, and her success in that field seemed a foregone conclusion due to her family's wealth and influence. She'd spent a semester interning in London at an investment firm called Stonehaven Wealth Management. Her love life was public; she'd dated a string of celebrities who appeared with her in paparazzi photos in gossip magazines. Her most recent boyfriend seemed to be a thirty-one-year-old technology guru named Kevin Walker.

Kami Washington didn't come from the same wealth as Monica. Her parents were computer programmers, and she seemed to have enjoyed a comfortable middle-class upbringing in suburban Texas. Her degree was in electrical engineering and she'd done two summer internships with engineering firms in Texas, and volunteered for the Red Cross. Her boyfriend for the past three years was a civil engineering student named Amir Bloomfield.

Nikki was summarizing the results of her research when the phone rang. Mario answered, the low grumble of his voice barely audible over the hum of the ventilation.

Minutes passed, and Mario's heavy footsteps tromped towards her. Nikki swiveled in her chair in time to watch him enter her cubicle.

So accustomed to Mario's disregard, his sudden proximity sent a surge of hot tension through her.

"What do you want?" she demanded, keeping her face impassive.

He stared for several seconds, breathing heavily through his nose. His face was flushed, lips pressed together, jaw working.

"You think you're so fucking special."

Mario was a big man, with decades of densely packed muscle and fat. He'd always seemed eager to leverage his size, to violate her boundaries. Three years ago, during her first weeks and months on the job, he'd jostled her in the hallways, shoving her against walls. Once he'd stumbled into her and grabbed her breast as though clumsily trying to steady himself. She'd decided long ago that she'd break his arm before she ever let him get that close again.

"Go back to your desk," she said.

He was blocking her egress, the closed space of the cubicle suddenly suffocating—the stink of garlic and heavy cologne masking a deeper, gamier odor. His gaze roved across her body, lingering on her breasts and coming to rest between her legs before flicking back to her face. He edged closer.

"You think you should have special rules," he said. "Special treatment."

"Not special rules." Nikki stood, prepared to fight him back if he took another step. Her arms twitched, primed to strike. "Just the usual rules; the rules that say you should do your job properly . . . that you should answer a call for backup from a colleague . . . that you shouldn't lie in an investigation to save your ass. You and I both know what you did. If you can't handle that, maybe you should find another place to work because I'm not fucking going anywhere."

For a moment, she thought he really would hit her. He stared, seeming to consider. Then, abruptly, he turned and strode from the office, door slamming behind him.

It took a while for Nikki's heart to stop hammering. She did push-ups and squats and kicks. For another hour she made an effort to work, then finally slipped on her motorcycle jacket and left the office.

She jogged across the base, cold air and sunlight working into her, surveying the pale yellow of the stucco buildings, the blocky concrete constructions and high metal fences. It was an ugly facility, but she'd always liked it: the structure and order of the military organization, and the sense of otherness that the Americans brought. Here, she'd become a professional investigator at Phoenix Seven—a job that gave her purpose. Not even assholes like Mario had affected her drive.

But now, something had changed. She felt a hollow place in her center, a sense of entering an empty room with only echoes and shifting shadows to remind her it had once been filled. The world looked different, too. Stripped of color.

She wanted to get back to the way things used to feel, but couldn't seem to find the map.

Her phone rang. She answered and heard Sonia's voice. "Are you here already?"

Nikki hated this feeling: like she'd missed a step.

"Where am I supposed to be?"

"I called the Phoenix Seven duty phone. Your guy answered. He said he'd tell you. We needed you at the station. We had a witness come in."

Silently, Nikki cursed Mario.

"I'll come right away."

"No. Not there. We've identified the victim: Claire Sexton, a nanny for a British family. They're scheduled to berth their yacht in Molo Luise this evening. The family can speak with us now. Meet me at the marina near Castel dell'Ovo."

The rain was starting again. Not yesterday's torrent, but a persistent drizzle. As Nikki rode down the hill from the airport into the city center and then along the waterfront, raindrops spattered her helmet, obscuring her vision.

Sonia stood near the harbor where local fishermen kept their dinghies. Nikki approached, past the bobbing rows of sailboats. Rain hit fiberglass decks, the gentle pattering sounds accompanying the metallic notes of cables striking the masts. Nearby, two white-haired men sat on crates, poles propped, lines in the water, a cut-off plastic bait jug between them.

Nikki apologized. "Sorry I wasn't at the station when you needed me."

"There are problems on your team," Sonia observed. "Your supervisor needs to get things under control before Phoenix Seven loses the trust of my colleagues."

Much as Nikki agreed, she wasn't about to trash-talk her team—even to Sonia.

"What did I miss?" she asked. Sonia gestured and Nikki fell in step beside her.

"Police report from Capri, and photo match with our victim," Sonia said. "Claire Sexton was working for Jayston and Fiona Lake aboard their yacht, *The Prophet*. She went missing Saturday night, along with some jewelry and cash. The Lakes filed a police complaint. The captain of *The Prophet* confirmed the ID at the morgue."

They made their way around the harbor, through the labyrinth of restaurants and sailing services, and past the rows of expensive sailboats. Nikki appraised and admired each one—and compared them all unfavorably to *Calypso*. She thought of Valerio. She should call him again, tell him to carve out time, ignore the bad weather, and sail with her into the grey-and-white waves.

Nikki followed Sonia through the glass doors of a restaurant. They scanned the faces in the dining room, then continued outdoors, where guests sat beneath an awning. Grey-haired couples drank coffee. Women with sculpted eyebrows and sunglasses drank Aperol Spritz. A goateed man nursed a Belgian beer, and his girlfriend sipped prosecco.

At another table sat a woman and a child of seven or eight. The woman had long chestnut hair and an eerie beauty that seemed less a gift of nature than of plastic surgeons—full lips, clear skin, and jutting cheekbones. By comparison, the child was awkwardly plain: short and chubby, with splotchy skin, crooked teeth, and a stubbed nose. Her eyebrows were bushy, and her straight mousy hair hung in a blunt, unflattering bob.

Sonia sighed. "I don't see the captain."

"Have you slept?" Nikki asked, noting the fatigued voice, tired eyes, and grey tinge to her skin.

"After this interview," Sonia said, then took out her phone and dialed.

Sonia's tough-mindedness was one of the reasons Nikki liked her, and why she'd accepted Sonia's gestures of friendship these past few months. They sometimes had coffee, or lifted together at the gym. And once, Nikki and Valerio had taken Sonia and her daughter sailing. Nikki had never been good at making friends—particularly with other women, who seemed to live by strange unspoken rules. But Sonia's rulebook was straightforward: honest communication and no bullshit. She also respected Nikki's privacy and need for solitude.

Nikki was about to offer to buy Sonia a coffee while they waited, when the homely child launched off her chair and came towards them.

"Are you the police?"

She spoke confidently with a refined British accent.

"Yes," said Sonia. "I'm Detective Sonia Dieng, and this is Investigator Nikki Serafino. Who are you?"

"I'm Audrey Lake," said the girl with an eager smile. She pointed. "That's my mum. Captain Henry said to watch for you."

Audrey led them to the table, and spoke loudly to the woman.

"These are the police, Mum."

Fiona Lake didn't respond. Clearly far into drinking, she seemed shaky, hand shifting a little late to steady her sloshing martini. She sipped, gazing across the water, where a cruise ship pulled out to sea. Beyond this, the dark form of Vesuvius was cloaked in a cloud.

"Signora Lake?" Sonia said. "Is there someplace private we can talk?"

When the woman still didn't answer, Sonia continued, "Perhaps inside?"

Fiona set down her drink and, taking out a cigarette, worked a lighter for several tries until the flame held.

"This is perfectly suitable," she said, gesturing to the nearby tables. "Interrogate me. Share my business with the world."

"We don't wish to disturb you," said Sonia.

Fiona glared, eyes slightly unfocused, and sucked on the cigarette. "And yet . . . here you are."

She drained her glass and gestured for the waiter to bring another.

"We really must talk to you," said Sonia.

"Do you have business cards?"

Sonia and Nikki took a moment to locate a card each. Fiona didn't look before tossing them onto the table.

"I'll instruct Henry to call you . . . or Jayston. I simply can't . . . not today . . . I just can't."

Nikki glanced between the disinterested face of the mother and the cheerful, expectant face of the child—a contrast that made her suddenly uneasy and acutely aware of the missing nanny.

"Ma'am," she said, leaning in and speaking quietly, "I'm sure this is inconvenient for you, but we wouldn't be here if it wasn't urgent. A woman has died."

She was going to say, "A woman was killed," but changed her mind at the last moment, glancing at the kid. Children made Nikki uncomfortable. She never knew how to be around them.

Fiona gave a bitter smile. "Yes. How utterly tragic for her. For Jayston. Yes. So very fucking tragic for Jayston."

"Who died?" asked Audrey in a small voice.

Nikki stared at the freckled face and wide eyes. Her stomach turned.

"Who died?" Audrey asked again, voice louder now. Quaking.

"Who do you think?" Fiona said with a dry, coughing sound that could have been a laugh. "Claire. Your nanny. Sneaky little cunt."

Audrey howled. A desolate, inhuman wail.

The low rumble of conversation around them stopped as every head turned.

Sonia dropped to a knee beside Audrey's chair.

"I'm so sorry, ma chère," she said gently. "We thought you knew."

The girl let out the last of her air, took a shuddering breath, and began to cry—deep, uncontrolled sobs.

"I didn't know!" She whimpered, shaking her head. "I didn't know. I didn't know."

Fiona ground her cigarette into the ashtray. "Oh, don't be dramatic! She was your nanny for less than a year. By the time I was your age, I'd had a dozen nannies. We'll find you another one."

Audrey howled again.

"That's quite enough!" Fiona sat upright with a jerk, voice low and threatening. "I will count. . . . I will!"

The girl clapped hands over her mouth, but the sobbing didn't stop.

Nikki wanted to take it all back, to somehow erase what she'd said.

No. More than that. She wanted to undo what had happened altogether—unwrite the reality of the small, bloodied form on the cold marble, and the little girl howling for her.

Fiona pushed away from the table, rising unsteadily to her feet.

"I'm counting now. One . . . two . . ."

Prickly with the sudden need to move, Nikki stepped between the woman and the child.

"Signora," she said, "can't you see how upsetting this is for your daughter?"

"And whose fault is that?" Fiona's rage turned on her. "You simply had to say that stupid thing. You're evidently too inept to do your job properly."

"What the fuck's wrong with you?" Nikki snapped, a rush of heat in her neck. She was vaguely aware of the pounding in her ears that seemed to drown out the screaming, and the restaurant noise. "You're a mother. Do your job properly, for fuck's sake. Take care of your daughter, or I'll file a complaint against you."

"You bitch! Don't you dare tell me how to raise my daughter."

Nikki opened her mouth to argue, but Sonia cut in with a firm hand on her arm.

"This is obviously a bad time, Signora Lake. We'll be in touch to arrange another interview. We need to speak to you and your husband,

and anyone else who knew Claire Sexton. In the meantime, you must stay in Naples."

"Oh, we have no intention of leaving," said Fiona. "Not until I retrieve my property. She pilfered from me. She was a thief!"

When they'd gone some distance up the pier, Sonia swung around and faced Nikki. Her tired eyes were hard. "What the hell was that?"

"What was what?"

"You know exactly what I mean. What the hell do you think you're doing antagonizing a witness? I thought I could trust you to deescalate."

"She was never going to cooperate."

"Well, she certainly won't now! First Angelo, and now you. Does everybody in Phoenix Seven need anger management training?"

Nikki protested. "That woman is abusing her kid. Do we just stand by and let it happen?"

"What abuse? She's healthy, well-fed. There are thousands of children in this city who have it far worse."

"Emotional neglect?" Nikki demanded. "Psychological abuse? Don't these matter?"

Sonia clasped her hands behind her neck and blew out, face to the sky.

"And you think that if you talk to her like that . . . shame her for being a bad mother—that will cure her? Or is it just possible she takes that shame and twists it, and turns it on her kid instead?"

Nikki was silent. The adrenaline was subsiding, leaving her weak and a little sick.

Sonia wiped a hand across her face. She looked defeated.

"You need to pull yourself together," she said. "I know things have been hard. I get it. I get that you're angry. But I can't have you on this case if you're going to be a liability."

Then she turned and left, striding across Via Partenope to where her police vehicle was parked. Nikki watched her drive away.

SEVEN

Valerio's phone was dead. Arriving at the station, he gave it to the techs to see if they could fix it.

Maurizio looked up from his paperwork when he entered the office.

"I'm happy to be wrong," he said. "Seems it went better than I thought."

Valerio stared blankly at his partner. "What?"

"Just some detective work." Maurizio grinned. "You're in your best shirt and shoes. You weren't wearing these when you left the office yesterday. But your clothes are wrinkled, and your shoes are ruined, which tells me you were out in the rain last night and haven't had a chance to go home and change. So, Maria was the real deal?"

Valerio felt a rush of irritation.

"No," he grumbled. Then, before Maurizio could say anything else, "I don't want to discuss it."

It was a quiet morning, with a full slate of catch-up. Valerio, usually annoyed with paperwork, was relieved to settle into the monotonous tasking.

Just before lunchtime, a tech knocked on the open door and strode into the office. He was a scruffy man with an overgrown beard, glasses, khaki pants, and an ill-fitting shirt.

"I can't believe I have to say this to you, an *important* capo," he announced in the dramatic voice of a TV presenter. "When you take your phone swimming with you, or store it in the toilet, it's very bad for the phone. Do you understand? It is not designed to operate in such environments."

Maurizio laughed. Valerio pushed up from his desk.

"Did you fix it?" he asked.

"I can't always perform miracles," declared the man. "This time you were lucky."

"I could kiss you," said Valerio. "Shave that ugly beard and I'll think about it. Right on the mouth. With tongue, if you ask nicely."

The phone took some time to boot up—and Valerio had nearly forgotten the password for the SIM. He made some failed attempts on his way to the toilet.

At last, the phone was unlocked, and he was annoyed to see that he'd missed a dozen messages.

He tapped on a number he didn't recognize. Someone had sent him several pictures. It took a moment to register what he was seeing. They were photos of his children—Davide and Gemma. The first two showed them on their way to school. The others were at the school entrance, as they greeted their friends and walked inside. All images had been shot with a telephoto lens.

Valerio was barely aware of himself as he rushed down the hall, down the stairs, and out of the building. It was only as he raced through the streets on his motorbike that he knew where he was going.

Luca Errichiello's home was nearly an hour's drive northeast from the center of Naples. Fueled with rage, Valerio barely noticed the winter countryside flicking by. He crossed into the depressed outskirts of Caserta, bled dry by the parasitic Camorra. Here, the asphalt was patched and torn, the spray-painted husks of abandoned buildings jutting like shipwrecks from the rising tide of trash.

Beyond these, as he approached the foothills and the compound of Luca Errichiello, doubt worked into him like a shard of glass.

Valerio had no excuse. No justification. Federico had warned him.

He owed Luca Errichiello a favor. And he knew what that meant.

He hadn't exactly forgotten Luca these past months. If anything, he'd been vigilant—hungry to learn any scrap of news or whispered intelligence about Luca's network and operations. He'd asked questions and listened in on briefings, dove into databases, and read the transcripts of trials involving Luca's peripheral network. But this investigator part of him, rabid and ravenous, had somehow quarantined itself from the man he'd been on that frantic summer night when he'd driven this road with Federico. Desperate to know if Gemma was tangled in the web, he'd gone straight to the spider. At that moment, Valerio had been entirely a father—filled with such clarity of purpose, he would have gladly traded his soul for Gemma's safety.

Until Federico's appearance this morning, Valerio had barely been conscious of the disconnect between father and investigator. Now, the walls of that separation began to crumble, flooding him with shame.

He keenly experienced the loss of his integrity, the bargain he'd made, and the revolting nature of the man with whom he'd made it. Worse, his decision had not secured the safety of his children.

Valerio shook himself. He couldn't afford to carry this burden through the gates of Luca's compound or it would get him killed. He needed to be sharp and responsive.

Worry about this moment, he told himself. *Only this moment.*

His approach took him through a vineyard to a high fence and metal gate, and he thought of that other visit months ago, and the armed men he'd seen at Luca's compound. On that occasion, Federico had called ahead to secure safe passage.

Valerio stopped his bike and called the number used to text him the pictures of his children. When a man answered, he said, "Tell Luca I'm here as he asked. Don't shoot."

The man didn't respond, but the gate slid open. Valerio drove through.

The winding road was picturesque, hemmed in on both sides by fruit trees—lemons and oranges. This far inland, the weather was clear and warm. The air smelled fresh, with a hint of woodsmoke.

Valerio approached another gate and was waved through by two men in combat gear with automatic rifles, and approached a sprawling mansion. It was constructed of grey stone and freshly painted stucco, with iron railing and red metal shutters, tile roof, and white pillars at the entrance. A square courtyard was formed by Luca's villa and two outbuildings, and in the center was a Baroque marble fountain, water pouring across the statue of a naked woman and a dolphin.

As Valerio drew close to the house, five men in black and carrying weapons came through the front door. The first man, broad-shouldered with sunglasses, pointed a handgun at him.

"Stay where you are," he ordered. "Turn off the motor. Hands raised."

Without the growl of the bike engine, the world fell suddenly quiet, the air thick with birdsong and the buzz of insects. Far away, a dog barked.

Valerio slowly raised his hands, and one of the armed men patted him down, removing the Smith & Wesson Bodyguard he kept in his waistband. This was his personal weapon. His service weapon was too bulky to carry without a harness.

"Be careful with that. I'll need it back," Valerio snarled as he felt the gun lifted. "Are we done?"

The obvious leader of the group was a lean, muscular man in his late thirties, with broad foreign features, pale mottled skin, and a thick crop of snowy hair. His posture was relaxed and he kept his weapon in his holster—a contrast to the alert tension of the other men, who flexed and gripped theirs. They looked to him, clearly awaiting instruction.

He gestured languidly.

"Come with me," he said in English.

Without looking to see if Valerio followed, he strode away.

They walked onto a gravel path on the outside edge of the house, under a bower overgrown with grapevines.

"People call me Ivan," said the man. "And you're Capo Valerio Alfieri, of the Naples police—the Sezione Falchi Squadra Mobile. Are you going to make trouble for me?"

He spoke with a thick accent, in a mix of English and Italian. Valerio struggled to decipher the words, then answered in Italian: "Is there a reason for me to make trouble for you?"

"Not at all," Ivan said. "I have many friends in your unit. We get along well. Who knows? One day, you might be grateful for a friend like me."

"You know what I think, Ivan?" said Valerio. "Liars and bullies are like mushrooms: everywhere. I'm never impressed by men like you. I put them behind bars. Who knows? One day, I might see you there."

Ivan laughed.

"The ego of a man who lies to himself!"

His pale eyes held a manic gleam. He said something in a language Valerio didn't understand. Then, in English, as if to let Valerio in on the joke: "If you listen to your own lie, you can't see the truth. See? I know you better than you know yourself. I'll enjoy this. I'll enjoy you, Capo."

Valerio glared back.

"If you know me so well, then you should know I don't respond to threats," he warned. "Keep out of my business, and I'll stay out of yours."

Ivan shrugged and continued walking.

They emerged to an elaborately tiled pool glinting blue in the sunlight, a handful of faded grape leaves curled on the surface.

Luca Errichiello sat at a tile-topped metal garden table, drinking Coca-Cola, a platter of salami and cheese before him.

As with their last encounter, Valerio was struck by the banality of Luca. He was an unremarkable man in his fifties with mild, forgettable features. Today, he wore leather loafers, a puffer jacket, and a tan felt hat. The unassuming, even features and bored expression gave no suggestion of what he really was. Luca exploited immigrants and refugees, cashing in on EU money for asylum seekers, pressuring and starving the most vulnerable: populating his brothels with them, and exporting sex and agriculture workers and domestic slaves throughout Europe and Russia. The only prosecutor able to get close to proving the case against Luca had been killed by a car bomb in Licola last year.

"Capo Alfieri's here," announced Ivan in a cheerful tone. "Want me to stay and protect you, Errichiello?"

"Fuck off," snapped Luca, the hot burst of irritation disturbing an otherwise expressionless face.

As Ivan strolled away, Luca ate salami and watched Valerio.

"You took your time," he said, voice flat. "I don't like to be kept waiting."

Valerio had meant to stay cool, but now he battled for control against his fury.

"Don't you ever, *ever* threaten my kids again!" he growled.

Luca stretched out his jaw with a click, like a snake preparing for a large meal.

"You appear to care for your offspring," he said. "Society considers this laudable. It only interests me as a means to achieve your attention. I see I have it. Next time, I expect you to come when I ask."

"You want something, you deal with men," Valerio said. "Leave the children the hell out of it, or I will hunt you down. I promise I will kill you."

"Pointless threats don't interest me, Alfieri."

"What the fuck do you want?" Valerio demanded.

Luca chewed. "You owe me a favor."

"I found my daughter without your help," Valerio said, even as he felt the futility of trying to constrain the borders of his debt.

"Yet, you asked for my help, and I gave it. And who knows what may happen to your daughter next?"

Valerio's rage flared. "Is that a threat?"

"Not at all," Luca said, picking something out of his teeth. "I only mean that young ladies have a way of wandering into a fox's den. You may wish to request my services again."

Valerio thought of Gemma, the knock-kneed little girl who transformed every day, becoming a woman. It should make him happy. Instead, he burst with near-constant dread, and a profound helplessness.

"What's your favor?"

Luca sipped.

"It's a very small thing, really. Not much at all."

"Tell me what you want."

"An eighteen-year-old boy was arrested yesterday. Gaetano Mancusi. Sweet kid. His mother works for me. Housekeeping. He was pulled over on a routine traffic stop. The idiot was carrying a very small—extremely small—amount of cocaine. Well, they arrested him. But the little fool wouldn't tell them about himself. So, they looked into his phone. And what do you think they found there?"

He seemed to expect a response. Valerio didn't give one.

"Well," Luca continued, "an app on his phone led the police to where Gaetano was living with two other boys. They found more drugs at this location. So all three boys are arrested. Gaetano says that these were not his drugs. I believe him. He's a good kid. I think the other boys are to blame."

"What do you want me to do?"

"I'd like you to speak with the magistrate . . . ask to release him until trial. You see, his mother is alone. She has cancer. Gaetano is her only son. She relies on him."

The anxiety in Valerio's chest was slowly easing. He'd been bracing, expecting something illegal or unethical. This was neither.

"And you can't help her?" he said, looking at the elegant garden and house.

"I can hire lawyers to reduce his sentence," agreed Luca calmly. "But what she really wants is her son back. Jail is no place for a young boy. You've been to Poggioreale. You must know that's true. Would you want your son there?"

Even without Luca's request, Valerio would have advocated to keep a teenager out of Poggioreale. He'd done this sort of thing before. The overcrowded jail was a law unto itself; young men, trapped with the wolves, were brutalized.

"I can't get the charges dropped," Valerio said. "The magistrate decides that. We can only give our recommendation."

Luca nodded. "I understand. Look, relax. What I'm asking from you is completely legal. One friend to another."

"Not friends," said Valerio.

Luca raised an eyebrow. "As you wish."

"I'll need to confirm what you're saying."

"Of course. Speak with Gaetano's mother. You'll agree, I'm sure, that you should talk to the general prosecutor's office."

Valerio examined him. Luca Errichiello's smooth, well-fed face looked nothing like the ancient, tortured apparition that was his brother. For years, Valerio had watched the anguish and fear of the old addict, and the daily labor he performed to keep up the small storefront salumeria. It contrasted disconcertingly with the luxury and ease of this life—and Luca's neutral, disinterested face.

"This is all you want?" Valerio asked.

"You do this for me, and I'll consider your debt paid."

"And you leave my family alone."

"You have my word."

Valerio was cautious. Alert. But relief eased his burning mind.

Luca's lips twisted. It could have been a smile. "You should see yourself. What did you think I would ask?"

Valerio grunted. "I haven't agreed yet. Give me the name and address of Gaetano's mother. I'll talk to her. I'll talk to the kid. If what you say checks out, I have no problem calling the magistrate."

Gaetano's mother lived in the Forcella district. There was a time, not long ago, when Valerio would have thought twice about walking alone down these streets, even out of uniform as he was now. The difficult neighborhood and Camorra stronghold had been cleaned up by a government eager to accommodate the tourist economy. A thriving contraband trade was still visible on the periphery, but Valerio was less likely to be attacked by thugs or jabbed by a discarded needle wedged between the cobblestones, or to catch a bullet from a random spray. Still, he preferred to be here in daylight.

Valerio called Maurizio when he arrived.

"Where the fuck did you go?" his partner demanded.

"Urgent call. Hey, I've been asked for a favor: to look into the arrest of an eighteen-year-old kid."

He described the situation, but omitted Luca's name.

"I'm here at his mother's house now—to see if the story checks out. Can you take a look on your side?"

"Fuck," Maurizio sighed. "You should have brought me with you."

"Can you take a look?"

"Yeah. Text me his details. I'll see what I can find."

The apartment was on the fourth floor of a large building with rusting railings and chipped concrete. Valerio buzzed the apartment number, but there was no response. He strode along the street, looking for another way in. The first open storefront was a cheap jewelry shop featuring twisted wire necklaces, beaded earrings, glass gems, and hundreds of cornicelli. The woman behind the counter had grey hair and a sour expression.

"We're not open."

"The door is open," Valerio observed.

"We're closed."

"I'm trying to get into number forty-one."

She took off her glasses and stared at him. "Who do you want there?"

"Ines Mancusi."

"You a debt collector?"

"What makes you think I'm a debt collector?"

"They're the only ones wanting forty-one."

"I'm not a debt collector."

"Well, whatever you want, she's not well," said the woman. "And her boy was just arrested. So, it isn't a good time to be bothering her."

"I may be able to help," he said. "I've been asked by a family friend to look into the situation of his arrest."

She looked him up and down, taking in the wrinkled clothing, the ruined shoes. She looked doubtful and Valerio thought she was going to kick him out. At last she seemed to surrender.

"She has a friend . . . a nurse who usually comes by around this time. Ravenna. She should be able to let you in."

Valerio waited by the building entrance. He felt worn out. Uncomfortable. A deep unease ran through his mind like a sewer beneath the city streets. For months, he'd carried the contamination of this obligation to Luca—whether he acknowledged it or not. Now that the corruption had worked its way to the surface, it itched. He wanted this to be over.

A group of teenage boys buzzed past on their motorbikes.

He waited and paced for nearly forty minutes, then strode into a nearby café for a cornetto and espresso, keeping an eye on the street and the door to the building. He ate rapidly, shoving the pastry into his mouth. He was brushing crumbs from his shirt when he saw a woman striding towards him—in her thirties, curvy, dressed in scrubs and sneakers and carrying a canvas bag. She had glasses and short, tightly curled hair.

"Ravenna?" he said, stepping forward.

She hesitated, looked him over.

"Sì?"

He showed his badge, introduced himself.

"I'd like to speak with Ines Mancusi. I understand you're her friend."

She shook her head. "Ines had her chemotherapy yesterday. She's very ill."

"It won't take long. I'd like to know more about the situation with her son."

She reached out for his badge and he handed it to her. She inspected it carefully.

"Am I required to let you in?" she asked.

Valerio sighed.

"No," he admitted. "But I'm here to help. A family friend asked me to look into Gaetano's situation, and see if there was something I could do."

"What can you do? He's arrested. He's in jail."

"If I'm convinced that he's no risk, that his mother needs him, I'll talk with the magistrate and see if they'll release him."

She examined him a moment more, and Valerio saw beneath the curtain of ringlets: her large soulful eyes and full cheeks. She reminded him of an angel painted on the altarpiece of a church.

She handed back his badge.

"Follow me."

The old building was dreary, the unfinished, rough concrete of the rectangular interior like an open box leading straight up to the grey sky and misery of rain. The floor was smoothed with grime. On the walls, patches of mildew erupted like an infection. Exposed rebar in the concrete leaked red.

Valerio followed Ravenna to the end of the hall and the entrance of a stairwell.

"I've known Gaetano since he was a baby," Ravenna said as they climbed the stairs. "I used to watch him for Ines."

"You're a nurse?"

"I am . . . now. But in those days, I was just a schoolkid. His babysitter."

"Ines was a single parent?" he asked.

"Her husband died just after the baby was born."

"What can you tell me about Gaetano?"

She took a few steps before answering.

"He has a good heart. But I worry about him."

"What are you worried about?"

"Well, there isn't much for a teenage boy, is there? The unemployment is bad, and the jobs for kids his age don't pay well. They can make so much more money dealing drugs, or working for the clans as transport or security."

"Is that what Gaetano was doing?" he asked.

She shrugged. "I don't know, Capo."

They climbed to the next floor in silence, accompanied only by the sounds of their footsteps and their breathing.

"I'm really trying to help if I can," said Valerio, feeling out of oxygen. "But I need to know: If I help to get Gaetano released from jail, can he stay out of trouble?"

"How much can any of us stay out of trouble?" said Ravenna. "We can do our best, but what happens when trouble comes looking for you?"

Ravenna let herself into the apartment and called out, "Ines, it's me. There's a policeman with me. He wants to talk to you."

She plucked a brown-haired wig off a hook and said to Valerio, "Wait for a few minutes before coming in. Don't make her ashamed."

The space was cluttered and untidy, and filled with an unwholesome odor: the smell of sickness, mildew, cigarettes, medicine, and cats. At the center of the clutter in a sagging armchair sat a thin woman with papery, sallow skin stretched across her skull. She was held down in the chair by tubes tentacled out from a nearby oxygen tank. Her eyes, sunk deep in their sockets, were shaded the colors of a healing bruise. The dark wig did little to change the skeletal appearance. If anything, it gave a disturbing contrast to the pallid grey complexion. But she smoothed it back with her long, narrow fingers, twisting the hair next to her ear. Her vanity reminded Valerio a little of his sister Penelope and of his mother.

"I don't have anything to say to you, policeman," Ines said. Her voice was rough but she held her head aloft, casting an imperious look. "How dare you take a son away from his sick mother?"

"Signora, I did not arrest your son—"

He was about to explain his purpose, but she cut him off.

"It's a vendetta," she rasped. "The police don't like me working for Luca—so they punish my son."

She coughed, then opened her fist and spat into the tissue clenched there.

"How long have you worked for Luca Errichiello?" he asked.

"Seventeen years now," she told him. "My husband, Azzo, was his driver. When Azzo died, Luca helped me out. They say he's a bad man . . . but would a bad man do that?"

"You do know what Errichiello does? He trafficks young women and girls. He puts them in his brothels. Sells them to men who abuse and kill them?"

Valerio hadn't planned to say this, but he couldn't play along with the fiction of Luca Errichiello as an upright citizen.

Ines brushed this away with a hand. "Lies. Ugly lies."

"You've never seen him do anything that worried you?"

"Not at all."

She breathed deeply, a harsh sound. The nurse lifted her wrist and measured her pulse.

"I thought your questions were about Gaetano, Capo," Ravenna said in a quiet, measured tone.

He looked at her and she returned his gaze, eyes wide and cautioning.

"When Gaetano was arrested," said Valerio, "I understand it was a drugs charge . . . he was arrested with two other boys?"

"Sì," agreed Ines. "I'm sure the other boys were responsible for the drugs. My son would never do such a thing."

"Gaetano wasn't living here when he was arrested?"

"No. He moved in with those two other boys during the summer."

"How did he afford to move?" asked Valerio. "Was he working?"

She coughed and coughed some more, narrow shoulders working hard as her chest heaved.

Ravenna stroked the sick woman's back.

"Would you get some water?" she asked Valerio.

In the kitchen, dirty dishes were in the sink. Valerio moved some of these aside to get to the faucet and fill a glass.

A list of numbers was taped to the refrigerator, alongside shopping lists. There were also snapshots of Ines and her son throughout the years. As a kid, Gaetano was dimple-cheeked, with a shy smile and an overgrowth of thick dark hair that seemed to never look combed. As the chubbiness of youth settled into a teenage heft, the smile vanished and he grew a sparse mustache. In the most recent photos, his expression had hardened into a distant, unsatisfied look.

The pictures of Ines were from an earlier era when her figure was slim and tight. Before her illness, she'd been a handsome woman, although an overlarge jaw and small eyes prevented her from being entirely beautiful. She had a clear complexion and long, dark hair. She posed for the camera, tossing her head and peering flirtatiously into the lens. There were also several photos of Ines next to a short, grey-haired man with a wide white smile and tanned, leathery skin.

Valerio took pictures of the photos and notes. For good measure, he checked the cupboards, where he found dishes, canned goods, pasta, an assortment of medicines, and a colony of shiny brown cockroaches.

Back in the living room, Valerio handed the water to Ines. She gripped it with skeletal fingers and drank, then was silent for a long time afterwards, staring straight ahead at the large flat-screen television opposite her chair.

A ginger cat had migrated to Valerio's seat in his absence. It ignored his attempts to shoo it away, so he picked it up and plopped it onto the ground. It hissed, then stalked to Ines's feet, where it stared malevolently at him.

Valerio waited.

"Gaetano was working for a local shop," Ines said, at last. "Deliveries."

"Do you have the name of the shop?"

She shook her head no, but Ravenna interjected, "He delivered produce to restaurants."

"How do you know this?" Valerio asked.

"I saw him around town," she said. "Making deliveries."

Valerio took notes.

"Do you know anyone he worked with?"

Neither seemed to know.

"What can you tell me about the other guys he was living with?"

"I don't know them," said Ines. "Just some boys."

"How did he know them? From school? From work?"

"I told the other police: I didn't know them!"

Her eyelids drooped and she seemed to crumple. Her head sagged against the chair and the water glass tipped. Ravenna took it from the sick woman's fingers and looked at Valerio.

"You should go," she said.

Valerio left his card, and was glad to escape the stink and clutter of the apartment.

Taking a deep breath in the cold air of the corridor, he'd started to head down the stairs when he heard a door close and someone said, "Capo!"

Valerio stopped and looked back.

Ravenna stood on the landing above.

"You didn't tell her," she accused.

"Tell her what?"

"You said you were going to try and get Gaetano out of jail. Is that true—or were you just saying that so I'd let you in?"

He shrugged. "It's true."

"Then why not tell her?"

Valerio shook his head. "Does it matter?"

Ravenna's dark eyes were wide. She took a step towards him. "She's dying, Capo. There's no help for it. The only thing we can offer is comfort."

The compassion in her face was a rebuke.

"You heard her," Valerio protested. "She works for Luca Errichiello, and she calls him a good man! Do you have any idea what he does? What he is?"

"So, you punish her for his sins?"

"I refuse to feel pity for someone who closes her eyes to the evil around her so she can take advantage!"

His voice sounded loud, echoing in the stairwell.

"She closes her eyes so she can survive," Ravenna replied quietly. "Have you never done the same when you were ashamed of yourself?"

The words stung.

She reached out a hand. "Come," she said. "Come back and tell her that you'll help Gaetano. Give her that, at least."

"I may not be able to get him out of Poggioreale."

"Tell her you'll try."

He gazed up into those dark eyes as she searched his face. A question hovered between them. He felt the pressure of it—as if she was invoking something from him, as if she expected or needed him to be more than he was. For a moment he wanted to be that person she was summoning. His neck felt hot. He broke contact.

"You can tell her, if you want," he said, then hurried down the stairs.

EIGHT

The world was turning grey when Nikki was awakened by a knock on the door and the buzz of the doorbell. A baritone voice sang out: "Ciao, bella! Nina! Nina! Nicole Angelina Serafino! Time to wake up!"

"Quiet!" someone from a neighboring flat shouted. "Don't you know the time?"

Nikki groaned and threw off the covers.

The cold tiles stung her feet as she marched to the entryway and turned the key. She pulled the heavy door wide, letting in a gust of frigid air.

"Babbo, what are you doing here?"

Raoul Serafino was wearing one of his two favorite suits: charcoal grey with a white collared shirt, open at the neck.

He kissed her cheeks, bringing the smell of outdoors and the tang of aftershave.

"Do I need a reason to visit my daughter?"

Nikki checked her watch. "It's not even six. What time did you get up? Four thirty?"

He clapped his hands and smiled in that way she remembered from long ago: a signal of adventure.

"He who sleeps catches no fish. Get dressed. Come. I'll buy you coffee."

"Okay . . . okay . . ." Her head was still foggy with sleep. "I need a shower first. My shift starts at zero seven thirty."

The city was starting to wake. A garbage truck rumbled along the cobblestones, two men in city uniforms jumping out to empty the bins. An old lady leaned out the door of her house, cigarette perched between her fingers. She waved and called to Raoul as he passed, and

Nikki waited while her father diverted to greet her and ask after her son.

"So good to have you back," she shouted as he walked away.

He started whistling.

This charged, ready-to-go, early-morning man was a familiar fixture from Nikki's childhood, but she hadn't seen this version of her father for a long time.

"What's gotten into you?" she asked.

"What are you talking about?" he said. "Oh good. Massimo's is open. Let's say hello."

A small crowd gathered at the bar where Massimo Fattore stood at the espresso machine, pulling coffees. Carlo sat at the cash register, the sleeves of his white shirt rolled, tattoos on hairy forearms.

Someone spotted Raoul, and a cry rose up.

"Raoul! Raoul Serafino! Where have you been? Good to see you!"

He was kissed and patted and answered questions from men whom Nikki barely recognized.

Nikki endeavored to keep a low profile, but this sort of attention was standard practice for her father, and he stood in the center of the adulating crowd, answering questions and saying things like "How's the leg, Luigi?" and "Has your wife had that surgery yet?" and "That motorbike was a bad idea. Anyone could see that. The engine was shot."

Nikki edged away from her father, crossing to Carlo, who gave her a smile and nod.

"What for you today, bella?"

"Cappuccino for me. And one for my father."

"I thought he preferred espresso," Carlo said.

"Does he?" Nikki hadn't remembered.

She was relieved to see that Massimo looked like his old self, dancing the familiar steps at the espresso machine. But it was difficult to put aside the recollection of him standing at her door the day before yesterday, shaky and confused.

Massimo winked at her. "Ciao, bella. Chocolate for you this morning? Will you take a cornetto?"

"Certo."

Behind her, Raoul's belly laugh was an echo of another era. It struck an ache in Nikki's chest.

Massimo called loudly, "Cornetto for you, Raoul? Chocolate? Crema?"

Raoul pivoted to Massimo, and his grin spread even further. "My doctor says no chocolate . . . but maybe just this once."

"What are you doing in the city?" someone asked.

"Oh, a little of this. A little of that."

"Don't be so mysterious!"

"Nothing mysterious about it! Just some business to attend to. You know how it is."

"Will you stay long?"

"It may take a few days."

He gave promises to stop by for coffee and to bring sweets to grandchildren.

Meanwhile, Nikki laid claim to a table and two plastic chairs, but Raoul sidled up to the bar and gestured for her to join.

"How are things going, Massimo?" he asked.

Massimo clucked his tongue and set two saucers on the glass bar, and two small spoons.

"Going, going . . ." Massimo leaned in, and spoke in a low tone. "What are you actually doing in the city? You can trust your old friend."

Raoul raised an eyebrow. "Some case from long ago floated to the surface. They want my advice."

"Of course, they need the best," said Massimo.

"Do you still have that spare room in your house?" Raoul asked. "It would help to have a place to stay a few days while I take care of my business. It's a long drive to Benevento."

Massimo hesitated. "Oh, I don't know, Raoul. It isn't very tidy."

Nikki was surprised. Her parents had always stayed with her when they came into Naples.

Raoul leaned on the bar with both forearms and spoke to Massimo in a confidential tone. "I'd ask Nikki or Gianni. But Gianni and Francesca have their hands full with the new baby. And I'm sure my daughter would like her privacy—"

"You're welcome to stay with me," she interjected.

Neither man seemed to hear.

"Alright, then," said Massimo, finishing the drinks and setting them on the saucers. "I'll ask my niece to help me clear it out."

"Good! I'll bring my bags around this afternoon."

Raoul drained his espresso and smacked his lips.

"That's exactly what I needed. Now, a cigarette. I'll come back for that cornetto and another caffè. Excuse me!"

Nikki watched him stride away. When did he start smoking again? He'd surrendered the habit years ago.

"You know," Massimo said, considering, "I wouldn't do it for just anyone. But your father . . . well . . . I know he's lonely since your mother passed. I think he could use an old friend."

Nikki nursed her cappuccino. A few more customers came in and Massimo busied himself. When he produced Raoul's second espresso and her father hadn't returned, Nikki took the cups and pastries and went outside to find him.

Raoul was seated at an outdoor table with two men. They were laughing and smoking as if it was the 1980s again and Raoul Serafino was known for his lively conversation, excellent memory, and fairness. On weekend mornings, he used to hold arbitrations here, listening to arguments between neighbors, between brothers, sisters, husbands and wives. People trusted his nuanced judgments and, more often than not, followed his advice.

After Adriano died, Nikki's parents moved away from the city, and retreated into the foothills of the Benevento countryside. Grief poisoned Beatrice. She became angry and closed, while Raoul seemed to simply surrender, as if all the air had left the room. The ebullient curiosity that had been so fundamental to him vanished. It was years before he gradually recovered some of his old enthusiasm. When Beatrice died, the scaffolding collapsed again. This morning was the first time Nikki had glimpsed her father as she remembered him. Not the shell of the man she'd come to expect, but fully alive and activated.

The two men sitting with Raoul stood up with exclamations of regret for leaving.

"I want to keep an eye on Massimo for a few days," Raoul told Nikki when they were alone. "He was always a good friend to your mother and me. I think he's lonely."

He bit into his cornetto, and leaned over the table to keep the buttery flakes from falling on his shirt.

"I came past Piazza del Gesù Nuovo on my way here," he continued. "It was cordoned off. And there was a police vehicle by the door of the church. What happened?"

"Someone was killed."

"Nobody would plan a murder in a church," he said. "Crime of passion, then. Did they catch the killer?"

"I don't know," Nikki said.

"They'll need a quick and quiet investigation, or it will chase away the tourists," Raoul said, then chuckled to himself. "Maybe it isn't a bad thing to lose a few tourists. . . ."

He finished his pastry and, looking thoughtful, lit another cigarette.

"Beatrice studied that church, you know?" he mused. "She was convinced there was a hidden message in the facade."

Nikki inhaled sharply. It had been months since Raoul had mentioned her mother. He never seemed to like it when Nikki talked about her.

"What was the message?" she asked.

He shook his head with a soft smile.

"She never told me. That's just who she was: a code breaker. Adriano was like her. He saw the patterns. She brought him into her world."

For a moment he seemed stricken.

Nikki glanced across the piazza, pigeons pecking at the stones.

Only since her mother's death last year had Nikki begun to realize the extent to which she hadn't properly known her.

Of course, she knew the family story well enough: Raoul had been a handsome carabinieri officer and Beatrice a beautiful twenty-four-year-old cryptologist translating for the United States Navy. They'd met on a joint operation, and began a love affair that lasted a lifetime. Beatrice left her career to marry Raoul and raise three children.

It was a beautiful fairy tale—but Nikki had spent her life intuiting the shape of her mother's secrets, and felt certain there was a lie buried in this truth.

Months ago, NCIS agent Durant Cole had talked about Beatrice—had said she was something more . . . something *special*. His words had brought a strange sort of relief, confirming an instinct Nikki had carried since childhood.

Violetta, he'd told her. *That was her code name. And what happened on Santo Stefano . . .*

It was possible he'd lied. Everything else had been a lie: the friendship . . . the trust.

Nikki had asked her father about it, but he'd brushed it off. "There were a lot of things about your mother I didn't know," he'd said.

Nikki had investigated as far as she could on her own. She'd filed requests for information from the US government. She and Valerio had also sailed *Calypso* to the island of Santo Stefano, hiked around, and talked to the locals. But it was a dead end.

"She brought Adriano into her world," Nikki repeated back to Raoul now. "What do you mean?"

"Oh," he sighed. "You know how those two were . . . like bread and onions."

Nikki remembered Adriano at the kitchen table while their mother cooked, talking politics and philosophy—the two of them speaking in that secret language they used.

Raoul clinked the small spoon around his empty espresso cup, scraping the remnants of sweet dark foam.

"Maybe I'll do my own investigation," he said. "I'll ask around . . . see what people say."

His eyes gleamed with replenished enthusiasm.

"Let the police do their job," Nikki warned. "They might not like you getting in the way."

"But the police don't know this place like I do. Tell me about the murder. What have you heard?"

"I can't discuss it," Nikki said.

Raoul looked surprised.

"So, you're part of the investigation!" he exclaimed. "And that means it involves the Americans."

"I can't talk about it."

She closed her lips to keep from swearing.

His face changed. His attention, which had roved around all morning, was suddenly focused, expression hard.

"I don't like you being in another murder investigation."

"It's my job," Nikki said.

"Can't they get someone else? Aren't there men on your team? Let them do it."

These had been Nikki's very thoughts when she'd gone to the station in the middle of the night, but hearing her father speak them aloud brought a current of irritation.

"So, it's acceptable for you to conduct your own unauthorized investigation, but it isn't alright for me to do my job?"

"It isn't the same thing. I just don't like the thought of my daughter being in a dangerous situation again. Your mother wouldn't have wanted it either."

"Adriano did dangerous work," Nikki said. "Would you have said this to him?"

"That was different," Raoul said loudly. "He was older."

Some door inside Nikki swung shut. "I'm older than he was when he died."

The words seemed to silence him.

"This is what I do," she said tersely. "And I'm good at it."

She didn't look back as she strode across the piazza and out of sight.

Nikki walked brusquely through the chilly city streets, rapidly covering the few blocks to the cathedral.

Two policemen stood at the entrance to the piazza on Via Benedetto Croce, directing foot traffic from the church square. A middle-aged woman in an oversize coat and orange scarf was shouting.

"You're stopping my business! How do you expect me to live, to feed myself?"

She patted the metal cart beside her—filled with boxes and bags and, strapped to the side, a folded card table and stool. Everything bristled with snips of bright ribbon and thread, and hundreds of rattling, shining charms.

One young officer with an artless expression was clearly uncomfortable.

"There's an investigation of a serious matter," he told her. "Can't you go someplace else?"

"Oh, say what it is," she shot back. "Everyone knows that there was a murder in the church! This piazza is where I work. People need to know where to find me."

She looked to the other policeman as if for reinforcement. But he busied himself directing people away. He gestured to a grey-haired priest, motioning him into the square.

"You let him through!" the woman shrieked. "Why him, and not me?"

"He's a priest," said the policeman.

"Why should that matter?" she said. "I'm as important as that priest. Ask your mother . . . your grandmother! They may go to him for confession, but for the things that matter—the things they truly care about—they come to Signora Dorotea!"

"Please, just go," he pleaded. "Nobody can come to you for advice in the piazza today. Nobody will be there."

Nikki sidestepped them and, showing her Phoenix Seven identification card, walked through, to the complaining protest of Signora Dorotea.

The cathedral was a brutal and imposing structure: a grey stone wall extending along a city block, faced in a bizarre, unrelenting matrix of stone spikes. This was interrupted by three doors, the center door flanked by marble Corinthian columns and draped in police tape.

A pale blue police cruiser was parked in front.

Nikki wasn't sure exactly why she felt the need to visit now. She'd been in the cathedral enough times to know the place where Claire Sexton had been murdered: the chapel just beyond the western transept. There was probably nothing left to see. Forensics had been collected; the scene combed for evidence and cleaned. But she wanted to fix it in her mind somehow, as if being in the church would give her the chance to talk to the dead woman herself.

She moved towards the uniformed officer in the car and, showing her Phoenix Seven ID card, introduced herself and asked to be let inside.

"Nobody's allowed," he said. "You'll need to ask the officer in charge."

Nikki turned to the center of the piazza, towards the enormous Baroque obelisk, the Guglia dell'Immacolata. Built in the eighteenth century to invoke the Virgin Mary's protection from the plague, the sides were decorated with saints and scenes from the life of Mary. Atop the column, facing the distant port and sea, stood the Immacolata herself—crowned, in flowing robes.

The place was usually filled with tourists, school groups, beggars, and vendors selling jewelry and flowers and umbrellas. It was empty now, and all the businesses—restaurants, a small bookstore and information booth—closed.

She was leaving the piazza when a loud, clear voice called, "You were betrayed!"

Nikki turned and saw the oversize coat and orange scarf of the woman who had been arguing with the police. She was at the base of the obelisk, and unstrapping her stool and table from the cart.

Nikki strode towards her.

"What did you say?"

Signora Dorotea's bleached hair was styled into large soft curls, her lips bright red. She beckoned with a manicured hand.

"You're a seeker. Come. I'll help you find what you're looking for."

She began unpacking her cart, hefting two boxes and a sizable canvas bag onto the cobblestones. Everything was bedecked in ribbons and trinkets: a dozen metal ex-voto cutouts used as offerings in the local churches; hundreds of the red chili-pepper-shaped cornicelli charms, the Neapolitan symbol of good luck and good sex; a plastic figure; and a bright silver talisman with a pair of twined snakes. Dorotea unzipped the canvas bag and rummaged inside, extracting a stack of shabby, damp-looking tarot cards. She snapped off an elastic band, and sat on the stool with a sigh.

"Were you here night before last?" Nikki asked.

"I see it," said Dorotea. "I don't ask for this gift. It comes to me. I see things."

"Did you see the woman who was killed?"

For several seconds Signora Dorotea serenely shuffled and sorted her tarot. Then she spoke in a matter-of-fact singsong: "I know that you're angry. He betrayed you. He let you think he was different than he was. Perhaps he wanted to be the man you believed. But it was impossible."

To Nikki's irritation, the woman's words triggered an electric chill along her spine. She saw the darkness of the cave, and the face of her former friend Durant Cole in the harsh light of the sizzling red flare.

O my dear Guide, who more than seven times hast rendered me security . . . do not desert me . . .

It's just a fucking trick, she reminded herself, hating the weak, hollow sensation in her chest.

Nikki scoffed, "Does that actually work? Say that to any woman, and she'll think of a dozen men who betrayed her."

Dorotea looked from beneath a fringe of false lashes. Her eyes were shiny and black, pale powder settled in the creases.

"But he was more than that. He was special to you, so his betrayal was a thief, robbing your trust."

She seemed to hear Durant's voice: . . . *in this nether world I will not leave thee . . .*

"I'm not playing this game," said Nikki brusquely. "I just want to know if you were here two nights ago when the woman was murdered."

The fortune teller seemed to consider. "Give me your palm and I'll tell you what you need to know."

"How much?"

"Fifteen."

Nikki sighed, then countered. "Ten."

The woman agreed with a grudging look.

Nikki stomped her feet against the cold, then surrendered her hand.

Dorotea snatched it, a cluster of sparkling bracelets jangling on her wrist. Her grip was cold, skin chapped as she spread Nikki's fingers wide, pulling back the thumb, and angling the palm close to her face.

"You do not trust," she said. "Walls of deception are built around you. Secrets . . . in your past and future. You're driven to root out those secrets. You systematize and analyze . . . to find your way through the maze of lies. You will find answers, but pay a high price. You're in danger—"

"That's enough!"

Nikki tugged her hand—gently at first, then wrenched it back. "I thought you were supposed to tell people about coming into riches, or finding good husbands."

"I tell you what I see," said Dorotea with a sly smile and a shrug. She pointed a finger heavenward. "What do you see there? When you look at the statue?"

"What do you mean?"

Nikki tilted her head to gaze at the statue high above. From where she stood, she saw the back side of the Virgin Mary, robes billowing behind her.

"On one side is the Immacolata—the face of the Madonna," said Dorotea. "But on this side . . . do you not see the hooded figure with the scythe? This is Napoli! Here, light and darkness are bound together. On the one side? Grace and mercy. The other? Death."

Nikki tried to calm herself, to bring back that measured control she used when responding to incidents, but her annoyance was tipping into anger. "What I'm interested in is what you saw at the church night before last. Were you here with your cards during the evening mass?"

"I was here," agreed the fortune teller.

"Can you tell me what you saw?"

Dorotea closed her eyes. "The young woman who was killed . . . she knew her killer . . . she was afraid. She wanted to keep something secret. She knew the killer would meet her."

Nikki's attention focused. She examined Dorotea's face.

"How do you know this?" she asked.

"I know," Dorotea intoned.

"Did she tell you?"

"She didn't tell me with words." The woman tapped a pink fingernail against her temple.

Nikki's irritation was a bright ember burning through her patience. She bent down to get on the level with Dorotea, and looked sternly in her birdlike eyes.

"I realize you need to make a living with this act," she said. "But a woman was killed. The murderer could kill again. Please stop your performance and tell me: Did you meet the victim? Did you speak to her?"

Dorotea was silent as she considered. Then she shook her head, chest puffed, and unfurled her hand.

"We did not speak."

Nikki dug in her wallet, found the bills and paid, then turned and strode away.

Signora Dorotea called after her. "You are a child of Napoli, full of light and darkness . . . the divine and infernal wrestling . . ."

In the office, Nikki was relieved to find that Pasquale was her duty partner today. Of all the men in Phoenix Seven, she preferred her shifts with Pasquale since he did his job well and was good company. Unfortunately, Angelo was also in the office. He summoned her when she arrived.

He stood behind his desk, leaning onto his fists, elbows locked.

"This isn't like last time," he said. A vein pulsed in his temple. "You don't get to take time off the schedule and pretend to be a detective. You work your shift, like everyone else."

"Excuse me?"

"You heard me," Angelo said. "Mario told me you got another by-name request to assist the police investigation yesterday. This has to stop. Your work is here. I can't have you prancing off anytime you want."

"I can't help it if the police ask for me," Nikki pointed out.

Spots of red were rising in Angelo's cheeks.

"Romano says you know that Black lady detective. He saw you on Via Toledo together."

"Detective Inspector Sonia Dieng?"

"Yes. Her. Is she your girlfriend?"

"And by that, you mean?"

"You know what I mean," he barked. "Don't pretend with me. Is she your girlfriend? Is that why she keeps requesting you?"

Nikki's incredulity was matched only by her outrage. But showing her anger to Angelo would only reinforce a perception she didn't want to feed. She kept her voice flat.

"If you'll recall, Inspector Dieng and I worked the Markham case together."

"You haven't answered my question."

Nikki took a deep breath. "Detective Inspector Dieng is not my girlfriend—but it wouldn't be your business if she was."

Angelo was working himself into a froth.

"It would most certainly be my business! Phoenix Seven does not permit conflicts of interest."

Nikki's words were ice. "In the past six months, Romano has dated two different carabinieri officers and a US Navy lieutenant. Would you consider these conflicts of interest?"

"I'm not talking about that with you," Angelo protested.

Nikki continued, raising her voice. "Mario's running a security consulting business as a side hustle. Would you consider that a conflict of interest?"

"Get out of my office."

Nikki maintained eye contact for a few beats before leaving Angelo, shutting the door behind her.

Not long ago, Nikki had believed she could get along with Angelo.

After the heat of summer had ended, after the admiral was released from hospital and returned to work and Nikki was recovering from the worst injuries she'd sustained in her fight with Durant, her suspension was lifted. Angelo had been courteous—commending her work and welcoming her back to Phoenix Seven. But the civility didn't last.

On the day Admiral Redford brought Angelo and Nikki to his office to award Nikki a medal, Angelo had bristled with indignation.

"It isn't appropriate to reward an individual investigator," he explained earnestly to the admiral. "Phoenix Seven works as a team—so the team should get the award."

He seemed incensed by Admiral Redford's refusal to listen to his reasoning, and afterwards became cold and dismissive towards Nikki.

Nikki's irritation with Angelo gradually transformed into disgust, and a hopelessness that anything she said would sway him. She also felt a sort of heady recklessness in their interactions, and an inability to play along and soothe his wounded ego.

Returning to her desk, Nikki checked her phone and messages and emails, and dug into overdue paperwork. She heard Angelo leave, but didn't look up as he stomped past, slamming out the door.

After a while, Pasquale pulled up a chair and chatted, discussing his family's plans for Christmas, and his wife's online business selling handmade lace. It was a quiet morning, and they left the office for a long coffee break at the outdoor café before heading back to work.

The morning stretched on, and neither Sonia nor Emilio called. Nikki, who expected to continue supporting their investigation, vacillated between disappointment and relief. Despite her defiant words to her father, she had ambivalent feelings about assisting the police in this particular case.

Before this past summer, before the Markham case and the investigation with Durant, she trusted her instincts and capability. When the world was ugly or unfair, when everyone else was losing their minds, she kept a clear head. But things had changed. Gone was the clarity, the calm. In its place, rooted like a parasite, was a persistent red glow of rage. Despite her efforts to get her emotions under control, the fury was growing—so intense, so close to the surface, it could erupt without warning. Yesterday, her anger towards Fiona Lake had become such an obvious liability that Sonia, for all her tolerance, had taken note. Nikki was ashamed to have lost control like that. Worse, she didn't trust herself to be able to stop it next time.

Nikki turned next to researching Claire Sexton, whose online presence was far less prolific than Monica's and Kami's had been. Her Instagram account consisted mostly of artistic scenery shots, or a grey cat named Mister Rochester. There were a handful of pictures of Claire herself: early twenties, a baby fullness to her cheeks and lips, smooth brown skin, and short hair in tight, springy coils. Her gaze was always turned away from the camera—so Nikki didn't have a sense of her eyes, only the shield of her long lashes.

After some searching, Nikki found a short video interview of Claire on the London-based Albion Nanny Agency website.

"Tell us a little about yourself and what made you decide to become a nanny," a woman off-screen said.

Claire's gaze flickered upwards only briefly, followed by a shy and awkward smile.

"Right," she said, and took a deep breath. "So, ever since I was a little girl, I've had this sort of . . . well, massive love for kids. I reckon I've never properly grown up myself, you know? I did a Level Three diploma in early years development, then moved to London. I was proper lucky, and found this amazing family to work for. And that's how my nanny career got started. I've moved on from that family, and now I'm with another lovely family."

Her words were slow but passionate. When she finished, she looked up at the interviewer, who said, "That was perfect," and Claire smiled fully, eyes gleaming.

Nikki was struck by the girl's innocence; so young and hopeful, her sweetness giving a bizarre contrast to Fiona Lake's characterization of the nanny as a "sneaky little cunt."

The interviewer continued. "What would you say to someone who was thinking about being a nanny?"

"Get ready for a ride . . . it's tough and incredible, yeah? You've got to stay strong, like, really embrace all the learning bits, 'cause there's a lot. And remember, like every single day, you've got this chance to make a proper difference in a kid's life!"

The video clip ended. Nikki copied and pasted the interview link in an email to Sonia.

The phone rang. It was Nikki's father.

"I've been speaking with Fons. You remember Fons, don't you? The butcher?"

It took a moment for Nikki's brain to latch onto the right gear. She vaguely remembered Fons De Luise—her father's friend. When she was little, he'd slip her a twisted paper of mortadella pieces while gossiping with her father.

"His shop is near Chiesa del Gesù Nuovo," Raoul continued. "He saw a man sprint past. Then, a second man, also running."

"Tuesday night?" Nikki asked. "Are you talking about the murder?"

"Exactly! Fons thinks they might have been the murderer and his accomplice."

"Or two guys trying to get out of the rain," she said.

He made a noise that could have been a grunt. "Perhaps. But he said they were running hard."

Nikki exhaled. "Okay. But after the murder, I'm sure plenty of people were running away."

"It happened before that."

She frowned. "Two men sounds premeditated. You thought this was a crime of passion."

A pause. Then, "Perhaps."

"Did he say what the men looked like?" she asked.

"He didn't get a good look."

"Did he tell the police?"

"They interviewed him. Fons doesn't think they took him seriously."

Nikki sighed. "What do you want me to do about it?"

"You should talk to him."

"I thought you didn't want me involved in this investigation," she said.

Another pause. Then Raoul said, "It's only Fons."

"Alright," she said.

"Good. We'll go tonight."

"I'm busy," she protested. "I'm teaching class."

"Nina!" That familiar scolding tone from childhood. "I thought you wanted to investigate this murder! Tomorrow, then. Francesca and Gianni invited us for dinner. We'll stop by Fons's shop on the way."

The station never called. It was only when Nikki was packing up to leave the office that a text message came in from Sonia on her personal phone.

Thanks for the information, it read. And thanks for your help on the interviews. Just so you know, we've decided to continue the investigation without Phoenix Seven.

NINE

The self-defense class started at 18:00 but Nikki liked to arrive early to arrange her gear and warm up before the students arrived. At 17:22 she parked her Hornet and made her way to the storefront studio. It was dark and the streets were chilly, a stiff wind gusting between the buildings.

The hours following Sonia's text had been unsettling and difficult. Nikki had closed up work and gone home for a quick bite and some time at the punching bag, her mind replaying the moment in the restaurant when her fury had taken control. The little girl's disconsolate wailing had given excruciating insight into who the dead woman had been to her. Nikki had some sense of Claire now—the animated kindness of that shy smile. She could picture her rushing in to comfort the girl. But Nikki hadn't helped anyone. Instead, she'd shouted at Fiona Lake *for fuck's sake* to do her job properly.

Shame washed through her in hot, uncomfortable surges. She'd never lost control so completely in a professional setting. She knew better—should have *been* better! Sonia had warned her that the credibility of Phoenix Seven hung by a thread, and what had Nikki done? Only pulled out the biggest, gnarliest knife she could find, and slashed the line. She'd squandered the only currency she carried: respect. Angelo's words echoed in her thoughts: *This isn't like last time. You don't get to pretend to be a detective.*

As she approached the studio doors, a dark figure in an overcoat peeled away from the shadows and stalked towards her.

Nikki tensed.

She seemed to know that posture, the boxer's frame filling the coat: the angular lines, the surety of his stride. Unbidden, her mind filled in the version of Tito as a teenager as he grew into that bulk. It was a sudden, visceral memory—the warmth of his body beside her, the cedar smell and pepper taste of him, that small twitch of his left hand, the rare flash of a sudden smile.

But the illusion of Tito collapsed the next moment, a trick of the light. The figure approaching her seemed to shrink, resolving at last into the compact form of Benedetto De Rosa.

"Signorina Serafino," he said.

Nikki nodded, keeping her face fixed.

"Signor De Rosa," she replied, crouching to unlock and heft the heavy metal grate on its rails. "I'd prefer you not meet me here."

His expression, always enigmatic, had a particular intensity this evening.

"The situation's changed," he told her. "We need to talk."

He isn't worse than Tito, she told herself. *Nothing could be worse than finding Tito here.*

But the sight of De Rosa cast a shadow in Nikki's already troubled mind.

She unlocked the glass door and he followed her into the cool empty space. It smelled of mildew and damp plaster. Nikki hit a switch and fluorescent bulbs buzzed and flickered.

In the sudden brightness, he was diminished even further, standing only a few centimeters taller than her. His features were delicate and refined. He wore a stylish dress shirt and grey overcoat with a bone-white cashmere scarf. So close, his heavily lashed grey eyes bored into her, and she smelled his cologne.

"You need to stop your classes," he said without preamble.

She faced him. "I'm not doing that."

From his breast pocket, he extracted one of Nikki's flyers.

"You've posted your schedule online, and advertised with these. This makes you an easy target."

"Easy target for whom?" she challenged.

He stared. A muscle flexed in his jaw.

"No," Nikki snapped, that familiar knot of anger forming in her throat. "Do you think it helps to tell me I'm being targeted, and not give some idea of the actual threat? I'm not a target, unless it's that fucker who attacked me—and I don't need your help with him."

De Rosa dismissed this with a gesture. "That man and his friends are no longer a problem."

"Then what's the danger? Who could possibly want to fuck with me?"

"I won't discuss that with you."

The intensity of his look jolted Nikki. Her heart thudded rapidly, the taste of metal and bile in her mouth. This class was her refuge, normalcy in a world that had become chaotic and ugly.

"Why am I a target?"

His tone was derisive: "You're not a foolish or ignorant woman, Nicole. Don't feign it now. It's no secret that you and Calandra were intimate once."

Intimate. Nikki pushed against the word.

She had once called Tito *caro, dear*—and she could still hear his voice, a whisper in her mind: *Mio piccolo mostro.* "My little monster."

"We were just kids . . . teenagers!"

"That may have protected you once," said De Rosa. "But you changed that. You! When you came to him . . . when you asked a favor."

"That doesn't make sense," she said. "I can't possibly be the only person asking Tito Calandra for favors."

His crooked mouth warped into a snarl. "Do you imagine that anyone can demand to speak with him, to be allowed into his sanctuary? To have him immediately grant so great a request? Calandra is known to be a man without weakness. Consider what he permitted with you! Consider who witnessed it!"

She would never forget the humiliation and fear of that night. Her brother Gianni, hunted by loan sharks, had needed fifty thousand euros to protect his family. She'd been forced to turn to Tito. De Rosa had been there; she'd followed him through a crowd of beautifully dressed men and women, seen the way they stepped aside at Tito's gesture, felt their eyes on her as she made her case to him.

"You're saying Tito has a weakness for me?"

"People interpret it that way," said De Rosa.

"That's ridiculous . . . paranoid. You think people watch so carefully—"

"Of course they do!" The words exploded with sudden emotion. "Rats are always the closest observers of the snake! Calandra isn't like other men. He must not be seen to be like other men."

Her cheeks burned.

"That was months ago," she protested.

"Enough time for whispers to spread," he growled. "Are you really so blind to the trouble you've caused?"

"It should be clear by now," she said. "Neither Tito nor I have any desire to see one another. If anyone really *is* watching, they'd notice this."

He seemed surprised. "You haven't seen Calandra since then?"

"Of course not!"

She'd tried to stay calm, but rage tightened her throat. She spat it out. "I never want to see Tito again. The only reason anyone could possibly believe Tito has a weakness for me is because *you* keep coming here. Leave me the hell alone, and maybe they'll lose interest."

As quickly as it had come, De Rosa's anger seemed to depart, his attention turning suddenly inward. He scanned the room as if hunting for an answer.

Nikki watched and considered him, her own anger retreating.

Benedetto De Rosa was so unlike the coarse thugs she knew from Tito's world. It was tempting to be lulled by the calm demeanor; the understated sophistication that belied the certain ruthlessness of the man. But he was Tito's right hand, and Tito chose his lieutenants carefully. As children, and then teenagers, Nikki had watched the way he culled the herd to find the brightest and best. The most loyal. The most merciless.

It struck her as suddenly odd that De Rosa would spend any of his attention on her—not once, but twice this week. After such a long silence from Tito, why send his deputy now?

"What's happened?" she asked.

De Rosa seemed not to hear.

"What?" he said, eyes flicking to her face.

"You said the situation's changed," Nikki said. "Why weren't you worried about this before now? What's happened?"

He began buttoning his overcoat.

"You've made your feelings clear," he said.

Nikki felt a shimmer of dread, and that whisper in her memory: *mio piccolo mostro.*

"Has something happened to Tito?" she asked.

His body was rigid, expression hard. "I owe you nothing."

He moved for the door, then stopped and glared at her.

"Change your patterns. Stop teaching. I won't tell you again."

Long after De Rosa was gone, Nikki stood frozen, crowded with the monsters he'd dragged in: their bullying weight and stinking breath, the catch of their claws. Some dark knowledge, which she'd long ago pressed into a cage, broke its bars.

Nikki had spent years removing every remnant of intimacy with Tito: a chaotic, anguished spasm followed by painstaking work to shield herself from his influence. It had once seemed impossible to separate who she was—who she really was—from him. They'd merged completely. Two sides of the same coin.

Now, alone in the studio, she seemed to feel him still, to hear his voice in her thoughts: *Don't do anything halfway,* he used to say. *Don't carry a gun unless you're prepared to pull the trigger.*

This knowledge seemed instinctive in Tito, whose response to his father's beatings had been to internalize the lessons of power. He had a profound capacity for observation, and tested what he learned methodically, with the patience of a laboratory scientist.

Perhaps she should have realized then what Tito was—guessed what he would become. Every child of Naples had some understanding of what il Sistema, the System, was. No doubt this was why her family had disapproved of her youthful affiliation with Tito's gang. But on the streets of Naples, the boundary between crime and survival had eroded so completely—a low wall to step easily across. And in those days, the police actions she learned about from her father and brother seemed disconnected from the petty crimes she witnessed—or the secret transgressions she committed daily with her friends.

Her brother Adriano, who'd worked in an elite carabinieri unit that dealt with organized crime and terrorism, had seemed to recognize the peculiar alchemy that brought boys like Tito inside, that fed off their desperation and ambition and ate them whole.

You must see—must understand the players and how they fit together, Adriano had told her.

He said that organized crime was like the mythical hydra, with new heads growing whenever one was chopped away.

It's never enough to just take a head, he said. *To kill the beast, you need to understand it completely . . . you must watch and learn . . . find its beating heart.*

Nikki stared at her reflection. The past few months had aged her. There was an emptiness in her eyes she didn't recognize.

Slowly, she pulled off her jacket. She was hanging this up when her phone buzzed. A text from Valerio: **Drinks tonight? Insurance papers to sign.**

Nikki was distracted and tired throughout class. She tried to focus, to become absorbed in the teaching. Instead, she kept looking at her watch, and the seconds sloughed slowly by.

Twelve minutes before the end of class, the door opened, letting in a gust of wind. Pushing through the doors was a short, squat figure wearing a blue puffer coat and bright pink beanie encrusted with sparkles. Assuming the kid belonged to one of the women in the group, Nikki turned her attention back to the class, and began correcting two teenagers who were practicing a choke-hold defense.

Above the scuffling sounds and conversation, a piping voice called out, "Nikki! Nikki! It's meeeee! Nikki!"

The child waved enthusiastically.

Nikki didn't like children on the best of days and couldn't imagine why this one knew her name. She excused herself and crossed the room, recognizing at last the kid whom she and Sonia had met in the port.

"Audrey, what are you doing here?"

Audrey Lake grinned up at her, showing rosy cheeks and crooked teeth.

"I'm here to . . . well, say hello."

Disconcerted, Nikki glanced through the glass doors, into the street.

"Where are your parents?"

"I'm here on my own!" she announced with pride.

"How did you find me?"

She held out a spiral notebook with Nikki's name, phone number, and the address of the studio in blocky, childish script.

"I took your business card from Mummy. I looked . . . online it said you were here. I took a taxi."

Nikki was astonished. Naples was no place for a child to be wandering alone.

"A taxi driver took you here?"

"I gave him money," Audrey said. "I told him you were my sister."

"Why did you do that?"

Another dopey grin. "Aren't you pleased to see me?"

"No," Nikki said. "You shouldn't be out alone. It isn't safe."

Audrey looked stricken and Nikki, remembering how loudly the girl had wailed at the restaurant, continued talking before any screaming could start: "You need to call your parents, and have them come get you."

The kid's lip quivered. "I don't have a phone."

Nikki took out her own phone, and unlocked it. "Use mine."

"I haven't got their numbers."

Fuck.

Nikki glanced at her watch. Ten minutes left.

She pointed at a metal chair in the corner of the room.

"Sit," she directed. "Don't move until I tell you. I'm going to finish teaching, and then we're calling your parents."

The kid looked stunned, and for a moment Nikki thought the wailing would start. But Audrey nodded humbly and complied.

When class was finished and the students began to filter away, Nikki called Sonia. After all, this was her case.

But Sonia didn't pick up—and neither did Emilio.

Fuck. Double fuck.

She left messages for them, and turned back to Audrey.

The girl hadn't left her seat; her coat and gloves and hat were strewn on the floor at her feet.

"Where are your parents?" Nikki asked.

"Dunno."

"They'll be worried about you."

"Nobody cares about me," Audrey insisted. "Can I come home with you?"

"Of course not."

There was the trembling lip again.

"For fuck's sake," Nikki muttered.

"You said a swear," said Audrey, instantly cheered. "Fuck's sake. For fuck's sake."

Nikki swore again, then made a decision.

"Come with me. We need to get you home."

Audrey followed Nikki around the studio as she shut off lights, and then out the door.

"Mum was so cross with you," she said, and imitated Fiona's drunken speech: *"Fucking bitch. I'll report her. Doesn't she know who I am?"*

It took twenty minutes to reach the Molo Luise marina. Nikki felt nervous with the girl on the back of her Hornet, her own helmet strapped on the kid, maneuvering carefully through the chaotic city streets. Audrey had no sense at all. Sometimes she gripped tightly onto Nikki, and other times didn't hold on. She leaned the wrong way in the turns, and babbled, words that Nikki had no chance of understanding above the engine noises, the horns, the blare of radios, and the shouting.

By the time she caught sight of the marina, Nikki was raw with tension—every nerve a charged wire. She drew the bike up on the pavement and parked. Maneuvering them both off the Hornet, she took the helmet off Audrey, whose face was red and sweaty, damp hair slicked to her head.

"That was fun," said Audrey, puffing out her cheeks.

The dozens of yachts berthed in the marina were eerily beautiful: Fairy towers lit against the velvet black of the sea, chrome finishes gleaming in the lamplight. There was the metallic slosh of water against the hulls, the clink of metal cables, the murmur of voices. It smelled of fuel, of cooked food, and of the sea.

Audrey said that she recognized the marina, but didn't know how to find her parents' yacht. Nikki chose the longest of the seven piers and they began to walk.

Audrey, who hadn't shut up until now, was oddly silent. Nikki was relieved for the change and almost didn't notice when Audrey's pace slowed and then stopped. At last, Nikki turned around to see the kid standing still, staring at her. She'd looped a lock of hair into her mouth and was sucking on the end.

"What happened to Claire?" Audrey said in a small voice. "Nobody will tell me."

Nikki wasn't sure what to say; how much truth to give.

"Somebody hurt her," she said at last.

Audrey stared, chewing on her hair.

"And that's why she died? Because somebody hurt her?"

"Yes."

Audrey blinked several times as if earnestly trying to hold back tears, but a few slipped past her guard. Her hands balled into fists, and her mouth pressed tightly shut.

Nikki felt horribly inadequate. She was suddenly angry at Sonia for not answering her phone, for leaving her to deal with this situation. She was angry at Fiona and Jayston Lake for not taking care of their kid, for letting her wander off alone into Naples.

"C'mon," she said, gesturing Audrey forward.

But Audrey didn't budge. She just stood, face contorted, and body rigid. Snot drained onto her upper lip. Her clear attempt to hold the emotion inside was somehow more awful than the wailing had been.

Nikki didn't know what to do. It occurred to her that the kid was an odd mix of independent ideas and compliant trust. On the one hand, she'd exercised some exceptional will to find Nikki and navigate her way through a foreign city. On the other hand, she'd implicitly trusted complete strangers: the taxi driver, and now Nikki. Was this the result of privilege—this sense of utter protection? She clearly had no idea of the danger she was in. The evening could have easily ended quite differently for the little rich girl.

"Bad things happen sometimes," Nikki said. "It isn't fair that you have to know this when you're just a kid. But this is why you need to be careful—why you need to stay close to people you trust. You can't just trust strangers. It isn't safe. You can't run off by yourself."

"Like Claire ran away?"

Nikki hesitated, then asked, "Did you know Claire was running away?"

Audrey nodded, and sucked on her hair.

"Did she tell you why? Did she say where she was going?" Nikki asked.

Audrey shook her head.

Nikki exhaled.

"Are you going to find the people who hurt her?" Audrey asked.

Nikki wasn't sure what to tell her. She wanted to say that she wasn't on the case anymore, but she heard herself saying instead, "Yes. I'll find them."

Audrey shuffled towards Nikki, and they walked together once more.

They were approaching the end of the pier when, in the dim light ahead, a tall, lean figure moved towards them with restless energy.

"Audrey," called a deep voice. "Is that you?"

"Daddy," Audrey called back.

Nikki shouted, "Mr. Lake?"

Despite the chill, he was in his shirtsleeves, and his stockinged feet struck the asphalt as he rushed forward with a sharp, almost aggressive precision. He came directly to Audrey and, crouching down, gripped her shoulders, scanning her face.

"Good god, Audrey, where have you been? I was preparing to phone the police."

"Mr. Lake," Nikki said. "Your daughter took a taxi into the center of Naples."

"You took a taxi!" he exclaimed.

Audrey started crying.

"I wanted to see Nikki," she sniffled.

"Nikki? Who's Nikki?"

He stood and fixed Nikki with an intense gaze. His face, sharply shadowed by the lamplight, was all hard angles and rugged lines, his skin weathered. He had high cheekbones, a stark jaw, and short, unkempt hair.

"Investigator Nicole Serafino," Nikki offered. "Phoenix Seven. I was with Detective Sonia Dieng when she spoke with your wife yesterday."

"Ah," he said. "Fiona mentioned you . . . she was quite upset."

"Yes," Nikki agreed. "She was."

Jayston Lake wasn't what Nikki had expected. This man was no polished marina regular with a leisure yacht and time to kill. In his late forties, he had the look of someone who'd seen his share of rough seas. His presence gave a sort of gritty reality to the serene boats and peaceful waters of the marina.

"You weren't with the police when they searched Claire's stateroom today," he commented.

Nikki nodded, stinging a little from the reminder of her exile. "As you said, I upset your wife."

"And my daughter came looking for you," he said. After a long beat, his expression suddenly softened. "Well, I should thank you for bringing her back safely."

He reached down for Audrey's hand, and she meekly gave it to him.

"Have a good night, Mr. Lake," Nikki said.

Relieved to be rid of Audrey, Nikki turned and strode rapidly away. She hadn't gone far when Jayston called out, "Ms. Serafino? I wonder if I can beg another favor of you?"

When Nikki had returned, he said, "Claire's passport is in my safe. I'd meant to give it to the police today, but it slipped my mind. Can I pass it along to you?"

TEN

Berthed at the farthest end of the long pier, the largest vessel in the Molo Luise marina was by far *The Prophet*. A sleek, white tri-deck. Nikki estimated the superyacht at eighty-five meters.

Jayston spoke into his phone as they approached.

"I've found her . . . no . . . no . . . she's fine. On the pier. Coming aboard now."

Nikki followed Jayston and Audrey across a short gangplank and onto the tail of the boat. They were met by a bearded man in captain's uniform. He greeted Jayston, then bent down to Audrey.

"Little madam," he said, "you had us all worried. Where on earth did you get to?"

"I took a taxi," Audrey said proudly.

"A little excursion in town," Jayston said, ruffling her hair. "Henry, would you take Audrey to my wife?"

The captain looked uncomfortable.

"Your wife is . . . indisposed."

"Very well. Would you please ask Shonda to put Audrey to bed?"

"Certainly," said the captain. He extended a hand to the girl, who, as she had with Nikki, complied without protest.

"And . . . Henry?" Jayston called after him. "Thank the crew for their hunt, will you? They'll see my appreciation reflected in their bonuses."

"Yes, sir."

Nikki followed Jayston. The yacht's luxurious interior was fashioned after a British country estate—walls alternately papered or paneled in mahogany, framed paintings, the floors polished hardwood and thick ivory carpeting. They passed up a set of stairs and into a comfortable living space—the main salon. A housekeeper was here, vacuuming. She switched this off when they entered, leaving without a word, taking the vacuum with her.

"There you are," said Jayston, snatching up a small pink rucksack from the sofa. He dug through the various compartments, coming up at last with a small coin, which he tossed to Nikki with a twitch of a smile. She caught it and turned it over.

"Tracker," he explained. "Not the first time Audrey's got the idea to run off, or hide. Whole damn crew's been looking for her . . . tearing the boat apart. I expected she would take her rucksack, though. She's supposed to keep her EpiPen with her. Peanut allergy. Terrifies me. Do you have children?"

Nikki shook her head.

"A delight and a horror," he said.

It was only now he looked down and seemed to notice his stockinged feet.

"Pardon me, won't you? I was in the middle of dressing when I learned my daughter had gone missing. Here—do make yourself comfortable. I'll fetch the passport at once."

He left the room with the same brusque efficiency that he'd done everything.

Nikki looked around the space. The furniture was leather and burgundy silks, the fixtures in gleaming brass. On one table, a profusion of orange and pink blossoms overflowed an enormous vase. Watercolor landscapes in gilded frames hung on the walls.

The elegance of the space was eased by signs of living: a jacket tossed on a chair, an unfinished puzzle on a table, a shuffle of papers with a clutch of crayons.

At one end of the room stood a sleek bar with a stocked wine fridge and a backlit display of high-end bottles. Nikki was facing this and didn't hear Jayston enter.

"Forgive me," he said. "I seem to have quite lost my manners. May I offer you a drink? Terribly sorry, I fear I've already forgotten your name."

Nikki turned. He was poised just inside the door, one hand resting on the frame. There was a graceful tension in his body that she recognized from the sailing community—a balanced readiness.

"Nikki Serafino," she said. "And, please, don't trouble yourself."

"Not a trouble, Nikki."

As his expression softened, she realized the intensity that had lived in those features only minutes ago.

"I just had a moment alone to think," he continued. "And I realized . . . you brought Audrey back from across Naples. No fuss at the police station. No spectacle. No demands. Merely a kindness to a child and her parents. I'm most grateful. Thank you."

Heat rose to Nikki's cheeks, and the familiar discomfort brought on by praise.

"No thanks needed," she said. "I really should go."

"Do join me for a drink, won't you?"

He strode into the room and opened the wine fridge, surveying the contents.

"A Livio Felluga pinot grigio? Or Meursault? There's a rather lovely Castello di Ama Chianti I've been waiting to open."

Nikki hesitated. He glanced up and flashed a smile.

"A whisky, perhaps?" he said. "I must say, a Lagavulin sounds just right."

She nodded. "Thanks. I'd love a whisky."

"Do take a seat."

Jayston slapped the passport on the bar and crossed behind it.

He leaned down, collected two heavy tumblers, and poured the amber liquid. Nikki perched on a padded stool.

"So, tell me about yourself, Nikki. Do I hear a trace of London in your accent?"

"Camden," Nikki agreed. "I spent a decade in London."

"Ah. And now you're in the police."

"I'm in a special liaison unit—Phoenix Seven. We work with the police."

She took out a business card, and set it on the bar. He glanced at it.

"I see."

He handed her a tumbler and raised his own.

"To you, Nikki. I'm in your debt."

They drank.

"And what is it you do, Mr. Lake?"

"Investments. I've been quite fortunate in that regard. I came into my inheritance as a young man, in the dot-com nineties, and took a bit of a gamble. Invested in some technology companies. Risky, but it turned out to be a stroke of luck. I've managed to build upon that initial success."

He looked around the beautiful room, and nodded. "Quite fortunate."

Then he glanced down at the passport on the bar between them and his expression shifted.

"This dreadful business with Claire has cast a pall on all of us, I'm afraid," he said. "It is quite impossible—truly inconceivable—to imagine why anyone would wish to harm her. She was such a sweet thing. Audrey adored her . . . we all did."

"Can you tell me about Claire, Mr. Lake?" Nikki asked.

"I've already spoken with the police."

"Oh," said Nikki, "I'm not part of the investigation anymore. You don't have to talk to me, if you'd rather not."

He took another drink, and swirled the glass, watching the liquid move.

"Young. Bright," he said. "Enthusiastic . . . keen to explore the world . . . a lover of books . . . and exceptionally caring. She had the correct credentials, of course. But beyond that, she had a natural affinity for children—really helped Audrey out of her shell. Claire joined us at our home in Kensington from July this year. Then, when we set sail, we simply couldn't imagine being without her."

"I understand that she went missing last week—in Capri?"

"Yes. Quite puzzling. We'd spent the day together: a bit of sightseeing and some shopping. After dinner, Claire brought Audrey back here . . . settled her into bed. When Fiona and I returned, Audrey was fast asleep, and we presumed Claire had retired to her quarters as well.

It wasn't until the next morning we discovered her missing. And Fiona noticed that her jewelry had also vanished."

"What jewelry was missing?" Nikki asked.

"A gold pendant . . . a diamond tennis bracelet . . . three or four rings. There may have been more, but Fiona couldn't give a good accounting. Fiona's memory is . . . faulty these days."

"Was there any evidence that Claire had taken the jewelry?"

He looked sharply at her. "No, you're quite right in observing that. As I mentioned to the authorities: Claire was genuinely good-hearted and kind. We compensated her fairly, and she looked after Audrey with great care. She was practically a member of our family. It's hard for me to believe she would have taken anything from us, or fled. Moreover, if she had been planning to leave, it doesn't make sense for her to go without her passport."

"What do you think happened?"

He leaned on the bar.

"I shared my theory with the police: I believe she was coerced. It's my suspicion that someone threatened her—or perhaps threatened Audrey. If Claire did take Fiona's jewelry, it's likely she was compelled to do so by this other individual."

"Did anyone see her leave the yacht?"

"No, but that's not particularly unusual. We were docked with only a minimal crew onboard. The rest of the staff were on the island."

He poured himself another substantial serving of whisky and offered to Nikki. She let him pour, but didn't intend to drink. With Jayston talking so openly, she wanted a clear head. Sonia had dismissed her from the case, but she didn't feel dismissed. If anything, she was more alert and energized than she'd been for months.

She'd told Audrey that she would find whoever had hurt Claire. She realized now that she meant it.

"How was she behaving . . . on the day she disappeared? How did she seem to you?"

A sad smile played on Jayston's lips. He stood upright and shook his head.

"Well, it really wasn't a good situation. Fiona, my wife, can be quite demanding and . . . well, unfortunately, rather suspicious. That day, she was exceptionally hard on Claire. I should have intervened. Put a stop to it. However, my past attempts to mediate only seemed to add fuel to the fire—worsening Claire's situation. This time, I chose not to say anything. In retrospect, I deeply regret not stepping in."

"So, if Claire was upset," Nikki said, "do you think it's possible she did run away—that she felt bullied and trapped and decided to take the jewelry and leave?"

"It is possible, of course," he said. "But I doubt it. It would be so unnecessary. There are formal ways to deal with this. She could have told me she wanted to leave—or told Henry, or the agency. We could have arranged to fly her back to London. There are clauses for termination we could have managed. No, it really doesn't make any sense at all. Which is why I keep returning to some hidden influence. Someone must have swayed her."

"Do you have any idea who this could have been?"

"I really can't say. Perhaps a friend. Perhaps someone she'd just met."

They were quiet for several beats. Then he glanced at Nikki with an evaluative expression.

"Audrey seems quite taken with you. You wouldn't by any chance be interested in a nanny position, would you?"

"Oh god, no!" The words were out before she could stop them. With a hot rush of embarrassment, she tried to explain. "I'm happy with my job. And I'm terrible with children."

Jayston didn't seem offended. He chuckled. Then the chuckle grew until he threw back his head and laughed.

He finished off his serving and poured another. He glanced up at Nikki, who raised the glass to her lips.

She didn't have a chance to taste the whisky, though, because a loud voice interrupted: "How perfectly precious!"

Fiona Lake strode towards them. She wore a long blue silk robe. This was open, revealing a matching lingerie set that barely concealed her breasts. Her face was flushed, eyes glistening.

"The liar and the bitch, having a laugh together," slurred Fiona. "Pour me some of that, won't you, darling? I need to phone the authorities and lodge a complaint about this . . . incompetent policewoman."

"Fiona." Jayston's voice was a warning growl. "Don't start. This investigator—Nikki—found Audrey, and brought her back to us. We're in her debt."

"Oh, that's rich," she laughed bitterly. "Masquerade as the doting father now, won't you? Suits you."

Seeming not to pay attention to Nikki, she crossed behind the bar and began opening and slamming cabinets.

Nikki stood.

"I'll get going," she said. "Thank you for the drink."

"Allow me to escort you," said Jayston.

He was silent as they moved through the boat, but unlike the relaxed silence of their conversation, Nikki sensed the tension in his body.

He stepped onto the pier with her. Nikki was about to extend a hand, and wish him a good night. But he seemed to come to a decision.

"I'd ask that you not judge Fiona too harshly," he said. "I'm aware she can be . . . somewhat challenging. But she's endured quite a bit. Perhaps it's best . . . well, you might as well know. Last year, we lost our son, Matthew. He was only four. It was a profound tragedy. I don't believe one ever fully recovers from losing a child. Fiona hasn't been the same. None of us have. And Audrey . . . it affected her deeply. She stopped speaking. Which is why Claire's kindness was so vital to our family. Under her care, Audrey really flourished. The thought of how Claire's disappearance might impact her is unbearable for me."

"I'm so sorry," said Nikki.

Jayston stared, a sudden pain in his eyes. Nikki didn't know what to say.

"Of course, we want to help the police," he continued. "But we'd like to get underway as soon as possible. I hope you can understand."

"Of course."

Nikki checked her watch as she left *The Prophet*. It was 21:14. She was late to meet Valerio. She texted him an apology and an ETA. He replied with a thumbs-up emoji.

She was walking briskly down the pier, focused on reaching her bike, when someone shouted: "Nikki! Nikki Serafino! Ciao, bella!"

The call came from the deck of a sleek twenty-meter yacht, where a man was smiling and waving. Nikki raised her hand to wave back before recognizing Vincente Di Pavola, father of her ex, Enzo.

She was suddenly hot, mind flexing. Her hand dropped to her side.

Nikki hadn't seen or heard from Enzo or his father since the summer, when she learned that Vincente had paid her debt to Tito Calandra. This was hardly an act of charity from the canny businessman, however; he'd meant it to pacify her after Enzo sent a thug to her house.

Vincente gestured her forward: "Come, come! Nikki!"

Then he seemed to register her mood. He held up a palm, shouting, "Please, don't go. Wait. I'll come to you!"

She watched, mind detaching a little as Vincente exited the boat and jogged towards her. He was well styled in slacks and a black leather jacket. And he looked so much like Enzo—those easy, muscular movements. Like a powerful cat. Also, like Enzo, he was handsome—but his tanned face was aging, wrinkles and folds set into characteristic lines, his thinning hair neatly trimmed.

"Grazie," he said as he approached. "Thank you for waiting. I'm glad to see you."

Her legs shifted, wanting to run away as he leaned in and kissed her cheeks in that familiar gesture she so disliked.

"Signor Di Pavola," she acknowledged.

"You're looking fit," he said. "I hope you're keeping well."

"I am."

He paused, and seemed to consider. "Let me be frank. I've wanted to come to you a dozen times. I was appalled to learn what Enzo did. I don't know what to say except that I'm so very sorry."

The apology was so spontaneous, so sincerely expressed, Nikki was stunned.

In the years she'd dated Enzo, she had met the shrewd businessman a few times—but she'd only ever really seen him through the lens of Enzo's perception, where he was hard and disapproving of his youngest son. Vincente Di Pavola had, through Tito's intermediary, paid sixty thousand euros to recompense Nikki for Enzo's attack, and Nikki assumed he'd viewed this as a business transaction, his responsibility towards her closed.

His expression now, far from what she might have expected, was open and warm and full of concern.

Those eyes were so much like Enzo's. The realization brought a pang—and Nikki understood how much she needed Enzo's apology . . . his remorse and tenderness.

Perhaps this was the closest she would ever come.

Some barrier in her chest seemed to soften.

"Please," he continued, motioning to the restaurants on the shoreline. "May I buy you a drink?"

She shook her head. "I have an appointment. I need to get going."

"I see."

His disappointment seemed almost childlike. Then his mood shifted. His expression turned suddenly serious.

"I want you to know," he said, "Barile doesn't work for me anymore. I was sickened to find out what he did—that he hurt you. It was inexcusable."

"It was inexcusable," she agreed.

"May I walk with you?" He gave a flourishing gesture. Nikki nodded.

As they approached her bike, Vincente continued: "I regret Enzo did something that can never be forgiven. I always liked you for him. You and I both know my son is weak. He takes after his mother. People like that need someone strong to look out for them."

Nikki stopped, and faced him. "Signor Di Pavola."

"Please call me Vincente."

"Vincente—I can't look out for Enzo anymore. We're finished."

"Oh, I know!" he agreed. "But I'm sure you can understand why I need to look out for him, now."

"Of course." She shifted, ready to leave.

"I worry sometimes," he continued. "Maybe someday Enzo will have an important business . . . or career in politics. I don't want the difficult moments of his past to haunt him. I'm sure you can see that—as his father, I must protect him. And I'm sure you don't want to harm Enzo. He is what he is, but you loved him once."

Nikki tensed.

"What is it you want from me?" she asked.

They'd arrived at her bike.

Vincente said, "It's typical in business to have something called a nondisclosure agreement. Just to close the door on this bad situation—make sure inconvenient details don't resurface and hurt Enzo's future."

Anger descended, locking up Nikki's chest, putting heat into her face and neck.

"It was inconvenient that Enzo cheated on me." She spoke in a low voice, heart thudding, fists and feet suddenly numb. "It was inconvenient that he stranded me on Capri. But then he sent a thug to break into my home and attack me. Would you call that inconvenient? Because that doesn't feel inconvenient to me. There's a different word I'm looking for . . . oh yes. Criminal. What he did was fucking criminal. And you want me to sign an NDA?"

Vincente lifted his hands in surrender.

"I can see you're upset." His tone was conciliatory, as if calming a skittish horse. "I'm just trying to come to a good resolution for everyone. In exchange, I would, of course, offer appropriate compensation."

She was trembling with fury as she strapped on her helmet and mounted the Hornet.

"Just think about it," he shouted as she started the engine. "Think about an amount that would make you comfortable. I'm a reasonable man. Just promise me you'll think about it."

ELEVEN

Via Toledo was thick with holiday shoppers as Valerio made his way home from work. The day had been clear and almost warm in the sunlight. But now the shadows stretched and the clouds moved in, and the air chilled, biting through his jacket.

Women in knee-high boots and belted coats, their faces framed in furs, bustled together in chattering groups. A month until Christmas, and the clean storefront displays teemed with sparkling lights, artificial snow, and holiday sales. Christmas music jangled discordantly from store doors as they opened to envelop every new batch of customers, mixing with the street sounds: a roar of voices and laughter, the shuffle and clomp of shoes on paving stones, the growl and hum of engines.

The glamorous commercial atmosphere of this street was only skin deep, Valerio knew. Like an old woman with her plastic surgeries and creams and thick makeup. Peel it back a centimeter and you saw the jagged bones and rough sinew of the city, the buzzing arteries of legal and illegal commerce mixing together until you couldn't distinguish blood from poison. The old heart still beat out its melody, but Valerio felt the weariness of that rhythm, the toll of sickness. Of course, the only way to diagnose the true health of the body was to look at its diseased waste—to look at the Poggioreale jail.

Maurizio had insisted on coming with Valerio to visit Gaetano in Poggioreale today and Valerio was glad for his company. This business with Luca had injected some venom in his blood. His native immunity to the city's infection was insufficient to preserve him, and he felt the fever of it. Maurizio was there to jab him with an antidote, to shock his heart and slap his face in the way only a partner could.

"You're lying," Maurizio said as they drove to the jail. "I thought it was that murder—and your mother finding the body—that this was the thing bugging you. But this business—this favor—trying to help this kid. Something stinks about it. Will you agree?"

"Yes," Valerio conceded.

"Will you tell me what it is?"

"I'm not sure I should."

He trusted Maurizio. Under other circumstances, he might have confided in him, but Valerio was compromised enough on his own. He wasn't going to drag his partner into this, too. Seeming to understand, Maurizio stopped talking for a few minutes, and chewed on his lip.

"You're a good guy," Maurizio said at last. "If you were corrupt, really corrupt—whatever this was . . . it wouldn't bother you. Just promise me something."

"Sure."

"Promise me you'll let me know if this will put any of us in danger. Me—or the rest of the team."

"I won't put you in danger," Valerio promised. "This is just something stupid . . . something I've gotten myself into. I just need to do this—help this kid—and then I can get out."

The boy in the interview room had looked younger than his eighteen years, with full cheeks and a tangled overgrowth of wavy hair. He wore a fresh bruise on his left cheekbone and his lip was split. He seemed scrawny and underdeveloped in his pilled brown sweater and sweatpants and scuffed sneakers. With the loose movements of a scarecrow come to life, he slammed into the seat across from them, big eyes darting between their faces. He smelled bad: mildew and body odor and toilet cleaner.

"I'm not saying anything," he declared with a bravado Valerio recognized from his own youth.

"We haven't told you why we're here," Maurizio said.

"Well, what is it?" Gaetano demanded, restless fingers thrumming and thumping on the metal table. When neither Valerio nor Maurizio answered, he slammed his palm down. "Fuck you. Fuck all of you. I didn't do anything. They're trying to pin this on me."

"It was a good arrest." Valerio's voice was calm and dispassionate, a deliberate step back from Gaetano's twitchy energy. "You and your friends had more cocaine in your apartment than you could use in a lifetime. I read your record and talked to the arresting officer. I also spoke with the magistrate. It doesn't look good for you—unless you can make a deal with them, offer them something they can use."

"I don't know anything," Gaetano replied, eyes defiant. "It wasn't mine. I didn't even know it was there. I don't know anything."

It was just possible he was telling the truth, Valerio thought. Maybe the drugs belonged to his roommates—maybe he hadn't known about the plastic bin under the kitchen sink. But as far as the law was concerned, the nuances of truth didn't matter when the burden of proof had been met.

This was how the clans ran their distribution network. By storing cocaine, heroin, marijuana, and pills in the homes of regular people, the mob eased delivery logistics, and distributed the risk of discovery and seizure. It had the added benefit of making local residents complicit in their operations, thereby decreasing the likelihood that anyone would resist, or report to authorities.

"How are you, Gaetano?" Valerio said. "Is anyone bothering you in here?"

The reply came with startling viciousness: "You can fuck yourself!"

Maurizio sighed. "He's trying to help you, little prick. He's your best hope right now, so I'd adjust my attitude, if I were you."

Gaetano didn't say anything to this, but his eyes flicked back to Valerio.

"I visited your mother yesterday," Valerio told him. "She seems to think you're a good kid in a bad situation. Of course, mothers are often blind to the faults of their sons. What do you think?"

Gaetano looked down and began pressing the fleshy web between his thumb and forefinger. He shrugged.

"I also met the girl who used to babysit you," Valerio said. "Ravenna. She says you have a good heart. She's worried about you."

Gaetano blinked and looked down at the table, where his hands were working, fingers twitching and roving. His nose started to run.

"During your validation hearing," Valerio continued, "the magistrate ruled that you and your friends should have a pretrial detention—which is why you're here now. This is usually only done in the case of substantial risks. In your case, she ordered you detained because of the quantity of drugs in your apartment. But you're a first-time offender, and you're young. Also, when I visited your mother, I saw how sick she is. I think I could ask the magistrate to reconsider your case on compassionate grounds—to let you stay with your mother until the trial."

The boy looked up and an expression flashed across his features, something much younger, much more vulnerable than the mask of his pretense. It landed on Valerio like a punch.

Naples made you grow up fast. Children as young as ten or twelve were used as lookouts for drug dealers. Just a few years older, and you were conscripted to push drugs or run errands for the clans. Boys playacted that they were tough, wise-minded businessmen, throwing their weight around. They swore and drank like men, fucked and killed like men. And the state treated them like men when they caught and sentenced them. But this boy was still a child. Valerio saw it in that expression—some naive and earnest flame that still burned. He'd seen the same expression in his own children—in Davide and Gemma. But if Gaetano was convicted, if he stayed in Poggioreale much longer, that flame would be extinguished. A sense of resolve fixed inside Valerio's mind. It relieved some pressure to realize that the right decision here was also the one he'd wanted to find.

"Before I ask the magistrate to reconsider," he said, "I need to know what you plan to do if they let you out."

"Dunno." He wiped his nose with his hand.

"Need to do better than that, pal," scolded Maurizio. "You need to tell us if you're working for the clans . . . and which clan."

Gaetano glared up at him, lips pursed.

Maurizio turned to Valerio. "He can't do it. It's no good. He'll just go back to them. He'll get arrested for something else, and then he's really fucked—and you're fucked, too. People will ask questions—they'll want to know why you picked this one . . . this stupid punk . . . to help."

"I won't." Gaetano's voice was clear and loud. They looked at him, and his next words came out in a mumble. "I'll go back to my mamma's. I won't . . . get into trouble."

Valerio exhaled.

"Ravenna said you had a job," he said. "Not for the clans. Another job. Is that true?"

The boy nodded.

"Can you work that job . . . stay out of trouble? Just work, and back to your mother's?"

"Yeah."

"If the magistrate does let you out, she may put you on house arrest. Then you'll have to stay with your mamma. Or she may make you check in daily at the local police station. Can you do that?"

"Okay. Yeah."

Valerio sat for a moment, considering. He was about to stand when he thought of something. He pulled out his phone and flipped through the pictures until he came to the photos he'd taken in Ines's apartment. He held the phone out to Gaetano. "The man in this picture," he said. "The man with your mother—can you tell me who he is?"

The boy looked surprised.

"You don't know?" he asked.

"Should I know?"

"Uhm . . . that's Paride."

"Last name?"

"Silvestri. Paride Silvestri."

"Okay. Thanks."

Valerio and Maurizio stood.

"Can you tell my mamma . . ." said Gaetano. "Tell her I'm sorry."

"Let's see what we can do to get you out, and you can tell her yourself," said Valerio.

Back at the office, Valerio spent nearly an hour trying to reach the public defender assigned to Gaetano before he finally got through; then more calls over the next few hours to encourage him to get the right paperwork filed with the magistrate. Midafternoon, he and the public defender went to the magistrate's chambers, where he summarized his visit to Ines Mancusi, talked about her obvious illness, and proposed that the magistrate release the young Gaetano on humanitarian grounds.

"I need a statement from Signora Mancusi's doctor, confirming her illness," she instructed the public defender.

Assured that the arrangements would proceed without him, Valerio returned to the office to close out his paperwork.

"Will it happen?" Maurizio asked. "Will they let him go home?"

Valerio nodded.

"Is it finished? What they wanted from you?"

"Yeah."

"Good. Now keep yourself out of trouble, you idiot."

Valerio expected to feel the burden lifted as he left the station and began the walk home. It was nearly finished, he told himself. In a few hours, Gaetano would be released from Poggioreale and the whole business with Luca would be behind him. He hadn't crossed any lines—nothing illegal, nothing unethical. Gaetano was just a kid, and the jail was the wrong place for him. If, instead of Luca, Ines Mancusi had asked for his help, he would have given it.

These thoughts comforted less than they should. He felt heavy and dull, a sensation worsened by the commercial cheer of the holiday shoppers. Unease jostled through his feet and hands, clamped onto his throat. Eager to escape the feeling, he made his way to Cosimo's pizzeria, where he filled up on a dinner of meaty pizza.

Fingers still a little greasy, he checked his phone, smearing the screen. He hadn't paid attention to it for a few days. Not since the night of the murder.

There were far too many texts.

He skimmed the group chat messages between Orlanda and Penelope as they diagnosed the psychological maladies of their mother, discussed whether they should insist she stay with one of them, coordinated bringing her dinner, and complained about Valerio's nonparticipation.

His ex-wife, Giorgia, had texted several times with news reports about the murder at the church, fishing for details.

His son, Davide, had texted, wanting money for new football boots.

Nikki had also sent him three texts since the incident at the police station—when he'd yelled at her boss. He wasn't proud of that moment. It wasn't like him to let his anger get the better of him, and he felt strange about it now. To his relief, Nikki didn't seem upset. She could get mad, but it was rarely about stupid things. He sent her a message, asking if she wanted to meet. There was insurance paperwork they needed to sign for their boat. Of course, he could have just emailed it to her, but he hadn't seen her for a while, and it seemed good to have her company right now.

He was looking at his phone when a text came through from a number he didn't recognize.

Ines says Gaetano will come home tonight. Is it true?

Valerio looked for a moment before writing back, **Who is this?**

Ravenna.

Yes, he typed. **It's true.**

There was a long pause, then she wrote, **I was wrong about you.**

Valerio stared at those words, and in his mind's eye, saw those tight brown curls, and the expressive dark eyes of the beautiful nurse.

As he thought this, as if she somehow knew his mind was on her, she sent him one more word: **Grazie.**

The uncomfortable sensation in his chest released. The pizza, which had sunk like lead in his belly, seemed to rest more easily.

The bar was called Point Break, named in honor of the 1991 movie that Dario, the bar owner, had loved. Dario was a childhood friend from the old neighborhood. Valerio had lost touch with him for the better part of two decades before running into him again in Quartieri Spagnoli after his divorce.

Dario was married to a woman fifteen years his junior named Graziella. Voluptuous and kind, she always painted her wide mouth red, as if to outline the large white teeth of her smile. Her perfume, citrus and cinnamon, made Valerio think of pastries. Her dark hair was cut in a flattering fringe, and she wore big sparkling earrings and necklaces.

"Buona sera, sweetie," she said when Valerio arrived, leaning in to kiss his cheek. She was soft and warm.

"Ooh, you smell like camping," she said with a throaty chuckle. "What can I get you? Peroni?"

"Sì, grazie!"

She glided back indoors, and Valerio shuffled behind one of the upright barrels that, balanced unsteadily on the slanting paving stones, served as an outdoor table. Point Break was little larger than a closet, with a counter running along the back wall. The interior was finished in dark wooden beams, shrinking it even further. There were only two cramped tables for indoor seating. Outside were three wooden barrels and wobbly stools. Christmas lights draped across spindly poles, providing lighting. Despite the hour and the chill, the street was full of people walking past them, up and down the hill.

Valerio sniffed at his jacket. The recent cold weather had prompted him to pull it out of his closet and he wasn't sure it was clean. It stank of woodsmoke and stale beer. He had vague memories of a long-ago fire on the beach, and beers with some of the guys from work.

Graziella brought his beer and a plate of olives and chips.

He relaxed as he drank, and chatted with Graziella, who had opinions about politics, about art, and about the old woman who lived in their building who had been trying to touch her belly ever since Graziella's pregnancy started to show. The evening grew chillier, but Valerio didn't mind. He had one beer, then another, and another.

Nikki was late. Dario showed up and had a beer with him.

By the time he spotted Nikki striding up the hill towards him, Valerio was relaxed for the first time in days.

"Ciao, bella!" He waved, and stood to greet her.

"You look like hell," he said as they hugged.

It was their joke, but this time it was actually true. She had that fiery expression that frightened devils away.

"So do you," she said.

"I ordered you a gin and tonic," he told her, then raised his bottle to

Dario, who was standing in the doorway, smoking a cigarette. "Another of these."

"Thanks," said Nikki, as they settled onto uncomfortable stools. "How's your mother? Sonia said she was the one . . . a witness . . . in the church."

Valerio drained the last of his beer, thought of the messages his sisters had left, and felt guilty for not checking in with them. He'd had time in the past few hours—he could have driven out and visited his mother, but it was just too much.

"Not good. Lots of praying. Trying to reconcile this with God, I think. My sisters are with her."

"I'm sorry," said Nikki.

"Yeah," said Valerio. "Me, too. Just when you think you're used to violence, something like this comes along and fucks you up."

For a moment, he considered telling Nikki about Luca Errichiello, but the thought felt heavy. Some superstitious instinct said that talking about it would grant it substance and reality. Besides, it was over. The whole fucking thing was over. For better or worse, he'd played his part.

"The weather's supposed to be nice on Sunday," he said brightly. "If you can get time off work, we could sail."

It had been too long since he and Nikki had taken *Calypso* out. Just the thought of getting away from here, of spending an afternoon on the waves, the creak of the hull and the flap of the sails, seemed to loosen some tension in his body.

Dario brought another beer, popped the cap, and handed it to him.

"We haven't taken you sailing yet, have we?" Valerio asked him. "You two should come with us sometime."

"He gets seasick!" Graziella said, playfully pinching Dario's side.

"How about it?" Valerio asked Nikki. "Let's get the hell out of here. Just for a few hours."

She shrugged. "Sure. Alright."

"How's the investigation?" he asked.

She exhaled. "Don't know. I've been cut out. Sonia's decided not to work with Phoenix Seven."

"Fuck," he said. "Sorry about that."

He meant it. Nikki's expression was stoic, but he could imagine her disappointment. He was angry with Nikki's supervisor. It wasn't her fault she was forced to work with that idiot.

"It's that boss of yours . . . Angelo," Valerio said. "He's a mess."

"Yeah, well," she said with a shrug. "I can't help that. Oh, that reminds me . . . I need to give you this."

She took something from her pocket, and set it on the barrel between them: a passport in an evidence bag.

"Jayston Lake wanted me to pass this to the police," she said. "Would you give it to Sonia?"

"And Jayston Lake is who?"

"The employer of our victim . . . Claire Sexton. When Claire took off last week on Capri, she left this behind in the yacht's safe."

"Why would she do that?"

"Jayston thinks she was frightened. He thinks she might have been coerced."

"Wait," said Valerio. "I thought you were off the case. Why were you meeting with a suspect?"

Nikki seemed reluctant to tell him the story, needing encouragement from the gin and tonic before he could draw it out of her.

When she finished explaining, Valerio chuckled at the audacious little girl who'd convinced a taxi driver to take her to Nikki.

"Kids are ridiculous," he said. "When she was seven, Gemma decided she would take a train by herself to visit a play park she liked. Thank god we found her before she actually boarded!"

He picked up the passport and turned it over in his hands.

"And you just happened to be carrying an evidence bag with you?" he asked.

Nikki flushed and gestured for Dario to bring her another drink.

"Of course," she said. "Don't you?"

"You're a better cop than most of the guys I work with," he said, realizing it was true. "What did you think about Lake? Could he have murdered Claire?"

"I wasn't exactly there to challenge his story," Nikki said. "I'm not part of the investigation anymore. It was awkward enough to get invited in for drinks after I yelled at his wife. I presume Sonia and Emilio checked his alibi, though. What makes you think Jayston is a suspect?"

"He knew her," he said. "Maybe he was having an affair with her, like his wife suspected. Maybe she told him she was pregnant. Maybe she threatened to tell the wife. Most murders are committed by someone close to the victim—look at the boyfriend or husband first, I say."

"True," Nikki agreed. "But if he wanted Claire dead, why do it publicly . . . and so brutally? Wouldn't it make sense to wait until they're out to sea . . . and oops—she vanishes overboard? No witnesses. Just an accident. Good way to hide a pregnancy, if she was pregnant."

"You've got a point there," Valerio acknowledged. "What about the wife? Could she have done it? Although, I suppose she'd have the same opportunity as the husband. If she'd wanted to kill the nanny, she'd do it at sea, too."

"It was such a high-risk attack," Nikki noted. "That's what surprises me. Why do it there? Public place and plenty of witnesses. And a stabbing death is messy. Too many opportunities to leave evidence. It just doesn't make sense to me that anyone from the yacht would take that risk when they had better options."

"You don't take that kind of risk unless you're desperate or insane," said Valerio.

Nikki was about to answer when a voice behind Valerio said, "Nina? Nina Serafino, is that you?"

Only when he swiveled around to look did Valerio notice how much he'd had to drink. The world seemed to track unsteadily. He was suddenly wobbly and a little sick. He swallowed to keep everything in place.

The speaker was a handsome, well-built man—a little older than Valerio and much fitter. His features were even and attractive and, much to Valerio's envy, he'd managed to keep all his hair. A thick mane of salt-and-pepper locks were combed in waves away from his face. He wore a long wool coat.

Nikki gave him a puzzled look. "I'm sorry, do I know you?"

"It's been . . . years," he answered. "More than a decade, now I think about it. You wouldn't remember me. I was friends with your brother . . . Adriano. We worked together."

Nikki, usually so quick, seemed to struggle for words. She looked momentarily stricken. In the pause that followed, Valerio stuck out his hand.

"Valerio Alfieri," he said. The man took it.

"Sandro Balestrieri."

If he'd been thinking clearly, Valerio felt sure he could sort through two conflicting opinions about the situation. His first feeling was annoyance with the intrusion. He'd been enjoying Nikki's conversation and didn't feel particularly inclined to share her with someone else. But this feeling contended with a powerful curiosity. Nikki was a deeply private person. What he knew about her personal and family history he'd patched together from the scraps she'd somehow forgotten to tuck away. He'd heard the name Adriano only once—as the beloved brother she'd lost years ago. Police records said that Adriano Serafino had died of a gunshot wound in November 2006 during a spate of Camorra-related violence. Twenty-year-old Nikki's statement was in the record, the only witness to the shooting.

"Pull up a seat, Sandro," said Valerio, indicating the spare stool. "Join us."

"Oh, I really shouldn't," he protested. "I'm just passing through. It's so strange to see you, Nina. It must be fate. As chance would have it, I think I saw your father earlier today."

"A Peroni for Sandro, here," Valerio called out to Graziella, who nodded.

"I think . . . I do remember you," Nikki said haltingly. She seemed to be regaining her composure. "Of course. Sandro! I remember you used to come by for dinner. You and Adriano went to school together, didn't you? Carabinieri Officers' College?"

"Yes!" Sandro exclaimed. "That's right. Then we worked together in the same unit until . . . he passed. The last time I saw you was at Adriano's funeral. How have you been?"

"I'm doing really well!" She said the words in an eerily chipper voice, without apparent irony. "Are you still in the service?"

"Yes." He made a slight gesture as Graziella brought out the Peroni. "I'm really sorry. I need to get home. Please give my greetings to your father. I'm sorry I didn't say hello to him in person."

"Of course," said Nikki. Rising to her feet, she didn't flinch or pull back as Sandro reached down to embrace her.

"Good to see you," he said. "Just wonderful to see you again."

The conversation didn't recover after that. Nikki seemed distracted and, after a few minutes, took out some bills and laid them on the barrel.

"I'll call it a night," she said.

It was only after she'd disappeared around a corner that Valerio remembered they hadn't signed the insurance paperwork.

Valerio's phone rang just as he reached the front door to his building, before he'd had a chance to pull out his keys. He needed to piss and was eager to get inside.

It was Luca's number. Fuck. He was too tired and too drunk to deal with this right now.

No sooner had he pressed the button to answer, a stream of abuse screamed from the speakers.

"You must be the dumbest fucking shithead on earth. What the hell is wrong with you, Alfieri? You tell me that! You answer me that!"

Valerio hung up.

The phone rang again. He answered and the abuse started again. He hung up again.

Answering a third time, there was a different voice.

"Alfieri?"

"Sì."

"Gaetano Mancusi is going to be released from jail."

"That's right."

"Boss is angry . . . off the chain."

"What the fuck is he angry about? I did what he wanted. We're done. Finished. There's nothing more to say."

"It's done when he says it's done. You should have told him."

"I'm telling him now."

There was a pause and Valerio heard muffled conversation before the man's voice was back on the line. "He wants you to go to the jail."

"No. I'm going to bed."

"Mancusi will be released at midnight. Errichiello wants you there."

"If it's such a big deal, he can go there. And who the hell does a prisoner release at midnight?"

"He wants you there. This isn't finished, Alfieri. Be there."

They were gone.

Fuck. Fuck.

Valerio rested his head against the door and pressed his fist into the surface until his knuckles throbbed. He wished he wasn't so drunk. He just wanted to piss and go to sleep.

Maybe two or three beers and he could have managed to get his motorcycle to the jail, but he'd passed that limit long ago—even stupidly switched to liquor at some point during the evening. His mouth was numb, face hot, joints loose. The world seemed to smear out, sounds echoing and amplified.

The taxi ride was a nightmare. He kept drifting to sleep for seconds at a time, only to be jolted awake as the car braked or turned, tipping him in his seat.

At last, they reached the relentless black silhouette of the jail, the high wall starkly lit by streetlights, the razor wire along the top like a rim of silver lace.

"We're here," said the driver, pulling up to the curb across the street.

"Good," said Valerio. "We wait, then you take me back home."

The driver turned on the radio. They listened together to the lament of some young singer, crooning about his lost love, and the plaintive accompaniment.

"Dimmi di riprovare, ma non di rinunciare," he sang. ". . . solo nel perdono cambia un uomo." *Tell me to try again, to never surrender . . . only in forgiveness does a man change.*

They heard the clanging jingle of a commercial next and Valerio was about to ask the driver if he would change the station, when he saw a shadow at the base of the tall metal door, and the slight figure of Gaetano Mancusi stepped out.

He looked even more like a scarecrow now than he had in the cell, so small against the high walls. He wasn't wearing a coat, just that ugly brown sweater, and he clutched a black plastic bag in his left hand.

Valerio patted the driver's seat-back twice, said, "I'll be right back," and stepped out.

He waved at Gaetano. The boy looked at him.

Valerio began to make his way across the street.

He'd only taken a few steps when a dark blue sedan screeched into the road before him, engine revving. He saw the shapes of three men in the car, the angular outlines of the weapons, the hot red sparks as the machine guns sprayed bullets. Gaetano's body danced and juddered as the bullets crashed into him, and he fell down down down, towards the hard concrete. Gaetano Mancusi, son of Ines Mancusi, eighteen years old, was dead before he hit the pavement.

TWELVE

The day was chilly, air heavy and damp. Pale sunlight filtered through the canyons of buildings, brushing the aged and crumbling edifices, flaked plaster, rust stains, and graffiti, glinting on the chrome of motorbikes and battered car paint. The cobblestones were uneven and hard. Slippery. Bad for running. But Nikki found her footing and raced, dodging traffic and crowds, breathing in diesel fumes, the odors of grease, coffee, fish, and baked bread. She pounded down narrow alleyways and side streets, past vendors with their racks of clothes; piles of oranges and persimmons and tomatoes and artichokes and peppers; ice-packed Styrofoam boxes overflowing with glistening tentacles, fins, and scales; stacks of purses and plastic toys; grocers and cafés and shoe stores and ateliers and pharmacists.

It was her day off and a rare opportunity to catch up on sleep. But Nikki had spent a restless night, then awakened with the feeling she'd lost something important.

Adriano had been in her dreams. His voice, his laugh. Throughout the night, she'd hunted through a maze of shifting streets, sure he was waiting just around the next corner. But it wasn't her brother she found—it was Durant Cole. The NCIS agent had such a strange sad smile, and she'd shouted, needing to tell him something. But he vanished into a mass of people, and the crowd dragged her along into Chiesa del Gesù Nuovo, where Claire Sexton's bloody form lay outstretched beneath the altar.

Nikki hadn't felt Adriano clearly for years. He'd faded so completely that in her waking life, she could never quite recall his face. But running into Sandro yesterday seemed to unlock a door inside, and she remembered the two men swaggering down the street together, talking and laughing. She'd been only nine years old when her brother graduated the Carabinieri Officers' College where he and Sandro had become friends, and to her, they had seemed like gods. Adriano had never ignored her—she was always his little buddy. But she'd wanted more than his affectionate indulgence. She'd ached to be part of that exclusive conversation—the laughter of the gods.

In memories, as in dreams, Adriano was always and forever just out of reach.

In that labyrinth of sleep, Adriano had vanished, and she'd found Durant Cole instead. Why? There was no connective tissue between them. Adriano had died sixteen years ago, in the seconds before she could reach him. Durant . . . well, Durant was different. In the cold of that cave, she'd grappled, fought against an impossible, terrible reality.

That was the difficult thing about remembering Durant. Her mind couldn't reconcile those last desperate moments of terror and pain with the warm feelings he'd evoked. She hadn't seen him clearly, never suspected the duality of his nature, and even now couldn't understand the darkness in him well enough to condemn him to it.

In her dream, there had also been Claire. Sweet face and shy smile. Soft voice: *I reckon I've never properly grown up myself, you know?*

Are you going to find the people who hurt her? Audrey had asked.

Yes, Nikki had said. *I'll find them.*

In the daylight she felt the helplessness of that promise. She was just another person with no insight, no authority, no access, no power to do anything.

She picked up the pace, sprinting down one block and then another until her lungs burned, until sweat poured down her face. Blood pounded in her ears, and her legs weakened.

At last, in a narrow alleyway, she slowed and stopped, bending to take in air.

Her phone rang.

Aunt Izzy.

"Is this a bad time?" Izzy asked.

"I always have time for you," said Nikki, realizing it was true. She was homesick for her aunt in a way she'd never let herself feel for her own mother.

"Preston suggested I call," Izzy said. "You know, he has good days still, and he can be quite sharp. Well, today he reminded me something about your mother."

Nikki's heart rate, which had begun to slow, quickened.

She'd told Izzy Durant's theory about her mother—his suggestion that Beatrice had led a secret life. In the months since, she and her aunt had worn out the topic.

Izzy continued. "Preston remembered the name *Violetta*. He remembers Beatrice mentioned it."

Nikki gripped the phone tightly. *Violetta*, Durant had said. *That was her code name.*

If he was right and Beatrice had led a secret life, then it meant her mother was a puzzle she could solve.

"Did Preston remember when this was?" Nikki asked.

"He thinks he saw the name on letters."

"Do you have the letters?"

"I'm afraid not."

Hope, briefly kindled, was quelled. Preston's memory wasn't a reliable source.

Izzy was apologetic. "I'm sorry it isn't much to go on."

Nearby, a woman in an oversize coat was tending to a votive shrine affixed to the plaster and concrete on the side of a building.

Like the hundreds of similar aediculae—street memorials—in the city, this shrine was made of a glass-fronted cabinet, set against white tiles, an arching piece of corrugated metal to protect it from the rain. The cabinet housed gold-framed prints of Jesus and the Madonna, and a painted wooden icon of San Gennaro, two bare light bulbs, candles, and a cluster of red plastic tulips.

Nikki recognized the bleached blonde curls and bright scarves, the fortune teller's cart with its baubles and ribbons.

"Signora Dorotea!"

Startled, the fortune teller stared wide-eyed, then made a show of reasserting control. She returned to her task, adjusting the items in the glass cabinet, locking it with a key that she kept on a wristband among the clinking bracelets.

"Ah, seeker. I knew you would find me," she said. "You wish for my guidance."

"I wasn't looking for you," said Nikki. "Just a coincidence."

"There are no coincidences," said Dorotea. "Your life is part of a greater dance. Look for the pattern. What wisdom do you seek?"

"I don't have money to pay for your wisdom today," Nikki said.

A flash of annoyance crossed Dorotea's face. She turned her back, arranging the items in her cart.

"Betrayal is the seed at the root of your rage," she intoned. "The pain of betrayal lives on in the heart of the child."

Nikki strode rapidly away.

She was approaching the end of her street when she spotted Enzo: a familiar figure seated at the same table at the same café where he used to wait for her after her shift. The well-groomed hair and beard, muscular build, and polished style was a sort of looping backwards, skipping to an earlier track. Her breath stopped.

She seemed suddenly to be constructed of many parts, not all in agreement about how to feel. Anger surged—a hot, unpredictable hostility that had built its home inside her. But alongside this was a peculiar longing. She'd been with Enzo, his passion, his companionship, affection, for three years. She'd loved him. At the end of a long night shift, her heart would thrill to see him here, waiting for her. They would talk, and he'd come up to her flat and make love to her in the early morning light. She remembered his arms around her, the smell of his sweat and cologne, listening to him breathe as she fell asleep. She hated herself for this weakness: sentimentality that urged her to hold him again, and pretend that the end of their relationship hadn't been so completely catastrophic.

She considered jogging past without a word. But that would be too much like hiding, and he obviously needed reminding to never come back.

"What the fuck are you doing?" she demanded, her back to the sunlight so that he squinted.

"Ah, Nikki, there you are."

He smiled, showing white teeth. Then he saw her face, and adjusted to a serious expression.

"My father said he'd spoken with you," he said. "I'm glad."

Nikki thought about Vincente Di Pavola, that same smile as he greeted her from his yacht, his kind empathy a pretext for the transaction he'd wanted—the NDA he needed her to sign.

"Why the fuck should you be glad?" she demanded. "What makes you think I would ever want to see you?"

She continued towards her building. Enzo pushed back from the table and followed.

"Listen . . . just listen," he said. "We were good together . . . you used to care about me."

She stopped and glared.

"I did. And then you fucked Carmela; you gave Raffaele Barile a key to my home so he could beat the shit out of me; you refused to help when I needed you—when they were going to kill Gianni and Francesca and the kids. There's no coming back from that, Enzo. This is when you leave and I never have to see you, never have to think about you ever again."

The cold words burned her throat, a scouring pain to remove any vestigial remnant of love or loyalty. She struggled to breathe.

"I need you to sign an NDA," he said. "Sign it, and I'll be out of your life."

"No," Nikki said, and continued walking.

Enzo followed. "I need this. My father needs me protected before he lets me take over operations."

Not long ago, she would have given anything to heal Enzo's desperate need for Vincente's approval. It was a bitter irony that father and son should unite around this.

"I can't think of a single reason why I should help you," she said.

She opened the gate to her building and stepped through, closing it behind her with a clang.

"He'll pay you," Enzo continued. "Anything you ask. I know things are difficult for you financially. You need help with the apartment . . . with *Calypso* . . . he can help."

She took the stairs two at a time.

Enzo called out, "Carmela is pregnant. . . . I need this, Nikki."

She hated the way her heart raced, how it ached . . . how her eyes burned.

Indoors, without waiting to take off her shoes, Nikki crossed to her training room. She slammed her fist into the punching bag, kicked and hit it again and again.

The anger ran its course, burning through her muscles, bloodying her unprotected knuckles, and bruising her shins.

Nikki showered.

She briefly considered eating chocolate for breakfast, then thought better of it and made a proper meal with bread, cheese, tomato, and avocado. Then she washed up, cleared the dining room table, and wiped away the crumbs.

She wouldn't think about Enzo, she decided. The best—the only—thing to do was to work. She wasn't part of the murder investigation anymore, but she'd promised Audrey Lake that she would find Claire's killer, and she'd meant it. Now, she needed to figure out where to begin.

She seemed to hear Adriano's voice in her thoughts: *You must see—must understand the players and how they fit together.*

The memory awakened a sense of Adriano again—the way he huffed out his breath, hands shoved in his pockets as he strode around a room, and their mother would say, *You don't solve a problem by moping. Think it through. Build a system. Analyze.*

Nikki located a stack of note cards and set them on the table. On these, she wrote the names of everyone she knew associated with Claire Sexton and the information she had for each. Next, she wrote the details she'd learned about Claire's murder, arranging this in a rough timeline across the table.

On Saturday, Claire had tucked Audrey into bed, then disembarked from *The Prophet*. She'd taken jewelry and cash, though not her passport. She left at night, unseen, and didn't tell anyone. Three days later, during mass, she was stabbed to death in Chiesa del Gesù Nuovo.

What was the connection between her silent departure and her death? Why had she left, and where had she spent those three days?

Nikki found and watched the video interview of Claire, and was struck again by her vulnerability—the tender naivete a vicious mismatch to the violence of her death.

Her phone rang—a British number.

"It's me. It's Audrey," sang the cheerful voice. "Daddy got me my own phone."

"Why are you calling me, Audrey?"

"Can you come over?"

"No."

"Why not?"

"You don't even know me. I'm a stranger to you."

"You're not a stranger. You're my friend. Daddy says so. He told Mummy leave it alone—she's a hero. He says you're a hero and . . . and . . . and . . . he should hire you."

"That's nice of him to say," said Nikki. "But I already have a job."

"Can you come over?"

"No. I have work to do. I need to go."

"Please!"

"I'm hanging up now."

"Please! I want you to come."

"Goodbye."

No sooner had she hung up than the phone rang again. She was about to send the call to voicemail when she saw it was Angelo.

"You need to come in," he said.

"It's my day off," Nikki protested.

"Admiral Redford wants to see you."

On base, Angelo waited for her outside the heavy concrete structure that housed the admiral's offices. His face was pursed. Disapproving.

"What haven't you told me?" he demanded, lunging a little with the words.

Nikki was taken aback. "What do you mean?"

"Don't pretend you don't know!" he snapped. "This is about the ambassador's case. I'm sure of it. What has your girlfriend said?"

Nikki hardened her expression.

"I don't know anything about the murder investigation," she said. "As I reported, the police no longer want the assistance of Phoenix Seven."

He didn't have a chance to respond; their escort had arrived, a US Navy lieutenant in a tan uniform, who brought them through the formidable metal turnstile.

The building was as grey inside as it was out, the smooth tiling and monochromatic walls reflecting the minimalist efficiency of the United States Navy. The only decorative elements were a wall with pictures of the military commanders of the base, each in service dress blues, each in the same posture, seated before an American flag. At the top was a photo of the US president, and just below was Admiral Redford's picture with the words "Commander, United States Sixth Fleet."

At the admiral's office, the lieutenant knocked on the open door and announced to the group inside: "Investigators Figliomeni and Serafino, Phoenix Seven."

Conversations paused and faces turned to them.

Apart from the admiral, Nikki recognized the defense attaché, and the pale face and white hair of Ambassador Lissom, wearing a brown cardigan and bow tie. Besides this, there were two uniformed men, and a man in a suit, vest, and tie; another man in a polo shirt.

Admiral Redford greeted Nikki with a warm handshake.

"Investigator Serafino. Always a pleasure to see you. I'm sorry it's not under better circumstances."

There was a flash of something in his face, a grimace so rapid it almost didn't register through the rigid mask of professionalism. For a moment, Nikki wondered if their proximity was as difficult for him as it was for her. On the rare instances when she spotted the admiral in his neatly pressed uniform, as he strode across the base with that characteristic confidence, as men and women stood at attention and saluted, she was abruptly reminded of those desperate moments of terror in the dark, clawing at the tape wrapped around his mouth, around his forearms and his wrists. She remembered him next to her, on the cold damp ground of the cave, while Durant Cole pointed his weapon at them. She was grateful they'd made it out alive, but she wished she could erase that vulnerability and fear and restore some former order to the world.

"Good to see you, too, sir," she said. "I'm fine, thank you."

He shook Angelo's hand next, with a curt nod. "Investigator Figliomeni."

Admiral Redford's office, lodged deep inside the command building, was harshly lit. Three flagpoles stood upright in a corner behind a heavy mahogany desk: the American flag, the US Navy flag, and the NATO flag. In lieu of windows, there were paintings of battleships in gilded frames.

Admiral Redford invited the group to sit on blue upholstered sofas and leather armchairs, then announced, "Go ahead, Paul."

The ambassador leaned forward, hands pressed together.

"I confess I'm at a loss," he said. "My daughter and her friend have been arrested for murder. They were merely in the wrong place, at the wrong time—and committed the sin of trying to help."

He ran an unsteady hand across his forehead, and turned to a suited man. "Advocate Ferragni," he said. "Can you tell them what you told me?"

The man spoke with a thick Roman accent. "I'm Advocate Ferragni. My firm is representing Ambassador Lissom's daughter in this case. Here is the evidence against Monica Lissom and Kami Washington: First, they were at the scene at the time of the murder, and had the blood of the victim on their hands and clothing. Second, the fingerprints of Signorina Lissom were found on the murder weapon. Finally, cocaine residue was found on the clothing of the victim and on Ms. Lissom and Ms. Washington. The chemical signature indicated it was from the same batch."

"It must have come off the dead girl," the ambassador interjected.

"Quite possibly," the lawyer said. "Both young ladies are being held in the Pozzuoli Remand Female Prison. The police will interview them again this afternoon."

"Phoenix Seven will support you," offered Admiral Redford. He turned to Angelo. "Investigator Figliomeni, I'd like you to assign Nikki Serafino to work with Advocate Ferragni on this."

Before Angelo could reply, the civilian in the polo shirt spoke, directing measured words to the ambassador: "The nature of this case—and your family's involvement—could well impact bilateral relations—"

"I'm aware of the implications!" the ambassador snapped. "I spent all night on the phone with Washington. I may very well need to recuse myself."

The man continued. "Well, you may also wish to consider that military support to your daughter's legal defense could violate the terms of existing agreements with the Italian government."

One of the uniformed men spoke—a navy captain in a dark blue jacket with golden stripes on his cuffs, gold buttons, and an eagle insignia above the ribbons on his chest. Nikki recognized him as the JAG, head of the legal office. He addressed Admiral Redford.

"Sir, it's questionable whether it's within the authority of Phoenix Seven to give support in a criminal defense case, especially one involving a civilian."

"Is it prohibited by the status of forces agreement?" asked the admiral.

"Not explicitly," said the JAG. "But it could be perceived as undue influence by the military. It may harm our credibility and perceived neutrality if this case draws unfavorable media attention."

The admiral nodded solemnly, hands clasped.

"I acknowledge the jurisdictional and protocol concerns," he said. "However, I must also weigh the broader implications for our base and personnel. It undermines trust if people perceive that one of our own isn't receiving adequate support in a foreign legal system. Moreover, whether or not we help, negative publicity from the case might foment anti-American sentiment—posing a potential security threat. We must proactively address these risks. By ensuring the case is handled with fairness and sensitivity, we protect not only the rights of Ambassador Lissom's daughter, but also the integrity and security of our operations."

He paused and looked at the ambassador. "It's up to you, Paul. I'd like to support, even if we're limited in what we can offer. As you heard from my JAG, we're skating on thin ice—jurisdictionally speaking."

The ambassador nodded. "I understand. Thank you."

Nikki's face was suddenly hot. She needed to say something, but was careful with her words around groups like these. She'd learned long ago to edit thoughts or opinions that might elicit her father's disapproval or the amusement of his colleagues.

"There's something else to consider," she said, voice weaker than she intended. "Phoenix Seven is neutral. When we interact with the police on behalf of US service members and their families, they perceive us as . . . fair. Unbiased. If the police see us working with a defense attorney on a criminal case, it may harm our ability to effectively do our jobs."

"Surely, there can be no more important job than defending an American citizen!" exclaimed Angelo with a broad gesture. "Clearly, Signorina Serafino doesn't feel up to the tasking!"

"I didn't mean—" Nikki began.

Angelo spoke loudly over her: "I humbly volunteer my services to defend the daughter of the ambassador. I will personally take charge of assisting the advocate. I will rearrange the shift schedule of Phoenix Seven to provide this assistance."

"That's very kind of you," said Ambassador Lissom. "Of course, I appreciate your support." He paused for a moment while Angelo nodded, before adding, "My daughter did tell me she felt most comfortable working with Investigator Serafino."

Placing a hand on his chest, Angelo bowed his head and gave the ambassador his most ingratiating smile. "Certainly. If it makes your daughter comfortable, Investigator Serafino can accompany me to the interview."

Angelo seemed pleased with himself, humming tunelessly to the radio as they sped along the Tangenziale in the Phoenix Seven duty vehicle towards the jail in Pozzuoli. They exited the tollway and navigated the side streets towards the port, and he turned the radio down.

"Your job is to assist the US military base commander," he said. "He makes a request and we say, '*Yes, sir!*' You embarrass me when you show your ignorance in such an important room."

"You aren't concerned?" Nikki protested. "The police are already shutting us out. If we assist in a criminal defense, they may start to think of us as the opposition."

"We help with defendants all the time!" Angelo scoffed. "Some stupid sailor is arrested for fucking a prostitute in the street and we must beg to have him released. '*Yes, sir, he violated laws . . . but he's a stupid boy—thinking with his dick. Don't make the Americans mad at us.*'"

"Of course," Nikki said. "But the police listen to us because they know we're not taking sides—just interpreting cultural misunderstandings. This is different. Don't you see?"

Angelo chuckled.

"You lack all understanding of the strategic level," he said in a tone of fatherly condescension. "A person must know their strengths. You focus on the tactical details, Nicole. This is your strength: day-to-day operations. Leave strategy to those in authority."

At the jail, Angelo and Nikki joined Advocate Ferragni in the interview room.

Monica Lissom had been crying. Her face was red and splotchy, eyes swollen nearly shut. At the sight of Angelo, her face contorted.

"No!" she shouted. "Not him! I'm not talking if he's in the room."

Angelo stepped forward. "Signorina . . . prego . . . prego. I'm here on the special request of your father. I promised him I will do everything in my power to help you."

Monica looked at Nikki, and then at the lawyer.

"Is it true?"

"Sì," agreed Ferragni.

She turned to Angelo, eyes fierce. "You called me a liar."

"Please accept my deepest apology," said Angelo. "I only desire to assist you."

Monica looked at Nikki. "Will you be there?"

"Yes," Nikki agreed. "Right here."

Sonia and Emilio entered, accompanied by their translator, a small, wiry man.

Sonia, seemed nonplussed to see Nikki and Angelo.

"We don't require Phoenix Seven at this time," she said.

Her voice was cold, face expressionless.

Angelo nodded, adjusting his posture.

"I'm here on the *special* request of the United States admiral and the United States ambassador," he said.

Sonia didn't wait for pleasantries. When they were seated, she passed across a paper with numbers and graphs.

"These are the results from the clothing swabs we took from you and Kami and from Claire Sexton. The cocaine we found on your clothing was an exact match."

"I told you," said Monica. "It must have gotten on us when we were trying to help."

"I know you said that," said Sonia. "We wanted to believe you. But your blood and saliva tests also came back."

She passed over another piece of paper.

"You and Signorina Washington both tested positive for cocaine use. Can you explain this?"

"I don't know," said Monica with a hiccuping sob, and she started crying again. Everyone waited for her to calm.

"We understand the victim was carrying a bag with her," Sonia said. "Did you notice a bag anywhere?"

"No."

"Did you happen to notice if anyone else was carrying a bag?"

"She was bleeding to death!" Monica exclaimed angrily, face flushing. "How was I supposed to notice?"

"You told us you didn't know the victim," said Emilio. "Is that correct?"

"I've never seen her before in my life."

"You may not realize this," said Emilio, "but smartphones are fairly stupid when it comes to deleting things. You take a picture with your phone, and it . . . moves around. Copies itself. So, when you delete a photo, it leaves a ghost behind. Our technicians are very good at hunting ghosts."

Monica was trembling. Emilio set an electronic tablet on the table, then dragged his finger across the screen to show a series of images.

"These pictures were on your phone and the phone of Kami Washington on Sunday night."

The photos were of Monica and Kami, both drinking cocktails—lit against a dark background awash in green and pink laser lights—flirting with men and with the camera.

Emilio stopped at a photo: a selfie of three women, their faces pressed together, full cheeks, eyeliner, and puckered lips—Kami and Monica and Claire Sexton.

Monica covered her face.

"This is your chance," said Sonia. "Tell us what you know."

Ferragni placed a hand on the table. "I need a word with my client."

Emilio and Sonia nodded and stood. Nikki stood, too, but Angelo stayed put until Ferragni gave him a hard look and said, "Alone."

Angelo dislodged himself and tromped from the room with the others.

They waited in the paint-chipped concrete hallway. Angelo seemed eager to get away from Sonia and took a few long strides, his hands clasped behind him, forehead creased as if in deep contemplation.

Nikki said to Sonia, "I need to apologize for losing my temper with Fiona Lake."

"It's okay," said Sonia.

"It really isn't. I should have been better. I will be better."

Sonia looked long, then nodded slowly. "Thank you for your apology."

"I lost my temper with Signora Lake, too," Emilio volunteered, grinning. "I thought Sonia would punch me."

The smallest hint of a smile twitched the edge of Sonia's mouth.

Relieved to have some restoration of their professional relationship, Nikki exhaled.

"If I knew I was meeting you today, I would have brought the passport myself," she said.

"What passport?" Sonia asked.

THIRTEEN

It was late morning by the time Valerio sobered up. The hours after the shooting had been grim and horrifying. His mind, dulled and disrupted by the alcohol, had been unable to think logically, and reality collapsed into a dark dream state, a jolting slurred mess of blood and guilt. Immediately after the shooting, he'd called for backup and rushed to the boy, but there was nothing left to save. Gaetano's young body was decimated—chewed up by machine-gun fire. Arriving on the scene, the ambulance workers seemed relieved that there was nothing for them to do; it was a dangerous business to save someone il Sistema had appointed to die.

Valerio had insisted on staying with the responding investigators. Only now could he comprehend that his drunken attempts to assist must have been thoroughly obnoxious, because at some point, his partner, Maurizio, showed up and took him home. There, Maurizio had pressed him to drink water, received his rambling sobs, and dragged him, stumbling, to the toilet to puke. Eventually, Valerio passed out.

He woke to sunlight through his open window and street sounds below. His mouth tasted foul, tongue swollen and sandpaper-dry, head throbbing. For one blissful moment the pain was only physical. Then the nightmare reasserted itself and, empty though he was, he wanted to throw up again.

Maurizio was in the living room, the fabric pattern from the sofa imprinted on his cheek.

Valerio collapsed into a chair, pressing palms against aching eyes.

"Did you know?" Maurizio asked.

Valerio shook his head. "Fuck no. I should have known. I should have . . ."

Words failed him.

He and Maurizio had both experienced plenty of violence. They'd seen murders and waded into the aftermath. This was different.

"He was only eighteen," said Maurizio. "I helped you."

Valerio thought of Davide. Thirteen years old.

"It was a fucking trap," said Valerio. "I walked right in. Like an idiot. I should have seen. I thought . . . fuck, I don't know what I thought."

"How did this get so fucked?" asked Maurizio. "Who did this? What did you do for them?"

Valerio felt like shit. His head hurt. His muscles and joints felt like they'd been pulled apart, and his neck . . . God, his neck!

He deserved it all—every dose of this pain. He clung to it as he told Maurizio everything.

"You're right," said Maurizio when he was finished. "You are a fucking idiot. You gave Errichiello your balls on a silver platter."

"I'll turn myself in," said Valerio. "Report everything, and take the consequences."

"That really would be idiotic," said Maurizio. "You know what your problem is? You see things so black-and-white. Right and wrong."

"This is black-and-white. That boy is dead!"

"And nothing you do now will bring him back," Maurizio said.

Valerio scrubbed a hand over his head. "I'll tell the truth. When I helped the kid, I didn't know what Errichiello had planned."

He thought about that benign and forgettable face, that beige hat. Errichiello had handled Valerio with the disinterested skill of a professional, only once displaying emotion—irritation—with his white-haired security chief. Wrapped around his own fear and anger, Valerio had unintentionally leaned into Luca's calm demeanor and the reasonable logic of his request.

"Nobody's interested in the truth," Maurizio sighed. "It's a political game—and you're shit at it. Let's say you march up to il Dirigente today and confess everything. Do you think he wants to hear it? Fuck, no. He's new. He doesn't know you—and he certainly doesn't give a shit about you. All he cares about are the numbers that make him look good. Until now, you've caught the baddies, and that makes him look good. If you fuck up his statistics, he'll throw you out on your ass. My advice? Don't tell him about Errichiello."

"But I'm a liability," said Valerio. "Luca Errichiello can draw a line between me and Gaetano's murder anytime he wants."

"Do you think you're the only one they've gotten to?" Maurizio laughed bitterly. "Of course not. If we kicked out all the crooked cops, everyone with friends and family tied up in the system, the building would be empty. It's the price of doing business. Look at my wife's brother—he's neck-deep. Always asking us for favors. One day, this is gonna bite me, and I'll be in the same situation as you."

Valerio leaned over and rested his face in his hands. He took a deep breath. Maurizio slapped his back.

"Get some coffee and head to the station. They'll need your statement. Then take a few days off. Get your head back in the game."

Maurizio left. Valerio took a shower, dressed, and walked outside. Squinting into the cool sunlight, he felt raw. Exposed.

He was hungry and nauseated, but didn't feel like eating. He took coffee at the corner café. Far from helping, the espresso seemed to set the pain in his head ringing.

The world was duller than it had been yesterday, as though he was seeing it through dirty glass. Something inside said, *Hadn't you noticed? It was always like this.*

At the station, he gave his statement to the investigating officers.

Against Maurizio's advice, he directed them towards Errichiello—stopping short of confessing that his work to help Gaetano had been at Luca's request.

Afterwards, he sat at his desk and tried to work. He couldn't seem to think at all. After a few hours, he was about to give up, when he was called into the director's office.

Valerio had only ever spoken to Dirigente Cristiano Bonetti once—a few weeks ago, during the director's first days on the job. Originally from Acerra, Bonetti had spent the past twenty years at the police headquarters in Trapani, Sicily.

Appointed as director only two months ago, he was already established in the office at the end of the corridor as though he'd spent his career here. Unlike the other offices, crammed with as many desks as could fit, and a jumble of excess and expired equipment and ugly metal lockers, his office was spacious and orderly, the polished wood desk organized—from the stack of active files to a neatly penned to-do list, and a row of Post-it notes in pastel shades. A bookshelf covering one wall was filled with judicial and policing review books—all alphabetized.

Bonetti gestured Valerio in with a curt nod, before returning to his computer and typing for several more minutes. At last, he pressed the Enter key with a little flourish, said, "There!" and turned clever, watchful eyes on him.

"It was not my intention to neglect you, Capo Alfieri," he said.

Valerio nodded.

Bonetti was a handsome man in a well-tailored blue suit and silk tie, black hair beginning to grey.

"Terrible business with this Mancusi kid," he said. "It's one of my priorities to begin to address these gangs of baby criminals—young Camorra boys acting like guerrillas, committing serious crimes, but spontaneously, without any real planning."

"Gaetano Mancusi was the victim of a targeted killing, not the criminal," Valerio said. "We can't know whether he was one of these baby criminals you're talking about."

"Ah, but he was in Poggioreale for a reason!" Bonetti exclaimed.

"He was only eighteen years old," Valerio said. "And he hadn't gone to trial. As far as I'm concerned, we should consider him an innocent."

"Hmmm . . ." Bonetti gave Valerio an appraising look. "That's a strange reasoning. He was arrested for drugs—and was clearly dealing for one of the clans. In a war, foot soldiers are never innocent. I understand you requested his release?"

It was no good denying it. Valerio nodded. "On humanitarian grounds. His mother is dying of cancer."

"I see."

Bonetti tapped his pen on the desk as if writing a message in Morse code.

"Our police and judicial actions are working," he said. "This creates a vacuum in criminal organizations. Young boys are trying to fill that void. They're drawn to crime. They inherit it. In these families, crime isn't seen as deviance; it's following the path of their father. When kids go to prison, there's no criticism from the parents—just acceptance. We need to change this, Alfieri. We've been too soft. We need to make crime unacceptable."

Valerio, not knowing what to say, nodded.

"I understand you witnessed the shooting?" Bonetti continued.

"Sì," Valerio agreed, and told the director the same thing he'd told the investigators. "I got a phone call last night—about the release. I took a taxi from my house. . . . I'd been drinking."

"You weren't warned that Mancusi would be killed?"

Valerio returned his stare. "No. But as I told the investigating officers, Gaetano's mother worked as a housekeeper for Luca Errichiello. They should explore the connection there."

Bonetti tapped his pen again.

"Yes," he said. "They told me about your suspicions. Do you have evidence that Errichiello was actually involved in Mancusi's death?"

"No," Valerio admitted. "But we know what Errichiello does; his name has come up in a dozen human-trafficking cases."

"Nothing that was ever proven!" Bonetti said. "As far as this office is concerned, Luca Errichiello is a law-abiding citizen."

"Tell that to the women and girls he's trafficked," said Valerio, who'd seen some of those cases firsthand.

Bonetti sniffed. "Have any come forward? Any willing to testify against him?"

"The ones who tried ended up dead," Valerio said.

"Without a live witness, my hands are tied," said Bonetti. "My predecessor may have done things differently, but I believe we should be careful . . . before painting someone with the brush of such ugly accusations! Now, back to the Mancusi case. We must investigate properly.

I hope you understand. It isn't personal, but we need to be thorough. We'll be examining your actions last night."

Valerio nodded. "I would expect nothing less."

"I'm placing you on administrative leave until the investigation is complete," Bonetti said.

Valerio raised an eyebrow. Administrative leave was reserved for extraordinary situations, like cop shootings. But if Bonetti expected protest, Valerio disappointed him.

"The kid deserves a complete investigation," he said.

Valerio sat in an outdoor café and had another espresso and rinsed it down with water, stomach churning. He thought about getting on his motorbike, riding to Luca's compound, and . . . what then? Scream impotently? Lay the murder of Gaetano Mancusi at Luca's feet—accuse him of being a cheat and a liar? He'd known what Luca was. Known it when he begged for his help, when he agreed to do what he wanted. And Valerio had done the one thing you must never do with a predator: exposed his throat. Luca had preyed on his obvious need to protect his children and clear his debt. He'd been stupid and blind, and Gaetano was dead.

His sister Orlanda called.

"You never answer!" she complained when he picked up.

"I'm answering," he said.

"You don't answer our texts. You don't come by. Mamma's too much to handle. You can't just leave this to Penelope and me. It isn't fair."

"I can't," he said.

"We're busy, too, you know," she said. "You're not the only one with obligations."

In the background, female voices were shouting.

"What's happening?" he asked.

"Giorgia came by with the kids; she has a date and wants them out of the house. She wants them to spend the night at Mamma's, but Mamma isn't well. Penny told her she can't just dump them here."

"She's saying this in front of Davide and Gemma?"

Fuck. That was the last thing they needed.

"It isn't Penny's fault," Orlanda defended. "I told you, it's been a lot."

"Tell Penelope to shut her mouth! Tell Giorgia to leave. I'll come and get them."

"But you're working."

"Not now, I'm not. Tell them I'm on my way."

Valerio heard raised voices as he walked along the landing, towards his mother's apartment.

"You've never liked me," Giorgia's voice rang out. "You hated me from the first day we met. You were jealous of me then, and now you're even more jealous!"

"Oh, get over yourself!" Penny scoffed. "Why the hell should I be jealous of you?"

Giorgia's voice: "Look in the mirror sometime."

Penny again: "You're right, I never liked you. That's because I know what you are: a spoiled, delusional bitch. My brother was too good for you, but he's an idiot and never saw you properly."

"Shut up, both of you!" screamed Orlanda.

The door opened and Davide stormed through, slamming it behind him, his face a mask of disgust. He crossed to the iron railing and leaned heavily on it. Then he turned and saw his father, and Valerio watched something wrestling in his expression.

Thirteen years old, Davide was nearly as tall as Valerio, voice deepening as he raced out of childhood. He'd always been such a funny kid—quiet and shy, intensely interested in music and football and extreme sports. He'd recently started to notice girls, and took painful care to douse himself in body spray, and to comb and gel his hair into a rigid crest. Easily embarrassed in front of his friends, he kept his distance from Valerio in public, telegraphing disinterest. But there was the tender child in him still, the little boy who had bad dreams and cried out for his babbo. This was the face Valerio saw now: the core of unshielded loneliness and grief. Valerio rapidly closed the distance to his son, and pulled him in close.

The feel of Davide in his arms was almost too much to tolerate.

Valerio's throat was tight with the pain of love, the image in his mind of a young body broken and bloodied in front of Poggioreale.

"Go get your sister," he said. "You're coming home with me."

Valerio's anger towards his sisters and ex-wife came out as revulsion. He couldn't stand to look at them.

Giorgia, in a skintight black dress and heels, hair curled and draped down her back, trailed behind as he marched through the apartment.

"If I'd known you would take them, I would have called . . . but you never have time for us! You can't just expect my life to stop—"

Valerio gave her a look and she shut up.

His mother sat in her armchair, a vacant expression on her face, the rosary clutched in her hand. He kissed her on the head before leaving.

They spent the rest of the afternoon in the city center, the kids dipping in and out of the shops on Via Toledo. On another day, Valerio would have left them on their own. But he didn't want them out of his sight.

There was one diversion: Sonia called, asking for the passport Nikki had given him, so he dragged Davide and Gemma to the police station to drop it off.

For dinner, Valerio took the kids to Cosimo's pizzeria, then, afterwards, back to his place. They were sitting together on the sofa, watching a superhero movie, when there was a knock at the door.

Not wanting to alarm the kids, Valerio turned up the volume and crossed out of sight before taking his Smith & Wesson from a cabinet in the entryway.

He approached the door cautiously, stood to one side of it. Another three knocks.

"Who is it?"

A female voice. "Ravenna. I'm looking for Valerio Alfieri. We met at the home of Ines Mancusi."

She wore hospital scrubs and white sneakers, an oversize coat and fluffy red scarf, and gripped a large canvas tote with two mittened hands. Her glasses glinted, and Valerio caught a distorted reflection of himself in the lenses.

He didn't understand his own reaction: a strange relief and gladness to see the wild frizz of her hair, those large dark eyes and full cheeks, the thin lips and expressive mouth. This feeling rapidly vanished, however, when he read the emotion in those eyes.

"You lied to me, Capo." Her voice was low and husky, eyes wide. "I accuse you. . . . You gave a dying woman hope . . . then you killed her boy. I don't care that you're a powerful man. I don't care what you do to me, but I must say it. Can you imagine her suffering?"

Tears pooled in her eyes, and she gave a little gasping sob.

Valerio was paralyzed, tongue dry and thick in his mouth. He stared as tears slid down her face.

"Babbo!" Davide shouted behind him amid the crashing sounds of a television battle. "Did you change your wi-fi password? I can't get my phone to connect."

The sound of his son's voice seemed to break Valerio's fugue state. He jolted and turned his head, calling out, "It's the same as before."

"I'll go now," said Ravenna with a little shudder. She took a step back.

Valerio involuntarily reached out, then caught himself and drew his hand back.

"I accept your accusation," he said. "I should have known—should have guessed what they would do. I'm responsible."

She seemed about to speak, then closed her mouth and stared, searching his face.

"You didn't know?" she said at last.

He shook his head. "No."

"So, you went to the magistrate like you said, got him released?"

"Yes. I didn't understand why they wanted him out—until it was too late."

He wasn't sure what to say next. He wanted to confess it all, to tell her about going to Luca for help to find Gemma—about his stupidity for not looking closer into what Luca asked; about those horrible moments outside the jail.

Gemma came up behind him and pressed against his back, peering on tiptoe over his shoulder at Ravenna.

"Hi," she said. "I'm Gemma."

Ravenna pushed the tears away and sniffed.

"Oh, Babbo!" Gemma said, squeezing around Valerio's middle, tugging him away from the door. "Don't just stand there like a big dummy. Invite her in! Can we do something for you? Can we get you water? Tea?"

Without waiting for an answer, she darted back into the living room shouting, "Davide! Turn off the TV. Babbo has a guest!"

Valerio stared at Ravenna, heat rising in his cheeks and neck. She looked at his hands and he noticed that he was still holding the gun. He tucked it out of sight.

"For safety," he mumbled.

"Are those your kids?" Ravenna asked.

Valerio nodded. "Gemma and Davide." Then, not knowing why, added, "I'm divorced."

After a long pause, he stepped back. "Will you come in?"

Her eyes were wide as she looked at him. Then, slowly, she nodded.

Valerio became suddenly, uncomfortably conscious of his apartment as Ravenna followed him: shabby secondhand furniture, posters on the wall masquerading as art, stacks of books and newspapers, wires looping out of boxes—entrails of dead electronics that he hadn't gotten around to burying. Dust on everything. It bothered him that it mattered what she thought of him.

In the kitchen, Gemma put the kettle on, and Davide slipped away into the back room with his laptop. Valerio pulled out a chair for Ravenna and she sat, clutching her bag in her lap.

"How do you know each other?" Gemma asked.

"We don't," said Ravenna. "We met this week."

"I like your scrubs. Are you a doctor?"

"Nurse."

"Babbo's a cop. Did he tell you?"

"Yes. He told me."

"He's really good at his job," said Gemma. Then, to Valerio, "Did you tell her?"

Valerio passed a hand across his face, and sat heavily in a chair. "I'm sure she isn't interested."

He looked around the room—dirty dishes stacked in the sink, the floor that needed sweeping.

Ravenna placed her bag on the floor next to her, and looked at him intently. "I'm actually very interested in the type of policeman you are. Are you someone who finds and punishes the murderer of a boy? Or do you put your head in the sand, and pretend not to see anything?"

"He sees everything," Gemma assured. "You should hear him. He's mad at anyone who pretends not to see."

"How is Ines doing?" Valerio asked quietly.

"How do you think?" said Ravenna with a flare of fury. Then she shook her head and closed her eyes. Her next words were quiet and earnest. "She's destroyed. I can't imagine the pain."

Gemma set two steaming mugs on the table, and kissed Valerio's cheek.

"I've gotta make a call," she said, and sauntered from the room.

Valerio watched her go, then returned his attention to Ravenna.

"What I don't understand is why," she said. "Why him?"

The difficulty, Valerio realized, was his own stupid slowness. Gaetano's murder had shocked him—in the truest sense of the word. It was so unexpected, so violent, so personal, it had stripped his ability to think. Overwhelmed by guilt, ashamed of his blindness, his ignorance, these were hampering him still—distracting him from the truth of the situation.

And what was the truth?

Gaetano had been killed for a reason. But Valerio couldn't imagine what that reason was. Had Gaetano been older, more savvy and powerful, there would have been ample explanations. When a well-liked deputy became too influential, the boss had an obligation to put him in his place or risk mutiny. But Gaetano was just a kid—too weak even to resist the unique tortures of Poggioreale. What offense warranted such a violent and public death? Drugs? No. Drug arrests were standard. They happened all the time. Besides, Gaetano's roommates were still safely ensconced. Gaetano had been singled out. Why?

"He must have known something that Errichiello didn't want getting out," Valerio realized.

"What was it?"

Valerio shook his head. "When I talked to him yesterday, he didn't think he had anything to trade. He may not have known, himself."

"I worried about him in jail," said Ravenna. "He was too soft. I thought he would die inside."

She clutched the hot cup, slowly raised it to her lips, her obvious agitation seeming to settle a little.

"If they were going to kill him," she said, "why bring him out of jail first?"

Valerio sighed. "An execution like that is meant to send a message."

"A message for whom?"

"Anyone involved with Gaetano—in case they had any thought of stepping out of line and . . ." He hesitated.

"What?" Ravenna pressed.

"Well, one message is for me, isn't it?"

"What do you mean?"

Valerio stood, paced the small kitchen.

"I owed a favor and I thought it would be harmless to help this kid. I thought it meant I could get out. But Errichiello was reminding me: You never get out. His brother tried to warn me."

Ravenna agreed. "You worked to get Gaetano released—and killed. That's what it looks like."

"Yes."

"But it isn't true," she protested.

"You thought it was true," Valerio said.

She pursed her lips and took a deep breath.

"What will you do?" she asked.

"There aren't many options. I can turn myself in and lose everything, or I can do what Errichiello wants."

Ravenna said quietly, "Isn't there any other way?"

"I don't have leverage," he said. "Nothing to stop Errichiello from coming after me and my kids . . . even if I do turn myself in."

"Oh." Ravenna breathed the word, realization emerging.

Valerio's mind was working, testing the walls, looking for a way out. Ravenna was clearly thinking, too, eyes focused on some distant point, forehead creased.

He gave what he hoped was a reassuring smile. "It isn't your problem. You didn't come here for this."

She looked at him, then nodded slowly.

"I should go," she said. "Thank Gemma for the tea, will you?"

Valerio watched Ravenna as she left, walking down the hall, then he closed the door.

Gemma, scrolling through her phone, glanced up as Valerio came into the living room.

"She seemed nice," she said with a grin. "A nurse is good. Nurses are interesting."

Valerio watched his daughter's broad smile for a moment before he understood the subtext.

"Oh," he said. "I'm not dating her."

"Sure, you're not," said Gemma, still smiling.

There was a knock on the door—a soft double tap. Distracted, Valerio nearly forgot to bring his weapon. But Ravenna called out before he could ask who it was: "It's me again."

He opened the door.

Her face was flushed, and she was breathing hard, as if she'd run back up the stairs.

"What if we found out?" she said.

"What do you mean?"

"What if we found out what Gaetano knew? Maybe it's enough to get Errichiello arrested . . . put him into jail or . . . I don't know. Maybe it's enough to give you leverage . . . so he lets you out."

Valerio thought. "I don't understand. What are you saying?"

She spoke slowly, as if trying out the idea. "I want to know what happened to Gaetano. I'm going to ask around . . . maybe it helps you if I find something."

"No," said Valerio. "Stay away. Leave it alone."

She looked stricken, and he softened. "I'll look into it," he said. "I promise."

She shook her head vigorously. "I knew Gaetano. . . . I know his girlfriend, Natale . . . and the kids Gaetano used to hang out with. I'm going to ask my own questions, whether you help me or not."

FOURTEEN

Music was playing loudly at Gianni and Francesca's flat—something with trumpets, twanging guitar, and tinny drums. A harsh female voice belted Spanish from the speakers.

The baby in Gianni's arms was wailing as he answered the door.

"Oh good," he said. "You're here. Can you hold Fredo?"

"No . . . wait!" Nikki protested as he transferred the screaming child to her.

He retreated rapidly from the room, shouting, "He'll be here any minute! Francesca, text my father. Tell him to bring more wine!"

Nikki stood rigidly, not sure what to do with the warm, squirming, noisy human. Children terrified her. The only other baby she'd been forced to hold was Bea, Gianni's first child, and she'd passed on that privilege as soon as possible. She looked around for someplace to put Fredo. He smelled bad, and was leaking.

Gianni and Francesca's posh flat had upscale furniture, a wide-screen television, speaker system, and personal temperature controls. Modern art on the walls included an oil portrait of Francesca in her wedding gown. Nikki couldn't begin to guess how they afforded any of this. Gianni owned an unremarkable clothing shop in a questionable part of the city that, by all accounts, was a spectacular failure.

She hadn't seen her brother since the summer, when Gianni had appeared on her doorstep, bleeding and delirious—tortured by loan sharks, begging for help.

The panic of that day, the terror she'd felt asking Tito Calandra for money, the frantic drive to Pozzuoli to deliver the funds, had been eclipsed in her memory by what came afterwards: the cave with Durant Cole. Those frozen minutes were etched into her. Sometimes the details arose with sudden, paralyzing clarity. Yet when she turned deliberately to it, ran her mind over those recollections, like running her finger over broken glass, she instinctively avoided the jagged edges.

Her phone rang. Nikki shifted Fredo to answer.

"Hi," chirped Audrey Lake. "It's me."

"Audrey, you shouldn't call me," said Nikki.

"We're not leaving," said Audrey. "We were supposed to go home, but the police say we have to stay."

"Really?" said Nikki, curiosity getting the better of her. "Why?"

"Mummy says it's because of the fucking drugs. Fucking drugs."

Nikki extracted herself from the call. Jostling Fredo to calm him, she phoned Sonia and told her what Audrey had said.

"We got the passport," Sonia said. "It tested positive for the same cocaine we found on Monica and Kami. It was good you handled it appropriately—but I wish you'd told Lake to give it directly to the police."

"I should have," Nikki agreed.

"Chain of custody should be fine," said Sonia, her voice softening. "But the Lakes are a powerful family and their lawyers are involved. We've put a judicial order on the Lakes' yacht, so they can't leave the country. And we're trying to get a search warrant, but they're resisting."

She was jolted by a loud rap on the door.

Nikki expected Gianni to return. When he didn't, she answered.

The man at the door was in his early forties. He had thinned brown hair, pale skin, and a rectangular face with jowls, eyes like buttons pressed into dough. He wore a suit jacket and checkered shirt, stretched over a barrel chest and hefty belly.

"You must be Nina!" He spoke English with a foreign accent, a wide smile pushing out his apple cheeks. "Gianni and Francesca didn't tell me you were such a looker. And there's Fredo! Hello, little Fredo."

He grabbed and waggled the baby's foot. Fredo's wailing intensified.

"And you are?" Nikki asked.

He snapped his heels together and saluted.

"Lieutenant Commander Mac van den Berg, at your service!"

"How do you know my brother?"

He gave a conspiratorial wink. "Mutual friends."

Gianni was back in the room now, rushing towards them. He brushed past Nikki and embraced the visitor, kissed his cheeks.

"Mac! Mac! You're here," he said in English. "Wonderful!"

Francesca followed close behind, gliding forward in a floor-length red dress slit to the thigh.

Nikki intercepted, extending the baby. "He needs a diaper change."

Francesca shifted deftly away. "Take him to my mother, will you?" she said, then, pushing past, greeted Mac with a kiss.

Nikki toted the howling Fredo into the kitchen, where Francesca's mother, Salvatrice, was slicing bread and scowling.

"Can't you see I'm busy?" she barked. "I spend the whole day cooking . . . cleaning. Tell Francesca this is her party. I'm not her slave."

The relentless screaming was starting to induce panic when the doorbell buzzed and Nikki heard her father's booming voice: "Sì, sì! Raoul Serafino. Pleasure to meet you. And this is Massimo Fattore, a good friend."

Gianni's voice: "Oh hello, Massimo. I didn't expect you. . . . Well, welcome, of course."

A shriek of joy pierced the air, then the pounding rush of little feet as three-year-old Bea raced through the flat.

Nikki entered the living room in time to see her niece flinging herself against Raoul, who bent to pick her up.

"Buona sera, bellissima," he said. "How was your day?"

Massimo, looking sharp in a velvet smoking jacket, came towards Nikki. Wordlessly, he lifted the screaming baby, bounced him gently, and made a "shh, shh" sound.

"Signore, what are you complaining about?" he said. "Oh, I see. You have a very stinky diaper . . . well, that's not something I can help you with. Come, let's find your mother."

He pursued Francesca and pressed the baby on her until she was forced to take him.

Gianni served beers and prosecco in the living room. He wore jeans, a stylish shirt, and a maroon jacket. He seemed to relish the role of host, ushering everyone to sit, and filling glasses. Nikki was glad to notice how much he'd healed. He looked the same as ever, although he limped a little, and wore a glove on his damaged hand.

"No alcohol for me," said Massimo with a sigh as Gianni extended a glass. "Too tricky with the insulin. Such a nice house you have."

"Yes!" Raoul agreed, looking around the space—the new furniture and electronics. "You seem to be doing very well for yourself. How's the shop these days?"

"I'm looking to expand," said Gianni. "Mac has some ideas about taking the business international. He's got some contacts in the Netherlands that we're exploring. There's a real market there. . . . We would need some initial investments, of course. . . ."

"Wonderful! Wonderful!" Raoul exclaimed, clapping Gianni on the shoulder.

Nikki wanted to shake her father. Despite his otherwise keen perception, he seemed forever blind to his son's schemes. He'd already poured tens of thousands of euros into Gianni, and would continue until it bankrupted him. Before she died, Beatrice had warned Nikki to stay away from Gianni's troubles—but that had proved impossible.

Raoul took a seat on the sofa. Bea climbed onto him. She searched his jacket pockets, coming up triumphant with two small toy cars and a wrapped candy.

In the next room, the voices of Francesca and her mother were raised, arguing about who should put the kids to bed.

"Fons was disappointed you didn't come this afternoon," Raoul scolded Nikki. "You need to keep your commitments."

"I couldn't come," Nikki said. "I was called into work. I texted you about it."

"All we have is our word," he said. "I thought I taught you that."

"How are you recovering?" Massimo asked Gianni.

"Fine. Fine . . ." Gianni replied, red rising to his cheeks.

"Yes, how's your knee?" asked Raoul. He turned to Mac and explained in English, "I'm sure you know: Gianni was in a hit-and-run last summer. They never caught the driver."

Nikki nearly spit her prosecco. She hadn't realized that this was the story her brother had been telling to explain his injuries.

Massimo, who knew better, raised an eyebrow. Then, pointedly to Gianni, said, "With your business going so well, I'm sure you've repaid Nikki the money you owe her."

Gianni gave a dismissive gesture. "Tito forgave the loan—so that's taken care of."

"What the fuck? That's not—" Nikki began.

Gianni spoke loudly over her in English: "Mac is a Dutch naval officer. Covert intelligence. Isn't that right, Mac? Doing some very important, very *secret* work for NATO."

Mac chuckled heartily.

"Well," he said. "That really isn't something I should talk about."

"What are they saying?" Massimo asked Nikki. She translated into Italian.

"What sort of idiot intelligence officer brags about his profession?" Massimo said derisively. "That's the problem with movies. Everybody wants to be James Bond. Real spies aren't glamorous. They're despicable moral cowards."

"What did he say?" Mac asked Gianni.

Gianni laughed. "He doesn't think much of your profession."

"It's a very important job," Mac articulated slowly in English to Massimo. "The public rarely sees the details of our operations. Unfortunately, we never get the credit we deserve."

Nikki translated this to Massimo, who snorted.

"Tell us more about it," urged Gianni. "Just the parts you can share, of course."

Mac looked as if he'd been waiting for just this invitation.

"Well, it's very elite," he said. "Obviously, I can't say much. But we're keeping an eye on some very bad actors, and we always need boots on the ground—eyes and ears. It's what we in the business call HUMINT."

He sucked air through his teeth and took a swig from his beer.

Francesca sashayed into the room with a tinkling laugh. "Oh, I'm pleased it's going so well! Come, Bea. Time for bed! No fighting. Give Nonno a hug."

Bea clung on to Raoul's neck, so that Francesca had to peel her away with much protest and tears. Raoul hugged her, and kissed her cheeks, then kissed them again.

Salvatrice came in from the kitchen, fanning her face with her hands. "It's boiling in there! Gianni, pour me a prosecco, won't you?"

She wore a tight, low-cut shirt, the crepey softness of her tanned skin bunching up at the pinched points.

"Raoul," she exclaimed as Nikki's father rose to his feet. "It's been far too long."

She kissed his cheeks, greeted Mac, and was introduced to Massimo.

"Will your husband be joining us?" Raoul asked.

Salvatrice pulled a pouting frown. "He has other priorities these days, I'm afraid. May I?"

She indicated the sofa. Raoul nodded and she settled in beside him. Gianni handed her a glass.

"He doesn't talk much about it," Gianni said to Mac, "but my father used to be in naval intelligence. He was the head of the Servizio Informazioni Operative e Situazione, SIOS."

"Oh, it's not called SIOS anymore," Raoul said.

"Tell us more," Salvatrice encouraged, placing fingers delicately on his arm. "It sounds fascinating."

"Oh, I retired nearly a decade ago," said Raoul. "I'm an old has-been."

She gave a gentle laugh. "I don't believe that for a moment."

"Yes, do tell us, Mr. Serafino," Mac encouraged. "Gianni said they called you out of retirement."

Raoul sipped his wine, and leaned back. "I'm consulting on an old case—from nearly twenty years ago."

"Tell us!" Salvatrice urged.

"Very well," Raoul agreed. "There was a man called Lotterio Patalano. Customs and excise official. Married. Two boys. We came to suspect Patalano of falsifying shipping documents. . . . I can't give details—but we became sure he was involved in smuggling operations. Some members of my team wanted to arrest him. Others, including myself, wanted to wait and understand his game."

"You were quite right about waiting," Mac interjected loudly. "It's important to find the criminal networks and how they operate."

Massimo muttered something under his breath.

"Sì," Raoul said, then continued. "The thing that puzzled us was this: The system was far more complex than Patalano's capability. He wasn't stupid, but he wasn't particularly clever—and this system was far more sophisticated than anything we'd seen."

"What did you do?" Gianni asked.

"We arrested him, and he agreed to cooperate. But his stories were outrageous. He claimed that he was just a pawn in some global conspiracy. He talked about agents inside the Italian and US governments, and inside NATO intelligence."

"You never told me this," said Massimo sharply. "Did you ever identify these agents?"

Raoul shook his head.

"NATO intelligence?" Gianni said, grinning at Mac. "What do you think of that, Mac? You have leaks in your organization."

"Counterespionage is one of our core capabilities," Mac said with cool confidence, then launched into the history of intelligence operations in Europe. Nikki translated for Massimo, who seemed increasingly irritated.

"If he's an intelligence officer," Massimo said, "then I'm the Queen of Denmark."

"Tell us more!" Salvatrice said breathlessly to Raoul. "What happened to this Patalano?"

"He ate a bullet. Just like that. We could never verify his claims, and the case fizzled out. It was shelved years ago. Then last week, something interesting happened—which is why they called me in. Patalano's widow died. As her sons were sorting through their mother's items, they came across the key to a safety deposit box in Rome. And what do you think they found there? Patalano's ledger! The bastard had detailed notes of all the work he'd done during nearly twenty years of smuggling operations. Of course, it's useless now. Expired long ago."

From a back bedroom, Francesca's voice rose: "I'm not going to say it again. Go to sleep!"

This was followed by the sound of a door closing, then a disconsolate wail. Francesca returned to the living room wearing freshly applied lipstick.

Gianni clapped. "Well, I hope everyone's hungry. My beautiful mother-in-law has prepared a fantastic meal for us tonight. Grazie, Mamma."

He gestured towards Salvatrice, who placed a gracious hand on her heart.

They migrated to the dining room. Nikki was about to sit when Francesca touched her arm and asked sweetly, "Can you help serve?"

According to everyone at the table, Salvatrice's cooking was excellent. Unfortunately, it was also full of meat and fish, and apart from a dish of zucchini, eggplant, and tomatoes, Nikki couldn't find much to eat.

"Vegetarianism isn't natural," complained Salvatrice as Nikki refused a meatball.

"I'll take hers," offered Mac, holding out his plate.

He grinned at Nikki. "Watching what you eat? You look like you work out. Spend a lot of time at the gym? Lift weights?"

Nikki stared back, unsmiling. "Does the Dutch Navy have fitness requirements?"

"Ha, ha," said Mac. "Funny, as well as hot. That's one thing about me, you know: Not a lot of men like strong women, but I do. I like a challenge."

"Tell me, does your father like the melanzane?" Salvatrice asked Nikki with a jab in her ribs.

"Excuse me?"

"Does your father like the melanzane?"

"I don't know," Nikki said.

"Well, ask him," urged Salvatrice.

Confused, Nikki turned to Raoul. It took a moment to get his attention. "Salvatrice wants to know if you like the melanzane."

"Delicious," said Raoul to Salvatrice, across Nikki. "The best I've tasted."

"You flatter me," she replied. "It's such a pleasure to cook for a man with refined tastes."

"Your brother tells me you're dating Tito Calandra," Mac said to Nikki with his mouth full.

Nikki flushed hotly. "What? No. I'm not. Why would you say that, Gianni?"

Her brother, red-faced, laughed.

"C'mon," he said. "Everyone's talking about it. Even Enzo says you are."

Nikki was incredulous. "Why the fuck are you talking to Enzo?"

Raoul coughed.

Francesca scolded, "There's no need for such language." Then, to Gianni, in Italian, "I told you she wasn't."

Nikki glared at her sister-in-law, who, she was fairly certain, had spent time in Tito's bed.

Gianni said to Nikki, "There's nothing to be embarrassed about. You and Tito dated for years. It would be perfectly natural for you to start again."

"Why should it matter to you?" demanded Nikki, rage rising.

"He clearly cares about you," said Gianni. "Look at what he did for you!"

"You forced me," said Nikki, trying, failing, to keep her voice calm. "I had no other options. And now I owe him. Do you understand? You did this, and now I can't get out."

This exchange was in Italian. Mac, clearly not comprehending the contention, smiled affably.

"Would you make an introduction?" he said in English.

"No," said Nikki. "My brother is misinformed. I'm not affiliated with Tito Calandra. I strongly recommend that you stay away. He's dangerous."

"You can ask," Gianni pushed. "He would take your call."

"Why don't you call?" she snapped.

Gianni glanced down and picked at the food on his plate.

"He's not taking your calls," Nikki realized.

Gianni turned red to the roots of his curly hair.

Francesca pushed back from the table, announcing, "I'll open another bottle of wine."

Nikki's phone pinged.

The message was from the landlord who rented her the Krav Maga studio. It was a picture of a building on fire.

Nikki barely saw where she was going as she sprinted out of Gianni's flat. Racing through the crowded streets on her Hornet, she heard only the engine and the rush of blood in her ears.

Fire crews were still battling the blaze when she arrived to stand with the watching crowds gathered in the rain. Smoke mixed with steam, the choking stench filling the streets.

A woman with frizzy grey hair, glasses, and a housecoat sat on the curb, barefoot, head in her hands, weeping as she looked up at the orange inferno.

"What happened?" Nikki asked, but the woman only stared.

She asked another bystander, dreading the truth before it actually emerged.

"Three men torched it," he told her. "It was il Sistema. The System did this."

She thought of the intensity of De Rosa's face when he visited the studio, and his threat: *Change your patterns. Stop teaching. I won't tell you again.*

De Rosa had warned her to stop teaching. She'd told him no. This was his response, Tito's response, to *no*.

It took only a few minutes to reach Tito's stronghold in the city. Last summer when she'd visited him, the building had been open, filled with music and company. Now, the giant gates were shut. Locked. High stone walls stretched up into the dark night.

She knocked. There was no sound or movement. She kicked the doors, slammed them, pounded, and screamed.

She'd been so naive to think she could be rid of him.

Tito contaminated everything—was everywhere. There wasn't a crime or mercy he didn't know about. Worse, he was inside her, in childhood memories, in her sense of her own body, his voice in her thoughts. She wanted him gone.

"Fuck you!" she shouted. "Do you hear me? Fuck you, Tito!"

Time passed, and as the anger drained away, she became aware of the passersby who slowed to watch, including a cluster of teenage girls filming with their phones. She strode past them and into a side street, where she sagged against a wall, breathing through the hot tears.

She didn't know how long she crouched like this in the dark, a creeping shame settling in where the rage had been.

Gradually, she became aware of her phone ringing.

She held it to her ear.

At first, all she heard was sobbing. Then her aunt Izzy's voice.

"Oh, sweetheart . . . Nikki. It's Preston. He's fallen. . . . Oh, darling, I don't know what to do. He's hurt so badly."

FIFTEEN

London was overcast; a plunge through grey clouds as the plane descended into Gatwick. Nikki navigated the crowded airport, took the train to Farringdon, and transferred to the Elizabeth line. She did this numbly, routinely, a muscle memory from the decade she'd spent in this city.

Emerging from the station, she walked along busy roads towards the hospital.

Whitechapel Market, alive with Saturday's lunchtime rush, barraged her with the scents of cut fruit and burnt sugar, spices and bread, hot oil, cooked meat, car exhaust, and the sour tang of trash. Nikki stepped around a heap of wilting cardboard and past the parade of spindly stall poles draped in green-and-white-striped tarps. Men and women in winter coats and sandals haggled over rugs and electronics, tunics and trousers, and crates of cabbage, pineapples, onions, radishes—while vendors and fishmongers hawked home goods and haddock.

The London streets were just as frenetic as Naples—chaotic and graffiti-tagged, a scrabble to gain or maintain a foothold in the slippery social landscape.

But these similarities were strangely superficial, and as Nikki's heart began to once again beat in time to the pulse of this city, she seemed to understand the way each environment nurtured and suppressed different things in you. London cultivated a peculiar stoic resilience: bracing against the dark chill of winter. Damp mornings and long stretches of grey twilight. Transplanted here long ago, Nikki had been forever changed from the girl reared in the furious sun and loamy earth in the shadow of a volcano.

She had a sense of that other self—arriving on Aunt Izzy and Uncle Preston's doorstep like a stray cat; feral, terrorized by loss.

They'd opened the door to her, and invited her into their hearts. An unbearable kindness.

At the hospital, she found Izzy standing next to Uncle Preston's bed, moistening his lips with a sponge.

His face was pale, twitching as he slept. A bandage covered his forehead, a blackened swelling around his right eye, his left leg bolted into a metal frame. His cheeks were sunken and his mouth gaped, a rasping sound as he breathed.

Izzy's white hair, usually meticulous, was mussed on one side. There was a shallow scrape on her cheek, and her clothes were rumpled. Worst of all was the look in those eyes. Nikki had seen the same expression in her mother's face in the minutes and days after she learned of Adriano's death.

For a moment, Nikki felt helpless as she looked on the scene, unsure of what to say, a desperate ache in her stomach, shuddering into her neck, her arms and hands. She wanted to run away. Instead, she willed her feet to move, and crossed to her aunt. They held each other. Nikki breathed in the familiar warm vanilla perfume and stale hospital odor, and Izzy cradled the back of her head in that way that reminded her of Easter visits and one time when Izzy had cared for her during a bad fever.

They sat in chairs by Preston's bed. On the bedside table, propped open, was a dog-eared copy of *Beowulf*.

"Bleeding in the brain," Izzy whispered. "They won't know the extent of the damage until he's awake."

"So he hasn't . . . ?"

Izzy caressed Preston's cheek. "Not yet."

"Do they know how long it will take?"

"No."

They sat in silence for a long time. She held her aunt's hand.

Nikki had always known Preston as a kind man. Too proper and British for hugs, he instead offered a sort of erudite scholarly affection, dressing his advice and comfort in the forms of his beloved authors. When she was a child, he'd taken a keen interest in her stories and thoughts, elevating them by drawing out their themes and comparing them favorably with the ideas of Shakespeare and Marlowe. In recent years, that scholar's mind had veered increasingly off track, and Nikki watched his attempts to navigate back by the light of his favorite books. As she gradually lost her uncle, Nikki couldn't tell whether her grief was about this loss, or for her aunt, who called him "my love," and read aloud to calm his agitation.

Izzy and Preston had repeated their love story enough times that it had become a fixed point, Nikki's mind supplying the details until she felt that she'd been there herself on that rainy afternoon in the British Museum. Izzy had been a concert pianist performing in London, and Preston was guiding a group of disgruntled young schoolboys on a tour through the Sutton Hoo collection, quoting Middle English poetry to them.

"I was intrigued. He was so handsome, and so intellectual," Izzy would say. "So of course, I stopped to listen."

This would prompt Preston to tell his part. "I was terribly awkward around women. But there was this angel suddenly before me . . . and what other words could I use, except from Chartier's 'La Belle Dame sans Mercy'? 'Love has bound me to be your man, and leave all other pursuits.'"

"I'm so worried about him, I can't think," Izzy said. "I know there's nothing to be done . . . but my mind is tied up in knots."

"He's strong," said Nikki. "And he loves you. He's fighting to come back. I'm sure of it."

Izzy nodded, and took her hand. "You're right. Of course, you're right."

"Have you slept?" Nikki asked.

Izzy brushed this off, and Nikki pressed, "You should get some rest. I'll take this shift."

Izzy squeezed her eyes shut. "What if he wakes, and I'm not here?"

Nikki didn't say the thing they were both thinking: that he might not wake up.

"I'll be here," Nikki reassured. "Go home, shower, and catch a few hours of sleep. I'll call if there are any changes."

It took some persuading, but Izzy finally agreed. Nikki walked her down the hall, then returned to Preston's bedside.

The hours passed slowly. She'd had a difficult night with little sleep, but her body flexed, agitated, and her heart pounded.

The hospital was anything but peaceful. The corridor was filled with people rushing past, conversations, beeps, rings, buzzings. A strange cold pressure in the air popped her ears every once in a while. Nurses came by occasionally to take measurements or administer medication, but there was no change in Preston's condition.

Angelo had been angry when she asked for time off to fly to London.

"I can't spare you," he said. "I've taken myself off the shift schedule while I support the ambassador."

At last, he'd capitulated on the condition that she coordinate the shift changes herself with the other men on the team before leaving. Nikki had made arrangements with her three most helpful colleagues: Pasquale, Iacopo, and Alfonso.

"Let me know if you need to stay longer," Pasquale offered. "I'll deal with Angelo. He can be an asshole, but he knows family is important."

It was difficult to sit here, looking on the dreadfully grey face of her uncle, terrified of what the next hours would mean for him and Izzy. Nikki did push-ups and lunges in the small hospital room while her thoughts spiraled perpetually inward, returning again and again to the fire in that storefront studio, the families displaced, homes reduced to ash. She still smelled the smoke, the acrid stink in her pores and nostrils. A sick, tight feeling flexed up the back of her neck as she considered the price those people had paid for her unwillingness to go along with De Rosa's demand.

Nikki understood Tito better than most, had been there as he formed and tested his rules—had fought him, pushed against him. He'd hated and loved her for it. Was that why she'd somehow imagined she was exempt from his laws?

When she was twelve years old and Tito had just turned thirteen, and the clans were recruiting for lookouts and sellers and couriers, everyone in Tito's gang talked incessantly about joining. It was tempting: Boys who worked for the System were paid in cash and given motorbikes. They talked big and swaggered, and carried guns—attracting respect and fear and favors, taking what they wanted.

Nikki lived in grim military housing with her brother Gianni and her parents—something she considered a hardship until she met Tito and his group, and saw where they came from. Theirs was a poverty she'd never imagined, and she could understand the intoxicating appeal of sudden riches. In their dares and games, they sometimes snuck into the expensive hotels and restaurants and resorts, marveling at the effortless elegance of the wealthy. They relieved patrons of their wallets and, pockets stuffed with hundreds of thousands of lire, considered themselves kings.

One day, an older boy of sixteen, Armo, approached them, and asked if they were interested in joining his group. All the boys wanted to say yes, but they waited for Tito to decide. He vanished for a few days while he thought it through—and nobody dared act without him.

When he'd made his decision, they gathered together for a discussion in the ugly back room of a mattress shop owned by the family of one of the boys. Mattresses sealed in thick cellophane were leaned against the wall. Others were stacked nearly to the ceiling.

They wrestled a couple to the ground so they could sit, the creak of springs and the rustle of plastic as Tito spoke.

"They'll pay us," Tito said. "But we're young, so they won't think we're worth much. There will always be a lot of boys who want to work for scraps."

Those boys were zanzare—mosquitos—he told them. They would take the attention of the police, sting and torment, give them something to chase, and take all the risk, while the real players got away.

The gang understood what it meant to shoulder risk. They had brothers, fathers, uncles, and cousins in Poggioreale, and yet others whose photos bleached and faded in the glass-fronted street shrines. Disreputable lives sanctified by violent deaths.

"Are we just mosquitos?" he asked them. "Is that all you want to be?"

There was an uncomfortable silence as everyone considered whether this might be such a terrible fate. One or two of the boys shouted, "Yes!"

"If you want to do it, then go," Tito said. "But if you decide to join them, then you're done here. No hard feelings, but you can't come back."

He looked so fierce, eyes like dark stones. There was muttering as everyone discussed this.

"What do you suggest?" asked Nikki.

She was personally relieved by Tito's pronouncement. She somehow understood that the offer to the group wasn't meant to include her, the only girl. She'd spent the past three years earning the respect of the gang, loved being a part of them, and hated the ominous feeling of change. She didn't want to be left behind. Moreover, she was gaining an understanding of what the System was. With her father and Adriano in the carabinieri, Nikki understood that if Tito decided to bring his gang to join one of the clans, she would be forced to choose between her family and her friends.

"We need to be more than mosquitos," Tito replied. "We need to have something valuable to sell them—so that we can work for ourselves and make them pay us more."

But he didn't know what that valuable thing was. Not yet.

Two of the boys, Loris and Brizio, left Tito and started working for the clans. Loris was a hothead and had always pushed against Tito's leadership, so it wasn't a surprise when he left. But Brizio was Tito's intimate, and the betrayal clearly stung.

In the weeks that followed, some of the other boys started muttering behind Tito's back. Nobody said the word *coward*, although it was clear that was what they meant. Nikki, who had seen Tito stand up to the hulking rage of his violent father, knew he wasn't a coward. She trusted him to come up with an answer. She didn't need money as desperately as her friends, but she knew that Tito's reputation and leadership depended on his ability to guide them all to wealth.

It was around this time Gianni was arrested for dealing drugs.

"It wasn't my fault," he whined to Nikki. "The lookouts didn't warn me in time."

Gianni was fourteen, and the case was heard in the juvenile courts. The investigating magistrate was initially inclined to jail him in detention, and Beatrice agreed, saying that Gianni needed to feel the impact of his actions. But Raoul didn't want his son's future tainted. He testified, promising to be responsible for him. The charges were knocked down to possession, and Gianni was released on probation into his parents' custody.

Tito seemed intensely interested in the details of Gianni's arrest, and questioned Nikki about it. The following week, he presented his idea to the group.

"If you're dealing, it's stupid to rely only on a lookout," he said. "Maybe the lookout is an idiot. Or maybe he gets distracted. Maybe he's busy taking a shit when the patrols come by. And, even if he does warn you, by then it's too late. You might still get caught."

There were other stupid risks, too, he explained. If you chose a clan, then you would be targeted when the clans fought one another. Also, he reminded them, their gang—about fifteen boys plus Nikki—wasn't from just one neighborhood. They couldn't simply join the Sanita gang, because it would leave out everyone from the Forcella neighborhood.

What Tito suggested was a new business model. "We won't work for just one clan. We'll sell something everybody needs: information."

Tito's idea was to map out the rhythms and patterns of local police patrols—to learn the names and behaviors of the officers who worked in certain districts, to predict where they would be and what they would do. This wasn't too different from the spy games they already played. But now there would be a real purpose for it, real stakes, and a real payoff.

Their first client was a woman who stood outside a community center in Forcella, selling contraband cigarettes from under a blanket. Their information was so accurate, so effective in keeping down arrests and fines, that their reputation spread. After a few months, the gang had nearly two dozen clients—from street dealers to shop owners. The money was beginning to pour in.

They could have continued like this indefinitely, slowly growing their wealth and importance.

But Brizio came back to visit Tito one day. Nikki saw them and snuck close to eavesdrop.

". . . you just need to stop," Brizio was saying. "He says you're cutting into his profits."

"That's bullshit," Tito replied. "He just doesn't like it because he's too stupid to do it himself."

"He says he'll fucking shoot you if you don't stop."

"Armo's all talk," Tito said. "He'd never dare."

But he was wrong.

On the day of the feast of the Immaculate Conception, a group of laundry women found Tito bruised and bloodied, unconscious, in an alley near his home. His arm and three ribs were broken, and his face was so swollen and purple and red, Nikki hardly recognized him in the hospital bed. But she recognized the glint of hardened steel in his eye.

"Tell me what you need," she said, anger and sadness making her voice shake.

He had the names memorized: the boys he'd recognized from Armo's group. He made her write them down.

"Find out where they live," he instructed. "Find out who their friends are. Find out where they park their bikes at night."

Nikki wanted to complete this assignment herself, but she didn't have as much freedom at night as the others. So, she recruited two of the top boys to help. In little more than a week, by the time the swelling in Tito's face was beginning to subside, the report was complete.

Tito thanked them all in that strange way he had: looking them each in the eye so solemnly while he spoke the words, so that you wanted more than anything in the world to volunteer for the next job, to take another turn at receiving those thanks.

But Tito didn't ask Nikki to complete the next part of the assignment. She only learned about it after the fact, when it was too late to argue against it or, as Tito likely feared, report it to her carabinieri brother.

On Christmas Eve, when the bells struck midnight, signifying that all of Naples had gone to mass, fires were lit simultaneously across the city. Five motorbikes burned, along with the homes of the couriers and anyone else foolish enough to stash their supply.

Nikki thought about those flames—which she'd only seen in her imagination. They danced, black and orange, against the night sky, thick smoke racing upwards like the billowing smoke of the studio fire.

Nikki picked up Preston's copy of *Beowulf* and read aloud to him, but this seemed to increase his agitation, so she stopped and sat silently for a long time, until fatigue overcame her and she half slept in the bedside chair.

In the late afternoon, the shadows lengthened and the windows reflected the fluorescent lights as the world outside darkened. Driven by hunger, Nikki left Preston's room long enough to find the hospital canteen and get a sandwich and small bag of salted macadamia nuts.

Preston was still asleep when she returned.

She went through her rucksack for her stack of cards, and peeled away the rubber band. The details were already in her mind—no need to reread what she already knew by heart. Instead, she tapped the pen, mentally sorting the pieces that still didn't fit. *What made Claire leave the yacht on Saturday night? What happened during those missing three days? Why was she at the church? Why had Monica thrown the knife?*

Then the new gaps—the lie about seeing Claire . . . the cocaine . . . the missing bag.

The facts were piling up, but they felt disconnected and wrong tonight, loose threads she couldn't grip. Her body was twitchy and restless, unable to calm, unsettled by the sight of Preston in that bed, and thinking about the bleed in his brain. She imagined it as a sort of invading force, decimating everything in its path: the works of Chaucer and Shakespeare and all the other poets who lived as friends inside his mind.

Nikki's phone chimed and she went into the hallway for a signal. She'd missed several text messages: a dozen from Audrey Lake—a series of laughing-face emojis and hearts interspersed with jokes:

Where do fruits go on holiday? Pear-is!

What did one wall say to the other? I'll meet you at the corner!

The final text message read, **Can you come over?**

I can't come over, Nikki texted. **Out of town.**

Nikki saw she'd missed a call from Izzy.

She called back and gave her report: "He's still resting. The doctor says he's stable. Did you sleep?"

"A bit," said Izzy. "I'm just getting ready. I should be there soon."

Nikki protested. "Please sleep in your own bed tonight."

Izzy's voice was tight. "He needs me."

"He'll need you when he wakes up," Nikki said. "Rest now. I'll let you know if anything changes."

The nurses arranged for a cot in Preston's room. Closing her eyes and drifting to sleep, the rigid canvas beneath her, Nikki watched the shimmer of orange flames.

Izzy arrived early in the morning, showered and reordered into that familiar graceful style, wearing a soft pale blue sweater and cream-colored slacks. She took her place of vigil at Preston's bedside, and clasped his hand.

Giving them privacy, Nikki left.

She changed, and brushed her teeth. In the mirror, her eyes and face were puffy, her short hair squashed on the side. She splashed her face, then combed water through her hair with her fingers.

Her neck and shoulder were cramped. She did some stretching, then found her way to an exit, squinting up into the dim sunlight of a clouded London morning.

After the detached isolation of the hospital, the sudden pulse of the world was invasive: a grinding roar of traffic, and a rush of people.

She started to move, jogging along the sidewalk and into the blocked-in maze of shabby-looking apartments around the hospital. She ran faster and faster, sprinting, body warming, until a sore spot in her knee made her stop.

At an intersection, she found a small shop selling cigarettes and sodas and beers, a money-transfer and travel-agency shop, and a dingy café smelling of mildew and grease, floors and tables of pressed wood.

She ordered a flat white and a grilled cheese sandwich and sat at a table to check her phone. Looking at her texts, she was chagrined to realize she'd forgotten her promise to go sailing with Valerio today.

"Shit."

She texted an apology and explained the situation.

There were twenty-six unread text messages from Audrey Lake. She didn't open them.

Nikki scrolled through Instagram without expecting much—Monica and Kami hadn't posted in days—but the comments had exploded. **Stay strong, girl! We love you.** and **Funny how people are quick to defend her. We all know what a total cunt she is. Money doesn't buy everything.**

Public opinion was rapidly splitting. It was the same over on Facebook. And a fundraiser for Kami's defense. Her mother's plea: **Help us give her a chance to prove her innocence, and bring her home.**

Claire's Facebook page was already filled with tributes, with the Albion Nanny Agency organizing a memorial: *Join us for a casual gathering, reflecting Claire's free spirit,* they wrote. *In lieu of flowers, bring a story to share, as we honor her together.*

The event was tonight at 18:00 in a pub in Gidea Park called the Three Horseshoes.

As she slowly ate the cheese sandwich and drank the watery coffee, Nikki thumbed through the images of Claire: pictures of her caring for children, those big brown eyes and that shy smile. There was a soft brightness, a sweet sincerity to the nanny. She'd been, what? Twenty-two, twenty-three? Impossibly young. It struck Nikki that she had been younger than this—only twenty years old—when Izzy and Preston had taken her into their home, kept her sane when she should have gone mad with despair and grief; loved her when she loathed herself.

She felt a strange light shining back on the person she'd been then, the memories more accessible in this moment than they'd been for a long time—as if this city had unlocked a cupboard where she kept that other self.

She'd been split down the center those days: she and Tito making two halves of a whole.

All those years, Tito had tunneled into the underworld of Naples. Nikki had tried to redirect him—suggested escape plans, fresh starts in Spain or France, or the United States. But his love affair with the System had felt like something inevitable, and she'd gone along with it because she didn't have the power or arguments to make him stop—and because he had been so much a part of her, it was impossible to conceive what it might mean to live without him.

She'd been too weak to truly resist or change him.

Then Adriano had been shot.

Everything exploded in that moment, rearranging itself so that the past and the future seemed to collapse into a single point of unbearable weight.

Her mother, who had always been so calm . . . distant . . . untouchable, was unmoored by grief. She raged insensibly, screamed and broke things, tore down walls and cabinets with her hands until her nails broke and her fingers bled. It was a terrifying exhibition from a woman who had never made a scene. Neither Nikki nor her father knew what to do; neither could find a way in. At other times, Beatrice would sit for hours in the dark of her room, motionless, as if she'd been turned to stone. One day, when Nikki had tried to draw her out of this state, she turned and hissed vehemently: "'If the devil doesn't exist, but man has created him, he has created him in his own image and likeness!'"

Those words had struck at Nikki, burrowed inside, and she knew that her mother had sent them like a curse, imprinting themselves on her mind forever.

Nikki finished her sandwich and coffee, locked her phone, put it in her pocket, and left the café.

Back in the hospital, she slowed, realizing that she dreaded reentering that room with her aunt and uncle, and the world between them that was slowly decaying.

A nurse brushed past her, jogging down the hallway. To Nikki's dismay, she rushed into Preston's room. She heard the commotion as she approached, her chest frozen mid-breath.

Then her aunt was in the hallway, a hand on her mouth. She looked at Nikki, eyes wide, and only then did Nikki see the smile in them.

"He's awake!" Izzy exclaimed. "He's awake!"

SIXTEEN

"I need new football boots," said Davide. "Mine are totally wrecked . . . like, seriously fucked up. They're too small anyway—they pinch—and now I can't even use them."

Valerio shuffled to the sink and emptied yesterday's coffee grounds from the Moka into the drain, rinsing the filter.

"Next paycheck," he said.

"Please!" Davide moaned. "We have a match next Saturday. The guys are counting on me."

"You can't use them for even one more match?"

"Like I said, they're fucked."

"Don't use that word," said Valerio. "It isn't nice."

"So what? You use it."

Valerio sighed and, tamping fresh coffee in the Moka pot, screwed on the top and started the flame on the gas stove.

His one-bedroom apartment wasn't really large enough to host both kids at the same time. Last night, he'd given Gemma the bed, and Davide slept on the sofa. Valerio had gotten a sleeping bag and fold-out army cot for cheap from a buddy at work. After this first test run of the contraption, he felt like his body had been worked over with a hammer. The shooting sciatic burn down his right leg was killing him.

"You snore like Godzilla," said Gemma, coming into the kitchen. "Davide, how could you sleep with Babbo's snoring?"

"Can I please get the boots?" said Davide. "I need them!"

"What do you want to eat?" Valerio asked.

"Let's go out to breakfast," said Gemma. "Can we go to a café, please?"

"This is a café," said Valerio with a sweeping gesture. "Caffé Alfieri. What can I offer? Toast? Juice?"

"I want a cornetto," said Gemma.

"Me, too," said Davide.

"That isn't food. It's sugar," said Valerio, who, in the ensuing argument, considered that he often had a chocolate cornetto for breakfast.

It was a matter of minutes before he capitulated.

"Okay. Fine. Go get dressed."

It was raining outside. A steady, miserable drizzle. He made everyone carry an umbrella.

At the café, while they ate pastries and looked at their phones, Valerio thought about Ravenna. He was strangely moved by her bravery. She'd been so frightened, had seen the gun in his hand, yet stayed to accuse him of Gaetano's murder.

"Hey," said Gemma, looking up from her screen. "Gina and Annalisa are on their way here. Can I hang out with them today?"

"I thought that we would hang out today," said Valerio. "Just the three of us."

"But it's Saturday!" Gemma protested. "Seriously, Babbo!"

Davide looked up. "Actually," he said, "a bunch of guys are heading to Fabio's house to play video games. I told them I would come."

Valerio tipped his empty espresso cup into his mouth, hoping for another drop. Nothing.

"Fine," he said, setting it back down.

His phone rang. Luca Errichiello. He sent it to voicemail.

"Can I have some money for shopping—and lunch?" said Gemma. "Please?"

"Yeah," chimed in Davide. "Me, too. And can I get the boots?"

Valerio opened his wallet and distributed the cash.

"We'll get the boots after my next paycheck," he promised Davide.

Watching them rush out of sight, Valerio was stabbed through with love and fear. He needed to protect them, yet felt the emptiness of his hands.

He sat in the café for another few minutes, then stood and started moving, a weird pressure inside his body propelling him through the misting rain.

He thought about Ravenna, about her probing questions, her drive to investigate: *What if we found out what Gaetano knew? If it was important to Errichiello, maybe it's enough to get him arrested . . . enough to give you leverage. . . .*

The idea glimmered in the darkness of his thoughts. Tempting as it was, Valerio resisted the relief it offered. Every condemned man has the delusion of reprieve.

Digging through the wreckage of Luca's crimes carried tremendous risk. If Luca found out, he might simply drop the blade. And this wouldn't just mean exposure and loss of Valerio's career and pension; Luca had killed Gaetano for whatever he had known.

Valerio's work had prepared him for the possibility of death, and perhaps that was why he was willing to take the risk. But Luca had made it clear that Davide and Gemma were also in the balance—and that was intolerable. Yet his children were in danger, whether he took action, or waited like a pig penned for butchering.

He had one advantage and it was this: Luca didn't know him. Not really. Not yet. The longer Valerio waited, the greater the opportunity Luca had to learn about him, to understand his tolerances, to pressure and corrupt him. He was compromised, but he wasn't corrupt. Not yet.

To his surprise, Valerio realized that, like a homing pigeon, he'd returned to his roost: police HQ on Via Medina. He greeted the door guard, took the stairs, and jogged the long hallway to his office. He unlocked the door to familiar odors of rusted metal, stale cigarettes and coffee, sweat, and yesterday's lunch. It felt empty without the other men. He sat at his desk and logged in to his computer.

He started with Gaetano's mother, Ines Mancusi, and the man he'd seen in the photograph with her. Valerio flipped through his notepad to find the name Gaetano had given him: *Paride Silvestri*.

There were a handful of police files on Ines—traffic violations. Apart from two anemic social media accounts, there was little about her online.

Silvestri was a different matter.

Valerio was surprised by the trove of information: articles and photographs spanning decades. With wealth that traced back to a foreign exchange trading firm in the Virgin Islands, he was rumored to be a billionaire. He owned villas in Sorrento, Rome, and Florence, where he hosted lavish parties attended by international elites as well as local and national government dating back to the Berlusconi administration. Movie stars and businessmen beamed beside him in photographs, his pearly teeth flashing against a deep, unnatural tan. At a recent art exhibition hosted by Silvestri, NATO men and women in military dress uniforms mingled with the black-tie crowd.

Silvestri's past was elusive. The name was Neapolitan, but the earliest records Valerio found were from the 1990s. One journalist claimed he'd been raised in Argentina and migrated to Naples, but Valerio couldn't corroborate it.

On paper, Silvestri was a saint. Not so much as a parking ticket. The financial police had investigated him a handful of times, but he'd come up squeaky clean. There was a solitary police report from 2008: a complaint from a woman named Agnese Cuomo, its contents sealed by a magistrate. Valerio recognized the name of the officer who had taken the complaint: Giuseppe Riccio—known by his friends as Beppe. Beppe had retired years ago, but Valerio found him on Facebook, and sent a message, inviting him for a coffee and catch-up. To his gratitude, Beppe responded almost immediately with a yes.

Valerio checked his watch. It was nearly lunchtime and he was hungry. He tapped his hand on the desk and thought for a minute before picking up his phone.

He'd kept the thing on mute and noticed now he'd missed several more calls from Luca Errichiello. Well, fuck him.

Valerio dialed Ravenna's number. She didn't answer. He thought about her for a moment—the way her eyes had flashed when she stood at his door. He texted, asking her to lunch.

He was just leaving the station when his phone rang. Giorgia.

"Are the kids with you?" she asked.

"They're off with their friends."

"Why did you let them do that? They were supposed to come home. They need to do their chores."

"That isn't fair," Valerio said. "You couldn't wait to get rid of them last night. You can't push them away when it's inconvenient for you—and then demand that they come back."

"And you can't just give them whatever they want!" she retorted. "They think you're so wonderful—but that's because you're always forcing me to be the mean parent. You don't respect me. Your family doesn't respect me—and they know that."

"If you need them home for chores," said Valerio, "then call and arrange that with them."

Cosimo's pizzeria was busy with the weekend lunch rush, but Cosimo waved at Valerio when he entered, and one of the servers hurried another customer out of a table.

He had just taken a seat when Ravenna came through the door.

Valerio had only ever seen the nurse in her scrubs and sneakers. Today she was dressed in a pair of well-cut jeans and black boots, tight dark ringlets framing her face. She removed her winter jacket to reveal a long burgundy blouse draping against her soft curves, a gold chain around her neck. Valerio rose to his feet and was surprised when she came close enough to kiss his cheeks. She glowed with warmth and smelled soapy.

They sat, and Valerio wanted to say something nice about how she looked, but words wouldn't come.

She leaned across the table and spoke quietly. "Who are we interviewing first?"

"What?"

Her face creased. "I thought that was why you wanted to meet—to investigate Gaetano's death."

Valerio hesitated. "I am investigating. But you shouldn't be. . . . As I told you, it isn't safe. You should stay away from this."

Cosimo was suddenly at the table, looking between them.

"Valerio, introduce me to your beautiful friend!"

"Ravenna." She offered a hand. "And you are?"

"Piacere, Ravenna. I'm Cosimo." He took her hand in both of his. "Welcome to my restaurant. You're a lucky woman—dating one of Naples' finest! And he is certainly lucky to have the pleasure of such charming company!"

He winked at Valerio, who, like a teenage boy, had the irrational urge to duck under the table.

When Cosimo had taken their orders and hurried away, Ravenna said, "I know you think I should be careful . . . and I will. But I can't just sit back and do nothing. I've never been able to just look away. I don't think you can either."

She picked at the corner of the paper tablecloth as she spoke, folding it back on itself in tight little patterns. Her fingers were nimble, bare nails trimmed short. Her forearms were muscular—Valerio guessed from the manual labor of her job.

"You're a nurse," he said.

"Sì."

"Why did you choose nursing?"

"I grew up in a big family—always scrapes and bruises and accidents. When I was ten, my brother broke his arm and I triaged it. I liked being able to know what to do when something bad happened. I think it was my way of being in control—not feeling helpless." She leaned forward. "That's what you do, too, isn't it? Help people?"

"I don't help people," Valerio said frankly. "I'm a cleaner. It's an ugly job, but functional. I find the filthiest places and clean them out. If I do my job well, nobody ever notices."

Ravenna said, "That's not true. Of course we notice!"

"I'm not saying it to complain," said Valerio quickly. "But the world is full of so much filth. I can only cage a few rats and clean up their shit. It isn't much. It doesn't really fix anything. There are always more rats."

"Why are you saying this?"

"Because I want you to understand that this is dirty and dangerous, but I've been trained to take this risk—I've spent years doing it. I know what I'm dealing with. If you wanted me to help with nursing, I'd hurt people and probably hurt myself."

"Not if I showed you what to do," said Ravenna. "You could rely on my expertise."

Valerio sighed, and found that he had started folding the edge of the tablecloth as well. He stopped and clasped his hands in front of him.

"Last night, you came to my house—and told me what you thought. You accused me of killing Gaetano. It was very brave of you. It was also very stupid. If I'd really been one of Errichiello's men, you might be dead now. I promise, I'll investigate what happened to that boy—but you need to stay away, for your own sake. And for mine. I don't want to worry about you."

A tight, hot knot closed his throat. He clenched his teeth.

Ravenna stared at him. "You're worried about me?"

Cosimo was back with their drinks—acqua frizzante for Ravenna and a Peroni for him.

For a moment, Valerio found that it was difficult to look at her, but he forced himself.

She was crying. Fuck. He'd done the wrong thing somehow. He didn't know how to fix it, so he sat uncomfortably with his beer.

Gradually she stopped, and wiped her eyes with a thin, waxy napkin.

"Okay," she said.

"Okay, what?"

"I can stay away. I can trust you to do this—and I'll keep my mouth shut. I won't go around asking people questions or accusing them of murder. But can you at least tell me what you're doing? Can I help with something—anything at all?"

Valerio exhaled and shrugged as he considered. She'd known Gaetano—at least peripherally. There could be value in having her identify connections in the boy's life, as long as she stayed out of the way.

"What do you know about Paride Silvestri?" he asked.

"That name sounds familiar. Should I know it?"

The pizzas arrived. While they ate, he told her about the photo on Ines Mancusi's fridge—and what he'd learned about Silvestri. Ravenna took out her phone and started searching.

"Wow," she said, taking a bite of pizza and scrolling. "It's like the Oscars. Everybody in Hollywood has been at his parties. . . . Oh! That's a gorgeous dress."

She held the phone up for him to admire a starlet in a slinky purple dress standing on a beautifully pillared balcony overlooking the sea.

"Where did he get his money?" she asked. "Exchange trading? Is that even real? It sounds sketchy to me."

Valerio didn't know. It was a mystery what the rich did with their money.

"The financial police have checked him out," he said. "They cleared him—but I guess that's different than saying he's legitimate."

Valerio realized that he'd been eating with his hands, rolling up the slices of hot and spicy meat pizza and shoveling them into his mouth, talking with his mouth full. He chewed, harvesting a handful of napkins to wipe his lips and fingers.

"What makes you think he's crooked?" Ravenna asked.

"I don't," said Valerio. "I just wanted to know who he was—since Ines had a picture on her fridge. It isn't a lead, really. Just a question. Gaetano gave me his name."

"Shall I ask her?"

Valerio shook his head. "Don't ask her any questions. Errichiello may have been responsible for Gaetano's death—but you heard her. She's in denial about him—what he is. I don't want her tipping him off about my investigation."

"Would you like to talk to Natale—Gaetano's girlfriend?" Ravenna offered.

Gaetano's girlfriend, Natale, worked in a leather goods store on Via dei Tribunali—close to Pio Monte della Misericordia, a chapel that drew tourists to its famous Caravaggio paintings.

The small shop burst with purses and satchels—stacked and

squashed on floor-to-ceiling shelves, hanging in colorful bouquets. A full-figured girl stood at a cash register. As they entered the shop, she stood rapidly as if she'd been caught.

"Hallo, Natale," Ravenna said warmly. "I'm Ravenna. We met a few months ago—with Gaetano at the McDonald's on Via Medina. Do you remember?"

"Oh." Natale glanced between Ravenna and Valerio, looking slightly stunned. She had a square face and heavy forehead and small eyes, long dark hair in a tight high ponytail. Beneath thick makeup, her face was splotchy, eyelids puffy.

"Yeah. I think so. Yeah."

She blinked several times very fast and then said, "Gaetano's dead."

"I know," said Ravenna. "I'm so sorry for you."

Natale squeezed her eyes shut and frowned. Her next words came out awkwardly loud: "Yeah, well, sorry doesn't do me any good. What do you want?"

"This is my friend, Valerio," said Ravenna. "He's looking into what happened to Gaetano. Can we ask you some questions?"

"Will it get me money?" Natale asked, eyes wide open now. "They don't believe I was his girlfriend so they won't pay me. They're going to pay his mother instead. And she hates me. If I was pregnant or had his kid, they'd believe me."

Ravenna looked at Valerio.

"I'm afraid not," he said. "But I believe you. I want to find out who killed your boyfriend."

Valerio's phone rang. He glanced down and saw Luca Errichiello's number before switching it off.

Natale gave him a disparaging look. "Isn't it obvious? You gotta be stupid if you don't know."

"Who do you think killed him?" asked Valerio.

"No," said Natale, suddenly aggressive. "You can't trick me. I keep my mouth shut. I don't need to be dead, too."

"Well, I'd like to find out why he died. Wouldn't you?"

She hesitated, then sniffed. "You the cops?"

"No," Ravenna lied without hesitation. "I used to babysit Gaetano—when he was little. He was a really sweet kid. He had a tender heart. I can see you cared about him, too."

"Of course I care!" Natale said.

"Can you please answer a few questions?"

Natale gave a small nod. Ravenna looked at Valerio.

"Did he ever talk about what he was doing?" he asked.

"Yeah. Sometimes," she said. "They gave him his own motorbike when he was fourteen. He made deliveries."

"Did he say what he was delivering?"

She shrugged. "Last year, he got his driver's license, and started driving properly—you know, driving people around. They had a big car for him to use."

"What sort of people?"

"Important people—you know, from the government, and businessmen." Natale picked at a sore on her jawline. "And he drove models to parties. He used to brag about that to me to make me jealous. He told me that one girl offered to suck him off, but I knew he was lying. That's why I picked him. He wouldn't cheat on me. He liked to show off, but none of those girls actually liked him. I saw him with them once, and they were making fun of him."

"Where did these models come from?"

"Modeling agencies."

"Do you know which ones?"

"Yeah. I asked Gaetano. Maybe I might want to be a model, too." She gave them a fierce look as if challenging them to contradict her. "They make good money. Alta Visione Talenti and Sogni di Moda. There were others, but I remember those."

Valerio made a note.

"You know Gaetano was arrested for cocaine possession," he said.

"That stupid thing!" She was suddenly furious. "That wasn't Gaetano! He wouldn't do that. He didn't need to."

"Why didn't he need to?"

"He was doing important work, wasn't he?"

"What important work?"

"Aren't you listening? The driving. They needed him to drive."

"Why was this important?"

She looked flustered for a moment as she thought about this.

"It just was," she insisted quietly.

"These parties he drove for—did he ever go in?"

"They didn't let him in, did they?"

"Do you know where the parties were?"

"Uh . . . Sorrento."

"Do you have addresses?"

"No."

"Did he ever tell you about what the parties were like?"

She picked at her skin while she thought. Scratching off a scab, her fingertips came back red. She didn't seem to notice.

"The night before he was arrested, Gaetano dropped a bunch of girls at a party. Then, they made him come back and pick up this girl. She was super high. Crying and bleeding everywhere."

"Bleeding?"

"Yeah. Her face was all bloody, he said. That happened sometimes."

Ravenna's eyes met Valerio's.

"The women would be injured?" said Valerio. "This happened more than once?"

Natale had been speaking confidently. Now, for the first time, she seemed uncertain.

"That's how rich people are, isn't it? Do whatever they want. That's what Gaetano said."

"Gaetano took women away from the parties when they were hurt?"

"Yeah."

Suddenly, she seemed to switch off, arms hanging limply, the light dimming in her eyes.

Valerio and Ravenna walked together in silence down Via dei Tribunali. Valerio was moved by the awkward teenager and her dead boyfriend. Natale exhibited the same type of reckless bravado that Gaetano had shown: a childish aggressiveness that must be a sort of barometer for the everyday terror they lived with. As if to convince themselves that they could survive a world where they were so out of their depth. Their desperate powerlessness felt horribly akin to his own, and he understood the need to lash out, to insist that he could solve this, that he could survive it.

Ravenna broke the silence: "What the hell kind of parties were they?"

They stopped at a café to duck out of the rain that had started during the interview.

Taking an empty table by the window, they ordered espressos and Valerio went to the toilet. On his way back, he stopped by the counter to buy a sfogliatella.

At the table, Ravenna was looking at her phone.

"Okay," she said. "I've found Alta Visione Talenti. Address in Rome."

She passed over her phone and Valerio flicked through the various pictures of beautiful young women, displayed like items on a menu. Each had smooth skin and parted lips, eyes seducing the camera. He was reminded, uncomfortably, of a photo some shithead had taken of his teenage daughter a few months ago.

One picture made him pause. He zoomed in, and examined the features before deciding he was right.

"I know her," he said slowly.

It was Maria. Raw vegan Maria.

"How do you know her?"

He opened his mouth to say—but was suddenly reluctant to talk about it.

"I went on a date with her," he admitted.

Ravenna's eyebrows raised. She took the phone back and examined the picture.

"She's very beautiful."

"She wasn't what I thought," he said. "She was looking for . . . a sugar daddy."

"Oh dear," said Ravenna. "And you didn't want a sugar baby?"

Valerio blew out through his teeth. The coffees arrived, granting a brief reprieve. He bit into the crunchy sfogliatella, scattering pastry flakes across the table.

"I wonder if she's still modeling for Alta Visione Talenti," Ravenna continued. "Maybe she knows about the parties. Do you think we could talk with her?"

Valerio shook his head. "I'm the last person she wants to hear from."

"Why?"

He described the dinner with Maria and the way it had ended. Ravenna laughed, her eyes sparkling with sudden merriment.

"You called her a prostitute?"

"She was asking for money!"

"Well," she said, "you're right. She won't want to talk to you again. Unless . . ."

"Unless what?"

"Maybe she hasn't been able to find another sponsor. She might want to talk to you if she thinks she has another shot at getting you to pay. Send her a text."

"I can't," Valerio protested.

"Sure you can," said Ravenna. "Unless she's already blocked you. What's the worst that can happen?"

Valerio thought for a moment and then messaged Maria: **We need to meet.**

"Not blocked," he said.

"What did you write?" Ravenna asked. Valerio showed her his screen. She smiled.

"You really don't know women, do you?" she said gently. "May I try?"

Valerio surrendered his phone, waiting with a strange anxiety while Ravenna wrote.

She showed him the result: **I've been an idiot. I met someone beautiful . . . perfect. A goddess. I should have worshipped her, but instead I judged her, and let her slip away.**

At his nod, she pressed Send.

To Valerio's amazement, only a few seconds passed, and a text bubble appeared.

I've been very angry with you, Maria wrote.

Ravenna typed, **Punish me. Please. I deserve it.**

I should, Maria said. **You were a very naughty boy.**

What would you do to punish me? To let me prove myself to you? Ravenna wrote.

Another text bubble appeared, then vanished—then appeared again.

Tomorrow night. 7PM. I'll punish you until you beg.

"There," said Ravenna, handing back the phone. "You have a date."

Several hours later, Valerio was smiling as he unlocked the door to his building.

He'd taken the kids for dinner before Giorgia picked them up. Despite his intention to part ways with Ravenna, he'd somehow never gotten around to it, and she'd joined them for dinner. Gemma and Davide had seemed unexpectedly comfortable with the arrangement, and laughed at her jokes. He hadn't wanted to say goodbye. He briefly considered asking her to come home with him before thinking better of it. Ravenna excused herself, saying she needed an early night for work tomorrow.

The attack came without warning: a sudden blow to the back of his head. Valerio staggered, stunned and temporarily sightless, flashes of light and color. Time stalled, and he fought to stay conscious. Battling the encroaching darkness, he scrabbled in his waistband for his weapon.

Then someone was choking him. A face close to his, features distorted, and the pungent stink of cigarettes and garlic.

"You stupid fuck," growled the man.

Valerio's fingers reached his gun. Struggling for air, he jammed the barrel into the man's gut, but his grip wasn't firm—he hunted for the trigger. The man suddenly released and stepped back.

Valerio saw the heavy black weapon aimed at him.

"Put your gun down," said the man.

"You first," wheezed Valerio. "I will blow your fucking head off."

He considered shooting anyway but he was too shaky and he couldn't see properly. His head was ringing from the blow, heart racing so hard it hurt his chest. He wasn't confident he could kill the man before he was killed first.

He took several panting breaths and, in that time, recognized the white hair and intense expression of Luca's thug Ivan.

"What the fuck do you want?" Valerio demanded.

"You work for us," said Ivan. "We call. You answer. You do as you're told."

"I did what Errichiello wanted," said Valerio. "We're finished."

Ivan's eyes lit with a manic glare. "You stupid fuck. We're a long way from finished."

SEVENTEEN

After waking, Preston seemed clear and calm, an outcome neither Nikki nor her aunt had imagined possible. He joked with the nurses and doctors as they did their evaluations. When they were finished, Preston held Izzy's hands and kissed her palms.

"'Thy sweet love remembered such wealth brings,'" he said. "'That then I scorn to change my state with kings.'"

By afternoon, however, his good humor and clarity were gone.

"He's not out of the woods yet," the doctor told them. "We'll keep him here a few more days. When he's stabilized, we'll talk about moving him to a rehabilitation facility."

Nikki offered to stay the night again but her aunt gently rejected this.

"I need to be here," she said. "I simply won't sleep without him next to me."

Nikki left the hospital and walked to Whitechapel station. Her mind felt stretched out. Wobbly. She considered going back to Izzy and Preston's house, but the thought depressed her. She checked her watch. It was 17:32. If she hurried, she would make it in time for the memorial for Claire Sexton at the pub near Gidea Park.

Nikki shucked her jacket as she entered the Three Horseshoes. A handful of people clustered in the dim space. These seemed to be locals—three middle-aged men in construction boots, a family of four, and a couple on a date. It smelled of fried fish, vinegar, and malty beer. There weren't any signs about the memorial—a shamble of papers pinned to a message board showed rooms for let, and declared the upcoming Friday as pub quiz night.

Nikki asked the woman at the bar, who said, "To the left and up the stairs, love."

The room upstairs was wide and deep, but felt cramped, due to a low plaster ceiling with heavy wooden beams. About two dozen people milled together, talking and cradling drinks. Others sat at tables, eating sandwiches and crisps. Most were in their twenties—friends or colleagues of Claire. They wore an awkward array of clothing—some in busty black funeral dresses, others in jeans and sweatshirts. A Taylor Swift album was playing.

One table near the entrance was draped in a white tablecloth and set with pink roses, artificial candles, and a condolence book. Nikki crossed to the book and scanned the notes and names, discreetly snapping a few photos with her phone before leaning in to write a message. Then she went past the beverage table and grabbed a bottle of Fosters to keep in her hand.

A woman in her early twenties sat alone. She wore an oversize sweater, jeans, and no makeup. Her cheeks were full and pink and dimpled. Her long, reddish-blonde hair was pulled back into two clips, frizzing a little with the humidity.

"Hi," Nikki said, approaching with a smile. "I'm Nikki."

"Sally," said the girl.

"How did you know Claire?" Nikki asked, taking the seat opposite.

"Went to primary school together, didn't we?" Sally's voice was oddly high-pitched and wispy. Nikki had to lean in to catch it. "So I've known her the longest. If anyone should be feeling sad, it's me, right? Not like everyone else here, all looking so tragic. Everyone pretending like they gave a toss about her. But they didn't really know her, did they?"

"So, you were close friends?"

"That's what I'm saying, right? Not like anybody cares what I'm feeling."

"Tell me about her."

Sally glanced at Nikki with hungry eagerness.

"We met when we were, like, eight years old. Her mum and dad split when she was six, and she was proper upset about it, yeah?"

"Is her mum here?" Nikki asked. "I've never met her."

"That's her over there. Lydia."

She pointed at three middle-aged women standing near an artist's easel where a large photograph of Claire was displayed. One of the women, wearing a cotton dress and jumper, bore a striking resemblance to Claire—with the same smooth skin and full, expressive mouth. Her eyes were swollen with crying and there was a hopeless agitation to the way she gripped her coffee cup, and shifted from foot to foot.

"Are you a nanny, too?" Nikki asked.

"Not a chance! That was Claire's gig. She was all about kids. Just mad for 'em. But I reckon I should've jumped on that bandwagon—'cause let me tell you, the dads Claire worked for were absolutely fit. Have you seen Jayston Lake? Absolute dish. Claire was all over him, too."

"Claire was interested in Jayston Lake?"

"Who wouldn't be?" She glanced at Nikki as if for confirmation, then added, "I mean, come on? He's proper famous. Can you imagine?"

"Did she ever tell you that she was interested?" Nikki asked.

Sally shrugged. "Blogged about it, didn't she?"

Nikki sat up straighter. "She did?"

"Not with her own name, 'course."

"What name did she use?"

"What was it?" Sally grabbed her phone and started scrolling. "Something proper weird . . . thorny . . . something. Ah! Yeah . . . Omygod. It's him."

It took Nikki a moment to follow Sally's attention, which was drawn away from her phone and to the entrance. Nikki half expected to see Jayston, but instead there was a startlingly good-looking man in his early thirties—refined features, hollow cheeks, and a mane of shining brown hair. He wore stylish black trousers and a skintight jacket over a clinging T-shirt. Striding into the room, he was welcomed by the crowd with exclamations and evident excitement.

"Who's that?" Nikki asked.

"Teddy Sexton. Claire's half brother. Isn't he fit? And he's dead clever. He's, like, some sort of genius inventor."

"He doesn't look like Claire," Nikki observed.

Sally made a snorting noise. "I said half brother, didn't I? Same dad—*white* dad."

"I should go," Nikki said, standing. She started to reach for a handshake, but Sally's eyes narrowed and she tossed her head, clearly taking offense.

"Fine, go on, then. Ain't nobody bothered about what I gotta say, anyway."

The women with Claire Sexton's mother had apparently left their post. Nikki was about to approach when Lydia seemed to gather herself and, with a look of desperation, slipped from the room. Nikki followed her—down the stairs, into the pub, and through the front doors.

Lydia Sexton stood alone in the cold outside, without a jacket, facing traffic on the noisy street. She dug through her purse for a packet of cigarettes and lit up, staring into the distance.

Nikki approached cautiously, sensing something fragile in that lost expression.

"Hi, Lydia," she said. "I'm Nikki. I wanted to say . . . I'm sorry for your loss."

Lydia nodded, seeming to make an effort to come back into the present.

"Thanks. Thanks for coming. It's nice, isn't it? Everybody here for Claire. It was decent of the agency to arrange this."

"Was Claire your only . . . ?"

"My one and only. She was something special, you know? Just brightened up my world. My angel. That's what I called her. My angel."

She was crying, but didn't seem aware of it. Tears slid down her cheeks and dripped off her chin.

"I can't imagine what you're going through," said Nikki honestly. She wondered how much Lydia knew about the way Claire had died.

She thought of Monica's hair painted in Claire's blood and, in her mind's eye, saw the photographs of the gruesome crime scene.

"How did you know her?" asked Lydia.

Nikki had considered a cover story, but the thought of lying to this grieving woman suddenly repulsed her.

"I didn't know her when she was alive," she confessed. "But, from everything I've heard, she sounds like a kind and caring person. My name is Nikki Serafino. I work for a unit called Phoenix Seven—we help the police sometimes. I was involved in the investigation of Claire's death in Naples. I'm not involved anymore, but I happened to be in the neighborhood and I wanted to understand . . . the person she was."

Lydia looked stunned, then she stirred as if waking up. Her eyes were suddenly intense.

"You aren't with the press, are you?"

"No. As I said, I'm with Phoenix Seven. I'm really sorry for intruding. Maybe I shouldn't have come. I know this is a special event."

"Do you have identification?" Lydia asked.

Nikki took out her ID and showed it to her, bracing, ready for her anger.

Lydia examined the card and seemed to consider. "No. I want you to stay. That's all I want, you know? Someone to give a damn that she's gone. Someone to care enough to find out . . . why anyone would do this to my baby. What do you want to know about my Claire?"

"I'm not on the case anymore," Nikki said. "I'm not able to formally investigate."

"But you want to investigate? You want to find out what happened to her?"

Nikki met Lydia's gaze. It was unexpectedly alert and determined.

She nodded. "I do."

"That'll do for me," said Lydia. She pulled a crumpled tissue from her purse and wiped her nose. "Tell me what you want to know."

"Okay." Nikki took a deep breath. "The police will already have asked you these questions, so I may repeat them."

"That's fine."

"Did Claire talk to you about her work?" Nikki asked.

"Some of it. She'd signed these business deals that tied her hands, couldn't blab about her work, but she still spilled to me."

"How often did you two talk?"

"A few times a week. We were tight. She'd drop me an email when they were out at sea—and then she'd ring up whenever they docked."

"Was she happy working for the Lakes?"

"Well . . . she was crazy about Audrey. Lovely little thing. And she was head over heels for Jayston. But the mother—Fiona—was a real piece of work."

"I understand that Fiona may have been . . . jealous. Suspicious of Claire and Jayston."

"Absolute madness, right? Jayston Lake was old enough to be Claire's father. Put Claire in tears when Fiona accused her. I told her it wasn't worth it. No amount of cash was worth putting up with cruelty. Folks like the Lakes—they think money buys everything. They act like they own you. I said, 'Darling, you can walk away anytime. You don't have to take that rubbish.' But she wanted to stay."

"Claire left the yacht on Saturday night," Nikki said. "In Capri. Did she tell you she was leaving?"

Lydia shook her head. "No."

"What was she like in the days before she went missing? Did she seem alright?"

Lydia put a hand to her forehead, and took a deep breath.

"I can't shake it off. She rang me the first day they docked—I remember it was Friday. She always did that. Normally, she'd be bubbling over about how fantastic everything was. But not this time. She sounded . . . different, you know? Not herself. She was in tears, saying she wanted to hop on the next flight back. I told her, 'Then come back, simple as that.' But she insisted she had to stay put. I just wish . . . I wish she'd come back. I wish I'd known what was eating at her."

"Did she say she was meeting anyone?"

"Who would she meet? She didn't know anyone in Italy."

"Was Claire romantically involved with anyone who might have met her up in Naples?"

"Nah. She was too shy for that. She was a natural with kids—more than that, brilliant with them. But she struggled with people her own age. She was more into books than boys."

"She'd never had a boyfriend?" Nikki asked.

"Just mates. I said to her, 'It's alright to take your time. You'll get there eventually. There's plenty of time for all that later on.'"

The words seemed to strike Lydia afresh, and she began crying again. Nikki excused herself and, returning with a glass of water and a handful of bar napkins, found that Lydia had been joined by a matronly woman in a long, pleated skirt.

"Oh, my dear," the woman said to Lydia. "What are you doing out here all on your lonesome? No wonder you're feeling down. This is meant to be a celebration of Claire's life. Come along. Let's fetch you something to eat."

Lydia nodded.

"This is Nikki," she said, accepting the napkins from Nikki and blowing her nose. "She's looking into what happened to Claire."

The matronly woman drew herself up. Her voice was sharp with indignation: "What are you doing here? This is completely inappropriate. This is a private event of the Albion Nanny Agency."

"It's alright," Lydia protested, but the woman stopped her with a hand and rounded on Nikki. "I don't know what dirt you're trying to dig up but let me make it perfectly clear that the ANA bears no liability whatsoever. You shouldn't be here."

"She can come—" Lydia started to say, but the woman interrupted her with a flutter of hands, shooing Nikki away.

"Get out! Go! You heard me. Leave!"

The pub was filling with the dinner crowd. Nikki chose a table, and ordered a beer, a vegetarian burger, and a plate of fried haloumi. She logged in to the pub's wi-fi with her phone and looked at the Facebook page for Claire's memorial event, where people had begun posting pictures and leaving messages. She scrolled through, cross-checking the names with those in the photos she'd taken of the condolence book.

Among the condolences, she found Sally Tate's name and the message, **Nobody misses you more than me. XOXO.**

Sally had also posted to the Facebook memorial page: eight selfies, three wide shots of the memorial, and a dozen photos of Teddy Sexton as he laughed with a cluster of women.

Nikki sent connection requests to Sally on Facebook and Instagram.

Next, she followed the tags of Teddy to his social media accounts, where she found a collection of pictures of the toned and handsome man: in an art gallery; drinking and laughing with friends; sitting beneath a blossoming tree and reading a copy of *Infinite Jest*; lifting weights at the gym; sparring in a boxing ring. From this account, she navigated easily to his other social media sites and to the website of a company he owned called Innovare MindCapsule, which boasted a "personal growth companion" offering "neurofeedback, time-capsule messaging, and cognitive training." The company had been featured in a few online magazines, and Nikki scrolled a range of testimonials from beautifully coiffed young men and women.

An architect called the MindCapsule "an absolute revelation." A PhD student described it as "grounding and inspiring," and a creative director said that it was "a game changer for anyone looking to push their creative boundaries." After a half hour of reading through the website and testimonials, Nikki wasn't sure she understood precisely what Innovare MindCapsule was offering.

Gianni texted: **You free? Mac wants to meet up. He's got some great ideas. You should hear them.**

She wrote back: **In London. With Izzy and Preston.**

Gianni wrote: **Yeah. Oops. Forgot.**

Audrey Lake had left a dozen text messages for Nikki. More emojis and then a series of crooked photographs of what she'd eaten for dinner: marinara pizza and chips and an orange Fanta and a tiramisu. Nikki texted her a thumbs-up emoji.

People started to filter out of the memorial at around 20:30. Nikki watched the groups of young adults tromp down the stairs and out of the pub. She had the idea of talking to Claire's mother again, but Lydia was firmly escorted out by the woman from Albion Nanny Agency.

Nikki paid her bill, and then went back upstairs into the memorial room. The space was empty and smelled stale. Bottles and glasses littered the tables, and a platter of forlorn sandwiches was decimated, leaving behind only crumbs and a few wilted slices of lettuce and ham glistening with mayonnaise.

Nikki's hands and face felt numb and cold—something she was starting to associate with death. It had been there at Adriano's funeral; and that peculiar sensation of distance—seeing things through the wrong end of a telescope.

She seemed to feel it now: the cold church on that December morning.

The funeral came nearly a month after Adriano's death because the police wouldn't surrender his remains until they'd finished their investigation. It calmed her to see the coffin, to know that her brother was, at last, back with his family, where he belonged. Rain had invaded Nikki's coat, her damp collar pressed icily against her neck. Her father wept openly and her usually lively mother stared empty-eyed, fingers like rigid claws at her sides. The posture reminded Nikki of a fairy-tale sorceress, as if any moment, she would lift her hands, casting a spell to rouse Adriano from his sleep.

The men from her brother's unit stood to attention by the coffin, so orderly in their dress uniforms; fitted tunics and capes and black boots. Nikki remembered the lean body of Sandro Balestrieri, grief twisting his features. After the service Sandro's pregnant girlfriend stood beside him, wrapping her arms around Sandro, tucked beneath his chin, and he'd kissed the top of her head. How Nikki envied them their consolation. Her own arms had lost the feel of Tito and, aching with emptiness, held only the memory of cradling Adriano long after he had slipped away.

She had learned to accommodate the peculiar ache of loss, grown around it until it became a part of her. Then, little more than a year ago, death returned to refresh the wounds.

The months and weeks leading up to her mother's death had been tumultuous. Nikki's relationship with Beatrice had none of the easy rapport that Lydia described with her daughter. Instead, Beatrice had been as stubborn and unyielding as Nikki, as unable to force her feelings into words. A natural tendency for detachment and secrecy had amplified over the years, and Beatrice became a solitary soldier, fiercely secretive and driven—fighting an enemy only she seemed to see. In unguarded moments of fatigue or surprise, however, the armor would slip and then Nikki would glimpse such a tender vulnerability and weariness in her, she wanted to wrap herself around her mother and keep her safe.

When Raoul called Nikki with the news in the dark of early morning, she had raced across Naples and to the mountains of Benevento on her Hornet. Some instinct told her that if she was fast enough, there might be a way to combat the insidious invader that had stolen her mother in her sleep.

Arriving at the house, and into her parents' bedroom, she almost cried with relief.

You made a mistake, she wanted to say. *It isn't her.*

Without the familiar animation, the warm movements, the resonant voice and laughter, the body of her mother had looked nothing like Beatrice Serafino.

Nikki and her father sat together in a strangely frozen vigil the rest of that night. They hadn't looked at each other, hadn't touched. Only stared at the body on the bed until the sun lit up the small bedroom, and the undertaker arrived to take Beatrice away.

Lost in her thoughts, Nikki was startled when someone said, "You alright?"

It took a moment to recognize the pale, handsome face of Teddy Sexton. He stood at the threshold, leaning back a little to look at her, as if he'd paused on his way someplace else.

"Yeah," she said. The memories were sticky. She wiped a hand across her face as if to brush away the cobwebs.

He took a step into the room.

"Are you one of Claire's friends?" he asked.

Nikki felt tired. She'd come here with the intention to investigate, but the prospect had become a stone in her throat. She was done here.

She sighed. "No. I was just leaving."

She moved to the door and he stepped aside to let her pass.

She wasn't far down the hall when he called out, "Wait," and jogged towards her.

He was older than she'd assumed from the Instagram pictures: a mature intelligence in his grey eyes that seemed to contend with the youthful image created by a toned body and rock-star attire.

Drawing close, he said, "You certain you're alright? I don't mean to intrude, but you seem a little . . . lost."

Her instinct was to reassert her professionalism, affirm her fitness for duty, but there was a razor truth in his words. She hesitated, feeling the cold of that church, and the roar of her motorcycle as she raced to Benevento, and the icy terror and despair that met her in a cave while the thunder crashed outside.

"My uncle," she told him. "He's in hospital. They weren't sure he was going to pull through. It's been a difficult couple of days."

Teddy gave a sad smile. "I'm a bit rudderless, too. This was a memorial for my kid sister. All her friends were here and I kept thinking she'd show up. Idiotic, isn't it? I still can't believe she's not coming back."

"I'm sorry," Nikki said. "Were you close?"

He shook his head. "She was actually my half sister. I was ten when she was born. You know how kids are. . . . I resented her for a long time. But she turned out to be really sweet. Introverted. Incredibly naive. Wanted to save everybody. She was a carer for children. That's why she . . ."

His voice shook and the words trailed off.

His face softened when he talked about Claire. After his trendy social media accounts, Nikki had been prepared to dismiss Teddy Sexton as entirely superficial, but his grief was clearly real and raw.

"It sounds like you loved her," she said. "What happened?"

"She was killed!" A sudden flash of viciousness lit up his expression. He shook his head. "Silly kid. Didn't understand anything. Didn't understand how the world works."

He shoved his hands into his pockets and shrugged with an agitated, disconsolate air. Nikki felt an impulse to reach out. She stopped herself.

"It feels terrible to lose someone like that," she said. "Sometimes I think that death should make sense . . . but I've never found it."

She considered saying more—telling him about her work, and describing the investigation into Claire's murder. But the words stuck in her mouth. She'd already misled him by omission.

He searched her face. "Can I buy you a drink?"

She glanced back into the empty room with its depressing decorations and empty bottles.

"I want to get out of here," she told him.

"Fair enough," he said. "It's Sunday night. Most places are dead . . . but I know a cracking spot in the city."

While they waited for Teddy's cab outside the Three Horseshoes, he smoked.

"I grew up around here," he said. "Hated it. Couldn't wait to get the fuck out."

"What did you hate?"

"Too cramped. Not only the place—the minds."

"How did you leave?"

"As rapidly as possible. If you want to succeed, you can't wait for opportunity. You create it."

He had a public-school accent, but Nikki had spent enough time in London to recognize the false notes. He'd clearly spent considerable effort purging Gidea Park from his life, but it clung to the edges of his words.

Almost as an afterthought, he said, "I'm Teddy."

"Nikki," said Nikki. The night chill seeped into her coat, and she pulled up the hood to block the unpleasant drizzle. "What opportunity did you create?"

"CEO of my own company."

"Impressive."

"Where are you from, Nikki?" he asked. "I'm trying to place your accent."

"Born in Naples—but I spent a decade in London. Camden."

"Love Camden. Excellent choice."

The easy camaraderie between them made Nikki increasingly conscious of her lie. She should have told him she was with Phoenix Seven—that she was investigating Claire's death—that she'd already done some internet sleuthing on him.

She redirected the conversation: "Tell me about your company."

Teddy put out his cigarette on the pavement.

"We all imagine that the human mind is restricted," he said. "We create these stories about ourselves and they just hold us back. The truth is: Success is your birthright. You can be—can have—whatever you want. You just need the right key to unlock your potential. That key is called MindCapsule. That's what we do—what my company, Innovare MindCapsule, does."

It was a practiced sales pitch—smooth and engaging. His eyes lit up as he talked. He offered her a mint and put one in his own mouth.

Their cab arrived and he held the door, helped her in.

As they rode, Nikki asked Teddy more questions about his company, listened, and pressed him when his descriptions were unclear. As far as she could tell, Teddy's app, *MindCapsule*, primarily included tailored meditations, tonal frequencies, and musical clips, and allowed the user to send encrypted messages, files, and videos to themselves at some future date.

"Payments are on a sliding scale—based on age and profession," he said. "I think everyone should have the opportunity to harness the power of their minds—especially young people. I wish I'd had something like it when I felt trapped. I gave my kid sister her own account on *MindCapsule*. Wanted her to think bigger, you know?"

They were sitting close together so they could hear each other over the sounds of the radio, the engine, and traffic, close enough for her to smell the clean musky undertones of his cologne.

"You're a very beautiful woman, Nikki," he said. "I had to say it. There it is."

He reached down and threaded his fingers through hers. His hand was warm and dry. His eyes, illuminated by the streetlights flickering by, were clear and grey.

The restaurant on the twenty-fourth floor of the business tower was a place to see and be seen. Chic customers and upscale staff contrasted the grubby feeling Nikki experienced inside her second-day clothing. This was a luxury she could never afford on her own, but Enzo used to take her to places like this, with sleek booths in soft fawn leather, dark lacquered wood, and a glass-fronted wall serving as a subtly glowing wine cabinet. A mirrored ceiling reflected the warm yellow lamps on the tables, and doubled the height of the windows, showing the soft lights of the cityscape below.

The waiter escorted them to a booth near a window. Nikki experienced a brief sense of vertigo looking out over the city.

Teddy ordered an Aviation cocktail. Nikki asked for prosecco, but Teddy talked her into an Oban instead.

When the drinks arrived, he said, "What are the odds I'd meet a beautiful Italian woman tonight, and enjoy drinks with her now?"

He ran his thumb along the edge of the crystal.

"I don't believe in luck," said Nikki, meeting his gaze.

"Neither do I."

They drank, and Nikki tasted the smoke and peat, the burn of the whisky. It seemed to amplify her fatigue. It was 22:03 and she'd spent a restless night in a hospital room. She needed sleep, but instead was enjoying the unfamiliar touch of Teddy's hand on her skin, his attention and interest. She swirled the tumbler, watching the golden liquid catch the light.

"What did it take to build Innovare MindCapsule?" she asked.

"A lot of hard work. It was my idea, of course. And I needed to scout for the right partners . . . the right talent."

"Did you find them?"

He smiled. "Well, if you want to *be* the next Zuckerberg and not fucked by the next Zuckerberg, you need to pick your bedfellows wisely."

"Tell me about your partners," Nikki encouraged.

He frowned and shrugged, then ran his fingertips along her arm. "I'd rather talk about you."

"What would you like to know?"

"Everything, international woman of mystery. Where do you work?"

Nikki considered the omissions she'd already made. They'd twisted her personal story too far; she could never bend it back to properly fit the truth. She borrowed from her own past instead, as if she were meeting Teddy years ago, in those days when the rage would slip out of her, uncontrolled and feral, when she would find a way to piss off the biggest guy in the club, daring him to take a swing at her; when she would choose her partner for the evening because she liked the vodka he drank, or his form during deadlifts, or the way he maneuvered his motorcycle. She tasted some of that recklessness now.

"Nightclub," she said. "Incendio."

"Wow," he said. "Are you a dancer? I mean, you look wicked fit."

"Bouncer."

He laughed. "Really? I believe it. You've got a magnificent tough-girl vibe. I love your muscles and tattoos. I'll be sure to conduct a full topological survey later."

He lifted her hand and kissed the tattoo on the inside of her wrist: a spiraling knotted pattern she'd once found on a grave.

He waved the waiter over and ordered seconds.

They talked about her work at Incendio, and as the minutes and hours slipped by, she told him a bit about Enzo—although not the specifics of how it had ended between them.

"He's an idiot," murmured Teddy. "I can't believe anyone would give you up."

Then he told her about his relationship with an actress that had just run its course.

"Can I be honest with you, Nikki?" he said during their next round of drinks. "I respect the work you do—but do you want to do it for the rest of your life? You're fucking smart. You shouldn't be working for anyone; people should be working for you. I see you more as a club owner."

Nikki tried to consider, but her thoughts were blurred. She'd had too much to drink.

"I'd like to kiss you," he murmured, leaning in.

Nikki let him, tasting cigarettes and rum. His lips were soft, teeth slick, tongue gently probing. She relaxed into the electric warmth and pleasure, reminded of the last time she'd been kissed—a green silk dress and the cooling island air of Capri, and a boat returned to the mainland without her.

But Teddy's mouth was not Enzo's mouth.

His hands roved upwards with practiced skill, and he pulled her firmly into him, ran fingertips through her hair, caressed her back and hips until something ignited inside and she stopped thinking about Enzo.

He was smiling when he pulled back.

Nikki caught her breath and shook her head. She was enjoying this—the way he touched and looked at her. She wanted him, wanted him to take her home and fuck her. But this was a bad idea. All of it was a bad idea.

"I should get back."

He leaned in, took her earlobe gently between his teeth. His hand was on her thigh, stroking, working upwards. He kissed her again.

"Let's get out of here," he whispered.

Teddy paid. Nikki stopped by the toilet on her way out. She rinsed her mouth and splashed her face with cold water. The mirror reflected her fatigue, but it also showed cheeks flushed with the alcohol and the heat of Teddy's attentions . . . and the lie.

Her deception had been like an armor. It made her feel invincible. Reckless, she'd leaned out over the edge, some part of her brain working to justify what she was doing—a vague sense that her lies and drinking and flirtation were in service to the investigation. But that wasn't remotely true. This was about something else entirely—an old familiar screaming pain that seemed to claw its way out of her chest whenever she stood still enough to feel it. She wanted it silenced, wanted to drown it in these moments of a numbly detached pleasure—the wordless physical act, the sense of connection and movement and momentary release.

"Fuck," she said aloud to her reflection.

She'd traveled down this familiar path as if it could take her anywhere besides misery. Until this moment, she'd deluded herself.

If this was for the investigation, then she was far over any ethical line.

"Fuck."

Here, she decided. *And no further.*

She found Teddy again outside the bank of lifts. Absorbed in his phone, he didn't look up as she approached. On the lift, he pocketed the phone and kissed her again. This time, he was rougher, his expression blank and hungry. He bit her lip and took both hands in his, squeezing until they hurt.

Outside, the business district was empty. No cars. No pedestrians. They walked alone through the streets. Coming around a corner, Teddy pressed her against a wall, kissing, grinding against her.

"That's enough," Nikki said, pulling away. "You're hurting me."

He pressed harder, trapping her. The cold concrete at Nikki's back scraped painfully through her coat—against her shoulder blades and spine. He was muscular and large, and clearly well trained. She was shorter than Teddy by several centimeters, and far smaller. He was crushing her.

"You're a fucking liar," he hissed in her ear. "You said you weren't there for Claire's memorial—but people posted pictures of you there. I saw them. Why were you following me? Who the fuck are you? What do you want?"

Gone was the easy sensuality between them, the sense of a shared joke. Passion had morphed into violence—but in some confusing and horrifying violation, the intimacy had remained.

Nikki was suddenly conscious of her vulnerability. Under other circumstances, she would never have let an attacker get behind her guard. He was so much stronger, and furious.

Her heart raced. She pushed against him—indignation to cover her terror.

"I wasn't following you. You asked me out," she shouted. "What the fuck? Let me go!"

He tightened his grip.

"Who the fuck are you? Don't lie to me. What do you want? Why are you stalking me?"

His right hand was clamped on her throat now, his face inches from hers. Panic and pain exploded in her body, contending with a rabid fury at letting herself be trapped like this.

Nikki twisted her torso rapidly to the left and down, rage and fear giving power to the action. This changed the grip on her windpipe. Using this momentum, she brought her right hand up and slammed her forearm down against his arm, forcing his hand away from her neck. This put him off balance and gave her the chance to put her right elbow into the side of his face. But he was strong and angry and her strike didn't take him down. He grunted and pulled his arm back for a punch, but she ducked and kept into him with her elbows and knees. When he came in again for an attack, she redirected his momentum, and he slammed headfirst into the wall with a sickening thud.

Nikki danced backwards, ready to defend herself. He swore—but didn't return for another attack. Instead, he was backing away from her. His hand went to his head, his eyes wide and shocked.

"Crazy fucking bitch," he shouted.

EIGHTEEN

It was a bad night. Valerio had needed several hours, ice on the back of his head, painkillers, and leftover wine to help him sleep. Once in bed, he discovered cookie crumbs and wrappers that Gemma had left behind, but he was too tired to change the sheets.

In the early morning, he was awakened from a shallow sleep by the clanging of church bells.

He made coffee, showered, took three paracetamol, and was out the door and on his motorbike before he had time to think about anything.

The weather was cooperating. Warm and clear. Good.

He made a brief stop at HQ to pick up some gear before heading out of Naples, taking the E45 south along the coast, Vesuvius in his periphery.

At an Autogrill outside Pompeii, he stopped to fill the tank and to piss. He was standing at a table, eating a crema cornetto and drinking espresso, when he saw a text from Nikki: **Can't sail today. Sorry. In London. Family emergency.**

He called.

"You okay?" he asked when she picked up. "What happened?"

Her voice was that cold, matter-of-fact monotone she used when she was frightened. "My uncle fell down a flight of stairs. Broken femur, and a head injury."

"Fuck!" said Valerio. "I'm sorry to hear that. You there now?"

"Yeah."

"Anything I can do?"

There was a long pause before she spoke. "Friday night—Tito Calandra's thugs fucking burned down my studio."

It took a beat for her words to register.

"What?"

"Friday night. They used an accelerant. Valerio, there was more than just my studio; it was the whole fucking building. People lived there."

"You sure it was Calandra?"

Another pause. "No. But Calandra's man—De Rosa—told me to stop teaching."

"What did you tell him?"

"What do you think I told him?"

Valerio sighed. "Okay," he said. "I'll look into it tomorrow. You safe now?"

"Yeah. I'm in London. How are you?"

Valerio looked through the windows, at the traffic hurtling along the highway. He was drained—a ragged and detached sensation. There was an emptiness inside, as if his thoughts wouldn't distill and take on weight. He touched the back of his head where a hard and painful knot had formed.

"Not great," he said honestly. "I'll be fine."

"Wanna tell me about it?"

He considered. On the boat or over drinks he would be glad to talk through the whole mess with Nikki. She had a measured way of seeing things, and gave practical recommendations. But it was too much to pass along over the phone.

"Not here," he said. "I'm on the road. Just stopping for fuel."

"You're not sailing?"

"Not today. We'll talk when you get back."

"Don't do anything stupid," Nikki said, by way of a sign-off.

"Don't *you* do anything stupid," said Valerio.

His phone rang as he was walking out to his motorbike. Luca. He sent it to voicemail, then, after a moment's thought, called Giorgia.

"What are you and the kids doing today?" he asked.

"Not that it's any of your business," she said, "but Bartolo invited us to his home in Posillipo this weekend."

Bartolo was the most recent boyfriend—a wide-mouthed and

accommodating man whom Davide called *personality-free* and Gemma referred to as *the dickless wonder.*

"Good," he said. "Will you stay at his place tonight?"

"That's none of your business either!"

"Well, will you?"

She seemed to hesitate. Then, "Yes."

"Good," he said again. "Keep an eye on the kids."

He couldn't be sure Errichiello wouldn't threaten the kids again. That was the biggest worry. But Giorgia's love life was difficult enough for him to track; it should keep Errichiello's men guessing.

The open road was a relief. In the bright sunlight, the growl of the bike beneath him, Valerio's mind loosened, and he was better able to remember, and to reason.

His thoughts churned, returning to Luca Errichiello, and that mundane malevolence: a calm, detached affect that never once signaled intent. Sitting by the pool, chewing salami, the unremarkable man in the hat had seemed tranquil. Bored, even. He'd played on Valerio's sympathy—discussing the plight of the jailed teenager and his sick mother—and, all the while, he planned to slaughter the boy.

Errichiello lived by the mathematics of the schoolyard bully. The nuances and depths of other men—their passions, loves, complexities—would always be reduced to two levers: pleasure and pain. Luca was probing, testing tolerances, trying to compress Valerio into these dimensions. If Valerio capitulated, Luca would use it against him the rest of his life.

Stupidly, Valerio had already demonstrated that he could be controlled by threats to Gemma and Davide. The real question was: How would Luca use this information? He guessed that depended on Luca's plans for him. If he saw him as disposable—good for only one job—Luca would lean heavily on this weakness. But Valerio guessed that Luca wanted to play the long game with him: a well-positioned asset within the police for decades. It was better for Luca if Valerio became a willing tool, and this required a lighter touch.

Luca's primary leverage was blackmail. Valerio's actions to free

Gaetano made him look guilty and could very well cost him his job and pension, not to mention prison time—if the evidence were twisted to make it seem Valerio had been complicit in the murder. But Valerio guessed that Luca wouldn't pull this trigger yet, since that would destroy Valerio's value before he could use it.

By refusing Luca's calls yesterday, Valerio had signaled that he wouldn't respond to the threat of exposure. Predictably, Luca had moved next to physical violence. Valerio wanted to make it clear that he wouldn't respond to this either. He needed to get free before Luca escalated again.

Silvestri's Sorrento home, perched on a rocky cliffside far from the center of town, was an elaborate stucco mansion. Valerio rode past the gate, following the winding road until he reached a turnoff where he could stash his bike and unpack his gear. From there, he hiked—sticking to the roads at first, then climbing stone steps into the hills, and hopping a fence into an olive grove. At last, he found the angle he wanted.

Silvestri's villa was the grandest in the neighborhood and commanded the best view of the bay: a profound blue, deepening at the horizon, where the hazy outline of Capri loomed like the head of a massive sea monster. Behind the villa, nestled among silver-leafed olive trees and flowering bushes, on a marble deck overlooking the water, two women in fur-trimmed coats and boots sipped coffee.

During today's visit to the police station, Valerio had borrowed a Nikon D6 with a telephoto lens—a camera he and Maurizio had recently used on a job. He took pictures of the property, zooming in well enough to capture the faces of the women before they returned inside.

Then he waited.

Two hours passed.

He ate a panino he'd brought from the Autogrill—more out of boredom than actual hunger. Not much happened except he was cold and started to feel a sunburn on his bare head. He also had several interactions with a large black beetle that seemed interested in his bags.

He was about to pack up, when movement caught his attention. A man in black combat gear stepped onto the deck. Valerio took several pictures. Five minutes later, the man stood suddenly at attention. Someone had joined him—Luca's white-haired thug, Ivan.

A clench of unease rolled through Valerio, his mind returning to last night: Ivan's face, close in the dark, and the rancid breath. His heart raced as he snapped photos. Here was the first solid proof that Errichiello and Silvestri were connected!

When the men disappeared inside, Valerio moved. He sprinted across the mountainside, ducking beneath olive branches, until he reached a new vantage overlooking the front of Silvestri's property. Then he dropped to his belly and waited.

Thirty minutes later, a green three-wheeled Ape truck pulled up, and the gate slid open to let it in. A barrel-chested man in work boots climbed out. Ivan frisked him while the other guard searched the vehicle. Then the man started unloading demijohns of wine and carrying them into the house before driving away.

Valerio snapped shots of him and the sign painted on the Ape: Cantina la Sirena. He also took photos of the large dark SUV parked in the driveway, zooming in on the license plates.

Fifteen minutes later, Ivan and the other man reemerged, got into the SUV, and drove away.

Valerio returned to where he'd stowed his things. His body was stiff, back aching from his time on the ground. He checked his phone: three missed calls from Errichiello. Loading his bags on his motorbike, he steered down the winding mountain road.

By the time Valerio arrived back in Naples, he was nearly an hour late for his appointment with Beppe. He'd texted about the delay but still felt guilty as he parked and jogged up the stairs to the front door of the concrete apartment.

Valerio remembered Beppe Riccio as a fat man. Well, not fat exactly, but chubby. With rosy cheeks and a broad smile. This was topped off by a shock of frizzy hair. He'd had the sort of easy personality that seemed to match: optimistic and cheerful.

The man who met Valerio at the door was barely recognizable: lean and sinewy, with sunken cheeks and a completely bald head.

"What happened to you?" asked Valerio before he could stop himself. "Are you sick?"

Beppe let out that familiar jolly laugh. "Went on a diet, man! No carbohydrates. No pasta . . . pizza . . . beer. Started running. You should try it."

"No pizza? Are you insane?" Valerio chuckled. "I hear the pope excommunicates people for that."

Beppe ushered him inside, where his wife, Carlotta, was busy with one of their grandchildren, helping the boy into his jacket and boots. She rose to kiss Valerio's cheeks.

"It's been too long," she said. "How are Giorgia and the kids?"

They exchanged family news, then Valerio followed Beppe into the kitchen, where he prepared fresh coffee.

They had a simple, well-kept home—a blend of ornate antiques and IKEA minimalism, everything neatly arranged on hooks, on shelves, and in plastic bins.

"No cookies, I'm afraid," Beppe said, handing him a cup. To Valerio's relief, he placed a bowl of almonds on the table. Valerio grabbed a handful.

"You may as well spit the toad," said Beppe. "Glad as I am to see you, I know this isn't a social call."

This was one reason Valerio had liked Beppe. He could gossip with the best of them, but when you needed something, he got exactly to the point.

"I didn't want to put it in a message," Valerio admitted. "I'm in a nice mess, and I don't want to draw you into it. If you call the station, they'll tell you not to talk to me."

"I see," said Beppe. "Well, it's decent of you to warn me, but I'm not worried. I'm finished with the bullshit—political games, pandering. And I'm on my pension now, so I don't have to pretend to like anyone anymore. But I've always liked you, Valerio. Truly. So, ask your questions and if they don't appreciate it, they can go to hell."

The resentment in the words contrasted so sharply with his pleasant tone, Valerio laughed. He had the urge to hug Beppe.

"Ah, I've missed you!" he exclaimed. "Alright then. Two thousand eight. You took a complaint from a woman named Agnese Cuomo about Paride Silvestri. You investigated, but the magistrate sealed the records. Do you remember?"

The smile faded from Beppe's face.

"Oh, I remember," he said. "But it's my turn to warn you. If you're looking into Paride Silvestri, you won't get far. He's protected at every level. Police . . . judiciary . . . government . . . you name it!"

"Is that why the records were sealed?"

"You guessed it. Officially, it was because a minor was involved."

"So, what happened?" Valerio asked. "Who was Agnese Cuomo?"

"Agnese ran a souvenir shop in Sorrento. Her daughter, Felicia, was a beautiful little girl. Remarkable. Schoolboys followed her around, proclaiming their love. She was thirteen when one of Silvestri's women spotted her."

"Silvestri's women?"

Beppe nodded grimly. "Yeah. We never identified her. But I think that's how Silvestri operated. The woman was a lure . . . claiming to be a talent scout. She told Felicia she had the looks to be a model and invited her to a photo shoot at Paride's home."

Valerio's stomach twisted. He didn't like where this story was going.

"The photo shoot was innocent enough," Beppe continued. "Nothing ugly there. But afterwards, the woman started asking questions. What did Felicia want for her future? Did she want to help her family? She told her that Silvestri could help her get her training and certification as a professional masseuse. Then came the next step: She'd need to demonstrate her skills on him."

Beppe stopped and looked down at his hands.

"That was the beginning," he said. "He abused her for several months before she finally told her mother."

Valerio had seen his share of violent crime scenes without flinching, but anything involving children always sickened him.

"I'm not a violent man," Beppe continued, rapping his knuckles on the table. "But if you ever left me alone in a room with Silvestri or any other pedo like him, I can't guarantee they'd walk out again."

They sat in silence for several seconds, digesting this.

"You investigated?" Valerio asked.

Beppe exhaled heavily. He looked suddenly older.

"It should have been straightforward," he said. "Felicia gave clear, consistent details. She was a remarkable kid—so brave. And her mother, too. They had nothing—barely making it to the end of the month—but they were willing to take on this powerful billionaire. I knew there had to be other victims; Silvestri's grooming was too well rehearsed. It should have been easy to build a case. But it was the hardest case I've ever worked. No cooperation. No support from my chain of command. They wanted me to shut it down before I could even get started. Even my own partner seemed to be working against me. And the magistrate wasn't any better. The entire system was stacked with people who wanted this to just go away."

"What did you do?"

"I investigated anyway," Beppe said. "Silvestri was already a big influence in two thousand eight. He threw these gigantic parties, with businessmen, politicians, celebrities. I knew I needed ironclad proof. But the more I investigated, the more resistance I got."

"It's hard without the support of your team," Valerio observed.

Beppe nodded. "I kept going. Kept pushing. Then, suddenly, I was accused of soliciting bribes. The charges were bullshit, but I was suspended while internal affairs investigated. Eventually they cleared me. But by then, little Felicia had taken her own life."

Beppe stopped, and pressed his lips together, then shook his head, and began scratching something off the table with his thumbnail.

"After that, there was no case against Silvestri," he continued. "Agnese and her mother closed the shop and moved north."

Valerio took a slow breath, holding down the sick feeling in his gut.

"Did you ever see any connections between Paride Silvestri and Luca Errichiello?"

Beppe seemed to think.

"There are similarities," he admitted. "Although Silvestri is considered a legitimate businessman—and everyone knows that Errichiello isn't. Both men seem to be involved in human trafficking. And both are untouchable. I can't remember a single case that's ever stuck on either of them. Can you?"

Valerio shook his head. "They're well protected."

"Not just that," said Beppe. "Impenetrable. Think about the biggest Camorra capos we've seen. There's always a chink somewhere: a prosecutor willing to take the risk, someone willing to testify. But with these two? Nothing. Silence."

Valerio agreed. "It's been almost twenty years since Agnese came forward and, as far as I know, Silvestri hasn't been investigated since. If he's still doing this, we'll find a lot more victims."

Beppe cautioned him.

"If you choose to investigate, keep it to yourself," he said. "Be careful who you trust. You could get burned."

It took Valerio the rest of the afternoon to shake off the nausea and disgust from what Beppe had told him.

The shadows were lengthening by the time he met Maurizio at the storefront kebab shop. Maurizio had invited him to his house but Valerio was too tired to deal with Maurizio's wife. She always wanted to know what was happening and participate in the conversations. He wasn't in the mood to argue with her.

As they ate greasy meat wraps at the plastic outdoor tables, Valerio recounted his visit to Silvestri's villa and his conversation with Beppe.

Maurizio gave a low whistle.

"You don't get into the normal sort of trouble, do you?" he said. "It's not enough to be in deep with Errichiello—you have to go looking for problems with Silvestri, too? If Beppe couldn't make a case stick against him, what makes you think you can?"

"Beppe didn't have the connection between Errichiello and Silvestri," Valerio said. "I didn't expect to find a connection either. There was just that one photo in Ines's house. I went to Silvestri because I didn't have a better plan. But now, I'm sure they're working together. Why else would Errichiello's head of security be at Silvestri's villa?"

He passed Maurizio the bag containing the surveillance gear.

"Would you run these plates for me?" he asked. "I'd do it, but I don't want to get into a fight with Bonetti about this administrative leave. If Beppe's right, I can't afford to attract attention. Also, can you run a facial recognition search on our white-haired friend? First name's Ivan. It would be good to get a full name and profile."

Maurizio took the bag. He looked worn out.

"I have a bad feeling about this," he said. "I don't like you pinning your hopes on a decades-old complaint against a billionaire. Even if there's a connection between Silvestri and Errichiello, it would take months—maybe years—to investigate. And you need a whole team working it. You're not some lone wolf."

"I don't have that kind of time," said Valerio. "And I don't need a full case against them . . . just enough to make him back down."

Maurizio shook his head. "Valerio—"

"Think about Gaetano," Valerio cut in. "He knew something important. That's why Errichiello killed him. I need to find out what it was. Silvestri's my only lead. Gaetano's girlfriend said that Gaetano used to drive women to exclusive parties in Sorrento. If I can confirm those parties were at Silvestri's villa, I know where to look next."

"Gaetano's dead for what he knew," Maurizio argued. "I don't see this helping you. And I don't want you to get killed."

Valerio opened his hands, and looked at his palms.

"I'm between the hammer and the anvil," he said. "If I wait . . . if I do nothing, Errichiello will force me. I need to find some way to push back before he gets his hooks in all the way. I have to try."

Valerio felt unprepared for his meeting with Maria. He'd intended to look the part of a sugar daddy, had showered and given himself a careful shave, but his clothing options were abysmal. His daily work required him to be inconspicuous—which usually meant sneakers, T-shirts, and hoodies. Besides, Gemma and Davide had taken his spare cash, and he hadn't bought new clothes for years. He had a decent pair of trousers that were only slightly too tight, and he could put some polish on his shoes, but he needed a shirt. Everything he owned was ugly—out of fashion, too small, or stained.

He considered asking Maurizio, but his partner was too thin. Then he thought of Dario, who always wore nice clothes. Also, Dario's proportions were closer to his own—with generous allowances to fit a comfortable belly.

Valerio called Point Break. Graziella answered.

She chuckled when he explained the problem.

"Come on over," she said. "Dario's a fashion fanatic, and I need an excuse to empty the closet."

He tried on seven shirts before finding one that met with Graziella's approval—dark pink, with a nice collar, and smelling of Dario's cologne.

She declared him "handsome" and "totally fuckable," which, alone with the pregnant Graziella in the intimacy of Dario's living room, both pleased and embarrassed him.

"Keep it," Graziella urged. "He'll never miss it."

The evening was cool and dry. Maria was nearly a half hour late.

Valerio waited outside the trattoria. Standing still, the city sounds wrapped around him like a blanket. He was exhausted, head pounding. He wanted to sit. No—he wanted to lie down right here on the cobblestones and take a nap.

He called Ravenna.

"Just compliment her," she reminded him. "She isn't looking for a partner—she wants a lapdog. She'll relax when she thinks she can control you."

Maria arrived like a fashion model—slender legs flashing, hips swaying, tanned and toned skin radiant in the glowing streetlights. He kissed her cheeks, inhaling the candy smell of her perfume. He was honest when he called her "bella."

The restaurant had been Ravenna's idea; she knew the owner and he'd saved a good table in an intimate corner, away from the bustle.

When they were seated and had ordered wine, Maria tilted her head, gazing from beneath a thick fringe of eyelashes, lips pouting. She traced a finger along the glass.

"I was very angry with you," she said.

"Yeah," Valerio agreed, suddenly warm with humiliation, remembering the text Ravenna had sent in his name: *Punish me.*

"I made a mistake," he said. "You're a very beautiful woman. . . . I should have appreciated you—treated you better."

Maria seemed uncertain.

Valerio knew he looked tired, and what he'd intended as a passionate plea sounded perfunctory. Wooden.

He felt absurd—sitting here, pretending to flirt, while he tipped with pain and fatigue, and while Luca and his thugs were preparing their next attack. He didn't know how to be the actor this situation demanded. Maria wanted the safety and comfort of a rich man, but he'd arrived in a borrowed shirt, unsure how he'd afford the dinner bill.

She blinked slowly and smiled.

Be a lapdog, Ravenna had said.

Valerio took a slurp of wine.

"So how does this work?" he asked. "I've never been a sugar daddy before."

Maria slid her hand across the table, and stroked his palm.

"I give you what you need and you give me what I need," she said. "Recurring wire transfers are best—so neither of us needs to think about it. That's it. You message me when you want to meet—and I'm all yours."

What must it be like for a man to have that kind of money, to escape the constant danger biting at your back, to stride confidently through the world, owning anything—anyone—you wanted?

"You make it sound easy," he said.

"It should be easy," she said warmly. "This is about prioritizing pleasure."

Valerio kissed her fingertips, and smiled.

The food was delicious and, he noted with relief, at a manageable price. Yet the atmosphere was sophisticated enough to satisfy Maria, and she found a meal to suit her special preferences.

As he ate spaghetti ai frutti di mare, Valerio regretted stuffing himself on kebab wraps earlier.

"Is there anything you'd like to know about me?" he asked.

"I'd love to know about your boat," she said.

Valerio considered lying—making *Calypso* larger and grander than she was. But he was proud of the little 9.5-meter Balanzone that he and Nikki had restored. He described sourcing the materials, repairing the hull and engine, bringing the decaying sailboat back to life.

To his surprise, Maria seemed genuinely interested. She asked the right questions and laughed at some of his stories.

"So much work!" she exclaimed.

A heat of pride rose to Valerio's cheeks.

"Well, it was Nikki, too," he conceded with a grin. "Stubborn little devil. She thinks she can save the world. You should meet her sometime. You'd like her. Once you get past her crusty exterior, she's a sweetheart."

Maria pouted. "Should I be jealous?"

Valerio chuckled. "She's just a friend."

He hadn't intended to mention Nikki at all. But talking about her made him aware that he'd bought into this illusion, blurring reality and fantasy.

What would Nikki think if she saw him playing this charade, lying, pretending? He imagined the disapproval on her face. She was the most honest person he'd ever known. She would urge him to tell the truth.

Now that Maria was comfortable, the conversation flowing, Valerio turned his attention to the real reason he was here.

"I'd love to know more about you. May I ask something personal?"

Maria hesitated. "Alright."

He lowered his voice. "What made you decide to become a sugar baby?"

She smiled, and tucked a strand of hair behind her ear. "It's a very boring story."

"I want to know everything about you," he said earnestly.

Her expression didn't change, but for the briefest moment, something flickered behind her eyes.

"I started modeling when I was twelve," she said. "It was a great opportunity. The agency flew me out to exotic locations. And models are always invited to parties. That's where I met my first daddy."

He nodded, biting the inside of his cheek to stop himself asking where her parents had been.

"Do you still go to these parties?" he asked. "Should I worry about someone stealing you away?"

"You should always be worried," she said with a seductive smile.

"So, tell me about this lucky guy."

"Oh." She brushed her hand through the air. "Ancient history."

He chuckled. "C'mon! Who was he?"

"His name was Alfeo. A big-shot lawyer."

"Lucky bastard!" Valerio exclaimed. "So this big-shot lawyer meets a beautiful woman at a party. He says the right thing, and wins you over. How long were you together?"

She shrugged and smiled. "Three years. We broke it off when I was sixteen."

"What the fuck?"

He hadn't meant to say it. The math hit him too fast.

Maria's face turned suddenly blank and he knew he'd made a terrible mistake.

He reached for her hand—but her fingers were limp and cold. He released his grip.

"I'm sorry," he said. "I'm not judging you. It's just . . . thirteen is so young. You must have been frightened. No child should . . . I just don't like to think about you being treated like that."

He meant it. His churning rage was for the sick motherfucker who had done this to her. He wanted to kick the bastard's teeth in.

She stared at her plate. Her breathing was shallow, rapid.

"Are you okay?" he asked.

Without looking up, she reached out and entwined her fingers in his.

"You have very nice hands," she said, voice flat. "You can tell a lot about a man from his hands."

She shifted and pulled away, and her hand fell heavily into her lap.

Then she glanced up. The look of grief was both far younger and far older than belonged on that face. It sent a shiver of sadness through Valerio.

"You aren't going to be my sugar daddy, are you?" she said.

Valerio shook his head. "No."

"I'm not what you want?"

"It isn't that," said Valerio. "You're amazing. Incredible. But I could never afford you. And . . . I'm a cop."

He continued carefully: "I catch and punish men who abuse thirteen-year-old girls, and try to call it a 'relationship.' Do you understand what I'm saying?"

He watched as realization settled.

"I understand that you lied to me," she said.

"Yes. And I'm sorry."

Maria nodded and sat back, staring at him.

The waiter appeared. Valerio shooed him away.

Maria's voice was suddenly sharp. "Why bring me here? Why lie to me? What do you want?"

Valerio met her gaze. "I want to stop them."

She flinched.

"I want to find out who these men are," he said. "I want to learn how they operate—so I can stop them hurting kids. I was hoping you could help me."

"It's my choice." Her voice was louder now, slack expression starting to reanimate. "How I choose to live my life is my decision."

"You've found a way to survive what happened to you," he said carefully. "You must be very strong. But it wasn't your choice when you were thirteen, was it?"

She glared.

"This is still happening, isn't it?" he pressed. "To other little girls."

No response.

"Can I ask you some questions?" he asked.

She shook her head. "It won't matter what I tell you," she said. "Or what you do."

"Why not?"

"Because you can't stop them."

"What makes you say that?"

Her words were bitter. "Because the men at those parties? They're like Alfeo. Lawyers. Politicians. Police. Celebrities. Businessmen. They're powerful. What do you think you can do? Arrest them?"

"Everyone has a weakness," said Valerio. "I just need to find it."

She studied him for a long moment. Then she pushed back from the table and stood.

"I can't think," she said. "Not here."

Valerio stood, too.

"May I come with you?" he asked.

She hesitated. Then nodded.

He signaled the waiter for the bill.

Outside, the air was crisp and cool.

Tense, agitated, wordlessly, Maria set a fast pace, heels clipping on the cobblestones.

Valerio let her lead, moving silently alongside.

Now that he knew what she was—what had happened to her—he saw the child in the woman. He understood the little details he'd noticed in their first meeting: the vulnerability, the polished aura of sophistication masking her fear.

She needed respect and care.

She needed to be in control right now.

He let her have that control.

For fifteen minutes, they strode wordlessly through the crowded streets of the city. Then her pace slowed and she gradually came to a stop. Her arms hung limply at her sides, and she swayed. Valerio worried she might collapse.

She turned towards him, but her gaze averted as she spoke.

"Other girls had it worse." The words came haltingly. "Alfeo wasn't so bad . . . but some of the other men could get rough."

"At the parties?"

"Yes. And . . . afterwards."

"These men—the important ones. Do you know who they are? Do you have names?"

She exhaled. "I know they were important and rich, because Alfeo used to talk about them. They never use last names, but I know their first names. And I've seen some of them on television."

"Were they local?"

"Most were Italian," she said. "But from other places, too. English, American, French, German, Russian . . . Spanish."

"I'd like to take you to the station," Valerio said. "Show you some photos, get your testimony on record—"

"No!"

The word was loud. Her eyes darted up to his—wide and full of anxiety. She shook her head and took a step back.

"No problem," Valerio said, raising his palms. "It's just you and me. Shall we find a place to sit?"

He scanned the street. He wanted to take her someplace warm, but was worried that having other people nearby would spook her. He pointed at a nearby café with outdoor seating—all empty, the chill having driven everyone indoors.

Maria pulled her wool coat around her, but she was shivering as he ushered her into a chair. Valerio gave her his scarf and she wrapped it around her neck. Then he took out his phone and placed it on the table between them.

"May I record this?" he said. "I've had a few glasses, and I don't want to forget anything you tell me."

She seemed to think about this for a moment, and then nodded.

"Allora," he said. "Tell me about the parties."

She stared at the tabletop. "They were beautiful, you know? Everything so sophisticated. Expensive. They gave us beautiful clothes, picked us up in nice cars. You could have whatever you wanted: wine, drugs, whatever. There was a part of me . . . that liked it. But the rest . . ."

She shuddered.

"Were the parties sexual?" Valerio asked.

"Not always," she said. "There were two sides, you know? One side was . . . glamorous—with the celebrities—everybody there for a good time. We were part of the decoration. But even at those parties, we always knew . . ."

"Knew what?" he urged.

"That anybody could pick us—take us into one of the rooms in the back. That we had to go along with it."

Valerio's throat was tight. "How did they force you?"

She looked past him, watching the street. "They didn't. It was just . . . you just had to."

"I don't understand," he said.

She sighed. "It isn't easy to explain. When I was little, things were hard. My father lost his job, and Mamma was sick and couldn't work either. I had four younger brothers. We were always hungry. At school, I was clever and got good grades, but my parents wanted me to quit, and go to work. One day, this older girl at school—Paola—she told me that she knew how I could make money. She took me to this place in the city—to this woman. The woman asked a lot of questions, then she drove me to this huge house in Sorrento to meet this man. He told me I was pretty enough to be a model. He had me take off my clothes so he could be sure."

Valerio was cold.

"He didn't touch me," Maria continued. "Just looked. Then he gave me two fifty-euro bills and said I was hired."

"How old were you?"

Her fingers gripped the scarf.

"Eleven. Almost twelve."

Valerio's chest was tight with anxiety. With fury. He tried to inhale, but the air didn't seem able to come in.

"It was the most money I'd ever had," she said. "It was like that. As long as we did what they wanted, they were nice. They gave us money, food. Sometimes drugs. They told us how lucky we were to be able to meet important people. We needed to do what the clients expected, and be cheerful about it. If we brought another girl in, we got a bonus. If you refused a client, the agency dropped you. We were all worried about losing our place—about being one of those girls."

Until now, her voice had been steady. She recounted these details factually, almost without affect. Now, her voice began to shake. Valerio felt an impulse to reach out and comfort her, but didn't want to stop her confession.

She continued: "I met Alfeo at a party. He wanted me exclusively. He made an arrangement. Then he paid for a place for me, and gave me spending money. At the parties, everyone knew I was his—so they left me alone."

When he was sure she'd finished, Valerio said slowly, "You were too young to make those decisions. You understand that, don't you? You should have been protected."

She squeezed her eyes shut. When she opened them, a grimace of agony painted her expression.

"I brought other girls to them," she said in a whisper, face turned away. "I was getting too old. They wanted younger girls. I knew what would happen to them, but I did it anyway."

Valerio fought back a crashing wave of nausea. He clenched his teeth and breathed through it.

"It's very brave of you to tell me this," he said.

She didn't speak for a long moment. She stared at the lights of a nearby restaurant.

At last, with a shuddering breath, she looked at him, fresh anger in her face. "What will you do?"

"I'm going to find the people who did this to you," he said. "I'm going to stop them. But I need you to tell me every name you know."

She nodded.

"Can you tell me the name of the man who made you undress that first time?" he asked.

She glanced to the end of the street. "That was Paride Silvestri. You can look him up. He's very rich. Very powerful."

Valerio kept his face blank, but the confirmation of the man's name dropped into place like a stone in his mind.

"And the woman who was helping him. What was her name?"

"I only know her first name: Ines."

NINETEEN

Nikki's phone was ringing. She hunted for it in the dark and checked the time: 06:30.

Consciousness brought pain.

Touching her bruised windpipe, she rasped out a difficult "Hello."

Her father's voice boomed: "Ciao, bella!"

It was like her childhood when he would bound, singing, into her bedroom in the predawn hours, flipping on the lights.

Nikki groaned.

"Did I wake you?" he asked.

"Yes."

"Izzy tells me Preston's awake. How is he?"

"Better than they'd hoped," she said.

She recounted what the doctors had said.

"Good, good," he said. "When are you coming back?"

"Tomorrow morning. I'm on duty in the afternoon."

"I'm at your place," he told her. "I can get in through the gate but my key for your door isn't working."

"What are you doing at my flat?"

He coughed, and made that little humming noise he used whenever he didn't want to explain himself. "I don't want to bother you. . . . I'm looking for something your mother may have left behind."

Until the flat was bequeathed to Nikki last year, her mother had owned the place for decades. There were still boxes, and cabinets full of papers and files Nikki hadn't taken time to sort through yet.

"I changed the locks," she said.

She'd never told her father about the home invasion that had necessitated this. Her mind flexed as that memory merged with the immediacy of Teddy's attack last night, triggering tension and filling her mouth with the tang of fear.

She sat, and felt for the light switch, squinting in the sudden glare.

"Oh." He sounded deflated.

He was silent a long moment.

"What do you need?" she asked.

"If you don't have the key for me, you don't have the key," he said, sounding irritable. "Fine. You should give Massimo a copy, though. He's watched over this place for decades. A man can be offended when he gives such loyalty and you shut him out!"

Nikki sighed.

"Valerio has the spare," she told him. "You can always give him a call."

He hummed again, the sound of deliberation.

"You'll be back tomorrow?" he said. "I'll come tomorrow."

Unable to recapture sleep, Nikki stomped to the toilet and then to the kitchen.

Tension and aggravation twitched through her body, and she wished she could work into her punching bag.

Izzy and Preston's home, usually tidy and welcoming, needed cleaning: dishes stacked in the sink, books and papers on tables and chairs. Nikki made coffee, set the porridge on to cook, chopped an apple, then cleared a space on the table and sat.

While the coffee brewed, she iced her throat and worked from her phone, writing an email to her students about the fire in the studio. Classes were canceled until she could find another location.

On Instagram, Sally had accepted her follow request.

Nikki typed a private message: **You told me about Claire's blog last night. Can you share a link?**

Sally wrote back immediately: **What did you do? Teddy is fuming about you.**

Nikki exhaled, throat suddenly tighter. She didn't answer.

Sally wrote, **Seriously. He thinks you're a supervillain. He's trying to find out everything about you.**

She sent a photo from the memorial where Nikki and Sally could be seen seated at a table together. Then a series of screenshots from a group chat where Teddy called her a "stalker bitch" and demanded information about her.

What did you tell him? Nikki asked.

As a security investigator, Nikki had careful social media practices; her accounts gave no clues to her actual identity. She was grateful for these protections now, although she didn't remember if she'd shared her full name.

Sally's response came almost immediately: **Don't know anything, do I? Who are you? I won't tell.**

Distrusting the proffered discretion, Nikki wrote, **a friend.**

She texted Izzy, asking if she needed anything from the house, then sipped coffee and ate, thumbing through the sparse notes from last night. Her brain was sluggish: a heavy press of ennui dulling her sharp edges.

The notes from her conversation with Teddy were especially unsatisfying. This annoyed her. Nikki thought about it for a few minutes, then searched her phone for a contact she hadn't used in a long time. It was doubtful the number worked after all these years, but she tried anyway.

Hi Ethan. It's Nikki, she texted. **Back in London for the day. Need your help with something.**

A few minutes passed before he wrote back: **Good god! Nikki! Haven't seen your name for an age. I take it you've joined the Foreign Legion, or started a cult. Would I say no to you?**

Nikki smiled, and told him what she needed.

It was nearly 08:00. She did the dishes, swept and wiped down the kitchen, showered, dressed, and headed out the door.

On her way to the station, Nikki's phone rang.

Not recognizing the number, she answered in Italian. "Who is this?"

"Hello," a male voice said in English. "This is Mac van den Berg . . . from Friday night. I think I made a bad impression. I'd like a chance to start over."

"How did you get this number?"

"Gianni gave it to me."

Nikki exhaled, hands flexing. Gianni had never respected her privacy. "I'm in the middle of something. So, whatever this is . . ."

"I know," said Mac. "Your uncle. London. Sorry about that."

"Gianni's sharing a lot," Nikki snapped.

"Oh, you shouldn't blame your brother," he said with a jovial chuckle. "I work in intel, remember? I have ways to get what I need."

Nikki stopped walking, irritation transforming into anger.

"Is that supposed to be a joke?" she said.

"This is what I do."

"What the fuck?" The words exploded. "Are you monitoring me? You think this makes me trust you?"

"I'm not asking you to trust me," Mac said. "Listen . . . I want to ask you something. Professionally. You're a security investigator. You track threats. You understand Naples. You know how power shifts when certain people are . . . out of the picture."

He paused, then coughed.

"If you have something to say, say it," she said.

"I just think sometimes . . ." He breathed heavily. "We're so sure we know the game, we forget to ask who benefits when a piece is removed . . . from the board."

The words, thick with implication, fed Nikki's anger. "What the fuck are you talking about? Is that a threat?"

He laughed. "No, no! God, no. Just an observation."

"I'm hanging up," she told him.

"If I needed to find someone," he wheedled, "someone *powerful* . . . where would you say I should start?"

"Not my problem."

She hung up.

Back in the hospital, Preston was serenading Izzy.

Nikki heard his voice as she walked the corridor to his room, a crooning love song she didn't recognize.

"This is the love of my life," he announced to Nikki when she came into view.

Izzy was by Preston's bedside, holding his hand in both of hers: tired but happy. Preston's expression was an ecstasy of love, his white hair spread across the pillow like the wisping tendrils of an undersea plant.

"How are you feeling?" Nikki asked.

He chuckled. "Feels like I fell down the stairs. Brain's a bit mushy. If you quizzed me, I'm sure I couldn't tell my Tacitus from my Pliny."

"I know the difference," said Izzy. "I put arthritis cream on your Tacitus every morning!"

They were like children, cackling and hooting in laughter.

About an hour later, a nurse came to take Preston for another scan, and Nikki walked Izzy to the hospital canteen.

The tea scalded Nikki's mouth.

Izzy didn't drink. Instead, she stared, fingers flitting around the edges of the paper cup.

"Preston and I have been together four decades," she said with a sigh. "You'd think that was enough time. That I should count myself lucky. But I'm selfish. I want more. He has good days—I live for those. And even on the bad days, he still remembers how much he loves me."

Izzy reached across the table and took Nikki's hand in both of hers.

"I'm so sorry about Enzo. Is it too soon? May I ask . . . is there anyone else?"

The words were ice, pressing into Nikki.

Izzy continued, squeezing her hand. "I do want someone for you, sweetheart. To have something of what I've had."

To love like that, you needed trust and openness. Those didn't exist for Nikki anymore. In their place, she found the aching echo of a dark cave, the choking black smoke of a building ablaze.

She implicitly understood the dimensions of the loss—as if a vital organ had been cut from her body, the pain of severed nerves to tell her where it should have been.

Pressure built in her chest; her heartbeat ached against it. She wanted to bolt.

"Oh, I'm a nosy old woman," Izzy said, releasing her hand with a pat. "You don't need to tell me anything."

They spent the next few minutes discussing Izzy's plans for moving Preston's rehabilitation. Nikki had researched a few options online, and tried to get her aunt to consider different scenarios—in case Preston didn't recover as quickly as Izzy hoped. But with the immediate danger passed, her aunt didn't seem interested in revisiting the fear of the past two days.

"You're so much like your mother," said Izzy, her gaze soft. "If you could only see how alike you two are."

"That's a nice way of saying irrationally stubborn," Nikki said.

Izzy laughed.

"No. I mean—practical, logistical. And clever enough to bury the pain. Clever enough to distract us. To keep us from the truth. Beatrice hid inside her games, her intrigues . . . so that we wouldn't see her grieve."

"I saw her grieve," Nikki said.

She would never forget the howling, the rage, the fierce isolation.

If the devil doesn't exist, but man has created him, he has created him in his own image and likeness!

"Too late, the dam finally broke," Izzy said. "It had to, didn't it? And when she lost Adriano . . . oh, Adriano. Beautiful boy!"

Her eyelids fluttered and closed, her right hand moving in the air as if to music, before coming to rest on her heart. She stayed like that for several breaths, then shook her head.

Her eyes glistened as she examined her cup.

"Beatrice always covered her pain," she said. "Always. You know, she was only seven when our mother left."

Nikki nodded. She'd heard the story. As a child it induced terror to realize that a mother could simply walk away from her children and never return.

"I was four years old. I cried for days," Izzy continued. "But Beatrice seemed to switch off. She was a Stoic. I think she was trying to protect me. She invented a secret language just for us, so our father wouldn't know what we were saying."

The secret language of Beatrice and Izzy had forever infuriated the young Nikki.

"She taught Adriano," Nikki said. "But she wouldn't teach Gianni or me. We went crazy, trying to figure it out."

"Of course I can teach you—it isn't that complicated." Izzy gave a sad smile. "That was your mother: a different language for each person in her life. She and I wrote all our letters in code. Never stopped. It got me into trouble once—in the nineteen eighties. In Prague. I was going to perform Rachmaninoff. They were inspecting my luggage and found a letter from Beatrice. Fortunately, it wasn't the nuclear launch codes. Just an update on you kids."

Izzy chuckled.

Nikki's relationship with her mother felt unfinished, as if she'd saved her thoughts and questions for some later time, when the wounds had healed and each could finally be what the other needed. That moment never arrived.

"When Durant said Mom was something special," Nikki said, "do you think it had anything to do with languages and codes—her cryptology job in the navy?"

"I wish I knew," Izzy said with a sigh. "Oh, but she had a gift for languages! Always brilliant at French and mathematics. I remember when Beatrice became fascinated by the Cyrillic alphabet. One of our father's colleagues was an expat from Moscow—helped her learn Russian. Set her up with a pen pal: his nephew in the USSR. I was so jealous whenever she got one of those letters—the thin paper and those stamps! Of course, with McCarthy and the Red Scare, it wasn't the best time to be friends with a Russian. But they were just kids."

She sipped her tea. "Oh, it's gone cold."

They made their way back up to Preston's room and were there when he returned from his scan. He'd shed his earlier exuberance, but gave a tired smile.

"You both look so concerned," he said. "'There is nothing either good or bad, but thinking makes it so.'"

After his rally, his energy and attention faded and he slept. A woman from social services visited and discussed his move to a rehabilitation facility.

At Nikki's urging, Izzy took a cab home for a rest and shower.

At 15:45, Nikki received a text from Ethan with the name and address of a restaurant. He wrote, **I've done your bidding, she-who-must-not-be-resisted. Eight-o-clock.**

By the time Izzy returned to the hospital, Preston was awake again, although more confused than before. He'd become suspicious and hostile towards Nikki, and seemed relieved to have Izzy back in the room.

"Have fun with Ethan," Izzy told her, hugging goodbye.

Nikki spotted Ethan across the restaurant. As she wended her way through the tables and chairs, he stood and, in a typically Ethan gesture of welcome, opened his arms wide.

He was tall and blond, with the muscular build of a Viking, and the confident energy of a drag queen. Today he was dressed in a tailored shirt and navy blazer with shining brass buttons, accented with an expensively understated silk scarf, a look he'd christened on social media as his "corporate fuck-boy" ensemble.

"Let's look at you," he said after their customary air-kisses.

In contradiction to his conservative upbringing, Ethan was a self-proclaimed huggy person, yet he'd always seemed intuitively respectful of Nikki's aversion to being touched. That he remembered now was strangely moving.

"You're looking delectable, as always," he said. "That haircut—so chic. Suits you with those luscious 'come hither' eyes."

"You're looking well, too."

She experienced a bittersweet wave of homesickness for that familiar face—the sparkling blue eyes, rough-hewn features, and slightly crooked nose. His hair, now decidedly turning grey, had receded into a swooping widow's peak.

Nikki had met Ethan more than a decade ago at a bar in Camden after she'd broken up with her then-boyfriend and didn't want to move back in with Izzy and Preston. They'd hit it off, and he'd offered to rent her the spare room in his flat. Back then, he was a party boy with the persona of a sexy vampire, and a fondness for illicit delights. The flat had been a revolving door of decadent personalities.

In spite of their vastly different tastes, Ethan supported Nikki's discipline—her daily gym sessions, and her Krav Maga training. In fact, it was Ethan who had set her up with her first job as a bouncer, enthusiastically recommending her to an ex-boyfriend who owned a club.

Ethan, too, had his own brand of discipline. He'd taken a First in economics at Oxford, his framed degree displayed ironically in their living room while he enjoyed what he called his *dissolute life*.

"Do you like my costume?" he said when they were seated. "Lestat gone undercover into sun-drenched respectability. I'd never survive if I took myself seriously."

"Working for *the man*, now," Nikki noted with a grin. "Your father would be so proud."

He sighed. "Alas, he is. Insufferable. I'd rebel, but the money's so damned convenient."

She picked up the menu. He put his hand gently over it.

"Don't even think about it. The chef is a friend. He's preparing something special for you."

He knew the waiter by name, an attractive twentysomething who served them water and prosecco and, in the next hour, brought out a series of vegetarian dishes, each more artful and delicious than the last: beetroot tartare, wild mushroom consommé, saffron-infused cauliflower panna cotta, artichoke and barley risotto. Ethan seemed pleased by Nikki's appreciation of the meal, regaled her with tales of his latest romantic escapades, and gently pried for details into her life.

Nikki, who was usually reticent discussing private matters, found herself telling Ethan about her job and family. But it was when she told him of Enzo's betrayal with Carmela, about the marriage proposal, and the man Enzo hired to attack her—Ethan's outrage flared. He unleashed a dazzling stream of creative insults, and suggested methods of appropriate revenge. His excess of emotion filled a hollow Nikki hadn't realized was there, an ache eased by his indignation.

Only when the plates were cleared, when the chef came out for their compliments, and coffee was served, did Ethan lean in, lowering his voice.

"I was intrigued by your cloak-and-dagger request," he murmured. "Nothing from Signorina Serafino for years. Then, suddenly, *I'm in London*, and *I need research*."

"Did you do it?"

"Amateur, am I? Perish the thought. I devoted the day to lurking in the finest clubs on your behalf."

Nikki grinned. "Don't keep me in suspense!"

He smiled and reached into his satchel, taking out a slim laptop and setting it on the table.

"Theodore Sexton," he started, scrolling through his findings. "Well connected, easy on the eyes, not entirely dim. Educated at Eton. Post-education, he's been remarkably unremarkable. Two years ago, Mister Sexton started an app: *Innovare MindCapsule*. Leveraged his connections for a bit of press—but no investors. I managed to secure a copy of the pitch deck."

He showed her the company formation documents for Innovare MindCapsule, which listed F. Deliso as the company's legal representative, and K. Walker as a founding partner. Then he flipped through a set of slides Nikki recognized from the Innovare MindCapsule website.

"Essentially," Ethan continued, "MindCapsule is a rather pedestrian attempt to capitalize on the pretentious personal-growth industry. Sexton pitched it to every VC firm in London. No one bit. And now? He's positively drowning in debt. A dreadful investment from the outset, but he kept pouring money in. And—surprise, surprise—he doesn't seem particularly inclined to roll up his sleeves for honest work."

Nikki nodded. In the uncomfortable brightness of the day after, she recalled there had been something about Teddy—a certain slippery sleight of hand that reminded her of her brother.

"This is very helpful," she said. "Were you able to find any connection with Jayston Lake?"

Ethan shook his head. "None whatsoever, I'm afraid. They move in entirely different spheres. Sexton did present MindCapsule to Lake's investment firm, but didn't clear the initial gatekeepers."

"What did you find out about Jayston Lake?"

Ethan blinked.

"Are you quite serious?" He let out a delighted laugh, then looked rapidly chastened. "Oh, you are!"

He composed himself. "Darling," he said. "You hardly need a clandestine investigation to uncover the affairs of Jayston and Fiona Lake. A glance at the tabloids should suffice."

"Even if I did read all the gossip columns," Nikki encouraged, "I couldn't see everything you see."

Ethan looked pleased.

"Very well, since you ask nicely, I'll spoon-feed you." He settled back. "Jayston's a media darling. Has been for ages. Simply gorgeous man, and shrouded in tragedy. Parents died in a plane crash when he was young—very sad, but it left him comfortably provided for. He ignored the lawyers and rapacious investment sharks, and charted his own course. Rode the dot-com boom to the top. Billionaire now, I understand."

"What do you think about him, personally?"

"I suppose I could tolerate his presence until breakfast."

"You think he's a good man?"

He smiled lasciviously. "Well, I wouldn't find him remotely intriguing if there weren't a whiff of naughty."

"Tell me about his wife," Nikki said.

"Ah, Fiona Cecil," he said. "The second Mrs. Lake. Jayston's first wife perished in a car accident—another tragedy for our ill-fated

Jayston. Fiona's old money. Always been rather . . . colorful, shall we say? Parties. Drugs. She did attempt to straighten up, but then tragedy struck again. Their son, Matthew. Drowned last year. There was an inquiry, and the press eviscerated her. Turned out that she'd been indulging in a tipple or two. Dreadful business, though officially ruled an accident."

He raised an eyebrow. "So, now that I've been a good little boy and given you everything you asked for, you must feed my insatiable appetite. Pray tell: What is your interest in Jayston Lake?"

Nikki considered for a long moment. If Claire's murder and her connection to the Lakes had already reached the tabloids, she would want Ethan's take. But there had been no press. This meant the Lakes—and the police—were keeping it quiet.

"I'm sorry," she said. "I can't talk about it."

He looked crestfallen.

"As soon as I'm able to discuss it," she promised, "you'll be the first to know."

TWENTY

Valerio stood beside his motorbike at the Capodichino airport pickup curb, his usual calm displaced by a restless energy and rare scowl. He greeted Nikki and kissed her cheeks. His whiskers scratched her, and she caught the sour waft of old wine.

"Ciao, bella," he said. "How's your uncle?"

"Better. What's up? What didn't you want to tell me on the phone?"

He handed her a helmet.

"Not here."

The air was warmer and more humid than in London, an intermittent drizzle flicking against them as Valerio navigated through the chaotic roar of morning traffic, down the steep streets into the city below. Nikki gripped onto him, rucksack slamming against her back as they jostled over paving stones, dodging vehicles and pedestrians. Valerio was one of the few people whose driving Nikki could tolerate. He was just as enterprising as every other Neapolitan motorist, but he handled the bike capably, and Nikki relaxed into the movement.

It had been strangely difficult to leave Izzy and Preston in the hospital. She had the sense of pressed flowers—every color and delicate fold carefully preserved, translucent, desperately fragile. Not one for sentimentality, Nikki had nonetheless experienced a pang of anxiety as they waved her out of sight.

Izzy had insisted, with a smile, "Oh, don't worry about us."

Nikki considered her aunt. The burden of Preston grew weightier every day, but she couldn't lift any part of this when Izzy made it clear she wanted to carry it alone.

Crowds thickened, slowing their progress as they approached Nikki's flat in the city's historic center. With several blocks to go, Valerio pulled up to the curb. Nikki dismounted and, removing her helmet, turned to say goodbye. But Valerio switched off the motor and took off his helmet, too—clearly intending to come with her.

Business had resumed in the busy Gesù Nuovo piazza, the sellers' stalls in their usual places: one hawking jewelry, another ceramic tiles, another black Pulcinella masks and dangling cornicelli. Beside these was an army vehicle in green camo and two uniformed soldiers cradling assault rifles.

The church doors were open again. Tourists joined the faithful in their slow march inside.

At the base of the Guglia dell'Immacolata, set against the iron railing, a makeshift shrine had formed, filled with handwritten notes, and carnations wrapped in cellophane. Assuming this was for Claire, Nikki drew near. But the framed photograph at the center showed a different young woman: large eyes outlined in kohl, and bleached curls.

Nikki stared for several seconds before recognizing Signora Dorotea—at least three decades out of date.

She paused, and whistled sharply for Valerio, who was bulldozing through the mob.

A plump woman with an umbrella stood at the shrine. She set a bundle of carnations on the ground, crossed herself, then pivoted to the church and crossed herself again.

"What happened here?" Nikki asked.

The woman turned. A scarf was wrapped tightly around her head, showing a broad face and arched eyebrows penciled into an expression of surprise.

"Signora Dorotea. God rest her soul."

"The fortune teller?"

"Sì," said the woman. "She had the sight. Assisto. Guided by the souls of the dead. She interpreted my dreams, and gave me my numbers."

"What happened?" Nikki asked.

The woman crossed herself again—a motion that seemed more compulsive than religious. "You haven't heard?"

"No."

"A robbery. In her home. They killed her."

Nikki's pulse quickened. Not even a week had passed since Claire's murder. A dreadful coincidence—if that's what it was.

"When was this?"

"Sunday. Pray for her soul."

The woman hurried off.

The memory of Signora Dorotea felt strangely present: the garish orange scarf and fierce eyes, the lipstick leaching into the crevices around her lips, and cool chapped skin as she gripped Nikki's hand.

Valerio had returned to Nikki's side and was following her gaze to the memorial shrine.

"Who was it?" he asked.

Nikki seemed to sense something hidden; some pattern of shadows she should be able to decipher if she looked carefully. She glanced from the shrine to the grey facade of the church, where her mother had once seemed to see a secret message. Her skin prickled with a sudden chill.

"Fortune teller," she said. "Murdered."

When they arrived at Nikki's house, Valerio diverted to the kitchen and began making coffee.

"Don't you need to get back to work?" Nikki called from the back room, where she was changing.

"I'm on leave," he shouted back. "Where are your espresso cups?"

Nikki pulled on a new shirt and jogged back into the kitchen.

"I'm antisocial," she told him. "You think I have cups for guests?"

She rummaged in cupboards and located shot glasses. Then she opened the window and metal shutter, letting in the morning light and street sounds.

"Did you know the fortune teller?" Valerio asked.

Nikki shrugged. "I interviewed her last week—after the murder."

"What did she say?"

"She claimed Claire knew her killer," Nikki said. "But then she admitted she hadn't even talked to Claire. I think she was just trying to trick me into paying more."

Nikki had been repulsed by the fortune teller's exaggerated playacting. Maybe that was why she hadn't followed up after those initial questions. She regretted this now. If Signora Dorotea had known more, she'd taken it with her.

"Predatory leeches," Valerio said with disgust. "My mother paid an assisto for years, for messages from my father. And the numbers, of course."

It was a prevalent, if secretive, superstition: that the dearly departed sent dreams with winning lottery numbers beyond the grave. Interpreting dreams had likely been a large part of Signora Dorotea's business.

"Did she ever win?" Nikki asked.

"No."

She cleared space on the table.

"So, why are you on leave?" she asked.

Valerio shrugged, and turned his back to her, checking the coffee as it heated slowly on the burner.

"I fucked up," he said, still not turning around. "Did a favor for someone I shouldn't have. A boy got killed."

Nikki studied him for a long moment: the hunch of his shoulders, the tension in his neck—and a purple bruise behind his right ear.

"What happened to your head?" she asked.

He leaned on the countertop, and gave a dark laugh.

"I'm really fucked," he said.

Turning to face her, he took a seat.

Last summer, he told her, his daughter had gone missing. He'd turned to the human trafficker Luca Errichiello for help. He said this calmly. Dispassionately. As if giving court testimony. If Nikki didn't know better, she might believe her friend was unaffected. But he seemed heavy, and his right hand pressed against the table as he talked.

He told her about his efforts to return Errichiello's favor, to release Gaetano Mancusi from jail, only to have Luca's men gun down the boy. He described his investigation into the billionaire socialite Paride Silvestri, and Silvestri's abuse of underage girls.

Nikki was cold with disgust.

"Silvestri . . . Errichiello—will they get away with it?" she asked.

"They have so far," Valerio said. "Like Beppe says: They have people everywhere—in the police, the judicial system. You know how it is."

This reminded Nikki of Adriano's words about the system: *To kill the beast, you need to understand it completely.*

"Do you have an idea which ones?" she asked. "Can you investigate? Can you build a case against them?"

Valerio sighed.

"I'll try," he said. "But that will take months—maybe years. I don't have that kind of time. What I need is leverage on Errichiello—to get him to back off . . . to keep Gemma and Davide safe."

There was something frighteningly raw in his usually unshakable demeanor. Valerio had never shared anything so personal, or so difficult.

"What do you need from me?" Nikki asked.

He stared for a long moment.

"You're not part of the police . . . no—I don't mean it like that. I just mean, nobody's watching you. We know there's corruption at HQ, and you don't have the same exposure."

She nodded. "Tell me what to investigate."

"I've found a link between Errichiello and Silvestri," Valerio said. "The head of Errichiello's security team, Ivan. I took a photo at Silvestri's place. Maurizio tried facial recognition, but he came up empty. Someone must know him."

He hesitated, searching her face.

"What?" Nikki asked.

"I wouldn't ask, but I'm running out of time . . . and I know you know Tito Calandra. . . ."

Nikki had sprung to her feet, chair crashing to the floor, before she registered that she was standing. Her heart raced. A high-pitched ringing in her ears.

She stared at the spot on the tiles where her brother had bled just months ago, begging her to save him and Francesca and the kids.

That had been the only time she'd turned to Tito. She regretted few things more.

Valerio rose slowly and silently, palms out. They locked eyes.

She should say something, but the words caught in her teeth.

When she finally spoke, her voice was shaky and too loud: "He burned down a whole fucking building because I wouldn't do what he wanted."

Behind Valerio, the Moka gurgled. He turned to switch off the flame.

A strange detachment settled over Nikki, and violent waves of heat. If it had been anyone else—*anyone*—she would have made them leave.

But this was Valerio. His comfortable manner and easy competence. There was a sort of unspoken agreement between them to put the friendship first—to never risk their mutual respect and understanding. He'd never pried into her life, never asked anything in return.

But she couldn't do it. She'd spent years carefully cutting connections with Tito, a painful surgery that required a sacrifice of healthy tissue to completely excise the disease. Now, the infection had returned, and she couldn't host it. Not even for Valerio.

Yet, he'd been there for her when it mattered. When she was fighting Durant Cole in the darkness of that cave. Against all odds, he'd been there.

"I'm sorry," she said at last, struggling to meet his gaze. "I want to help . . . I really do. But not Tito . . . I can't. You know that, right?"

He nodded. "I understand. I had to ask."

He tucked his chair gently into place beneath the table.

"I'll get going."

"What will you do?" Nikki asked.

"Ravenna is meeting me after lunch, to take me to Ines. If she's the woman Maria remembered, maybe she knows more than she's saying. It's worth a shot."

She walked him to the door. He'd stepped across the threshold when an idea occurred to her.

"What about Sandro?" she suggested. "From the other night—at the bar? He and my brother Adriano were friends in the carabinieri. Maybe he can find your guy."

Valerio exhaled, and smiled, an expression that didn't reach his eyes.

"Sure. That's a good idea. I'll text you the picture."

Nikki didn't have a number for Sandro, so she rang her father to see if he did. He answered on the third ring.

"Are you at home?" he asked.

"Yes."

"Great! I'm on my way."

"Wait!" she said, but he'd already hung up.

The coffee in the Moka was hot. Nikki poured herself a cup and, righting the toppled chair, sat and opened her phone.

As usual, there were dozens of messages from Audrey Lake, who seemed undeterred by Nikki's nonresponse.

There was a video message from Izzy, who thanked her for her visit and said that they loved her.

On Instagram, there were several messages from Sally Tate:

- Teddy is on the war path
- He's seriously connected
- You'd better watch out
- He says he'll report you to the police

Her most recent message from only a few minutes ago read: Seriously. Who are you?

Nikki messaged: Can you please send me the link to Claire's blog?

Sally responded immediately: If I do, will you tell me who you are?

Nikki wrote: I'm an investigator. Trying to find out what happened to Claire. You were her closest friend. I need your help.

Sally wrote: **Holy shit. I knew it! Is Teddy a suspect?**

Nikki wrote: **I can't talk about that. Would you please share the link?**

A few seconds passed. Then, to Nikki's relief, Sally sent it.

Claire Sexton's blog, *Thornfield Manor Secrets*, looked like the cover of a novel—white roses on a pale coral background. The page opened on the most recent post, dated the day before Claire vanished off the yacht in Capri.

> His eyes, deep and piercing, penetrate my soul. How I long to cast aside this pretense. Why must we play these games? I swear he can read my mind with just a glance. Please, Rochester. I need to talk to you alone.

It went on like this for pages.

Nikki shifted uncomfortably as she skimmed the intimate confessions. She felt like an intruder—as if she'd found a stranger's diary.

The entries stretched back to August, shortly before the family set sail on *The Prophet*. As Sally indicated, Claire had been infatuated with her employer. Most entries read like the thoughts of a typical young woman, but when Claire wrote about Jayston, whom she referred to as "Rochester," the language was florid—as if she were the heroine in a romance novel.

The fixation seemed to originate at a restaurant where Jayston noticed she was cold and loaned her his jacket.

> SO thoughtful. And it SMELLED like him! Heaven! Incredible.

Beyond this, Claire described only professional interactions with Jayston; nothing sexual or inappropriate. Given Lydia's account of her daughter's shyness and inexperience with men, Nikki wondered whether Jayston was even aware of Claire's limerence.

Apart from her overwrought declarations about Jayston, Claire was enthusiastic in her descriptions of life aboard the yacht—exploring Greece and Croatia, and playing with Audrey. She loved and enjoyed the awkward little girl, and sympathized with the trauma of losing her younger brother.

Audrey's tendency to run away or hide on the yacht seemed a frequent occurrence, which Claire attributed to her parents' battles, and Audrey's unmet need for her mother's attention.

Claire had created the blog well after the start of the hostilities with Fiona, and by then was already clearly distressed by the adversarial relationship. The topic appeared frequently and, as Fiona's criticism escalated, Claire's posts darkened.

> She says she's hired private detectives to get dirt on Rochester. She says *I know why you're really here. Don't think you're the first one, Princess*. Like she actually knows. She's a liar. I know that. But I need to be more careful. She'll never let him go.

Yet there were hints that their interactions had once been warmer. Claire mentioned clothing and jewelry that Fiona had once loaned her—until their rapport soured and Fiona demanded them back.

Nikki startled as the door buzzer sounded. She stood and shut her laptop.

Nikki's father was on the landing, rocking back on his heels and finishing a cigarette. He stubbed it out on the iron railing.

"Ah, Nina! There she is!"

He kissed her cheeks and followed her inside, rubbing his hands together.

"Sì, sì, sì," he muttered.

"Do you remember Sandro Balestrieri?" Nikki asked. "Adriano's friend from the carabinieri? He said he saw you in the office."

"Of course! He's a big man now in the agency. I had coffee with him yesterday."

Nikki exhaled. "Good. I need his contact information."

"What for?"

"There's a man who doesn't show up in the police facial recognition search. I thought Sandro might have access to different databases."

"What man?" He was suddenly interested. "Show me."

Nikki texted him the photo Valerio had sent.

Raoul put on his reading glasses and studied the image, squinting. "Don't recognize him." He sounded disappointed. "Looks Slavic . . . Eastern European."

Nikki smiled. "Are you supposed to recognize every criminal?"

"I could—at one time," he said, with a matching grin.

"So, will you ask Sandro?"

"Make me coffee, and you have a deal!"

Nikki rinsed the small Moka and started a fresh pot. Raoul didn't seem inclined to wait. As soon as he'd made his calls and gotten Sandro's contact details, he bolted from the kitchen and Nikki heard him tromping through the flat as she made a message to Sandro.

Raoul's mission was underway when Nikki joined him in the living room. He carried in a stack of boxes, setting them in front of the sofa. They stank of dust and mildew.

"Start with that one," he said, pointing.

Nikki sat and opened the first box. "What am I looking for?"

"Your mother's notes. Letters. Anything with her handwriting. Just set it aside."

He bustled away again.

By the time he was finished, the space was littered with dusty boxes: old family memorabilia, left by Beatrice when she and Raoul moved back to Benevento. Under other circumstances, Nikki would have left her father to sort through these himself. But the conversations with Izzy yesterday about Beatrice's secret life made her wonder if she could find evidence about that mystery here.

They excavated decades of sediment—old photos, school records, personal letters, Christmas cards, and geological formations of souvenirs. Nikki paused at a photo of her mother after boot camp, wearing Navy service dress blues, a stern expression on her childish face—large, intelligent eyes and Romanesque nose. Her lips, pressed closed tightly in that moment, had always been so ready to curve into a laugh. Nikki saw that smile in other family pictures—beachside holidays, and poorly lit Christmas dinners.

The longer Nikki searched, the clearer it became: There was nothing mysterious here. No key to unlock the enigma of her missing mother. Instead, she was unexpectedly confronted by the immediacy of a familiar grief—the faces of her mother and Adriano, memories so far faded, faces so young and hopeful, they seemed to belong to another life.

After a few hours, they broke for lunch.

At a nearby trattoria, they ordered panini and insalata, settling into an outdoor table to enjoy the sunlight and respite from the rain.

After the meal, as they drank coffee, Nikki asked, "What exactly are you hoping to find in Mom's stuff?"

Raoul stared for a long moment, then took out his phone, and scrolled through photos before handing it to her.

"I'm probably hunting chimeras," he said. "It was a long time ago, and my memory isn't as good as it once was."

Nikki squinted at the screen—at a photo of lined paper and handwriting scrawled in thick blue ink: numbers and dates and names.

"What am I looking at?" she asked.

He leaned forward.

"This is from Lotterio Patalano's secret ledger," he explained. "He kept track of shipments for the mob. See the vessel names and the code for the manifest?" He pointed. "And the port, the date. And there, on the far right—the name."

Nikki zoomed in, sounding it out. "*Damascus.* They were shipping to Syria?"

He shook his head. "I thought that at first. But these records are sea routes. Damascus isn't a port—it's in the middle of the desert. Also, it doesn't make sense in the context. I think it's a code name for someone."

"Someone inside Syria?"

"I wondered that, too, but I don't think so. I've been working with some young analysts—they're very eager . . . very bright. We can't find any link between this name, and shipments to that region during that time. If there's a connection, we're not seeing it."

He flicked to the next picture. "Now, look at the names here."

Nikki zoomed in again. "Diogenes," she read. "Another code name? Who's Diogenes?"

Raoul pressed his lips together and wrinkled his nose. "Diogenes was a Greek philosopher. He carried a lamp, saying he was looking for an honest man."

"Okay," said Nikki. "I'm not seeing what you're seeing."

"When I saw the name Damascus, I thought it rang a bell, but I couldn't place it. Then I saw Diogenes. Those two names together—that meant something to me. Diogenes and Damascus. Not a natural pairing. But your mother . . . she used to talk about them. Yesterday, I drove back to Benevento, went through all her notes and records. Nothing. I told myself it was a coincidence."

He felt in his pockets, took out a cigarette, and lit it.

"One more name," he said. "Scroll to the next picture."

Nikki found it. "Zosima."

"Zosima was a monk in Palestine in the fifth century," he said. "Beatrice connected those names: Diogenes, Damascus, and Zosima. Three names. They shouldn't go together, should they? Two points . . . two names . . . they can be a coincidence. But all three? It's like celestial navigation—three stars to tell you where you are!"

"What does it mean?" Nikki asked.

He shook his head. "Your mother knew things."

"What things?"

He squinted and looked across the street while he sucked on his cigarette. "This was after Adriano. . . . She thought that he . . ."

He didn't finish, only shook his head.

"Tell me," Nikki pressed.

Raoul seemed suddenly older. He slumped in his seat.

"They caught the boys who killed him," he said. "Stray bullet. Manslaughter. They went to Poggioreale."

Nikki clenched her teeth and didn't say anything. She nodded.

"Beatrice didn't think Adriano's death was an accident," he said.

Nikki was suddenly cold. Her father's face seemed to retreat—flattening into an abstract image.

"Why didn't you tell me?" she asked.

He sighed. "You two had your own problems," he said. "You fought like tigers. Then, after you went to London with Izzy, it seemed like you'd finally found some peace."

"What did Mom believe?"

"You know how your mother could be . . . obsessive. I couldn't talk her out of it. She thought the official investigation was a cover-up. She investigated on her own—talked to people, asked questions."

Nikki's mind raced.

She thought of Beatrice after Adriano's death—distraught and vicious, incapable of her usual compulsive planning and analyzing.

"She never gave up," he continued. "I stopped listening, I think. I didn't mean to—but I did. I regret that. Beatrice saw things I couldn't."

He put out his cigarette and lit another. "I can't find her records. She kept everything—big files—on a shelf in our bedroom. I asked if I could put them into storage. She never let me. I don't know where they are now. Maybe at your place. That's where I remember those names: Damascus, Diogenes, and Zosima."

They walked back in silence.

As they approached the gate to her building, Nikki spotted her brother and his new Dutch friend, Mac.

Raoul waved. "Good! You made it!"

"What are you doing here?" Nikki demanded.

Gianni shrugged. "Babbo said you were going through Mamma's things. Thought I'd have a look."

She stiffened. She didn't want Gianni in her home, especially not with Mac. But Raoul was already leading them through the gate, and up the stairs.

"I can't have you here," she protested. "I need to leave for work soon."

"We won't stay long," Gianni said, then laughed. "What's with the laundry?" He pointed to her clothesline. "You wear anything besides black T-shirts and hoodies? What are you, a twelve-year-old boy?"

Usually inured to his jabs, Nikki nonetheless tensed in annoyance.

"Fuck off," she said.

"Gianni, be respectful," Raoul scolded indulgently.

Mac chimed in with, "What a great old building. So much character."

"Mamma bought it in the seventies." Gianni's voice oozed with nostalgia. "I have so many memories here."

Nikki rolled her eyes.

"What memories?" she challenged. "We lived in military housing. Mom kept renters here."

Gianni shrugged. "Fond memories."

Inside, Gianni helped himself to coffee, rifling through the kitchen and shouting for Nikki to tell him where she kept the sugar and to ask if she had biscuits.

Nikki snapped, "Don't fuck up my kitchen. You have ten minutes."

She darted towards her bedroom.

To her irritation, Mac followed her into the narrow hallway.

"Hey, Nina," he said. "Do you have a moment?"

She shook her head. "Not really. I need to get to work."

But he didn't leave. Instead, he drew in closer.

"You're plugged in around the neighborhood, aren't you?" he asked.

So near, she saw his pores and the flare of his nostrils, and smelled his breath—onions and fish.

"What do you mean?"

He leaned against the wall and smiled.

"I mean . . . a smart, beautiful woman like you. Doors would open."

Nikki blew out. "What are you getting at?"

"Have you thought about leveraging your access?"

"What?"

"You see things," he coaxed. ". . . know things. You could help a lot of people out if you share what you know."

He brushed fingers lightly against her arm. She recoiled.

"You should leave," she said.

Rapidly, angrily, she prepared for work.

At 14:20, she returned to find everything in disarray—neatly organized stacks upended. Papers scattered. Gianni shuffled through a pile of old photos.

Mac, thumbing the contents of a manila folder, smiled at her.

"This is a great location," he said. "Center of the city. Good access. Good lookout points. Good security options."

"Yeah," said Nikki. "Time to go."

"Hey." He leaned in. "Your father says you need my help with biometrics. Facial recognition."

"I don't want your help," she said. "Everyone needs to leave. I'm going to work."

Raoul, deep in a notebook, didn't look up. "Go ahead. I'll lock up when we leave."

"You don't have a key," Nikki reminded him, then, turning to Gianni and Mac: "You need to go."

Gianni, who seemed not to hear her, guffawed. "Check this out."

He held up a photo of the two of them as children at the seashore. Eight-year-old Nikki had built a sandcastle, while a scrawny ten-year-old Gianni with a bush of curly hair stood over it with a grin and a bucket of water.

"What a little chunker you were," Gianni said.

Her father exhaled loudly.

"Give me your key, Nina," he said, pinching the bridge of his nose. "I'll make a copy. You should have more copies."

Nikki hesitated. Had he been alone, she might have agreed, but no way was she leaving Gianni and Mac unsupervised.

"If I give you my key," she told Raoul, "you'll need to meet me at midnight after my shift."

She watched his face as he did the calculation. Her early-bird father sighed, and stood.

Despite her best efforts, it was another twenty minutes before she herded them out.

At the door, Mac made a show of chivalry, holding up her jacket and bag.

"Maybe we should have dinner and talk things over," he murmured.

Nikki snatched her things from him.

"No."

As she drove them down the stairs, she noticed Gianni carrying a plastic grocery sack stuffed with papers.

She asked about it, and he yanked it out of reach.

"You got the whole house," he whined. "And you're griping about me bringing home a few mementos?"

She didn't have time to argue.

Beside her, Raoul was talking. "Just give Mac your photo. He can access NATO facial recognition databases."

"I don't want his help," Nikki said.

"Don't be unreasonable," he said. "In intelligence, you need as many allies as possible."

"He's not my ally," she said.

"Well," he said with measured calm, "may I share the photo with him?"

Nikki sighed. "Do whatever you want."

TWENTY-ONE

Valerio strode from Nikki's apartment feeling uncomfortable. His neck and head were stiff and painful from Ivan's attack three days ago. He'd been so distracted he'd forgotten to drink the coffee—leaving the Moka steaming on Nikki's stove.

Yesterday had been complete shit. He'd been heading to the gym for some much-needed weight training, when he was called into HQ and spent hours going through mug shots. The CCTV footage of Gaetano's shooting hadn't captured the men in the sedan, so Valerio was the only eyewitness. But he was loath to finger anyone when he didn't trust himself. He'd been far too drunk.

The investigators used the interview room with the two-way mirror—a procedure Valerio didn't like at all, but that they said had been insisted on by Director Bonetti.

Afterwards, Bonetti himself strolled casually in, acting for all the world as if he just happened to be stopping by instead of having watched the entire exchange.

"How are you holding up, Capo?" he asked, putting a hand on Valerio's shoulder.

"Fine," Valerio said.

It was never good to be completely honest with a boss—particularly one inclined towards politics.

"That's a nasty bruise," said Bonetti.

Valerio shrugged. "Just catch the bastards and let me get back to work. Have you looked into Errichiello?"

"There's no reason to suspect his involvement," said Bonetti. "He has an alibi."

"He's scum," said Valerio. "Look again."

Bonetti gave a hard stare.

"That sounds like a personal grudge," he said. "Is there anything I should know about?"

"You should know that he trafficks girls and women," Valerio said.

"Last year, I took a course about confirmation bias," said Bonetti. "We must be constantly on our guard to ensure our feelings don't drive our policing. Go home, Alfieri. Let *us* worry about the investigation."

Valerio stopped by Maurizio's desk on the way out.

"Did you run the plates?" he asked.

"Looks like they're stolen. It's a dead end."

"How about our white-haired friend? Any hits on facial recognition?"

Maurizio shook his head. "None. Sorry. I've sent it to a friend at Europol. Maybe he'll get a match."

This morning, Maurizio had called with the bad news: no hits in Europol's databases. This surprised Valerio, who couldn't believe that the white-haired Ivan had a clean record. He was a clever and experienced operator, and had likely moved in criminal circles for a long time. There had to be an ID somewhere. Valerio wondered if the problem was in organizational information sharing—everybody with their own system and data.

If he'd had any other option, he wouldn't have asked Nikki. Thinking about her violent reaction, though, how she recoiled at Tito Calandra's name, he regretted his request.

Last summer, he'd been so surprised to see her coming from Calandra's place, carrying a bag full of cash. He guessed that, like him, she'd been desperate—willing to make a deal with the devil. He'd wanted to bring it up with her, to ask what had happened that night. But she never mentioned it, and as the months went by, the subject became more difficult to broach. Nikki was a private person and he didn't want to pressure her. If she wanted to tell him, she would tell him.

But he was also an investigator and, curious, he'd made some inquiries. The rumors shocked him: that Nikki Serafino and Tito Calandra had once been in a relationship. He'd wondered if this was true, and whether Nikki maintained her ties to the powerful Camorra capo.

Now, he was ashamed for asking. Nikki believed that Calandra had burned down her studio, and that was hardly a sign of affection.

Well, he wouldn't ask again.

After Ivan's ambush last Saturday, Valerio made it a point to take different routes home, and practice good countersurveillance. These careful efforts were wasted today, since the white-haired thug and two buddies loitered outside the entrance to his building, with no attempt at subterfuge.

Valerio strode to them, speaking loudly, with more confidence than he felt: "Are you really this desperate? Coming to my home in daylight, where I've installed surveillance and have guys waiting nearby?"

Of course, he'd done none of these things, although it occurred to him now that they might have been reasonable precautions.

Ivan, wearing sunglasses on this overcast day, pushed back from the wall where he'd been leaning.

"You don't answer your phone. That's not smart."

"What isn't smart is you giving me a bruise for the whole station to see. If you wanted to keep this low-key, you're really fucking up."

A group of tourists coming down the narrow street must have sensed the tension. They rapidly changed direction.

"What do you want?" Valerio demanded.

"Just a little job," said Ivan. "A small document we need you to recover from your boss's office."

"Boy, your intel must be shit," said Valerio. "After you shot up Gaetano Mancusi in front of me, my boss put me on leave. I have no business going to the station until it's over."

Ivan smiled. He held up his phone and Valerio heard a recording of his own voice: *Tell me what you want.* Then Luca explaining his request for help with Gaetano Mancusi. He wasn't surprised they'd recorded this.

"So what?" he challenged. "I've done nothing illegal. If this is blackmail, you're shit at it."

Ivan lashed out with surprising speed.

Valerio fought back, and was able to return some solid hits before they grappled him into submission, gripping tightly while Ivan punched and kicked.

The thrashing was predictable, Valerio told himself as it was happening. As if this knowledge somehow made it more tolerable, as if he'd chosen it himself. He noticed, with detachment, the practiced nonchalance of those expert blows and kicks.

He heaved and vomited from the gut punches.

They dumped him on the pavement, then one of the men wrestled his hand open, forcing his fingers around the handle of a gun.

Ivan crouched next to Valerio, and spoke in his ear. "Two women were shot last night. Your fingerprints are on the murder weapon. How's that for blackmail, Capo? I'll text your instructions. You go to Bonetti's office and get the file we want."

When they left, Valerio worked his way to the wall, then pulled himself to sitting. He stayed for a long time, assessing the damage, and trying to catch his breath.

From the balcony above came the thin voice of his upstairs neighbor, Agata.

"Valerio, have you seen my little dog? He left his basket and hasn't come back."

It took a handful of paracetamol, and ice on his kidneys before Valerio thought he might be able to leave his apartment again. He moved like a ninety-year-old man—gingerly, every movement bringing pain.

He considered it a good sign that they hadn't hit his face. This meant they still believed they could control him, and so needed to keep his face intact. This new pretext for blackmail was also a good sign, since it took the target off his family. Well, he could take a thrashing if that meant they were paying attention to him instead of his kids.

If it protected Gemma and Davide, he'd turn himself into the biggest fucking punching bag in the world.

Ravenna was wearing hospital scrubs when she met him a few hours later at Cosimo's pizzeria.

She apologized. "I didn't have time to change. What's so urgent that you couldn't discuss it on the phone?"

Valerio searched her face—glad for those bright eyes and full cheeks, the mobile expression brimming with curiosity. He actually liked the shapeless purple nursing uniform. It seemed to express something essential about her: determination, competence, compassion.

He had a sudden fantasy of being Ravenna's patient: this angel bustling into the room, tucking him in, and leaning over to adjust equipment; the warm fragrance of her perfume, her laugh when he reached up to caress and kiss her, pulling her down onto the bed with him. It was a ridiculous daydream that, given his dire situation, he couldn't possibly act on yet. But it made him grin.

She returned his smile.

"Are you hungry?" he asked.

"Starving. You?"

"I'm always hungry when I'm upset . . . or happy . . . or sad," he said with a chuckle, fighting back the pain of his bruised and tender torso—and his kidneys! He was pretty sure one of his ribs was broken. It hurt to breathe. And his stomach clenched, an ache he didn't think pizza would resolve.

Cosimo was at his shoulder.

"Ah, the beautiful Ravenna! A pleasure to see you again. This big oaf isn't bothering you, is he?"

She laughed. "Not at all!"

Cosimo leaned in and kissed her cheeks. "If you get tired of him, you know where to find me."

He took their orders and winked at Ravenna before hurrying away.

"What happened with Maria?" she asked. "Is that why you're worried?"

"I'll tell you more about that in a minute. Can you answer a few questions for me, first?"

She nodded.

"Ines Mancusi," he said. "You've known her a long time. What kind of person is she?"

Ravenna's face crinkled.

"Did you have a good mother?" she asked after some thought.

The question called Leonora to mind. Not her face—perpetually turned upwards to the Immacolata—but her hands, strong and capable, bulging at the knuckles, and always moving: chopping, stitching, scrubbing, repairing, tucking . . . holding.

"Yes," he said. "A very good mother."

Ravenna said, "That must have been nice. My mother wasn't good. I can see that now. She must have had a very bad childhood to give me one, too. She was . . . difficult. And there was never enough . . ."

Without realizing or intending it, Valerio reached out. Her fingers were cold. He squeezed, giving her his heat.

"It's okay," Ravenna said. "I'm fine. Really. I survived."

She laughed uncomfortably, then continued. "It wasn't easy to grow up in that place, you know? When you don't have much, kindness doesn't come easily, does it? And I was an ugly little girl. Chubby. Nearsighted. Ines was friendly—she pulled me in, fed me, asked questions. Made me feel special, you know? Her husband died right after Gaetano was born. I was thirteen . . . and I started helping out."

"Did she pay you to watch Gaetano?"

Ravenna shook her head. "She didn't have money . . . none of us did!"

"Besides babysitting Gaetano, did she ever ask you to do other types of work?"

"No."

"Did she ever talk about the work she did for Luca Errichiello or Paride Silvestri?"

She shook her head.

"I didn't know about Silvestri," she said.

"And Errichiello?"

"She talked about him all the time: what a great man he was. I honestly didn't know . . . the things you say he did."

"Errichiello said she was his housekeeper. Does this seem right to you?"

Ravenna's eyes narrowed. "What do you mean?"

"You've seen her home. Does she look like a woman who knows how to clean?"

Ravenna pulled her hand back. "She's sick, Valerio! Have a little compassion."

Valerio nodded. "But she wasn't always sick. Did she ever clean? Alright . . . I'll ask another way. What did she wear when she would go to work for him?"

Ravenna seemed to think.

"She was always a beautiful woman. Slender. Long hair. Men liked her. She dressed nicely." She paused, then stared intently at Valerio. "You aren't saying she was a prostitute?"

He shook his head. "No. I don't think that."

Valerio realized he was reluctant to tell Ravenna what he'd learned. Telling her would change things. And he didn't want things changed. Not yet.

He'd spent his life peering into dark places, digging through the sewers of human nature. He was never surprised to find filth—disappointed, but never surprised. But Ravenna, with her cheery disposition, seemed determined to look for the best in people. She'd worked her way out of the slums of Forcella to create a better life, yet returned regularly to minister to a sick old neighbor. He wished he could shield her from what he suspected. Better to keep your illusions and live with whatever peace you'd achieved than to know that every truth you treasured had turned to shit.

The pizzas arrived.

"Let's set this aside," he said. "We'll talk about it after lunch. Buon appetito!"

They ate, and Ravenna chatted amiably about her work. Valerio listened with real interest. He wished this could just be a nice meal where they talked about themselves, or made plans for the weekend together. He would ask to take her sailing on *Calypso* when things calmed down.

At last, it could be delayed no longer. With the pizza sitting like a rock in his gut, he gave Ravenna a summary of what Beppe had said—and then played segments of the recording he'd made of Maria's confession.

When it was finished, Ravenna sat in stunned silence.

"Those poor girls," she said.

Her hand shook a little as she lifted her glass of water.

"Did you ever hear anything about this?" he asked. "Did Ines ever invite you to Errichiello's or Silvestri's house?"

"No! I mean, there were always disgusting old men who wanted to look at you . . . or do things. That's life . . . that's just what happens. But Ines would never do that."

"Are you sure?"

"Of course!" she insisted. "It must be someone else."

"Would you come with me to ask her?"

Valerio smelled the cats as they approached the entrance of Ines's apartment. Ravenna turned the key, and pushed the door. An overwhelming stink wafted out, and two cats streaked past them onto the concrete landing, racing down the stairs.

"It's me," Ravenna called out.

A moan came from within, and a weak voice. "Ravenna! Sweet girl. Oh, help me!"

The house was just as disordered as before, Ines's armchair a throne in a kingdom of clutter. Ravenna busied herself opening windows and shutters, letting in grey light and fresh air, city sounds, and a view of the chipped paint and plaster of the building across the alley. Ines limped towards a window, dragging the cart with her oxygen tank behind her, her skeletal frame silhouetted against the light through her thin nightdress. She lit a cigarette.

"It's dangerous to smoke with your oxygen," Valerio warned.

She gave a baleful stare and sucked her cigarette, leaving lipstick marks on the filter.

"My son is dead," she wheezed. "Tell me what I have to live for now. He was my only child!"

She began to sob. A dry, hoarse sound. Her body curved around it. Ravenna gently took the cigarette from her fingers, putting it out in an ashtray.

"Sit down," she urged, helping the frail woman back to her chair.

At Ravenna's instruction, Valerio cleared the seat—picking up a thick photo album. Ravenna tucked Ines in, and he opened the book, glancing through the pictures of Gaetano as a child.

He was suddenly full of the pizza, and sick with pity and the stench of the room. His stomach wrenched.

"Ravenna tells me Gaetano had a good heart," he said, handing her the album. "I'm sorry for your loss."

"You can't possibly understand my loss," she moaned. "Only a mother whose heart is broken like mine."

Valerio still saw the juddering form of the boy as the bullets tore into him.

"I want to find and punish whoever was responsible for Gaetano's death," he said. "Will you answer my questions?"

"What questions could you possibly have?" she keened.

"I need you to tell me what you do for Paride Silvestri."

"I don't know what you're talking about," she snapped with a sudden appraising look.

Valerio opened his phone, and showed the picture of Ines and Silvestri together.

She examined it for a moment, then exhaled and shrugged. "He's a friend of the family."

"You weren't working for him?"

"As you've already pointed out, I work for Luca Errichiello."

"You didn't arrange for Gaetano to work for Silvestri?"

"No!"

"You weren't grooming little girls?" Valerio said. "Serving them to Silvestri?"

She stared, her eyes narrowing. "How can you torment me at a time like this?"

Her hands reached into the air as she spoke, as if she wanted to grab onto him. The book slid to the floor, spilling papers and pictures.

"Capo," Ravenna said, rushing in to tidy up, "that's enough."

But Valerio was watching Ines as carefully as she watched him. He knew what it was when a woman lied to him. He'd grown up with two sisters whose deceptions he readily detected, and an ex-wife whose lies had taken longer to spot. Ravenna might be blind to whatever Ines was hiding, but he didn't have time to play these games.

Without asking for permission, he strode from the room, and into the dark apartment.

"Where are you going?" Ines shouted after him. "You can't go there. Stop!"

Ravenna caught up to him as he opened doors in a back hallway where he found more clutter, and a box of cat litter, brimming with shit.

Three cats came from the bedroom as he switched on the lights.

"What are you doing?" Ravenna protested. "You can't invade her privacy!"

This room was tidier than the rest of the house, the mess stacked into piles along the walls.

The bed was lavish and oversize—the headboard carved and gilded wood. A fat ginger cat curled atop a baby-blue satin coverlet.

On the dresser sat an open jewelry box—overflowing with gold bangles and necklaces and rings. A dozen framed photographs displayed a well-dressed Ines Mancusi at parties throughout the years—each with a different celebrity. There were also several images with the tanned and smiling Paride Silvestri, his arm draped across her shoulders, looking directly into the camera while Ines laughed.

As Ravenna examined the photos, Valerio moved to the wardrobe. Inside were designer dresses—labels of Prada and Ferragamo and Hermès. Many had clearly never been worn.

He turned his attention next to a mountain of boxes stacked to the ceiling. One box revealed a 950-euro pair of heels, the price tag still visible. The next, a 1,300-euro pair of boots. Another, a Gucci handbag.

"Look at this," Ravenna said, holding up one of the pictures. It showed Ines and Silvestri with three girls in skimpy dresses and heels, heavy eyeliner and bright lipstick—none of which could camouflage the full cheeks and knobby knees of youth.

"But I don't understand," she said. "If what you're saying is true . . . she never did anything to me."

"Didn't she?" Valerio said, staring at the woman who had spent her childhood so desperate for attention and care that she'd been manipulated into raising another woman's child without a penny of payment or word of thanks. Meanwhile, Ines Mancusi hoarded blood money and fed her own vanity. That Ravenna had escaped the fate of those other girls was only due to the separate purpose she served the grotesque witch.

Gripping the picture to her chest, Ravenna marched from the room.

She was trembling and pale as she held the photo in front of Ines.

"How old were these girls?" she demanded.

Ines hunched in her chair, waving a hand as if shooing it away. "It isn't what you think. It isn't what he said."

"I heard it for myself," said Ravenna. "You brought girls to Silvestri . . . and other men."

Ines fumbled for her cigarettes and struggled to light one. She took a couple of puffs, her head turned away from Ravenna and the photo.

"What future did they have here?" she said at last. "What future did any of you have here? At least I gave them a chance."

Ravenna's lips were rimmed in white, her eyes wide.

"A chance at what?" she demanded. "Exploitation? Rape?"

"Do they look unhappy to you? Look at those faces. They're smiling. Let me tell you something: They fought for the chance to stay. They wanted it—to meet wealthy men . . . important people. Those girls may look sweet, but let me tell you: They were hungry, self-serving . . . little rats."

"How old were they?" Ravenna demanded.

Ines shrugged. "Don't judge me. Men want what they want. It's the way the world is."

"What was the arrangement?" Valerio said. "Tell me how it worked."

She glared back. "Why should I tell you anything? You killed my son."

Ravenna's usually soft voice was icy: "He didn't kill Gaetano. Errichiello killed him."

"Lies!" Ines hissed. "Luca would never hurt Gaetano—"

"Errichiello called me himself," interrupted Valerio. "He wanted me to watch as his men gunned down an eighteen-year-old boy. Wanted me to appreciate what he could do."

Ines's face writhed—self-pity shifting into confusion. "But why would he do that? Why?"

She crumpled, hollow eyes roving, as if searching for an answer.

He couldn't muster any mercy for her, knowing what she was.

Ravenna's face was fixed in a rictus of disgust. Slowly, deliberately, she moved forward, crouched in front of Ines's chair, and gripped her bony hands.

"Gaetano had a good heart," she murmured. "You remember how sweet he could be? How he used to sing himself to sleep?"

"He was his mamma's little boy," Ines agreed, her face twisting. A tear worked down her wrinkled cheek. "Oh, how could they give a mother such grief!"

"He deserves peace," Ravenna said. "You can give him that peace now. You need to tell us: What were you doing for Errichiello?"

"Azzo worked for Luca. That's how we met," Ines told them. "I was *irresistible*—that's what he called me: *irresistible*. Couldn't keep his hands off me. Of course, the pregnancy changed that for a while—Luca likes his women slim. After Azzo died, I thought Luca would be pleased to be a father. But he was different than other men . . . he didn't have the same inclinations, I suppose. Never wanted to see the baby . . . never let me talk about it."

"Gaetano was Luca's son?" Ravenna asked.

Ines held her head up. Proud.

"He acknowledged him, too," she said. "When the boy was ten, he said, 'You may as well bring him in and let me take a look.' After that, he let me bring Gaetano to work."

"What sort of work were you doing for Errichiello?" Valerio asked.

"He didn't keep me around out of pity, if that's what you're thinking," she snapped. "You should know that he isn't that type of man. He's very . . . efficient. He knew I was talented. He needed me."

"What did you do for him?" Valerio pressed.

"The girls could get . . . restless. I kept them calm—let them know what was best for them."

She leaned forward.

"The modeling agency was my idea," she said. "In the beginning, I found them. But then they started coming to me, you know? Begging to be part of it. A good business. Everybody gets what they want."

"Tell us about Paride Silvestri," Valerio said. "How were he and Errichiello connected?"

"Oh, the girls were for Paride," she said. "At first, he only needed a few—but then he found other men with his preferences—and we needed more."

"How many?"

She smiled. "I need my cigarettes, Capo. Would you hand them to me?"

After she lit another cigarette, she said, "How many men are in your police station? How many men do you think you know? Good family men? Show me a good family man and I'll show you what he really is—what he really likes."

Without intending it, Valerio's mind went to his friends—the good-hearted Dario, and the tall and solemn Maurizio.

"Have you never wanted a young sweet thing, Capo? I could find you a perfect little cherry."

She laughed at whatever she saw in his expression.

"And what did Gaetano do for Errichiello and Silvestri?" Ravenna asked.

"When he was little, the girls liked to take care of him. Play with him. But when he got older, Luca didn't like having him around. Luca doesn't like needy things. But I said to Luca, 'You'll never find a more loyal man. Give him an assignment.'"

"And did he?"

"Luca put him with his couriers. Gave him a motorbike. But the other boys didn't like him. So Luca put him to work in the warehouses—but Gaetano could make mistakes. So, I made him get his driver's license."

"Was that all he was doing for Errichiello? Driving?"

"Sì."

"He was arrested with cocaine," Valerio said. "Was he moving cocaine for Errichiello?"

"Of course not. The little idiot. Those other boys put him up to it."

"What did Errichiello think of Gaetano? Did they have a good relationship?"

She shrugged. "Luca doesn't have those instincts. And Gaetano was . . . disappointing. Always trying to fit in. Always pretending. Always groveling."

"Was Errichiello disappointed in Gaetano?"

"Yes," she said.

"How do you know? Did he tell you this?"

"Two weeks ago, Gaetano drove Luca to a dinner. A long drive—to Salerno. Gaetano had to piss. He went into the restaurant to use the toilet. Luca was furious. The Ghost dragged Gaetano out, and hit him—actually hit Luca's son! He called me. Crying. I told him to find another place to piss. Then Luca stopped letting Gaetano drive him."

"The Ghost?" Valerio asked.

"That's what everyone calls him: il Fantasma—the Ghost—because of his white hair. He runs security for Luca."

"What's his actual name?" he pressed.

She shrugged.

"How long has he worked for Errichiello?" he asked.

She considered. "He came to Luca three years ago."

Valerio pictured the ungainly boy tromping into the sophisticated restaurant. He could imagine Luca's annoyance, and Ivan's ready violence.

"Who was Errichiello meeting?" he asked.

Another shrug.

"Do you know the name of the restaurant?"

"No."

"I want names," Valerio said firmly. "Anyone else who worked directly for Errichiello or Silvestri."

She rattled off half a dozen names—cooks, managers, housekeepers, and serving staff.

Valerio switched off the voice-recording app on his phone, and started dialing Maurizio.

"I'm bringing you to the station," he told Ines. "You're going to tell the police everything about Errichiello's operations."

She laughed.

"The police already know," she wheezed. "Everyone loves Silvestri's parties. They especially love the girls. The younger the better. That was the point. That was always the point. Don't you understand? If the police wanted it to stop, it would be over."

She turned to Ravenna. "Bella, get me a glass of water. I'm parched."

Ravenna's face was white, lips pressed together, fists clenched at her sides. She gazed back at Ines, and Valerio saw something he'd never thought could exist in that sweet face: hatred.

"Never," she said. "Never again."

Then she turned and strode rapidly to the door. Valerio followed.

"You can't judge me!" Ines screamed. "You can't judge me!"

The screeching followed them onto the landing and down the stairs.

As they left the dank concrete hallway and emerged into the daylight, amid the sounds of traffic and city noises, Valerio thought he could still hear her.

TWENTY-TWO

Angelo and Mario were in the Phoenix Seven office when Nikki arrived seven minutes late for the 15:30 shift.

Angelo held up his watch, frowning.

"It's important to be on time," he intoned. "Everyone needs to pull their weight, signorina. Not only when it's convenient. While I'm focused on the American ambassador, I rely on the professionalism of this team."

"What's happening with the ambassador's daughter?" Nikki asked.

"You've been out of the loop," he said, scarcely suppressing a grin. "The world doesn't simply stop when you're away."

"Would you brief me?"

"It's *need-to-know,*" he said. "You're not on the case anymore."

Nikki could see his deliberation—the pleasure of keeping the information from her contesting with his compulsion to showcase his superior knowledge. At last, he tipped his head as if the balance had shifted.

"The police found forensic evidence that Signorina Sexton was in the apartment rented by the ambassador's daughter, Monica, and her friend, Kami."

Nikki was surprised. "She was in their flat?"

"Perhaps even staying with them."

She thought of Valerio's words: *You don't take that kind of risk unless you're desperate or insane.*

"If she was staying in their flat," she said, "why not kill her there? Why wait to kill her in a church with potentially hundreds of witnesses?"

"Precisely my thoughts!" agreed Angelo, clearly unable to hide his excitement.

"What does Monica say?" Nikki asked. "Did she tell you what Claire was doing at her flat?"

"She denies it."

"She must be lying."

Angelo's chin tilted, face flushed. "As I told the detectives! I knew she was lying. My instinct is never wrong. I understand Americans. There are subtleties in such knowledge. The police could learn a thing or two from this humble investigator."

"Why do you think she lied?" Nikki asked.

"I believe she's afraid."

"What could be more frightening than facing a murder charge?" she asked.

He leaned forward, rising on his toes. "That's the question!"

As they talked, Mario had been noisily packing his bag. Now, he hefted it onto his shoulder with a grunt.

"Are you coming?" he asked loudly.

Angelo's face, which had been animated, froze. He glanced at Mario. "On my way."

These last words were spoken in the same abrupt tone Mario always used.

"Is Iacopo here?" Nikki asked, remembering that his name was on the duty roster for the afternoon shift.

"He's going to be late," Angelo said and, handing her the duty phone, followed Mario out.

Nikki settled into her cubicle and checked Angelo's notes from the morning. It had been quiet. No break-ins or accidents. Nobody arrested.

It was a relief to have the office to herself, and nothing on the agenda. She could think about the case.

Rummaging in her rucksack, she grabbed the notecards, the edges starting to soften, removed the rubber band, and laid them out. She reviewed these and digested the new information.

Two young women, educated, privileged—facing murder charges.

They had lied about knowing Claire. Why? What connected the three women?

Whatever it was, it had to be more frightening than murder charges.

The most obvious clue was the cocaine. Drugs introduced the specter of organized crime. Had the women been smuggling drugs for the Camorra?

She shuffled the cards slowly, pausing on the interview with Claire's mother.

Lydia said that Claire had been afraid: *She sounded . . . different . . . not herself. . . . She was in tears . . . wanted to hop on the next flight back.*

If Claire had been involved in cocaine trafficking—if she'd even brushed up against the Camorra—it might explain her distress.

Nikki scanned the pale pinks and peaches of Claire's blog site, searching for confirmation of this hypothesis. But Claire seemed to have been more child than woman, her naive infatuation with Jayston dominating her writing.

Nikki winced a little as she reread the post: *Oh, please, Rochester. I need to talk to you alone. There must be some explanation.*

She doubted Claire possessed the subterfuge to maintain a secret self—one that smuggled cocaine while maintaining the appearance of a sweet-natured nanny obsessed with her employer.

What could have possibly induced Claire to compromise her future, her work for the Lakes, the proximity to her beloved "Rochester"—for the risky proposition of drug smuggling?

Unless it was Jayston himself who had brought her into it.

Sonia answered on the second ring.

"How's your uncle?" she asked.

They discussed Preston and Izzy for a few minutes before Nikki said, "Angelo tells me that forensics puts Claire in the same flat as Monica and Kami."

Sonia sighed. "It's not looking good for them."

"Do you think it's tied to the cocaine?"

"We do."

"Have you read Claire's blog?" Nikki asked. "She was infatuated with Jayston. He could have influenced her—maybe even gotten her involved in drug smuggling?"

"We searched *The Prophet* yesterday," Sonia said. "No evidence of drug transport. The cocaine came from Signora Lake's personal supply. Fiona confessed—and Jayston confirmed that his wife has had long-term issues. It looks like Claire took the cocaine when she left the yacht in Capri, along with Fiona's jewelry."

"To sell it?" Nikki asked.

"Yes. We think this is how she met our suspects—selling cocaine at a club."

"But why leave the yacht so suddenly?" Nikki asked. "Why steal Fiona's jewelry and drugs, and run? She was such an innocent kid. It's completely out of character."

"It seems Fiona was cruel to her," Sonia said.

"But she'd been cruel for months," Nikki said. "Claire hated her. And why not tell Jayston or the agency?" She hesitated. "Her mother said that Claire called from Capri—that she sounded frightened. She wanted to come home."

A long silence. Nikki checked the connection. "Sonia?"

"What were you doing talking to Lydia Sexton?"

"I went to Claire's memorial in London," Nikki said. "I saw the notice—and it wasn't far from where I was staying."

Another pause. Nikki suddenly realized she should have reached out sooner.

When Sonia spoke again, her words were clipped. "You had no authority. No jurisdiction. Do you realize how badly this could hurt our investigation? At trial, they'll say you were tampering with witnesses. And the British police won't be happy when they hear you overstepped. What the hell were you thinking?"

Nikki was suddenly hot. She peeled off her hoodie.

"I'm not on the case," she said. "So, I wasn't under the authority of the Naples Police or Phoenix Seven. I acted as a private citizen. I was fully transparent with Lydia Sexton about this."

"Did you talk to anyone else?"

Nikki told her about Sally Tate and Teddy Sexton. She was honest about the latter, painfully so—including the social media fallout.

Her mind replayed it, face and neck burning. She'd put herself in such a vulnerable position—hadn't anticipated or prevented his attack. If she ever decided to interview a witness undercover again, she would be better prepared.

"I can write it up for you," she offered.

Sonia exhaled. Her voice was dry. "The last thing I need is a paper trail. Theodore Sexton's lawyer called the station this morning, demanding to know which Italian detective attacked his client. Of course, I told him he was mistaken. I didn't believe for a moment you'd do such a thing."

Nikki hadn't expected Teddy to be so motivated to track her down, although she might have anticipated it if she'd thought more carefully about his sudden aggression in the empty after-hours London streets. He was a man used to winning. His violence had been reflexive, an instinct to restore his sense of control the moment he realized she'd lied to him.

He'd been fighting for his ego; Nikki had been fighting for her life.

"I didn't attack him," she said. "I defended myself."

She could still feel his palm on her thigh, the warm alcohol taste of him, his tongue in her mouth. Pain and panic as he gripped her throat.

"I see that," said Sonia. The edge in her voice vanished as quickly as it had come. "Did you give him your name?"

"My first name."

"Did you file a police report about the assault?"

"No," Nikki admitted.

Sonia didn't say the other part, the part Nikki was thinking. Self-defense only mattered in a courtroom. It wouldn't stop Teddy from filing a complaint. It wouldn't stop an investigation, a suspension, or worse. And she definitely couldn't afford a lawyer. Teddy Sexton could destroy her without ever throwing a punch.

At last, Sonia sighed. "Hopefully, I put him off. He may drop it."

Nikki paused, then asked: "How badly did I hurt your investigation? Is Teddy a suspect?"

"His alibi checked out. He was in London when Claire was killed. I have to go. We'll talk later."

Iacopo arrived while Nikki finished her call. Sullen and silent, he didn't bother explaining his lateness. After a few minutes, he stomped out, muttering something about coffee.

Clipping the duty phone to her belt, Nikki also left.

The air was cold and dry as she crossed the base's central spine.

Her personal phone pinged. A text from Mac: **I'd really love to buy you dinner.**

No, she wrote back.

You don't even know what I'm offering, he wrote. **We can help each other.**

Not interested, she replied, and blocked the number.

It was 16:45, the end of the workday, and personnel moved across the concrete courtyard towards their cars. She maneuvered past them and was through the glass doors of the shop when she heard a shout—someone calling her name.

In the café adjacent to the shop, the defense attaché sat with Ambassador Paul Lissom. He stood as Nikki approached, his voice discordantly cheerful.

"Investigator Serafino! Just the person we need! Can I buy you a coffee?"

He glanced at his empty cappuccino cup and, beside it, the ambassador's untouched espresso.

"No, thank you," Nikki said. "I thought you'd both be back in Rome."

"We'll stay as long as we're needed," the attaché said, though he looked like he'd rather be anywhere else. As the official link between the State and Defense departments, he was responsible for the ambassador's visit. But an army colonel likely had more pressing duties than babysitting a diplomat.

Nikki turned to Ambassador Lissom. His cardigan and red bow tie were neat, his posture erect. But he was hollow-eyed, face puffy and red.

"How are you holding up, Ambassador?" she asked.

He nodded distractedly. "Advocate Ferragni is doing what he can. . . ."

Then he leaned forward, voice rasping too loudly: "They need to understand. My daughter didn't do this."

Nikki became acutely aware of their surroundings—two uniformed lieutenants, three women in jeans and sweatshirts, café staff cleaning up for the evening. Music from the local radio station crooned from the speakers.

"Maybe we should talk somewhere private," she suggested.

But the ambassador continued. "Monica is innocent. The murderer is still out there."

"I have confidence in the investigators," Nikki said quietly. "And your lawyer will protect Monica. We have to wait and see what comes out."

"You don't understand," Lissom said. "You need to tell them that she wouldn't do this. I know my daughter."

Days ago, he had spoken about stepping back, handing operations to the deputy chief of mission. But the attaché presence at his elbow told Nikki he hadn't done it. She wasn't an expert on US diplomatic politics, but she knew an ambassador couldn't function properly while his daughter faced criminal charges in an Italian court.

"What does the admiral say?" she asked.

"He supports me, of course."

"I work for Phoenix Seven," Nikki said. "So, I support you, too. But I'm not assigned to Monica's case. Angelo's the lead—"

Lissom interrupted. "Keith told me what you did. You hunted down that killer. You stopped him. He told me. . . . I need you to do the same for my daughter."

His desperation was palpable. And suddenly, Nikki was overwhelmed with the burden of his expectation. She wasn't authorized to investigate. Neither Angelo nor Sonia wanted her near this one. And after London—after Teddy—she wasn't sure she trusted herself to get involved.

"I want to help," she said carefully. "But I'm not a detective. I did what I could when Admiral Redford was kidnapped, but I made mistakes and it nearly got us both killed. I don't want to make mistakes with Monica."

"She trusts you," he pressed. "Talk to her. Talk to her friends. Her boyfriend. They'll tell you."

"The police don't want me interfering."

"The police aren't talking to her friends," he shot back, suddenly irritable. "At least try. Get to know her. You'll see—this isn't something she could do."

There was a severity in his usually mild face that reminded her of her own father.

She took a deep breath. "Do you have names and contact details?"

Lissom sorted through the papers in his briefcase and produced a sheet of hotel stationery, sliding it across the table. A dozen names were scrawled, the press of a blue ballpoint pen leaving ridges on the flimsy paper.

"My wife put this together," he said. "Everyone we could think of."

Nikki scanned the list. She was about to fold it into her pocket when one name caught her attention.

"Kevin Walker," she murmured. "Where do I know that name?"

Lissom followed her gaze. "Until recently, Kevin was Monica's boyfriend."

Now she remembered—he'd been mentioned in an online gossip column. And she'd seen the name someplace else, as well.

"I'll try," she said. "But I can't promise anything."

She turned to leave when she had a thought.

She asked in a low voice, "Do you know what she's lying about?"

His eyes narrowed. "What do you mean?"

"She lied about knowing Claire—there was a photo of them together at a club. She lied about the cocaine. I don't know why or who she's protecting. But she needs to tell the truth."

His expression darkened. "Whose side are you on?"

Back at the office, Nikki's mind tugged at that name: Kevin Walker. She remembered reading about him in an article about Monica's vibrant social life. But there was something else, some other place. . . .

She ran a search, but the ubiquitous name effectively anonymized him. She scrolled through social media platforms, but nothing stood out.

Iacopo returned, notably less irritable than before. He was telling her about a business he wanted to start with his brother-in-law, when it hit her.

She knew where she'd seen Kevin Walker's name before.

Tracking down Lydia Sexton was a challenge. A search of directory services led nowhere, and the receptionist at the Albion Nanny Agency was equally unhelpful, reading aloud from a carefully lawyered statement about Claire.

Nikki broadened her search, cross-referencing the name with the areas around Gidea Park. A Lydia Sexton turned up—an early years teacher at a local primary school. When Nikki called, the office manager told her she was in luck; Lydia was just about to leave the office.

"It's Nikki Serafino," she said when she heard Lydia's voice. "We spoke at Claire's memorial—outside the pub."

A sharp intake of breath, then, "Oh, I—I'm not supposed to talk to you!"

Nikki tensed. "Who told you that?"

A shuffling noise, then Lydia's voice dropped. "It's just that . . . Claire's father is suing the agency for damages. Everyone's really wound up."

"Please," Nikki said. "Just a few questions."

"I'm sorry," Lydia said.

Worried she would hang up, Nikki said urgently: "I'm trying to find out who killed your daughter. That's all I want. I need your help."

A long pause. Then, softly, "What do you need?"

"Claire started working for the Lakes last July," Nikki said. "How did she get the job? Was it an agency placement?"

"Oh, that was Teddy . . . Claire's half brother," Lydia said. "He got wind of it. He was very sweet. He made a few calls and sorted her out with the interview. And of course, they took to her. Everyone loved Claire."

Sonia didn't answer her phone or respond to Nikki's texts.

Irritated but undeterred, Nikki grabbed her coat and gloves, and told Iacopo where she was heading. As she stepped out into the cold, she called and texted Ethan. No answer.

It was 18:42 when Sonia answered Nikki's knock.

"I called Lydia Sexton," Nikki began.

Sonia put up a hand. "Not here."

From within the flat, Nikki heard the murmur of Sonia's parents' voices. A rich fragrance of sautéed onions and chili peppers drifted into the hallway.

Sonia stepped out, shutting the door behind her with a firm click. "I told you to stop," she said. Her voice was low, and vibrating with anger. "Wasn't that clear enough? If you were working for me, I'd write you up."

Nikki had never seen her so irate.

"You have every right to be angry," she said. "But hear me out first—"

"You've fucked with my investigation!" Sonia continued. "I told you to leave it alone. I don't know how to fix things when you don't listen to me. I just got a call from the office—Theodore Sexton knows who you are. Claire's mother identified you from the memorial, and now his lawyer is asking for information about you."

Nikki's phone buzzed. She glanced down. Ethan.

"I think you need to hear this," Nikki said. "Can I answer?"

Sonia exhaled sharply. "Fine."

"Hello, gorgeous," Ethan said when she picked up. "Sorry I missed your calls . . . busy sucking my boss's dick. Not literally, you understand. He's an ugly old Rasputin and even I have standards. What can I do for you?"

"I need to ask a question about what we discussed yesterday. May I put you on speaker? I'm here with Sonia Dieng of the Naples Municipal Police."

"I live to serve."

Nikki held up the phone.

"Yesterday, we talked about Teddy Sexton's business, Innovare MindCapsule," she said.

"We did indeed."

"Teddy wasn't doing this on his own, was he? As I recall, there was a business partner. Can you tell me who he was working with?"

"Didn't I say? An old friend from Eton. I assume they bonded over the tragedy of being middle-class. It's on the company formation documents. I thought I sent them to you. Just a moment . . ."

A clack of keys, then a pause.

"Here we are. I'll send it over. Teddy Sexton's business partner worked as a broker for Stonehaven Wealth Management before they launched MindCapsule. Lad named Kevin Walker."

Nikki's pulse spiked.

"You're amazing, Ethan."

"I know, darling."

"Is this supposed to mean something to me?" Sonia demanded.

"Kevin Walker," said Nikki, "is the connection between Monica Lissom and Claire Sexton."

TWENTY-THREE

"It isn't enough," said Valerio. "Even if Ines cooperates, the investigation could take weeks . . . months. Also, she may be right about people protecting Errichiello and Silvestri."

Valerio and Ravenna huddled beneath the inadequate protection of the awning of a closed wine café in Piazzetta Divino Amore. They'd been caught here when it started to rain.

Ravenna didn't respond. Valerio followed her gaze across the small piazza, to a trattoria preparing for evening customers, arranging chairs and tables beneath a plastic cover.

They were silent a long moment.

"I didn't know what she was," Ravenna said at last.

"I'm sorry," Valerio said.

Emerging from the horror of that disgusting apartment, he felt the residue of childhood nightmares: old fairy tales and witches who ate children. He wanted to take a shower, wash away the hideous woman's filth.

He took Ravenna's hand. It was cold and trembling. He pulled her close—an instinct, a need to offer comfort, and receive it. She seemed to feel the same, and the voluptuous warmth of her body pressed into him, her dark curls against his face. He breathed the lilac fragrance of her shampoo. Then her caresses found the fresh bruises. He inhaled sharply, but didn't pull back. Instead, he kissed her cheek, and she kissed his. With calm deliberation, she turned to him, and looked into his eyes for a long moment before kissing him on the mouth. It was like nothing Valerio had ever experienced—at once erotic and deeply comforting. He remembered being lost as a child—wandering for hours in the cold city before catching sight of a familiar street. There was something of that in Ravenna's kiss: a feeling that he might, finally, find his way home.

"Grazie," she said, and tucked back into him again.

They stood like this for a long time. Then the rain let up, and they walked together.

She left him near the Obelisco di San Domenico. He wanted to invite her home with him, lay her gently on his bed, undress her, feel her against him, pleasure her—but Luca's men had been waiting at his house earlier today, and he didn't want her in danger. He said this. She kissed him and said, "There will be time later. This has been a heavy day. I feel it in my heart. I hope to see you soon, Capo."

He kissed her again, a feeling of longing and loss as she left the piazza—as if he were losing something precious before he'd had a chance to warm it in his hand.

He continued thoughtlessly along Via Benedetto Croce, until he came to the open air of a piazza. Preoccupied as he was, it took a moment before he realized that, without meaning to, he'd arrived at the stone wall of Chiesa del Gesù Nuovo. He'd avoided this church, wondered if he'd ever feel comfortable walking through this piazza again. Exactly a week had passed since he'd seen the young woman, bloody, stretched out on the cold marble.

He hadn't intended to go inside but, as he drew near the entrance, he followed a sudden impulse and stepped into the church.

It was strange to have the cathedral open again—priests in purple and black in the dark wooden confessionals; the pious kneeling in prayer; tourists strolling, heads tilted up towards the spectacular views. Everything was as it should be: gentle, contemplative motion, echoing sounds of footsteps and quiet conversations.

The edifice was like a giant train station, passengers moving in and out of life—families and friends to greet them or bid goodbye.

He didn't cross himself, or kneel at the pews. Instead, he strode forward, glowering at Mary with her cherubim. He thought about his mother's prayers, the way she wheedled and bargained with God as if he owned the corner shop and could be persuaded to make her a better deal.

He stared at the gaunt form of Jesus on the cross, at the agonized, inhuman expression.

"I don't expect you to save me," he told God. "I've gotten myself into this mess, and I need to get myself out. But I could use some help, if you don't mind."

Valerio thought about Errichiello, and considered his options.

He understood better what Luca was doing, but didn't have enough to sway a magistrate. He needed something he could use—a solid piece of evidence that couldn't be ignored. And he needed it soon—to keep Luca away, or somehow get protection for his family. Even with evidence, though, he wasn't sure how, precisely, to extract himself. The System was a lifetime membership—the only way out, at the wrong end of a gun.

Suddenly ashamed of his superstition, yet wary of discarding it entirely, Valerio turned and, shoving his hands into his pockets, strode away.

At the church entrance, he paused. He did know one man who had done the impossible—who had gotten away.

Federico Errichiello wasn't in his salumeria, so Valerio went to his home—a one-bedroom apartment in Secondigliano. Valerio had spent time here a few years ago, when Federico had a sobriety lapse and, worried his addiction would drive him to return to his brother for drugs, begged for Valerio's help.

Federico didn't open the door when he knocked, but Valerio could hear the muffled sounds of a television program. He knocked again. The sounds from the program stopped—but there was no other noise.

Valerio knocked again, this time harder, and shouted, "I know you're in there, Federico. It's no good pretending."

The door opened, and Valerio saw the barrel of a shotgun.

"Fuck," he said. "Put that thing away. It's just me. I need to ask some questions."

"You're not welcome here," Federico growled.

Valerio considered. He'd helped the old addict in the past, but Federico had long since paid back that debt.

"That's fair," he agreed. "I knew you didn't want anything to do with your brother. I knew how hard you worked for your sobriety. But I pulled you back into the worst addiction of all. And I never thanked you for helping me."

The barrel dropped a centimeter.

"I don't need to come in—and I don't need any favors," Valerio continued. "But I want to know: How the fuck did you get out? How did you get Luca to leave you alone?"

Federico lowered the gun, then turned and stepped inside, leaving the door open for Valerio to follow.

Everything in Federico's sparsely furnished apartment was threadbare, as if he'd salvaged the pieces from dumpsters, mended and polished them into use again. Even the television was reclaimed—a gouge on the side of the monitor. Yet, it was all tidy, scrubbed, with the faint piney odor of disinfectant.

Federico set the gun on the table, and gestured for Valerio to sit.

"I warned you," he said. "Told you not to get involved with Luca."

"I know."

"He doesn't have feelings like a regular person. He's psychopathic . . . cruel because he can . . . because he likes it. We're insects to him—he wants to pull the legs off."

"Yeah," Valerio said, rubbing a hand across his head.

"What does he want from you?" Federico asked.

Valerio told him about Gaetano Mancusi—and about the visits from the Ghost and his friends, the order to retrieve evidence in Bonetti's office.

Federico scoffed. "He doesn't know how to use you yet—or what you're good for. He just wants to know he owns you. You're his new plaything."

Valerio had wondered whether the random demands and jabs were part of a systematic strategy. They had the feel of a cat toying with its food.

"How do I stop being his plaything? How do I get away?"

"You don't," said Federico. "You can't outsmart him, and you'll never overpower him. He has people everywhere—and I mean *everywhere.*"

Valerio thought of the rich and powerful men at Silvestri's parties. If even a few were part of Luca's system, they could easily cripple any legal action.

"How did you do it?" Valerio asked. "Why did he let you go? Why aren't you dead?"

Federico sat calmly for a moment, oversize hands in his lap, his glasses and skull reflecting the glare of the overhead lamp.

"I was there from the beginning," he said. "He knows my weaknesses. Used them for years—controlled me. But I know his weaknesses, too. What he is. How he works."

"What weaknesses does such a man have?"

Federico gave Valerio a pitying look. "I can't afford to lose my own protection—and it won't cover both of us."

"Well, give me some idea of where to search!"

"Luca has agreements with other clans," Federico said slowly. "But my brother is ambitious. Unsatisfied. Wants to rule. Always maneuvering and cutting, strategizing, undermining. He's useful, so the other capos don't attack directly, but they don't like it. Don't trust him. It would be better for them if someone else took his place."

Valerio considered this. Had Federico taken something from Luca—something he could threaten to use against him?

"You offered something to a competitor!" Valerio realized with surprise.

The thin man raised a bushy eyebrow.

"A direct offer would mean war," he said. "Then I'd be fucked. No. It's only the threat of sending Luca's information to his enemies. I check into an electronic program every week, and enter my password.

If I don't check in—if I'm drugged or dead—then the documents are sent. You see, it isn't brotherly love that stops Luca killing me."

Valerio laughed. He'd never taken Federico for a clever man. He'd always seemed to possess the sort of grasping desperation common to addicts, and Valerio assumed that the drugs had also done their share on Federico's brain. Yet here was cunning and strategy that outstripped his own.

He clapped him on the arm. "I've underestimated you! Can you tell me about the information you have?"

Federico shook his head. "The more I say, the greater the risk."

"I understand," said Valerio. He rose to his feet. "Thank you for telling me."

At the threshold, Valerio stopped and turned.

Federico had stayed where he was, staring blankly into the distance.

"Tell me about il Fantasma . . . the Ghost," Valerio asked. "Who is he?"

Federico seemed to emerge slowly from his thoughts. "Never met him. He came to Luca after I left."

"What do you know about him? Do you know his name?"

Federico clicked his tongue. "I know Luca doesn't like him."

"Why not?"

Shrug.

"Why keep him around if he doesn't like him?" Valerio pressed.

Another shrug.

"He's working as a go-between with Luca and Silvestri. Do you know why?"

"No—but you should stay away," Federico warned. "From what I hear, he's as psychopathic as my brother."

Outside, it was pelting rain. Valerio hunted for cover to wait it out.

He was beginning to understand Federico better now, to appreciate the strength of mind and character that had gotten him free of Luca.

It had been a stormy winter night like this—nearly a decade ago—when he'd first met the old man. He hadn't thought about it for a long time.

Valerio had been on his way home from work when the squall hit. Ducking into a doorway, he found it already occupied. The strange tall man exuded instability. Danger.

Federico had been tweaking—sweating, hands roving, and his voice had been rough: "You a cop?"

Rather than risk confrontation, Valerio stepped back into the rain.

But Federico called to him: "I need a cop."

"Yeah?" Valerio said. "Why do you think you need a cop?"

Federico scratched ferociously at his neck. "Girls in trouble."

Valerio had been reluctant to listen at first. But Federico told him about two cargo trucks parked in a warehouse on the outskirts of Rome. They were part of Luca's smuggling operation, he said, abandoned when the Rome network was compromised.

"Luca's waiting," he told Valerio.

"Waiting for what?"

"Waiting for the heat to die down. But it's been two days. Fuck. Fuck. Those girls."

"What girls?" Valerio pressed.

"You gotta get them out," Federico insisted. "They're gonna die in there."

With dawning horror, Valerio understood.

By the time the police broke into the warehouse and opened the cargo containers, it was already too late for two of the women.

Of the seventeen women and girls they rescued, the youngest was thirteen.

Federico had assisted throughout the rescue and investigation and, battling for sobriety, had begged Valerio to lock him up. Instead, Valerio got him into a treatment center.

Valerio was nearly a block away when he heard footsteps and his name called.

Federico wasn't wearing a jacket.

"What will you do?" he asked, rain glancing off his thick eyeglasses.

Valerio shrugged. "I've run out of time. I can't allow Luca and his Ghost to hurt Gemma and Davide. I have to turn myself in—tell them what I know, and the part I played."

"You think you're safe with the police?" Federico exclaimed. "You won't make it past the first night."

"I trust the guys I work with," said Valerio.

"Luca will shoot your family first," Federico said. "To remind you of your mistake. You'll be in jail, and can't do anything to help them. He'll keep you alive for a while to make sure you feel it. Then he'll kill you, too. Painfully. To make an example."

Federico's eyes were wide with concern, his strangely large hands moving in the air, as if trying to unwrite this future.

"Tell me what to do, then," Valerio said. "I don't know what else to do."

Federico's hands hovered before him, reaching for an answer. None came.

Valerio clapped the old man's shoulder. "You warned me," he said. "I should have listened."

Giorgia answered the door in a housedress.

"What do you want?" she demanded.

"Are the kids here?" Valerio asked.

"Why should they be here? They have friends, don't they?"

The disappointment was a boulder suddenly on his chest. He hadn't realized how much he wanted to see and touch them, how precious it was to hold them in his arms.

He nodded, not trusting himself to speak.

At last, he said, "You need to call them and make them come back home. Leave town for a few days. Don't fly. Take the train or drive. Go north. Rome or Siena. Or drive up into France."

She brushed this aside. "You know we can't afford to go anywhere. Where would we stay? What would we eat?"

Valerio had emptied his savings—745 euros that he gave to Giorgia now.

"This is what I have. Try to make it last as long as possible."

She thumbed through the bills. Realization slowly emerged, and her face filled with rage.

"Fuck you, Valerio. What did you do?"

"It's a police matter. I need to make sure you and the kids are safe until it blows over."

"Isn't there police protection?" she demanded. "If it's that serious, there should be some sort of protection."

"Not this time."

"It's the middle of the school week."

"Tell their teachers there's an emergency . . . a death in the family. Will you do as I say, and just leave?"

She fought him for a few more minutes, but it felt to Valerio that this was from habit, or perhaps a need to exert control over her shock. But he could see that understanding was gradually taking hold. He saw the moment Giorgia's fear and self-preservation made up her mind.

"Fine! We'll go!" she snapped.

"Tonight," said Valerio. "Leave as soon as possible. Don't tell anyone where you're going—not even your boyfriend."

He went next to his mother's apartment and let himself in with the key.

He was met by the sounds of the television blasting. Leonora was going deaf, and always watched with the volume up.

The smell here was familiar—a comfortable, lived-in mixture of cooked food and cleaning products, and the perfume his mother had worn since he was a child.

Out of habit, he crossed into the kitchen, and opened the refrigerator. At the sound, Orlanda's voice called out, "Valerio, is that you?"

"It's me," he shouted back.

He scanned the contents of the fridge, peeling back the foil covers of dishes to see what looked good.

He wasn't really hungry. The lunchtime pizza had been greasy and filling and, besides, he'd been eating too much lately.

But he wanted food. Something to shove down this desperation surging through him.

He grabbed a fork and peeled the tinfoil off a ceramic dish with noodles and sauce, eating it cold as he strode into the living room, where Leonora and Orlanda were watching a documentary. His mother was crocheting—fingers moving automatically across the edge of a red yarn quilt, hardly looking down to check her stitches. A small Christmas tree was on a table in the corner, glowing with colored lights, and covered with the handmade ornaments Leonora had collected from her children and grandchildren over the decades.

"Mamma," he said, "I need to talk to you."

Leonora didn't look up. She motioned at the screen.

"That man thinks the Vatican had something to do with it," she shouted with an expansive gesture. "It isn't possible!"

The two of them sitting there together like that, the Christmas tree, and the half-finished blanket in his mother's lap, reminded Valerio of another winter's evening long ago—when his father had gone out "to pick up a few things" and never returned.

Valerio's appetite left him. He set the plate down and took a chair facing them.

"Mamma," he said again.

Orlanda picked up the remote and paused the program. Only then did Leonora—blinking up—seem to notice him.

"What is it?" Orlanda asked.

Now that the moment had arrived, he realized that the truth was impossible.

"I wanted to check on you," he said. "How are you feeling?"

Leonora's face was suddenly radiant.

"Oh, Valerio, my sweet boy!" she exclaimed. "How thoughtful to check on your old mother."

Orlanda rolled her eyes.

Ignoring the spasm of guilt, Valerio scooted his chair closer to his mother, repeating, "How are you feeling?"

"Every day a bit stronger," Leonora said. "I talk to Costanzo. He reassures me. He says that my son will catch the devil who killed the girl."

"I'm not part of that investigation, Mamma," he said.

"Do they know who did it?" Orlanda pressed.

"They made an arrest," he told her.

Leonora stopped crocheting, and patted his hand.

"Costanzo has faith in you. So do I. I pray for you every day. *My Valerio—he leads with his heart,* I tell the Virgin. *He acts without thinking, so you need to keep a special eye on him.*"

"Do you need anything, Mamma?" he asked.

She shook her head and reached out, caressing his face.

"If you're offering," Orlanda said, "the sink in the bathroom needs to be fixed. It's leaking."

Valerio rose from the chair, and leaned in to kiss his mother's cheeks.

"Love you, Mamma."

Orlanda launched from the sofa and followed him into the kitchen.

"What's going on?" she demanded.

"Nothing," he said.

He covered the dish and put it back.

As he shut the door to the fridge, she was standing before him, blocking his exit, arms folded across her chest.

"You're lying," she said. "You don't just stop by for nothing. And you have this stupid expression on your face . . . like you're going off to do something noble and self-destructive."

"I need to take care of something," he said.

"Is it dangerous?"

"It'll be fine," he lied.

Federico had said that if he turned himself in and told his colleagues what he knew, he would be buried alongside the truth. But he didn't know what else to do.

The sight of his sister's desperate face made him ache. It had been a mistake to come.

"Do you know what's actually noble?" she said. "Showing up for your family . . . doing dishes and laundry . . . shopping. Sleeping at your mamma's house so you can wake her up when nightmares make her scream."

Orlanda's features contorted. He saw the wrestle of love and pain. He pulled her in, and hugged her, even as she stood rigid against his affection.

"Take care of Mamma," he said.

She followed him to the door, standing on the threshold as he crossed into the fading light.

"Don't you dare die. Don't you fucking die."

Valerio was already out of the neighborhood when his phone pinged.

A message from Federico: **I have an idea.**

TWENTY-FOUR

Nikki sat in the waiting room of the Pozzuoli women's prison while Sonia argued with Advocate Ferragni, their voices raised in the next room, muffled by thick concrete walls. It was 21:43, and both Ferragni and the prison staff were clearly unhappy about the late hour of this interview request.

Nikki shuffled her cards and was laying them out before her, matching the information she'd captured against what she knew, when Emilio strode in.

"There she is!" he announced. A smile crinkled his eyes. "Our resident troublemaker."

"Sorry to disrupt your evening," Nikki said.

His grin broadened, and he scratched the stubble on his neck. "I was losing my multiplayer game. This gave me an excuse to bail early."

It was the first time Nikki had seen Monica and Kami interviewed together. She thought of their Instagram photos, posing in front of the Eiffel Tower, flirtatious in heels and satin. The contrast was jarring. Here, in the dreary room with its ugly furniture, chipped paint, and stale stink, both women wore sweatpants and sweaters. Monica was sallow, acne spreading across her cheeks, greasy hair pulled into a stringy bun. Kami's face was puffy, eyelids heavy.

"I have to say," began Sonia, "I've had trouble understanding how two bright young women with such promising futures landed here . . . with murder and drug trafficking charges. You haven't made things easy for yourselves. You've repeatedly lied. And you've obstructed our investigation."

Kami returned Sonia's gaze, but Monica stared at her hands, picking at her nails.

"I've received new information this evening," continued Sonia. "It changes how I view this case."

She pulled out a file, and opened it flat on the table.

"Monica," she said. "Last year you interned at Stonehaven Wealth Management in London. There, you met a broker named Kevin Walker, whom you started dating. We know this from press articles. And your parents confirmed the relationship."

Monica pressed her lips together.

"Walker cofounded a company called Innovare MindCapsule with Theodore Sexton, brother of Claire Sexton," Sonia said. She flipped a page. "Their business was failing. They had loans they couldn't repay. No investors. They were desperate. Theodore recruited his sister, Claire, to nanny for Jayston and Fiona Lake. Lake owns an investment firm. We think Theodore wanted Claire to persuade Lake to invest in their company."

She stared pointedly at Monica. "It's clear you coordinated your arrival in Naples. Claire disembarked from *The Prophet* on Saturday, the nineteenth. Then, you and Kami arrived and rented an apartment on Via Montecalvario. We know Claire was with you that evening. Possibly, she stayed with you. We know cocaine was involved."

Monica began chewing her thumbnail.

Sonia continued. "We've checked the flights into Naples. Kevin Walker arrived from London on Tuesday. That night, Claire was murdered in Chiesa del Gesù Nuovo. The following day, Walker flew back to London. Here is what I need you to tell me: What agreement did you have with Signor Walker?"

Monica and Kami exchanged glances.

"Walker's partner, Theodore Sexton, is in custody in London," Sonia said. "He's being questioned right now."

Kami's head snapped up. "What about Kevin?"

"A search is underway."

"So, they haven't caught him?"

Sonia's tone remained level. "As I said, a search is underway."

Kami leaned forward, placing both hands on the table.

Monica whispered, "Don't. Kami! Please!"

"We need protection." Kami's voice was fierce. Her gaze bored into Sonia. "I don't need to get knifed in the shower—and neither does Monica."

"That depends on what you have to say," said Sonia.

"Promise you'll protect us, or we're not talking."

Monica began to sob.

Sonia studied them. "Why do you think you need protection?"

"Because the night you brought us in," Kami said, "some guy put a gun to my head. He told me to keep my mouth shut about Claire. The same thing happened to Monica."

Sonia's expression didn't change, but Nikki saw her fingers stiffen on the file.

"Is this true?"

Monica nodded, still crying.

"Who was he?" Sonia asked. "Can you describe him?"

"He was a policeman," Monica whispered. "Behind me. I couldn't see his face . . . just the gun."

"You're sure he was with the police?"

"They were the only ones there that night," Kami said, suddenly angry. "And the ambulance workers."

"And here in jail," Monica added. "We've gotten threats here, too."

"They say they'll hurt my mom and sisters if I cooperate with the police," Kami said. "They knew their names and where they go to school."

Sonia's voice was measured: "Your family in Texas?"

Kami nodded. "Yeah. And my boyfriend, Amir. They threatened him, too."

Sonia turned to Advocate Ferragni, switching to Italian. "Did you know about this?"

"My client didn't tell me," he said, spreading his hands.

Sonia looked at Emilio. As if reading her intention, he stood and strode to the door.

"I'll start making calls," he said.

Ferragni turned back to Sonia. "I want my client removed from general population."

"What about me?" Kami demanded.

"Sì," agreed Sonia. "Both of you. Tonight." She held up a hand. "But you need to tell me: What was the plan? What were you doing with Kevin Walker and Theodore Sexton? What did you know about Claire Sexton?"

Monica looked at her lawyer. He nodded, and she took a shaky breath, wiping her eyes with her sleeve.

"We didn't know about Claire," she said. "I swear. Kevin was supposed to meet us up in Naples. We were just gonna have fun. Then, on Saturday, he calls . . . says his friend's sister is stuck in Naples, and can she stay with us until he gets there?"

"So, Claire stayed with you?"

Monica nodded. "She slept on the couch. She was sweet. Super quiet. Shy. We asked her questions, but she didn't want to talk. We thought she was backpacking across Europe—"

"But she wasn't the type," Kami interrupted. "No way was she out on her own. She was an indoor cat. Nervous all the time. Scared."

"We talked her into going with us to a club," said Monica. "Sunday night. She hated it. Couldn't wait to get back. It was like she was hiding."

"Did she say from what?"

"No. She hardly said anything."

"Tell me about the cocaine," Sonia said.

"We freaked out when we found out she had it," Monica said.

"She needed cash, okay?" Kami interrupted. "So yeah, we bought some. We were just trying to help out."

Sonia flipped to a new page. "Her backpack. Did she leave it with you?"

"No. She took it with her wherever she went."

"What happened at Chiesa del Gesù Nuovo last Tuesday?"

Monica started crying again.

Kami answered. "We were supposed to meet Kevin at the church."

"Was that his idea or yours?"

"His idea."

"Was Claire with you?"

"No. She stayed at home."

"Did you meet Kevin Walker at the church?"

"We were late getting there. He didn't answer his phone, so we went inside to look for him."

Monica's sobs deepened.

"Claire was on the ground . . . covered in blood. A knife sticking out of her chest," Kami said. "Kevin was standing over her. He saw us and . . . just ran. It was like a nightmare. We tried to help her. We really did."

"Why would Kevin do that?" Monica sobbed. "Why would he kill her?"

Sonia's voice was cold. "Have you heard from him since?"

Both women shook their heads.

"You have to protect us from him," Kami said. She was trembling. "He's gotta be super mobbed up or something. He knows everything about us."

At 01:48, Nikki returned late to the offices at Phoenix Seven. Iacopo had already gone, and Pasquale and Romano were seated at their desks. She gave them the duty phone, briefed them on the evening's events, and left.

Nikki's phone jolted her awake.

It was Angelo: "I hope you're pleased with yourself, signorina!"

She blinked at the screen: 07:32. Fuck. She needed more sleep.

"Is there a problem?" she said.

"Oh, that's magnificent." He spat the words. "Don't play innocent with me. I know exactly what you are!"

Nikki sat up, mind racing. *What the hell happened?*

"What's going on?"

"I refuse to tolerate insubordination like this!" he barked. "There is such a thing as respect, Signorina Serafino. There is such a thing as chain of command. But you—you think the rules don't apply to you. You go behind my back. You . . ."

Words seemed to fail him. The guttural noise he made was feral, his breathing ragged.

Nikki had dealt with Angelo's anger before, his contempt. But he prided himself on maintaining a professional demeanor. She'd relied on his dignity to protect her from his disdain.

She'd never seen him so enraged.

"I'm sure there's a misunderstanding," she said, trying to steady herself. "If you could just explain . . ."

"You go to the police." His voice dropped, furious. "Without informing me. You know this is my case. *My case!* I'm the official liaison with the ambassador. I can't tolerate such insubordination!"

Understanding hit like a cold slap. *Monica Lissom.*

It hadn't even occurred to her to call him last night. It had been after hours, and a standard work task. But she should have known better.

Angelo's fledgling rapport with the US ambassador was the jewel in his crown, and she'd stolen his moment to shine. Harm to his status—his self-regard—was an injury he could never forgive.

"I should have called you," she admitted.

The words only stoked his fury.

"I know your games," he exploded. "I tolerated them because I thought I could make you a better investigator—but some people cannot be taught. Clearly you lack the decency and respect this job requires."

She started to respond, but he shouted, "You will *listen* when I'm speaking!"

She clenched her teeth. "I'm listening."

"I can't afford to be short an investigator," he said. "I'll give you three weeks—time to post your job and find your replacement. I suggest you start looking for another position. You're finished at Phoenix Seven."

Nikki was out of bed and pacing. She unlatched the window, shoving the metal shutters wide. They clattered against the side of the building. The day was chilly, morning traffic loud, weak sunlight filtering through the buildings.

Her breath came in short, sharp gasps. She slammed a fist against her ribs to force her lungs open.

It didn't work.

"Fuck."

She was angry at herself for not catching this in time, for not restoring the uneasy camaraderie with Angelo she'd worked so hard to establish. This collision felt inevitable. Like an asteroid hurtling towards the planet. She'd seen it coming from far away, and had been powerless to stop it.

Three years ago, the Americans had lauded Angelo for hiring the first-ever female investigator in Phoenix Seven. Proud of himself, he'd used the American euphemism "equal opportunity" and paraded her around as his special project, telling everyone he was taking her "under his wing." But, for all his talk of mentorship and equality, her increasing competence clearly grated.

Until now, she'd been able to maneuver around Angelo's fragility. But events last summer had disrupted the power dynamic.

That he had never viewed her as a serious investigator had been her protection. This was gone now.

She considered calling him back. But if she reasoned with him, if she protested, or fought, he would only dig in. To be effective, she would need to be repentant. At one time, she could have feigned this. But something had shifted and, desperate though she was to keep her job, she didn't think she could force herself to kneel.

Nikki worked the punching bag and lifted weights until she was drenched, muscles burning, then scrubbed her kitchen.

Her stomach was too tight for food, so she drank espresso while shuffling through unopened mail.

Among the bills was an unmarked envelope. Inside, a stack of legal papers.

She skimmed the first page—an NDA.

A note was clipped on top—in Enzo's handwriting: *If you ever loved me, please sign.*

She dropped it in the rubbish bin.

Her phone pinged. Another message from Audrey. A selfie. Close up. Pink freckled cheeks and bushy brows.

Nikki texted back: **Never send anyone pictures of yourself. It isn't safe. Show this message to your dad and tell him to talk to you about online safety.**

Audrey texted: **Can you come over?**

No, Nikki typed, and set the phone down.

It buzzed again. She almost didn't check it—but then saw that the message was from Sandro: **I found your guy.**

It took her a moment to remember what she'd asked him for. Then it hit: the man from Valerio's photo. **Great! Thanks so much. Who is he?**

He wrote, **Better discussed in person. Coffee?**

The clouds had been threatening all morning, rain dripping in fits and starts. By the time Nikki reached Piazza San Domenico Maggiore, the sky cracked open, and people scrambled for cover. She ducked into Massimo's café, joining the crowd pressing into the humid space.

The scent of espresso and damp clothes mingled with the acrid cigarette stink from the men smoking outside, sheltered beneath the awning. Competing conversations echoed in the small space, and the air thrummed with the beat of ambient music, the hiss of the steamer, coffee grounds slammed out, ceramic cups clinking.

Sandro had already arrived, and reserved a small table overlooking the piazza.

He stood as she approached, leaning in to kiss her cheeks.

It was an odd feeling to see him; a profound recognition and familiarity tempered by the strange newness. Sandro had been such an integral part of her childhood, Nikki couldn't remember their first encounter; she'd been only six or seven years old at the time. He and her brother Adriano had met during their first year at the Scuola Ufficiali Carabinieri in Rome—and Adriano had brought him home on weekend and holiday visits. She remembered youth in that handsome face, and eyes bright with possibility. There was a gravity to his features now; experience etched in the grooves around his mouth, sorrow in those eyes, and alert focus.

Adriano would be the same age now, she realized. The image came unbidden: her brother with a lived-in face, kindness in the lines of his laugh, and the bend of his body.

"You're looking well," Sandro said, after they ordered. "Tell me about yourself, Nina. Married? Any kids?"

She shook her head. "Not for me. You?"

"Divorced. Two sons," he said. "They have good hearts—but my youngest has a wild streak like his father. Needs to get it out of the system."

His smile was heavy.

Their coffees arrived.

"Sixteen years, isn't it?" Sandro said.

Almost exactly. Last week was the anniversary she hated. The date she never forgot.

"After Adriano," Sandro continued, "I should have visited your parents more. They were always good to me."

"They left Naples," Nikki told him. "Moved back to the mountains. Benevento."

"That's understandable," he said. "It was an awful time. Adriano was the best of us."

She nodded, but couldn't speak.

"I heard you went to London," he said. "Then I lost track of you."

They talked about Izzy and Preston, about the years Nikki had spent building a life in London, her martial arts training, her return to Naples, her work at Incendio, then Phoenix Seven. It felt so natural telling him, and Sandro listened with careful attention. Only when she'd nearly finished did Nikki realize how much she'd said. Her neck burned—a sudden hot flush of exposure.

Out the window, rain pooled in the slick black paving stones, and a parade of trainers and umbrellas marched past.

"I'd always seen you following in his footsteps," he said. "I should have known better. You were always your own person."

"What about you?" she urged.

"After Adriano . . . I thought about quitting the service, but I'm glad I stayed. I've done well for myself."

"I'm glad for you," Nikki said.

He nodded towards the window. "Rain's clearing. I need to get back soon."

He set a file on the table.

Nikki flipped it open. Printed photographs. The white-haired man from Valerio's picture.

Sandro's voice lowered. "He's known as 'the Ghost'—we believe his name is Yasen Lazarov. Former Bulgarian special services. We learned about him during a joint operation two years ago. He's wanted by INTERPOL. Red notice. Cop killer. Dangerous fucker. You aren't mixed up with him, are you?"

"Not me. A friend."

"Tell your friend to be careful," he said. "We'd love to get Lazarov under lock and key. Would your friend talk to someone on my team?"

"I'll ask," Nikki said.

He slid his cup aside and pushed back from the table. "I'm glad to see you, Nina."

"There's one more thing," Nikki said, and he settled in again. "My father's been visiting your offices recently."

"Yes." His smile was kind. "It's been good to see him again."

"Did he happen to mention what he's working on?"

He nodded, then leaned in, dropping his voice. "He's telling everyone about your mother's theory: that Adriano's death was an assassination. A *conspiracy*."

Nikki cringed at the unadorned description.

"I don't mean to disparage your father," he said, expression softening.

"I have tremendous respect for Raoul—but he's been off the pitch for a while. He's knocking on doors, and shouting in the street. Even my most patient colleagues are getting fed up."

"You don't think there's anything to find?" she asked.

"I don't." His voice was steady. "Raoul asked me to pull the records, so I did. I read every piece of evidence very carefully. Let me be clear about this: Adriano's death was a tragic accident. Wrong place, wrong time. They caught the guys, Nina. Ballistics matched. They confessed."

Nikki had testified in the trial. Stared them down across the courtroom. If she'd had a gun, she might have shot them herself.

"So . . . the code names he found? Diogenes, Damascus, Zosima?"

Sandro shook his head. "Raoul asked me that, too. I couldn't find much. Diogenes was a code name from a case in the eighties. Source went cold decades ago."

"And the others?"

"Nothing in our records. Damascus is just a city in Syria."

"And Zosima?"

"As far as I can tell, Zosima was a character in a novel: a priest."

"Which book?"

"*The Brothers Karamazov.* Dostoevsky."

Nikki was suddenly hot, the need to move flexing into her body. She wanted nothing more than to run and keep running.

"I don't know what your father is hunting," Sandro said. "But I don't think it has anything to do with Adriano's death."

Nikki clenched her hands beneath the table. "I see."

"I'm sure it hasn't been easy for him since your mother died," he said. His expression was kind.

She agreed. "It hasn't."

They sat for an awkward moment.

Sandro looked at his watch. "I've got to get going."

After Sandro left, Nikki said a quick goodbye to Massimo and Carlo, then stepped into the cool drizzle.

Several blocks away, her phone rang—an unfamiliar UK number.

Wary of Teddy Sexton, she hesitated, then answered.

The voice was friendly. "Good afternoon, Investigator Serafino. Jayston Lake speaking. Do you have a moment?"

She said that she did.

"Audrey just showed me the . . . numerous texts she's been sending you. You've been exceptionally patient and kind. I wanted to extend my gratitude, and to apologize for any trouble."

"It's fine," Nikki said. "But I do recommend you educate her about online safety."

"I quite agree," he chuckled. "You rescue us yet again!"

"How is Audrey?" Nikki asked.

"I fear I've done her no favors by bringing her on this cruise. She's lonely and in need of a proper carer . . . and friends her own age. We're eager to get underway."

"You're still in Naples?"

"Regrettably, yes," he said. "Still entangled in this unfortunate business with Claire. We're doing our best to be patient, but it's unsettling. Are you certain I can't tempt you with the nanny position? Audrey would benefit from someone of your caliber."

"I'm flattered," she said. "But caring for children isn't for me."

As she put her phone away, a text from Sonia appeared: **British police have Kevin Walker in custody.**

Nikki called. Voicemail. Sonia texted again: **Busy.**

Nikki stopped by the shops for some vegetables to sauté for lunch. She'd returned home and was unpacking groceries when Sonia called.

"Teddy Sexton hasn't reached out to you, has he?"

"No," Nikki said. "Why?"

"Sexton's lawyers got him released from custody a few hours ago. Now he's missing. We need to find him. Kevin Walker was just stabbed in jail."

"Fuck. How bad?"

"He's at the hospital, and it doesn't look good. I need all the help I can get."

"Did they interview Kevin?"

"Yes. He swore he didn't kill Claire. Said he saw the stabbing, panicked, and ran."

TWENTY-FIVE

Weak rays of early-morning sunlight kissed the hilltops as Valerio drove south along the E45. The road was still dark and he accelerated carefully, the moan and clank and rattle of the small engine asserting its speed limitations. He'd borrowed Federico's little Ape, the three-wheeled truck he used to make countryside deliveries. It was a rickety, flimsy thing, reeking of diesel, and he worried it might not make it all the way to Sorrento as they'd planned.

"If you want to be an idiot and throw your life away, that's your business," Federico said when he'd returned his call last night.

"You told me you had an idea," Valerio urged. "What is it?"

"Not on the phone," Federico grunted. "Come here, and I'll tell you."

In his apartment, the old man had said, "My brother's a careful man. Splits hairs in four. If he wasn't a psychopathic killer, he'd be an accountant."

"So?" said Valerio.

"So, he keeps good records," said Federico. "Can't help himself. Luca's got every detail of his operations documented: distributions, clients, routes. It's a business to him, see? He's proud. He thinks he's some sort of CEO. Believe me, he's hoarding all the evidence you'll ever need."

"Even if that's true," Valerio said, "I don't have enough for a warrant, and I doubt my witnesses will testify. Besides, building a criminal case would take months. And you yourself told me that there's corruption in the police. They could warn him—he'll clean everything before we have a chance to search."

"I've been thinking about this Silvestri fellow," said Federico, tapping a broad hand against his leg. "Luca doesn't like partnerships. He thinks other people are sloppy."

"That's probably why Luca sends his security team to visit Silvestri," Valerio said. "To keep things tidy."

"I'm sure," agreed Federico. "But do you think Silvestri likes that arrangement? He's rich. Important. He lives a comfortable life. Do you think he likes Luca's thugs at his place? No. Believe me, he blocks them—pushes them out whenever he can. Your best chance for evidence is there. At Silvestri's house. Papers . . . documents."

"But Silvestri's protected, too!" said Valerio. "I'll have the same trouble getting a warrant for his place. Besides, searching Silvestri would tip off Luca."

Federico's eyes were huge behind the thick lenses. "Then don't get a warrant. Don't let him guess he's been searched."

Valerio was starting to understand. He thought it through. He was willing enough to kick in doors alongside his team, but those skills didn't transfer well to cat burglary.

"How would I get in?"

"You're a clever man. Figure it out."

They talked for hours, examining the photos Valerio had taken when he'd reconnoitered Silvestri's place. There was a high fence and cameras along three sides of the property, steep cliffs on the fourth. Had Valerio been a much younger man, he might have attempted a scrabble along the cliffside, but his *Mission: Impossible* days were behind him.

"They didn't really look at the delivery guy, did they?" said Federico, inspecting the picture.

"I can't go through the front gate," Valerio protested. "If Errichiello's men are there, they'll recognize me."

"The Ghost might recognize you," said Federico. "If you see him there, then get out. But nobody ever sees me when I'm making deliveries. I'm just a guy in a hat and coveralls. Besides, you said that Luca's security team was only visiting. They might not even be there."

"They frisked the driver," said Valerio, straining to remember the details of that interaction. "And they searched his vehicle. They'll know I'm armed."

"So don't bring a gun."

They worked out the details. To pose as a deliveryman, Valerio needed to deliver something—and a lot of it—to justify loitering in Silvestri's house.

Not wanting to waste good wares on a reconnaissance mission, they loaded items Federico had rescued from the trash: wine and olive oil dumped by a beach club after spoiling in the heat; cases of sardines and tuna past their expiry dates; velvety boxes with Belgian chocolates long since melted into misshapen wax.

Federico hummed discordantly, seeming to relish the task. He bustled around crowded storage rooms, yanking out this or that item.

"I knew these would come in useful," he said with a grin.

"Give me some bottles of good wine," said Valerio. "And a few other items. I've got to have something nice, in case they want to sample the goods."

In his shop, Federico picked through and prepared a box of cheap—though not spoiled—wine, twenty eggs, a thick slice of shrink-wrapped pancetta, and two bags of fresh mozzarella. He nestled a demijohn of local brew among the goods, and prepared a full sales receipt for Valerio to carry for signature on a clipboard.

This complete, Federico located a set of zippered jumpsuit, and a cap with a wide brim.

The thick blue canvas coveralls were clean, but stained in paint, suggesting their use in a previous incarnation.

Valerio slept fitfully on Federico's threadbare sofa, which, no doubt liberated from some junkyard, smelled unpleasantly of mildew and dog.

He woke when it was still dark, and made espresso on the stove. He drank this down with a generous helping of sugar and checked his phone.

Orlanda had written several texts, demanding information.

He typed back, **I'm fine.**

Maurizio had written about his continued search on the identity of the Ghost. Two words: **No Joy.**

But where Maurizio had failed, he was surprised to see that Nikki had succeeded. She sent several photos of the white-haired man, and the text: **Yasen Lazarov. Former Bulgarian special services. INTERPOL has a RED notice on him—cop killer. Dangerous. Be careful.**

Not *Ivan*, Valerio noted with interest. He sounded out the name: "Yasen Lazarov."

Despite his fatigue and worry, Nikki's message made Valerio smile. He loved that she'd managed to squeeze drops of precious information from this dry stone.

"Little devil," he muttered.

Federico was still sleeping when Valerio climbed into the Ape and headed off into the unusually quiet city streets.

From the cliffsides of Sorrento, the wide expanse of the bay was a tumultuous blue, the occasional gleam of sunlight breaking through the dark rainclouds, glistening on the roiling waters. The Ape complained and whined as he pushed it, clattering, up the steep roads.

Early morning was the best time for police raids and arrests. Cocooned behind locked doors, deep asleep, people were vulnerable. Startle them with chaos and noise, and their brains took a while to make sense. Confusion created mistakes; they might spontaneously confess, implicate conspirators, or unlock cabinets and safes.

Valerio was operating with few advantages in this poorly planned scheme, and considered this early-morning arrival a necessity. As he approached the gate to Silvestri's villa, however, he doubted himself.

He considered calling Maurizio and asking for advice, but his partner would try to talk him out of it. Valerio didn't want to waste time arguing, or to implicate Maurizio in what he planned to do next.

Valerio stepped from the Ape, and pressed the button on the speaker. When nobody answered, he pressed again.

A sleepy male voice said, "What is it?"

"Delivery for Silvestri."

He was loud, efficient, looking into the camera and gesturing towards the Ape.

A pause, then, "It's very early."

"My apologies, signore. I have a full schedule today."

A buzz, and the gate slid open. Valerio drove through.

To his relief, the courtyard was empty—no armed guards pouring from the house.

Silvestri himself opened the front door.

A large black rottweiler bounded forward, putting its paws on Valerio as he stepped from the Ape.

"Down, Brutus," ordered Silvestri.

"He just smells the pancetta," said Valerio, and held up the box with the cured meats and eggs and mozzarella.

He approached Silvestri, holding out the clipboard for signature, then nodded back to the Ape. "Where do you want these?"

Valerio had reviewed footage of Silvestri last night: television appearances and interviews. He'd laughed and joked, seeming robust. Lively. Now he was shrunken. Centimeters shorter than Valerio. The characteristic smile from his photos was missing. His tanned face was thick and leathery, eyes swollen and sleepy. He wore velvet loafers and a silk bathrobe, boxers visible beneath—and a rounded potbelly.

Silvestri checked and signed the delivery list, then led Valerio into the extravagant cliffside villa. The floors and staircase were in artisanal hand-painted tile, and the furniture was in leather and ropy canvas. White plaster walls displayed large canvas oil paintings in ornate gold frames.

They arrived in the kitchen, and Silvestri pointed. "Put that there."

Valerio set the box on the marble countertop.

Continuing through the villa, Silvestri led him down stone steps into a cellar with a metal grate.

"Put the wine and other goods in here," he instructed.

The dog, Brutus, followed Valerio on his first few rounds, before settling on a carpet in the living room area to watch. To extend his time in the house, Valerio unpacked and moved slowly, carrying fewer boxes each time.

Despite his best attempts at loitering, there was no opportunity to look around. Silvestri stuck close, preparing coffee, tracking his comings and goings.

When the Ape was nearly empty, Valerio stopped at the kitchen, where Silvestri sat at the table with his espresso, talking on the phone.

"Toilet?" Valerio asked. Silvestri gestured him away.

This was it. His single opportunity to find what he needed. He strolled out of sight, then moved rapidly, silently. He darted to the stairs, taking them up two at a time, then strode along the hallway, opening and closing doors. He wanted to find an office—someplace Silvestri might keep documents.

His heart was pounding so hard, he could see the movement through the canvas coveralls. His hands were slick with sweat, the back of his neck hot and electric. He was running out of time.

At the end of the hall, he opened the door to an enormous bedroom with plush white and gold furnishings—and stopped short at the sight of a teenage girl sitting on the edge of the large bed.

She wore an adult-size T-shirt. It bagged, brushing her bare thighs. Long hair hung down her back, tangled and matted from sleep. Bony-kneed, full-cheeked, flat-chested, she was younger than Gemma. He didn't think she could be older than thirteen-year-old Davide.

The room was clearly Silvestri's: his clothes draped on the furniture and crumpled on the floor.

A sick and violent anger gripped Valerio. The fucker was abusing a kid here. Now.

He had nothing. No gun, no protection, no authority. He was operating far outside the law.

Reason told him to leave, to find the evidence incriminating Luca, to call for backup—live to fight another day.

Well, fuck reason.

"Are you okay?" he asked gently.

She stared at him, expression flat, unsurprised to find a strange man standing in the room.

"My name is Valerio," he said. "I'm a policeman. I'm here to help. Do you want to leave?"

Her body tensed. Her hands clenched into fists. She nodded and stood.

Valerio didn't want to frighten her by approaching. He gestured her forward.

"Come. I'll get you out of here."

She came slowly towards him.

"We need to hurry," he urged, reaching out.

With his other hand, he felt in his pocket for his phone, and dialed Maurizio. He was far outside any operational rules—but he'd worry about that later. What he needed now was to get this kid someplace safe. Idiot that he was, he'd decided to leave his personal weapon behind. He regretted this now. He needed backup.

The line was ringing, phone pressed to his ear, as he felt the girl's warm hand grip his. He gazed into eyes that were wide with terror.

"I got you," he said, and tugged her from the room.

He'd planned to hustle her down the hallway and stairs, to get them both into the Ape and out into the street before Silvestri noticed. But he was too late.

Silvestri was in the hallway, blocking their egress, the muscular dog at his side. The girl gasped, hand tightening in his.

"I knew it!" Silvestri shrieked. "Ines warned me about you! I knew it!"

He was carrying a gun—silver, and too large. He handled it awkwardly, like an accessory instead of a weapon. Valerio hoped he was right in guessing that Silvestri had no fucking clue what he was doing—or this would never work.

Pushing the girl behind him, Valerio released her hand. Then, in three rapid steps, he shoved the weapon aside and plowed his right fist into Silvestri. The smaller man gave no resistance, his body moving with the punch and slamming to the floor. The gun skittered away on the tile. That might have been it. That should have been it. But the dog, defending his master, jumped on Valerio, who raised his arm to protect his face and neck. The pressure and pain of the dog's teeth clamped onto his right forearm. Valerio roared.

Behind, the girl let out a high, thin whimper of despair.

"Get out of here," he shouted at her, but she was blocked in by the thrashing bodies and had nowhere to go.

Valerio shook the snarling animal, punched it. Its jaws did not release. He slammed it against the wall. Again and again.

This was shit. This had all gone to shit.

That was when Silvestri shot him.

Maurizio had been shot once, in the shoulder. He'd told Valerio that he'd never even felt it—that the adrenaline had numbed the pain, and that it had taken someone noticing the bleeding for him to know what had happened.

"It wasn't that bad," he'd said. "Like someone punched me in the arm."

Valerio remembered this as the bullet slammed into him, and realized: Maurizio was a fucking liar.

Fire tore through Valerio's leg, a searing agony in his hamstring as he collapsed to the floor.

He fell onto the dog, which had released its grip at last, the warm body limp beneath him. Through a miasma of pain, Valerio understood that the dog had also been shot—that this was why it had released its jaws.

Silvestri shouted and gestured with the gun. "Not Brutus. No. No. No!"

"Put that down," Valerio ordered. "I'm a cop. You shot a cop. They'll be sending in a team any minute now. They'll shoot you if they see you with that."

This last part was a lie, but Valerio had been calling Maurizio when

Silvestri confronted him. Despite his own idiocy, despite everything, he desperately hoped that Maurizio had picked up, had heard—would find him, and send backup. But that was wishful thinking. He needed to get himself out of this somehow.

The first priority was to assess the damage. Stop the bleeding.

It hurt. Fuck, it hurt.

"Call emergency services," he told Silvestri. "This doesn't need to get any worse."

Silvestri rose to his feet and, trembling, blood spattering his silk bathrobe, stumbled down the hall towards the stairs, still gripping the gun.

Valerio rolled off the motionless dog and looked around for his phone. He didn't see it. At the end of the hallway, crouched against the door, the little girl stared at him.

"It's okay," he told her. "It's going to be okay. Can you see my phone?"

She didn't answer. Valerio glanced around. He couldn't find it, and didn't have time to look.

"He'll come back," he said. "Get into that room."

She did as she was told and Valerio followed, half crawling, half dragging himself down the tiled hall.

Inside Silvestri's room, he shut the door.

"Do you have a phone?" he asked the girl. "Call one-one-three."

Propping himself against a wall, Valerio peeled back the coveralls. Beneath, he was wearing yesterday's clothes—a T-shirt and corduroy pants. Gingerly, he felt his thigh below the buttock where the bullet had gone in, then felt for an exit wound. The back of his pant leg was warm and wet, the pain exquisite. He unbuckled and stripped off his belt. Threading this around his leg, he guessed by the pain where he needed to tighten. His hands, slick with blood and shaking badly, kept losing their grip. He swore as he cinched the leather tight.

No sooner had he managed this than he heard pounding footsteps on the stairs. He cracked the door open to see.

His briefly irrational hope for rescue was doused when he saw the black clothes, muscled body, and white hair of the Ghost.

TWENTY-SIX

After lunch and before heading into work, Nikki visited a secondhand bookshop near Piazza Dante.

"We only have it in English," the bookseller told her apologetically as he retrieved the fat hardbound text: *The Brothers Karamazov* by Fyodor Dostoevsky.

She brought the book to a nearby café, ordered an espresso, and scanned the pages.

Izzy's description of her childhood, and about Beatrice's interest in the Russian language, had jostled Nikki's memory. She recalled a copy of *The Brothers Karamazov* on her mother's bedside table, and other Russian language books on the family bookshelves—an afterimage of Beatrice's navy career. Nikki had spent most of her life adamantly incurious about her mother's passions, and so never read Russian literature. But Sandro's comment about the book made her wonder if some secret was buried here. She'd probed the idea throughout the night, working it like her tongue on a sore tooth.

Now, flipping through the pages, she hunted for the name Zosima. It appeared in the fifth chapter. He was a spiritual leader called an "Elder."

"What exactly is an elder?" Dostoevsky wrote. "An elder is someone who takes your whole soul and your will into his soul and his will. Having chosen an elder, you renounce your individual will and surrender it to him in complete obedience and full self-abnegation."

She continued reading and found more references to Zosima, but these shone no new light on her mother.

Before leaving the café, Nikki checked her phone, hoping for more information from Sonia. Nothing.

She pinged Valerio, who had apparently read but not responded to her text about the identity of the Ghost, Yasen Lazarov.

He didn't answer.

Glancing at her other messages, she noted with relief and a small pang that Audrey's usual barrage of emojis and pictures was absent today.

Nikki arrived on shift at 15:30 sharp.

Angelo was on the phone, his office door open, bombastic voice filling the room.

"Sì. Sì. Ambassador, I understand. Believe me when I say we are doing everything in our power . . . Sì."

Crossing to her desk, Nikki was mortified to find an enormous bouquet of flowers, the vase so large her keyboard and files had been shoved aside to accommodate it.

"It's unprofessional," came a voice at her back.

Romano stood at his desk, peering over the grey cubicle wall.

"Excuse me?"

"Having flowers delivered is unprofessional."

"I didn't order them."

She walked the vase away from the cubicles and set it beside the office door, before spotting the handwritten card nestled among the pink and orange blooms.

In gratitude for your care of Audrey. Do let me know if you change your mind and decide to come with us.—Jayston.

"Get those out of here," ordered Angelo. He strode towards her, aiming his finger.

Nikki started to speak: "Where do you want—"

"Out of here," he barked. "You will keep your personal life out of this office!"

The last thing she needed was another fight with Angelo. Hefting the unwieldy bouquet, she left. The flowers were utterly impractical—so huge she could barely carry them, let alone bring them on her bike. The only reasonable destination was the dumpster. She hesitated briefly at the exit, then turned and walked rapidly down the service road.

Two blocks away, someone called her name.

She turned to see the stout figure of Mac van den Berg jogging towards her. He was in uniform: a dark blue jumpsuit and black beret, rank displayed on his gold-stitched shoulder shields. His shirtsleeves were rolled, showing hairy forearms.

"I tried to call—I couldn't get through!" he panted, drawing alongside.

"That's because I blocked your number."

He grinned.

"Oh *ouch*. You hurt my feelings! Gianni said you liked to play hard to get."

Fuck you, Gianni.

"This isn't a game," she said. "I'm not playing. You may be Gianni's friend, but you aren't mine. You aren't welcome in my home or my life."

He chuckled. "Okay, okay . . . I get it. You're pissed off."

They'd reached the dumpster. Nikki hoisted the vase over the edge. The glass shattered as she turned and strode back the way she'd come.

Keeping pace, he said, "Hey . . . I think you should give me a chance. I have a professional question. It's about your ex, Calandra . . . super high-level top-secret shit . . . hey . . . slow down."

He grabbed her forearm.

She responded instinctively, years of training giving speed and direction to her anger—stepping towards him, raising her elbow above his wrist, then swinging her arm rapidly down. He grunted in pain and surprise as he released her, and she danced away, hand up in warning.

"Back off," she growled through gritted teeth. "I told you to leave me alone."

"Shit!" he shouted, rubbing his arm. "What the fuck is wrong with you?"

Angelo was gone when she returned to the office.

"Did they release the ambassador's daughter?" she asked Romano.

He shrugged. "What do you care? You're leaving anyway."

Nikki texted Sonia, asking about the status of the case.

Sonia wrote: **The Brits are still looking for Sexton. Without Walker, we can't drop the charges against the women.**

Nikki texted: **What happened to Walker?**

Sonia replied: **Died at the hospital.**

It was a slow afternoon in the office. Nikki answered emails, finished paperwork, and checked the jobs website to see if Angelo had posted the vacancy notice for her position. He had.

Nikki looked on her social media accounts, and messaged Sally Tate: **Do you know where Teddy is?**

Sally responded: **What's it to you?**

The police need to talk to him. Do you know where he is?

You set the POLICE on him? Sally wrote. **He told everyone you're a psycho stalker bitch—and he's right. LEAVE HIM ALONE!**

With those words, the intimacy and viciousness of Teddy's attack seemed to surge through afresh. Nikki gently touched the bruises on her neck. Then, shoving down the discomfort, she invited anger to take its place.

She wrote: **He has information to help find Claire's killer. If you know where he is, tell the police.**

Sally didn't answer, but she didn't block Nikki either—a good sign.

The phone on her desk rang. It was the guard at the front gate.

"There's someone here asking for you: Orlanda Alfieri."

Nikki had met Valerio's younger sister a few times: twice for drinks with Valerio, and she'd once come sailing on *Calypso*. Nikki didn't know much about her, except that she'd recently ended a bad marriage.

Nikki spotted her as she exited the base. Orlanda looked a lot like her brother—the same bright eyes and playful mouth. But these were contorted with anxiety.

Orlanda apologized. "Sorry to come in person, but I didn't have your number, and I didn't know how else to reach you. Have you heard from Valerio today?"

Nikki checked her phone. Valerio still hadn't responded to her texts about the white-haired Yasen Lazarov.

"What's happened?" she asked.

"Oh!" Orlanda gestured forcefully. "My brother's an idiot. He came by last night and—I don't know . . . I had a really bad feeling about it. I just knew he was going to do something stupid and dangerous. I can't stop worrying about him, and he won't answer his phone. I called his ex-wife, Giorgia. She says he gave her money and told her to get away with the kids. He didn't tell her why."

"Have you reached out to his partner, Maurizio?" Nikki suggested.

"I called the station. They wouldn't put me through."

Nikki thought about the bruise on Valerio's head, and what he'd told her yesterday about Luca Errichiello and Paride Silvestri. *I fucked up*, he'd said.

"I'll get my bike," she told Orlanda. "We'll go to the station together."

It had been months since Nikki had visited the public reporting entrance of the police station. The last time she was here, she'd come to report the attack carried out by the thug Enzo had hired. Then, the place had been chaotic, crowded after the riots. Today, the room was subdued and orderly. A handful of uniformed cops filling out forms or taking statements.

Orlanda didn't seem able to stand still as they waited for Maurizio. She fidgeted, picking at the skin on her arms, and rocking backwards on her heels. Her anxiety seemed to seep into Nikki, whose own body tensed and thoughts raced, an ill-formed worry latching onto her mind.

"Where are Giorgia and the kids now?" Nikki asked.

"She wouldn't tell me." Orlanda shrugged. "Good for her. Giorgia may be a bitch, but she knows how to survive."

When Maurizio arrived, he listened attentively to Orlanda's concerns.

"Valerio called me this morning," he said in a low voice when she was finished. "It was zero six thirty, and my ringer was off—so it went to voicemail."

He played the recording. Nikki and Orlanda leaned in to listen to the confused and noisy exchange—somebody shouting, a dog barking, scuffling, then a clatter before the recording stopped.

"What's he saying?" Orlanda asked.

"I can't make it out," said Maurizio. "His phone's been switched off ever since. I had the techs work out where he was—that call came from Sorrento."

Nikki couldn't get the image out of her mind: Valerio's face as he told her, *I'm really fucked.*

Her mind replayed everything he'd said—the favor he'd agreed to with Errichiello, the death of the boy Gaetano, and Paride Silvestri's abuse of underage girls.

"Paride Silvestri has a home in Sorrento," she told him. "Valerio surveilled him before. He might have gone there again."

Maurizio glanced uncomfortably around the room and nodded towards the door.

"Let's discuss it over coffee," he said.

He led them from the station onto the noisy throughway of Via Medina. In a piazza on the back side of the station, they found outdoor seating at a café.

"Valerio's been on administrative leave since the Mancusi shooting," Maurizio told them. "That means nobody's very worried about him being out of comms. I talked to my boss this morning, and played him the voicemail. He isn't convinced it means anything."

"Valerio's in danger," Orlanda insisted. Her voice was tight and unsteady. "He certainly thinks the kids are. Why else would he tell Giorgia to leave town?"

Nikki weighed in with what Valerio had told her about Silvestri and Errichiello, and showed the photograph of Yasen Lazarov, the Bulgarian Ghost. She felt guilty repeating this. Valerio must have had his reasons for telling her and not his partner or sister. She hoped he would forgive her.

"Valerio told me about surveilling Silvestri," Maurizio said. "I looked into him, but he's clean. And I searched the pictures Valerio took, including this image of—this Ghost—but I couldn't get a hit. Now that I have a name—Yasen Lazarov—I'll see what we have on him."

Orlanda, who had been pinching her fingers, leaned forward and grabbed Maurizio's arm.

"Can't you get a warrant for this guy—Silvestri?" she asked.

Maurizio shook his head. "There's not really enough to convince a magistrate, even if I can confirm the identity of this Ghost. Valerio didn't tell me what he was doing, and he hasn't been missing long enough to get anyone here worried. I'll get some local cops over to the property, knock on the door, see if there's anything I can put on the warrant. If I'm successful—and that's a big *if*—it would be at least twenty-four hours before we could get inside."

Nikki's stomach turned. She looked at her watch: 17:31. Eleven hours since Valerio's voicemail. A lifetime, if he was in trouble.

"Did Valerio tell you anything?" she asked Orlanda. "Anything Maurizio can use to get a warrant?"

"No!" Orlanda started crying. The emotion seemed to make her angry and she pressed her palms to her eyes. "He's such an idiot. He doesn't tell me anything. What if *I* go to Silvestri's house? What if I bang on the door and make him let me in?"

Maurizio said gently, "That could put you in harm's way. Valerio wouldn't want that."

She shoved the tears back. Her eyes narrowed.

"There was a man," she said. "He came looking for Valerio at Mamma's house, the morning after that woman was killed in the church. Could he have anything to do with this?"

"Did he give a name?" Nikki asked.

"Federico . . . yes. That was it. Federico."

Maurizio seemed to think. "Tall skinny guy? Old? Glasses?"

She nodded.

Maurizio exhaled. "I may know who he is: an old addict Valerio helped a long time ago. I've met him a few times. He owns a shop not far from here."

He turned to Nikki. "I'll text you Federico's address. You start there. I'll head back in the office and see what I can do. It's the end of the day, and Valerio gave me a big fat *nothing* to go on, but I'll see whether I can get a magistrate to issue a warrant."

"Is there someplace you can go?" Nikki asked Orlanda after Maurizio left. "If Valerio was worried about Giorgia and the kids, you may also be at risk. You should take your mother someplace."

Orlanda glanced around, as if the threat was lurking around the corner.

"I'm not sure where we could go," she said.

Nikki dug in her bag, and pulled out her house key.

"Take her to my place until we find Valerio. I'll call you when I know anything."

Nikki wove her Hornet in and out of traffic, moving rapidly through the crowded streets. Her mind was with Valerio, wherever he was. He was a competent and highly trained capo. She told herself he was just fine. So, what was this bad feeling that kept climbing up her throat?

He'd come to her yesterday, asked for her help. There was no precedent for this. Valerio had never asked her for anything. She should have offered more—agreed to whatever he needed. Not long ago, as Nikki fought for her life in a cave by Lago d'Averno, Valerio had defied reason, defied odds, and found her. If he'd waited . . . hesitated . . . she would be dead.

The address Maurizio gave for Federico was in Forcella. It was a difficult neighborhood, and Nikki always removed her helmet when she rode through, for fear of being misidentified and shot.

The tiny salumeria was filled with rush-hour shoppers.

The proprietor was busy. Old and slightly hunched, with thinning grey hair, papery skin, and thick glasses, the man was impossibly thin. His large bony fingers worked the meat slicer, weighing prosciutto on the scales. Nikki tried to flag his attention, but in the thick crowd, everybody making their order, she had to take a number and wait her turn.

"Are you Federico?" she asked when she reached the counter.

The slight tilt of his head could have been a nod. "What can I get you?"

"I'm looking for Valerio Alfieri."

He grunted and glanced over her shoulder to the chaotic queue behind her.

"You need to place an order, signora."

"My name is Nikki. I'm his friend. He's been missing since this morning."

He coughed and spoke in a loud voice. "Allora. Sì. Pancetta . . . what quantity?"

His eyes, huge behind his glasses, were bright and staring. She understood.

"Enough for pasta tonight," she said.

He nodded, then sliced and weighed the meat, typed and printed a sticker, wrapped and taped the bundle, and dropped it in a sack.

"Next!"

Nikki paid for the meat at the cash register, then walked out of the shop. Two blocks away, she stepped into a doorway and examined the package. Next to the weight of the meat, 213g, Federico had typed, *Basilica. Venti minuti.*

The church closest to Federico's salumeria was the Basilica della Santissima Annunziata Maggiore. The large Baroque structure was badly deteriorated, and had been shuttered when the Camorra ruled this district. A few years ago, the city had made an effort to clean up this neighborhood. Syringes no longer littered the sidewalk, but you could still buy contraband from street dealers. The church, which had been used as a dumping ground for decades, was cleared out, and its doors opened to the impoverished community it served.

Not wanting to attract attention by loitering, Nikki strode through the church gates and up the stairs into the dreary interior.

It was empty. Alone in the fading light, she walked halfway up the nave, breathing in the musty odor. Taking a seat in a wooden pew, she glared at the crucifix. Never one for religion, she nonetheless felt irrational anger towards the figure on the cross.

"Don't let him be dead," she said.

Federico stole silently into the church, the thick soles of his trainers making no sound. Crossing himself, he took bowlegged strides towards Nikki, and slid into the pew beside her. He smelled of meat and cigarettes and bleach.

"You're Nikki," he said in a low voice. "Valerio talks about you."

"Do you know where he is?" Nikki asked.

He nodded. "He went to Paride Silvestri's house, looking for evidence against my brother."

"Why? Who's your brother?"

He stared. "You don't know?"

"No."

"My brother is Luca Errichiello."

Nikki understood now.

"I need you to talk to Valerio's partner, Maurizio," she said. "He's trying to get a search warrant—the police need to get into Silvestri's place and get Valerio out."

Federico shook his head. "It's too late. He won't be there anymore. Silvestri's not the one to handle it. If Valerio's still alive, they've taken him to Luca."

"Then tell the police!" Nikki exclaimed.

"I'm out," he said. "I promised myself I'd never go back . . . never get involved again."

"At least tell Maurizio."

He looked thoughtful.

"How much do you trust Maurizio?" he asked.

"I trust him . . . fine," Nikki said. "He's a good man."

Federico sighed. "The police will do nothing. Even if this Maurizio is a good man, as you say, there will be problems. This person says to wait . . . that person says there is not enough evidence . . . and so it goes. Believe me, the police will never come to Luca Errichiello's door. They say that my brother is a human trafficker, but this is not the point of what he does."

"Then what's the point?"

"The secrets, of course. Luca deals in secrets. If you own a man's secret, you own the man."

Nikki considered. "Then what do we do?"

"There's nothing to be done," he said. "Valerio knew the risk. I warned him. He understands the wolves he's hunting, and he did it anyway."

Nikki thought about Valerio, the relaxed kindness of his company. She'd become so accustomed to having him close, to easy conversations, to lazy, sun-drenched days together on *Calypso*, and the backbreaking work they did to keep their boat running. This new thought, the idea that Valerio might not be in the world, was like coming suddenly to the edge of a chasm. She simply couldn't tolerate it.

"I need to call Maurizio," she said. "Can you wait?"

He nodded.

Federico was right. She knew it before she even dialed Maurizio's number.

She stood on the steps of the church, phone pressed to her ear as she explained what Federico had told her.

"I'm trying, but I keep hitting walls," said Maurizio. "I can't get anyone interested in doing their fucking job."

"But Federico confirms that Valerio was going to Silvestri's house this morning," Nikki pressed. "We know that's where he was."

"I understand," said Maurizio. "But it doesn't do us any good if I can't get someone to sign a warrant to search the property."

"What if Federico's right and they've moved him to Errichiello's place?" Nikki said.

"Fuck," said Maurizio. "If he's alive, I'm gonna fucking kill him."

Nikki's mind churned as she walked back into the church. She couldn't give up. Valerio would never give up on her. If he hadn't come looking for her that night . . . well, things would have been different.

Federico was sitting where she'd left him, posture rigid, staring ahead towards the altar.

"They won't help, will they?" he said.

She shook her head.

"Nobody likes to hunt wolves," he said with a sigh.

Nikki's heart was racing. There was a sick taste in her mouth. She looked down and realized she was still gripping the package of pancetta.

"What about another wolf?"

TWENTY-SEVEN

Pain reminded Valerio that he was alive. He held to it grimly, stubbornly, as the car jostled and jolted along the rutted roads, clenching his teeth to keep from crying out.

The trunk was leaking. Rain soaked the foam liner, sopping his clothes, and the small space was filled with the powerful stink of mildew and exhaust. He lay on his left side, hands zip-tied behind his back. It was excruciatingly uncomfortable—arms contorted, circulation cut, pressure on his twisted shoulder. These mundane miseries somehow amplified the agony of the gunshot wounds in his thigh, and his forearm, which had been crushed and ripped by the rottweiler.

When the men arrived, he'd fought back, and done what damage he could. But injured, without a weapon, he'd been laughably ineffective.

The Ghost had aimed his gun, a detached assessment in those grey eyes, and Valerio had the sudden disorienting realization that he was seen as a rabid dog to be put down.

But Silvestri protested with a wail.

"Not in my house!" he screeched, looking with dismay at the white and gold furniture already spattered and smeared with Valerio's blood. "Do it someplace else! Get him out of here."

As they dragged him away, Valerio turned, straining, to verify that the girl was still alive. She sat on the floor, backed against the wall, skinny arms wrapped around her knees. He wanted to shout to her, urge her to get away, but she'd just witnessed his failed rescue attempt, and he knew his words would be empty.

He shouted anyway. "Don't give up!"

Trussed in the trunk, shivering from damp and blood loss, he was glad that he'd had a chance to bind his leg and stem the bleeding. Yet Valerio had no illusions that he'd survive what came next. Errichiello no longer had a reason to keep him alive. By getting himself shot, he'd spoiled any usefulness he might have as an inside man with the police.

Raging at his idiocy and impotence, Valerio's chest constricted, as if to keep his thrashing heart where it belonged.

It wasn't despair, exactly. But something of that flavor. And a sense of fate, as if all the moments of his life had led inexorably to this one. Time itself seemed to stretch out, unwinding like an enormous snaking rope trailing on the ground behind him. And Valerio's thoughts took on an unfamiliar sheen—as if he saw things clearly for the first time.

To his surprise, his thoughts were of his father, whose life and character never really deserved the sainthood that Valerio's mother assigned him after death. Costanzo Alfieri had been an affectionate and enthusiastic man, and the boy Valerio had loved him fiercely. But his father had also been fickle, spending money and time he should have saved, forgetting promises, and forever disappointing his wife and three young children. Valerio's mother had always been the one to put the pieces back together, to make do and make excuses, to soothe the ragged wounds in her children's hearts.

On that night, Valerio had seen his father at the kitchen table, right hand thrumming, and that irascible expression he had: a sort of mischief tucked into the left corner of his mouth. Five-year-old Valerio had climbed onto his father's lap. Enveloped in the familiar smell of beer and cologne and cigarettes, he mimicked his father, thrumming fingers on the table.

Costanzo laughed and squeezed him, and set him down.

"Go to bed," he said. "I'll be back soon."

He'd broken that promise, too.

Valerio wondered if he'd managed to be a better father than his, and was reminded of all the times he'd disappointed Gemma and Davide. With an urgent pang, he suddenly wished he'd used his savings to buy Davide those football boots he needed.

The thought of leaving his children now—like his father had left him—was a molten core burning through his chest. And his mother, whose husband had vanished, would lose her son in the same way.

My Valerio, she'd told the Virgin. *He acts without thinking.*

She was right, of course. That was what had landed him in this mess.

Well then, think, you fool.

If he was going to have any chance of fighting, he needed his hands.

Maneuvering as much as he could in the small space, he struggled to pull a hand free. But his wrists were bound too tightly, fingers swollen and numb. By the time he gave up, his skin was raw, hands slippery with sweat. He wondered if there might be something in the trunk with him, something sharp to cut the thick plastic zip tie. But he was facing the back of the trunk, and it was too dark to see what was here. He hunted behind him with his fingertips, feeling the surface of the trunk door. There wasn't much here—just the door and latch. This wasn't useful if he couldn't work it open. Then his fingers found a small edge of jutting ragged metal: a broken piece of trim. It wasn't much—certainly not sharp enough to cut the plastic on his wrists. Valerio squeezed his eyes shut and concentrated. He traced the ridged contours of the zip tie up and around the jagged piece until it hit the locking mechanism. Carefully, fighting the motion of the car, he worked the pointed end of the metal into the small square hole. It was painstaking, frustrating—like threading a needle—every jostle and shudder causing him to slip and reorient. His arms were fatigued and shaking when, suddenly, the locking mechanism was released, loosening the zip tie by a few centimeters! He wriggled his left hand free, and then his right.

The success of his improbable attempt gave Valerio a rush of exhilaration, and relief so overwhelming tears and snot streamed down his face. Pain flooded his body as he pulled his arms around front, flexing his fingers and rubbing his wrists to bring the circulation back. It took him a minute before he could use his hands again.

Now, for the next priority: He needed a weapon.

Valerio scrabbled at the back of the trunk, hoping to locate the tire iron but finding only more of the drenched foam liner. He peeled this back with his fingernails, and found the edge of the floor panel. Beneath it, he might find the spare tire and tire iron. But his weight was on the panel, and he couldn't negotiate the space well enough to remove the pressure of his own body.

He continued running his hands along the edges, pulling back the liner—finding a roll of duct tape and a plastic sheet. Then his fingers gripped a hard piece of Styrofoam. He picked away chunks of this until he touched something cold and metal. Frantically he dug, until he could run his fingers around its dimensions. Rotating himself slowly with gritted effort gave him just enough angle to pull it out sideways. Heaving and grunting, he wrenched it free: the hard metal of a car jack. The cold heft was the first comfort he'd felt all day.

The vehicle was beginning to slow. He had only seconds to decide how to use his small advantage.

As the car parked, he shifted position—facing the lid, and arranging his hands behind his back as though they were still tethered, the metal car jack tucked beneath him, gripped in his fists.

The trunk opened, letting in the cold and rain, blinding Valerio with the sudden wash of light.

He breathed fresh air, then grunted as two sets of rough hands yanked him out by his elbows, dragging him to his feet. Two men.

This was exactly what he'd needed. Standing on his good leg and using the momentum of the upward movement, he swung the heavy metal tool up and around, smashing it into the face of the man on his right with a sickening thwack—before ramming the full force of his weight into the other man, knocking him to the ground. They crashed down together into the mud and rocks, and the man grunted as the air left him. Valerio piled on top. Punching. Grappling. Slamming the man's head onto the ground.

A painful explosion close to his head set Valerio's ears ringing. He didn't know if he'd been hit, but it didn't matter. If he stopped now, he would die. He wrestled, punching blindly and taking punches. Rain blurred the world, the thick and slimy mud making it difficult to maneuver. There was no way he could stand—not with his leg like this. So, he dragged his enemy down every time he tried to rise, and they rolled through the mud like pigs. Then, suddenly, there was a black gun in the man's grip. Valerio grabbed for it, fingers closing around the barrel and shoving it aside, sending the shot wide.

They struggled for the weapon. His opponent was young and strong and muscular, while injury and terror had weakened Valerio. But Valerio's heart surged with fury, and the desperate need to return home to his children. When he managed to get the weapon in his hand, he didn't hesitate before shooting the other man in the head.

No sooner had he done this than a bullet smashed into the bumper of the car, narrowly missing him. Valerio glanced up to see Ivan taking aim again.

No. Not Ivan. Yasen Lazarov was shooting at him.

Valerio hit the ground and rolled to the side of the vehicle, putting the tire between himself and his attacker as another bullet crashed into the car. His hands, slick with mud and rain, were shaking. He tried anyway, turning and aiming the gun and pulling the trigger.

Nothing.

Fuck.

He tried again. The gun was jammed. Two more bullets crashed, one of them hitting the car and causing it to judder.

Fuck. Fuck.

"You and I need to talk, Lazarov!" he called out in English. Another bullet hit the ground nearby. Then, to his surprise, there was a pause.

"Lazarov!" he called out again, trying to remember what Nikki's message had said about the man. "Yasen Lazarov, we need to talk!"

An eerie silence filled the air, broken only by the patter of rain.

Then Lazarov's voice: "How do you know that name?"

"I know more than your name. I need to talk to you, Lazarov. Don't shoot. We're on the same side."

Another pause, and Valerio's mind worked furiously to fill in the lie. He glanced around, trying to work out where he was. They were in a field that looked as if it had once been a factory dumping ground. Enormous rusted machine parts rose up on all sides, hulking and bare like the fossilized skeletons of monsters.

Valerio calculated. There had been five men in Silvestri's house, and two vehicles at the property. But he'd only seen three men here: Lazarov and his two buddies. He'd killed one of the men, and badly injured—or killed—the other. He hoped this was all—that the other vehicle wasn't following close behind. The odds were better now than they had been. But he needed luck. He needed the gun to work.

"Who are you working for?" Yasen shouted.

There wasn't a good way out of this.

He needed time. That was all. He needed to live just a little bit longer. He'd figure out the next step later.

Mouth dry, Valerio gambled: "Did you think you were the only one sent to keep Errichiello and Silvestri in line?"

Another pause, then the voice was closer than before. "How do you know my name?"

The response brought a surge of hope. Lazarov hadn't called his bluff.

"Let's stop playing games," Valerio shouted. "You know I can't discuss my mission with you. If you let me die, it won't be the Naples police you answer to."

"You're a bullshitter, Alfieri. Prove it."

Valerio scoffed, warming to the role. "Fuck you, Lazarov. *You* prove it. That idiot Silvestri shot me—I need medical attention. Make whatever calls you need to make to confirm that what I'm saying is true. But stop shooting, and let's get the fuck out of here."

When Valerio saw Lazarov, he knew his words had found their mark. The clever, brutal face was full of suspicion, but there was also a reluctant agreement in his eyes. His hand gripped the gun still, finger on the trigger.

"Put that thing down," Valerio said, reaching towards him as if he expected support. "And help me up."

"You killed my men," said Lazarov. "Put down your weapon, and get back in the trunk."

"I'm not going back in there," Valerio snarled.

"Then I'll shoot you now."

"Fuck it, Yasen. I'm bleeding out. I don't have a lot of time. Get me out of here."

Yasen was close enough for a head shot, but Valerio didn't dare use his jammed weapon again. He offered the handle to Lazarov, as if a peace offering.

"Cuff me if you need to," Valerio said. "But I'm riding in the front. And you'd better get someone out here to get rid of those bodies."

Lazarov took the gun and stared at it for a moment as if considering. He squatted down and looked Valerio in the face. There was a frenzy in those eyes—dark and chaotic. Valerio felt the calculation of the moment. Lazarov might decide to kill him after all.

"I don't like you, Alfieri," he said. Then, holding the gun like a hammer, slammed it into Valerio's cheek. It was so sudden, so brutal, Valerio didn't have time to brace. His head jerked back, something crunched in his cheekbone.

"Get back in the trunk," Lazarov said. "I won't ask again."

Trapped once again in the dark and stink, Valerio vomited. He tried his best to keep it in—but there were some things out of his control right now, and this was one of them.

He took deep breaths and tried to slow his heart rate. The last thing he needed now was a heart attack.

"Worry about one thing at a time," he told himself.

At least his hands were free this time. He used them to investigate his wounds. His leg was still bleeding and excruciatingly painful. It was swelling badly and was hot. He felt around in the trunk for the roll of duct tape he'd located earlier. Then, adjusting the belt he'd secured earlier as a tourniquet, Valerio wrapped his leg tightly in tape. The blood and the damp and the mud made it tricky work, but he managed to get several layers secured. He hoped this would slow the bleeding. He used the rest of the tape to stop the bleeding from the dog bite on his forearm. He felt the rest of his body. He was bruised, and his cheekbone was fractured, but those injuries weren't life-threatening.

Keep thinking, he told himself. *What do you know? What do you have? What can you use?*

He was alive. He'd killed two men, and somehow convinced Lazarov not to kill him.

Now, he thought more carefully about the lies that had bought him more time.

We're on the same side, he'd told Lazarov. *Did you think you were the only one sent to keep Errichiello and Silvestri in line?*

He'd acted instinctively, guessing and bluffing in equal parts—and the gamble had paid off. Why exactly had he said that?

Valerio had watched Lazarov's interactions with both Errichiello and Silvestri—the disdain and entitlement he seemed to have towards both. The attitude made some sense when it came to Silvestri, since Lazarov owed the rich old pedophile no allegiance or respect. He'd been merely a tool—useful for his connections and proclivities—and Lazarov had treated him accordingly.

But Lazarov had also been contemptuous towards Errichiello, and this had surprised Valerio from the outset. Lazarov had treated Luca like a nuisance, not a benefactor. Luca had clearly bristled at this, telling Lazarov to "Fuck off."

It made little sense for Lazarov to disrespect his employer.

The power structure had felt off. And Valerio realized: Errichiello wasn't actually in charge.

So, who was?

Was Lazarov actually in control—the mastermind of this operation?

No.

Valerio had met men like Lazarov—talented in a kinetic operation. Quick to assess an opponent, with a reactive instinct. He'd combined these skills with a taste for brutality. But a natural physical prowess was its own vulnerability. He relied on strength and fear to rule the men who worked for him; fear to dominate his prey. But reliance on his physical abilities meant he was never forced to think creatively—and you needed to think creatively if you were in charge.

No, Lazarov liked to be close to power, was drawn to those who could appreciate and harness his vicious skills, yet he lacked the finesse and patience to claim real power himself.

Lazarov was the sheepdog. And that meant there was a shepherd.

So, who was the shepherd?

Valerio's mind felt out the edges of this missing piece—rough outlines in the dark. There was just enough here to know that it was bigger than the individual players.

Whoever it was, Valerio felt certain that it was connected to his name. He'd introduced himself to Valerio as Ivan—and was known in the underworld as il Fantasma. But he'd clearly been surprised when Valerio called him by his name: Yasen Lazarov, the Bulgarian operator wanted by INTERPOL.

Valerio had bought himself time by claiming affiliation with Lazarov's master. Maybe Lazarov believed him, maybe he didn't. But he wouldn't kill him until he knew for certain that Valerio was lying.

Valerio was shivering badly by the time the car slowed, tires crunching on gravel, and stopped. He was wet, his hands frozen, fingers numb, when the trunk opened.

Lazarov wasn't taking any chances. He stood a meter back, gun aimed at Valerio.

"Get out," he ordered.

Eager though he was to escape his cage, Valerio was also stiff, leg badly swollen, every movement an invitation to agonizing pain. He maneuvered gingerly, easing over the rim of the trunk. He balanced on his good leg, and leaned against the car.

They were in a narrow gravel area close to Luca's compound. Through the trees, Valerio could spot the pool behind Luca's house, a winking patch of blue.

Valerio spoke urgently: "I know you don't want to fuck this up any more than I do. But Luca's ambitious and self-interested—this could blow up in our faces. You're here to make sure he doesn't fuck up. That's why I'm here, too. Let me go. Let me get back to my mission."

He didn't have a chance to see if Lazarov believed him. Two men came around the side of the house, weapons drawn. They glanced between Lazarov and Valerio.

"Put him away," Lazarov ordered.

"I've been shot. I need medical care," Valerio said.

But Lazarov strode off. The men grabbed Valerio harshly. Finding he couldn't walk, they dragged him down a stone path into the trees—to a small windowless concrete outbuilding with a padlock.

"I need water," he told them. "If I die, you'll have a big fucking problem to deal with. Your boss won't be happy."

As they approached the building and opened the door, Valerio struggled, shouting, hoping someone on the nearby property might hear—might think to report this to the police.

"Lazarov isn't telling you everything," he told his captors as they shoved him inside. "You don't know who you're working for!"

TWENTY-EIGHT

The car park was in a vineyard, grass and flowers wending through concrete slats, twisted vines teeming with leaves. It was drizzling, and the air was humid, thick with the earthy smell of plants, and diesel from the nearby road. Peering through the bars of the high metal gate, Nikki saw only luxury vehicles: Ferraris, Lamborghinis, and a Bugatti.

"This is it?" she asked Federico.

Behind her, on the motorcycle, the old man gripped tightly.

His voice was muffled by the helmet. "That's what they told me."

Nikki, who never considered she might need to find De Rosa, hadn't known where to look. But Federico made some calls, and they were directed to this thermal spa in the rural hills of Campi Flegrei.

On the other side of the high concrete wall and gate, Nikki heard men speaking, and the sounds of a television program. She shouted, and the voices stopped. A muscular figure in a T-shirt stepped into view. More bull than man, with a large forehead and burly forearms, he was chewing something. He gazed for a moment, then scooped his large hand through the air, pushing them along.

"No loitering."

His voice was gravelly.

Nikki worked against the mad thrumming of her heart to keep the words steady: "We're here for Benedetto De Rosa."

"He expecting you?"

"Yes," she lied, meeting his gaze.

He chewed for a moment, evaluating. Then smiled.

"You're not his type, sweetheart."

"Call. Tell him Nikki wants to talk."

"Nikki . . . Nikki . . ." he muttered, strolling away.

Nikki pulled the bike to the curb.

When the guard returned, he pointed at her as the gate screeched slowly open on its rails.

"Just you. The old man stays here."

Leaving Federico, Nikki followed the man through the gate and car park, past flowering gardens and a pond, to a glass-fronted building among the trees. A guard in a Kevlar vest sat by the door, rifle propped on his knees.

Her beefy escort stopped, turned, and said, "Arms up."

He frisked her, hands lingering a little on her thighs and buttocks, then said, "Give me your phone."

She handed it over, noticing that she'd missed two calls from Phoenix Seven.

Inside the building, a woman with long hair and immaculate lipstick hurried to greet them. She gestured with an impersonal smile and nod.

"This way."

They followed her into a high-ceilinged room with rows of white lockers. It was warm, smelling of hot stones, eucalyptus, and bergamot, with the underlying stink of sulfur and sweat. They walked past two young men in towels and flip-flops, and a tattooed old man with an overhanging belly, drying his hair with a towel.

The woman handed Nikki a key on a lanyard, and indicated a locker.

"Undress and put your things in there."

"I'm not going into the spa," Nikki protested. "I just need to talk to Signor De Rosa."

"Those are the rules," said the guard. "Take off your clothes and shoes, or De Rosa won't see you."

"I don't have a bathing suit," Nikki told him.

She looked to the woman for support. There was none.

The guard stared openly at her.

She'd come this far. She refused to quit now. Moving mechanically, she unlaced and kicked off her shoes, peeled away her socks, her jacket and hoodie, unbuttoned her shirt, then folded and placed these neatly in the locker. Face burning, she stripped off her belt and trousers.

She secured the lock and slipped the stiff shoestring lanyard around her neck, the cold key tapping the skin between her breasts.

Standing in her bra and underpants, she stared at the guard, daring him to say more.

He took a good long look, then ambled away.

"Follow me," the woman instructed.

They marched down labyrinthine tiled corridors that echoed with the efficient clip of the woman's shoes, past massage rooms, into a hot and humid antechamber. Here, light filtered in from a filmy window showing concrete walls stained green with algae. Men in Speedos reclined in blue canvas beach chairs, staring as they walked past.

Her guide stooped, and whispered to one of the men. He answered, gesturing to the room beyond.

In the next chamber, the echoing din of water drowned out all other sound. Men moved chest-deep in a swirling pool, skin reflecting the eerie green light.

Here, the walls were composed entirely of the bare rock face of the mountain, black and pitted, water dripping down. A heavy door was set into this, dark and glossy wet.

The woman pointed.

"In there."

Behind the door was blackness and an assault of heat and steam. Nikki gasped, struggling to breathe.

As her eyes adjusted, she was dismayed to find herself in a narrow volcanic tunnel, the walls uneven and shiny with moisture—black rock scraped away with crude tools, striations still visible, streaked with lines of calcium grey. The soles of her feet burned on hot wooden planks, beneath which came the roar of rushing water, superheated from the volcano.

A bright flash of lightning struck in her memory, the screaming sizzle of an orange flare, and the crashing terror of a thunderstorm in the dark. Her body tensed, ready to fight, ready to tear apart the nightmare waiting for her in the shadows of that cave.

Paralyzed, heart hammering, Nikki told herself to breathe, but the hot air seared her lips, burning her lungs. Chest constricted, panicked, she sipped the air. Closed her eyes.

O my dear Guide, who more than seven times hast rendered me security. . . . do not desert me. . . .

Gradually, her breathing began to adjust. Yet the heat, unrelenting and stifling, carved desperation along the boundaries of her mind. She wanted to run. Instead, she wended through the narrow passageway, heat growing with every step, until it opened into a cavern lined with wooden benches.

Two men sat side by side on a bench, skin slick in the dim light of a single bulb. The beautiful younger man held a long branch of eucalyptus. He stroked this against the back of Benedetto De Rosa, who was bent forward, elbows resting on his knees, eyes closed, the tattoos on his muscled back and arms moving gently as he breathed.

Both seemed lost in their own struggle with the heat and didn't seem to notice Nikki until she was standing before them.

"Signor De Rosa."

She spoke loudly to be heard above the relentless rush of water.

De Rosa's eyes opened, and he leaned backwards, resting against the rough wall. His companion adjusted to the new arrangement, giving Nikki an unfriendly stare.

"Signorina Serafino." De Rosa's expression was blank. "Why are you here?"

"I've come to ask for your help," she said.

Uncomfortably conscious of her body, she squared herself to him, as if this was a professional meeting, as if she wasn't so exposed.

He didn't answer, but he looked at her. She took this as invitation to continue.

"I understand Signor Calandra has agreements with Luca Errichiello," she said.

He raised an eyebrow, and she continued: "Signor Errichiello is holding one of my friends. I'd like you to help me arrange for his release."

"Why should I help you?" De Rosa asked.

Nikki trembled, a surge of rage overcoming the fear and heat.

"You fucking burned down my studio, that's why."

De Rosa's expressionless stare raked her.

"That was not my doing," he said.

Nikki opened her mouth to protest, but thought better of it. If he didn't accept responsibility, she was in no position to force the matter.

"Tell me what you want from me," she said.

"You'll do what I ask?"

The heat nauseated her. She felt unsteady, a rush of blood in her ears, terror and sweat pouring from her skin. But her thoughts seemed to travel far away. They sought out Valerio, the easy movements of his body as he clambered over *Calypso*; the sense of having him beside her, of him joining her in the darkness of that cave as she grappled for her life, the ringing shot that saved her.

"Yes."

"I thought you didn't deal in favors," said De Rosa.

Nikki's heart slammed against her ribs. When she didn't answer, he stood.

His eyes fixed on hers, body so close, they were almost touching. He seemed to be looking for something. She stared back, breathing in his exhalations.

"Follow me," he said at last.

Sweating, body glowing with the heat, Nikki almost collapsed with relief as they exited into the relative coolness of the echoing antechamber. Beneath a steel showerhead, De Rosa pulled the lever. Water slammed down, soaking him.

De Rosa's companion handed him a towel. He wiped his face and chest, and Nikki followed him through the spa and out a set of double doors. The noise of the water was abruptly cut, and they passed into a garden with a large pool, steam rising from the surface.

Wrapping the towel around his waist, De Rosa indicated for her to join him at a small table in the misting rain. She did this, and the cool air and rain, the cold chair, came as a relief.

Nikki watched as De Rosa looked out over the view.

"Luca Errichiello is an unscrupulous man," he said after a long silence. "If your friend has gotten into trouble with him, I pity him."

"Please," Nikki said. "I need your help . . . if you could just make a call. Luca's brother, Federico, said that Tito has agreements with him."

He gestured. "That's finished."

There was a hard edge in his voice.

Then, as if he'd just heard what she said, he sat suddenly upright and looked at her. "You have contact with Errichiello's brother?"

"Yes."

"I thought he was dead."

"He might be dead to his brother," said Nikki. "But he's alive, and he still knows people. That's how I knew where to find you. He says he has information for you."

"Where is he now?"

"Outside the gate."

They didn't require Federico to undress, as they had Nikki. The old man took unsteady, loping strides as he followed the gate guard down the path.

Federico glanced briefly at Nikki, seeming unsurprised to see her stripped.

He turned to De Rosa.

"Are Calandra and my brother still trying to kill each other?"

The hint of a smile played on De Rosa's crooked lips. "What have you heard, old man?"

"Luca broke the truce when he tried to have Calandra killed. You must have known he would. He's a malignant fuck. Ambitious. And Calandra's standing in his way. If you let him think he's won, he'll only get more vicious."

"You're well informed," said De Rosa.

"Be informed, or be dead," said Federico.

"Anything else I should know?" asked De Rosa.

"Just suspicions."

"Such as?"

"I suspect Luca's made friends with some big dogs," said Federico. "He doesn't have the teeth to attack Calandra on his own."

De Rosa leaned back and tapped on the glass window behind him. His beautiful young companion came to the door, and stuck his head out.

"Bring me my phone," said De Rosa.

When the young man returned with the phone, De Rosa scrolled through, and handed it to Federico.

"You know this man?"

Federico examined the screen, then shook his head. "I don't know anyone anymore. I just talk to old friends sometimes."

Federico looked at Nikki. "Ask her."

"I've already asked Signorina Serafino to look," said De Rosa. "She doesn't wish to be contaminated with our business."

Nikki remembered De Rosa in the dark and rain, outside the studio, holding out his phone, and her desperate compulsion to look away. She didn't want to see, to know. But closing her eyes to the reality hadn't helped her.

Federico clucked his tongue. "Try to stay out of it . . . try to stay out and it pulls you back in."

The city's entrenched criminal systems were terrifying: a reef beneath black waters, impossible to navigate without knowing where to look. It could break you into pieces. Maybe somewhere, right now, Valerio had wrecked against this hidden hazard. If she could feel along the edges, map its shape, maybe she stood a chance of finding a way through—like Federico had.

Nikki put out her hand. "Show me."

The picture was a still from a CCTV camera, in black and white: a man wearing a Kevlar vest and carrying an assault rifle. Immediately, she recognized the white hair and cold eyes of il Fantasma.

"His name is Yasen Lazarov," she said. "Also known as the Ghost. He's wanted for the murder of a Bulgarian police officer."

"Where did you get this information?" De Rosa demanded.

"I won't disclose that," she said.

"Bulgaria," he said. "Is that what the authorities think?"

"You think different?"

"He's a link," said De Rosa. "As the old man says, Errichiello needed sharper teeth. The question is: Who is the big dog with those sharp teeth? I want to know who this Ghost is working for."

"My friend was surveilling the billionaire Paride Silvestri," said Nikki. "Lazarov was there—and also at Errichiello's place."

De Rosa looked interested. He glanced between Nikki and Federico. "Tell me everything."

TWENTY-NINE

Trapped in the dark, mind foggy, pain pulsing through his body.

The smell was intolerable. A choking, foul odor—human waste and something worse. Valerio took short, shallow breaths to stop himself from gagging.

Then there were the flies. Swarming. Crowding his face and hands, coming into his mouth when he tried to breathe.

Valerio did his best to calm the rising panic and assess his situation.

He started with his injuries. His face, head, arm, and belly hurt—but most urgent, most likely to kill him, was his leg. He didn't think the bone had been hit. The bullet seemed to have torn through the muscle. He felt it, trying to tell if the bleeding had stopped. But everything was wet, and he wasn't sure how much of this was blood.

He turned his attention next to his prison. His eyes adjusted to the pitchy blackness, light filtering through chinks in the masonry above. He was in a rectangular structure about four meters across, with a cement floor and drain in the center—where the smell originated.

He scooted to a corner of the structure and, grunting, straining, used the walls to push himself up, balancing on his left leg. Experimentally, he touched his right foot to the ground. Pain shot through—so intense, he shouted, eyes watering, and nearly collapsed.

Maneuvering unsteadily along the wall, he began a slow investigation.

Concrete blocks formed the walls to about head height—and, reaching above, Valerio felt heavy wood beams. Outside, beyond the frenzied insect buzz, he heard birdsong. Along one wall, two metal rings were fixed into the concrete, grooves worn into the block below, where the rings had dragged across the surface. Valerio pulled hard at the fixtures, trying to loosen or twist them around. They didn't budge.

Suddenly, everything seemed to tilt and tumble, a sort of disorienting nausea. He lowered himself, and sat with his back against the wall. His mouth and body were parched—an aching burn and a straining for water that eclipsed the other miseries.

The small space was humid and cold, and his teeth chattered. But he was also feverish.

He tried to slow his breathing, push down the panic. He couldn't afford to numb up or lose his mind.

He continued investigating the edges of the structure, running his hands along the space between the cement floor and the blocks forming the outer wall, looking for weaknesses—perhaps a crack he could exploit, or a loose block. He didn't find this, but after several minutes, he came across a small, delicate piece of wire. He held it up, squinting, but couldn't make out what it was. He ran it between his fingers. It took him several moments to realize: It was a woman's earring.

Understanding settled like a boulder in his belly.

The iron rings affixed in the walls and the drain in the floor should have told the story—but he'd somehow refused to see it. This delicate earring was the clue that made it impossible to interpret this any other way. He wasn't the first prisoner here.

Who had she been—the woman with the earring? Had she been imprisoned here last week while he met with Luca—only steps away—his only concern ridding himself of his obligation?

He lost consciousness. The first time, it was like falling asleep, but so rapid he couldn't be sure. Then it happened again. And again. He didn't know how to prepare for or prevent it. And each time he awoke in agony, disoriented, struggling to think.

The involuntary escape, the relief from pain, was difficult to resist. Part of him welcomed it.

"Stay awake," he told himself.

He'd set himself beside the door—and ran his hands along the bottom, and up to the latch. He knelt, putting his eye up to the small gap beside the bolt. Nothing.

He didn't know how long he was there, drifting in and out of awareness. Every once in a while, desperation would get the better of him and Valerio would shout and slam his fist on the door. There was no response.

If they forgot him—without water, without medical care, he would die.

He awoke as the door opened. A flashlight beam found him.

"Water," he said to the dark figure. "I need water."

"Smells like shit in here," someone exclaimed in Italian.

Men dragged him out.

Unbearable, exquisite, crystalline pain.

Valerio heard groaning and was ashamed to realize the sound was coming from him.

At last, they dumped him in a heap. Valerio wanted to move, to fight, but his body was sluggish, unresponsive.

He struggled to sit.

The area was brightly lit by electric lamps. Beyond this, blackness.

Men pointed guns at him. Lazarov wasn't one of them.

Nearby was the sound of splashing water—a stone fountain and, beyond that, Luca's house. As Valerio watched, a door opened, and the strains of distant jazz music drifted out.

Luca Errichiello paced towards Valerio, feet crunching on gravel.

He was dressed casually, hair glossy with pomade and stinking of cologne.

"You are one dumb motherfucker," Luca said, squatting down. His face was inexpressive. "You just had to do what you were told. Look at you now. What a dumb fuck."

He was so close—Valerio considered attacking. But how? And what then? It would be suicide.

"You killed Gaetano," he croaked.

"It was necessary," said Luca with a small shrug.

"He was your son."

Luca grimaced and sighed, then stood.

"You are burdened with sentiment for your children, Capo," he said without affect. "I've never suffered from that affliction."

"You have other weaknesses," said Valerio. "Yasen Lazarov, for one."

"Who?"

"Il Fantasma. Your Ghost. Except he doesn't work for you, does he? You aren't the boss at all. You work for him."

Luca kicked him. The movement was fast and vicious. Valerio toppled, and the strikes continued. Valerio balled up, trying to protect his head and middle. But Luca was in a frenzy, and a few of the blows landed badly—one on his head, near his broken cheekbone, and another on his cracked ribs. At last, Luca stomped on his wounded leg. Valerio roared in pain.

When Luca had exhausted himself, he stood back, breathing hard.

"Even a dumb fucking animal knows better than to run towards danger," he said.

Then he swiveled around as a headlight beam cut across them, and a new sound: a car engine and the crunch of tires on gravel.

It pulled to a stop, and a door opened, then Lazarov's voice in broken Italian: "What the fuck are you doing, Errichiello? He's no use to us dead."

Valerio's head was ringing, the world closing in around the edges.

"Not now," he said, struggling to stay conscious.

Everything faded to black.

He was wet, dripping. Someone had tossed water on him. He tasted it on his chapped lips.

Gradually, he became aware of the sounds of screaming.

His eyelids were heavy, but he forced them open.

She was centimeters away, face twisted with crying, tears streaking her cheeks, dark eyes wide and full of terror.

"Valerio!" she shrieked. "Valerio!"

He'd been a thinking man once, full of plans and observations. He'd had ideas. But there was no more strategy left. Only terror. It overwhelmed him. He was drowning. Desperate.

"Ravenna! No!"

He reached for her, but someone grabbed Ravenna by her hair and dragged her back. She screamed and fought, clawing at the man.

He punched her, and she bent over, coughing.

"Ravenna," Valerio called. "Look at me! Stay calm. I'll get us out of this."

"There you are," said Lazarov, grabbing Valerio by the collar and yanking him upright. "Time to answer some questions. You know this woman? Good. I found her at your apartment. Who is she? Girlfriend? Wife? Sister?"

"What do you want?" Valerio demanded.

"Tell me the truth, Alfieri. That's all I'm asking. The truth."

Slow as he was, weak with blood loss and infection and pain, Valerio knew better than to tell Lazarov the truth. The truth was desperate and stupid and pathetic and would get them killed. The truth was: He'd gotten himself into this mess, and managed to drag Ravenna into it, too.

The truth was: Nobody knew where he was. Nobody was coming to save them.

"Alright," Valerio said. "Don't hurt her. What do you want?"

"How do you know my name?"

"They gave me your dossier," Valerio lied.

"Who?"

"They don't exactly hand over their ID cards," Valerio said.

"Why? What does he want you to do?"

Valerio hesitated. Had he heard correctly? Not *them*. *Him*. The shepherd Valerio had imagined, the hidden force behind Lazarov. Maybe it was a trick—Lazarov testing him.

He took the gamble anyway: "He doesn't trust you to get the job done properly."

Lazarov scoffed. "And he thought *you* would? You're a mess, Alfieri. A fucking mess. Of course he trusts me."

"Not after Gaetano," Valerio said.

Lazarov stopped laughing.

It was something about what Luca had said—that it was necessary to kill Gaetano. What was necessary about it?

Valerio strained to get his thoughts in order, trying to remember what Ines had told him. Gaetano had seen something. Lazarov had been angry about it. What had he seen? Valerio didn't know. A secret meeting between Luca and Lazarov—and someone else?

"Two weeks ago, in Salerno," Valerio continued. "When Gaetano came into the restaurant. He wasn't supposed to be there. He wasn't supposed to see . . . that was why you punched him—and why Gaetano needed to die. He was young . . . sloppy . . . undisciplined. The stakes were too high and *he* couldn't take the risk."

Lazarov's silence told Valerio that he was on the right track.

"*He* won't be happy if you kill us," Valerio continued. "I promise you that. Lazarov, I'm in trouble. I've been bleeding out. I'm not going to last. Ravenna is a nurse. Let her treat my injuries."

His attention was on Lazarov, watching that cunning, cold face. He saw the clockwork behind those pale eyes. For the briefest moment, it was as though the air pressure had changed. The calculation Valerio needed him to make was slotting into place.

Then everything fell apart.

The loud *bang* of a gun shattered the calm. Valerio turned to the sound and saw that Ravenna had somehow gotten hold of her guard's handgun. The guard was on the ground, writhing, shouting, blood gushing from his stomach.

Ravenna pointed the gun around towards the other men, a terror in her face.

"Let him go," she said. "Just let Valerio go . . . let us leave. Valerio, please. Come with me."

But he couldn't go anywhere. He couldn't stand or walk—and he was far too weak.

It was obvious Ravenna didn't know how to handle the weapon. Her hands shook violently. She'd shot the first man at point-blank range, but it was clear she wouldn't be able to hit anyone else.

Valerio said her name.

She looked at him—was looking at him—when Lazarov put a bullet in her head.

THIRTY

De Rosa's agreement to help had been in his own fashion. After Nikki and Federico answered his questions, he left them outside in the clinging rain. Two hours passed before he returned, clean, freshly shaved, hair combed. He wore leather gloves, a cashmere sweater, and a motorcycle jacket.

"Take me to wherever you think il Fantasma is," he said. "I'll confirm Lazarov is there."

Federico shook his head. "You should bring all your men . . . an army. Luca has an army."

"I'll go alone," De Rosa said firmly. "This isn't a war. I merely want confirmation of what you say."

"We can't wait," Nikki protested. She was frozen, wet, feet numb against the paving stones. "What if Valerio is hurt?"

De Rosa's voice was ice.

"Permit me to be clear about my intentions. If Lazarov is there, as you believe, we will extract him. If you wish, you may also look for your friend—but I don't take responsibility for you nor him. This is a coincidence, not a favor. You have not earned my favor."

Nikki was shivering violently, teeth banging together as she returned to the locker room. Retrieving her clothes, she carried them to one of the small dressing rooms. Within the limited privacy provided by a blue canvas curtain, she slammed her palm against the wall, and took big gulping breaths. Her heart was racing.

"Get control," she told herself.

It wasn't over yet. She couldn't afford to fall apart now.

Her skin prickled with the cold, underpants and bra damp as she pulled her trousers and shirt and socks back on.

The gate guard handed her the phone on her way out. There were several text messages from Phoenix Seven—beginning with **Where the fuck are you?** and ending with **I'm telling Angelo.**

Angelo called after that—then four more times—voice messages informing her she was fired.

Nikki felt cold and detached. She didn't return the call.

It was dark by the time Nikki climbed back on her Hornet, Federico hefting himself behind her. He hadn't spoken since leaving De Rosa, and he remained silent as Nikki made adjustments and started the engine.

She saw the struggle in him—loyalty and fear for Valerio wrestling against his terror. He hadn't wanted to speak with De Rosa. Nor did he want to follow where they were going next. Yet here he was.

Nikki felt his discomfort and resistance in the rigidness of his body as he sat upright behind her, tension turning his arms into blocks of wood.

"This is suicide," he muttered, as Nikki navigated the Hornet onto the empty road, De Rosa following on his Ducati.

Federico directed Nikki towards the Tangenziale and they traveled north, turning off at Lago Patria and heading northeast through Aversa, towards the mountains of Caserta. The world vanished around them, until reality existed only in the patches of yellow headlamps and the uneven smatters of distant houselights. Federico led them onto increasingly rural roads, up into the mountainside.

Nikki felt sure they must be getting close when De Rosa flashed his lights and passed them. She fell in behind and followed him for another kilometer, when he exited onto a dirt road and into the shelter of thick trees. He switched off his bike, and removed his helmet.

Nikki followed suit.

"Who did you bring with you?" he demanded, striding towards her. His gun was out, pointed at the ground.

Nikki looked around.

Without the engine sounds, or the bright illumination of the headlamps, it was suddenly very dark. Quiet.

"Nobody," she said. "What do you mean?"

"A grey Škoda has been following us since Arco Felice. He isn't one of mine."

Then they heard it: the rumble of an engine. Through the trees behind them came the jostling light of an approaching vehicle.

"If you have a weapon, prepare yourself," said De Rosa.

But Nikki wasn't armed.

She and Federico moved rapidly off the road, taking cover in the trees as the car came into view.

The night was torn wide by the double report of a weapon—the first shot disabling the tire, the second striking the windshield. The car swerved and braked, and began to reverse, but De Rosa was in the headlights, and took aim, firing a single shot.

The windshield shattered. The car slowly rolled backwards, stopping when it hit a tree.

De Rosa moved rapidly in, and opened the door, aiming his weapon at the driver.

"Don't shoot!" a man said in English.

"Get out," said De Rosa in Italian.

When the man didn't answer or follow the instruction, Nikki edged closer, and repeated the command in English.

He was bleeding as he staggered out, left hand clutching his right elbow. Blood was coming through his shirt at the shoulder and down his arm.

"I'm shot," he moaned.

"Mac!" exclaimed Nikki.

She hadn't known what to expect, but certainly not the Dutch naval officer. He was out of uniform and wore a white cotton shirt, a cardigan draped around his neck. He sobbed and fell to his knees.

"Nina! Take me to a hospital. I need a hospital!"

"You know him?" De Rosa said with a suspicious glance.

"He's my brother's friend," said Nikki. "He doesn't speak Italian."

"Translate for me," De Rosa told her. Then, to Mac, "Why are you following us?"

Sweating heavily, Mac rubbed a palm shakily across his face, smearing blood. "We want to talk to Tito Calandra."

"Who?" De Rosa demanded. "Who wants to talk to him?"

"I work for an elite Dutch intelligence organization—MIVD."

De Rosa gave a humorless laugh. "How elite can it be if you're one of them? Why do you want Calandra?"

"The assassination attempts," Mac stammered. "We know Calandra's been shot. We'd like to meet with him—make an arrangement."

At his words, Nikki forgot to translate. She turned to De Rosa. "Has Tito been shot?"

She hadn't considered—hadn't let herself consider—that Tito could actually be injured or killed. The possibility was a meteor strike. She reeled from the impact.

De Rosa stared at her. "I won't discuss this with you. You've already made your feelings clear. Tell me what he's saying."

"People know where I am. They'll be looking for me," said Mac, seeming to gather his courage. "Nina . . . Nina . . . you know me. I'm friends with Gianni. We've had dinner together."

"Why would an intelligence officer be friends with my brother?" Nikki asked, realizing the answer as she spoke. "Because he's connected to Tito!"

"Tell me what you're saying." De Rosa insisted. Nikki told him.

"Tito's my nephew's godfather," she explained.

"Ask the Dutchman how he knew where to find us," said De Rosa. "We can't continue if they're following."

Nikki asked.

"Your bag," Mac said. "I put a tracker in your bag . . . at your house."

"Why?" Nikki demanded.

"We hoped you'd lead us to Calandra."

Nikki told De Rosa.

"Get it," he instructed.

Nikki retrieved her cross-body bag, rifling through the contents in the car headlamps. She couldn't find anything.

"Show me," she said, handing the bag to Mac. Hands quaking, fumbling, he worked a small piece of metal from the bag's lining.

"Here . . . here . . ." he said, extending it up to Nikki. She passed it to De Rosa. He examined it, frowning.

"Tell him I won't do it again," said Mac between sobs. "I won't tell anyone. I promise."

Nikki translated this to De Rosa, who looked thoughtful.

Then his face seemed to lose all expression as he turned to Mac, who raised his hands in supplication. De Rosa's lips parted and Nikki prepared to translate whatever he would say next, but he lifted his Beretta and emptied two shots into Mac's surprised face. He tossed the tracker onto the lifeless body, turned, and strode away.

Nikki couldn't move. She was suddenly heavy. Tired. A strange, overwhelming sense that she might fall asleep. Her eyes fixed on that pudgy pale face, red pockmarks on his forehead leaking blood.

Federico was at her side. He tugged her arm. "We need to leave."

"He killed him," Nikki said, stupid with the reality of it.

"I know."

"I didn't want this."

He glanced over his shoulder. "This isn't a game, bella. What did you think would happen if you went to this man?"

Nikki nodded and followed along automatically. De Rosa started his Ducati and waited for them.

She mounted her Hornet, then followed Federico's directions as he led them back out onto the main road.

Her mind lurched as she followed Federico's instructions, giving everything a strange stuttering quality: the growl of the engine beneath her, the inertia of the bike, and the cold air on her face. She told herself not to think about what just happened, yet it repeated over and over in her mind. Had she not realized the seriousness of De Rosa's intent?

No, that had been obvious. He'd opened fire on the car expertly and decisively. Why would he not do the same with the driver? Perhaps she'd deluded herself into believing she would have more time—more influence—to stop him from killing Mac.

The night was still as Federico directed her into a wooded turnout.

"We go the rest of the way on foot," he told them.

Federico took them off the road, and staggered up the mountain with unsteady strides.

In the darkness of thick trees, the only light from a half-moon, the ground was treacherous. Nikki stumbled twice. De Rosa turned on the light from his phone, and Federico hissed at him to switch it off.

After twenty minutes, Nikki wasn't sure he actually knew where he was going. De Rosa clearly had his doubts as well.

"Where is it, old man?" he demanded.

"The entrance is watched. Guarded. We're going around the back."

After nearly a half hour of climbing, there was a loud *clack*. Nikki hit the ground, De Rosa beside her as bright lights flooded the hillside in a weird fluorescent glow, revealing the grey outlines of a stainless steel security fence among the trees. Only Federico remained standing, continuing his loping stride up the hill along the fence.

They rejoined him at a small gate, where he examined a keypad lock.

"They never replaced it," he scoffed. "It's faulty."

Taking a long switchblade from his jacket pocket, Federico jimmied it into the locking mechanism. There was a click, and the gate swung to.

They passed inside, navigating the tangled undergrowth and trees until they arrived at an outcropping of rock above the compound, an unobstructed view of the buildings below.

The main house was an ornate stucco structure, with marble pillars and tile roof, manicured gardens, and a swimming pool. At the front of the house was a courtyard with a marble fountain, and two large buildings. Four vehicles were parked in the drive—a dark sedan and three black SUVs.

From her vantage, Nikki could see an armed security guard in the courtyard, and another two pacing around the buildings.

Nikki and Federico and De Rosa stayed for more than an hour in their uncomfortable perch, watching the guards conduct their patrols. Then De Rosa stepped away and Nikki heard the low murmur of his voice on the phone.

"Would they be holding Valerio in the house?" she asked Federico.

"Doubtful," he said. "Luca doesn't like messes."

He was silent several minutes, then continued, this time in a low voice, glancing in the direction of De Rosa. "Take care of yourself, bella," he said. "He's lying to you. This isn't only a reconnaissance mission."

"He's trying to find Lazarov," Nikki said.

"Yes. And when he does, do you think he can afford to wait . . . to let him get away?"

"What can he do on his own?" she whispered. "If he was going to take Lazarov tonight, he would have more men with him."

"Tito Calandra was shot," Federico said. "That doesn't happen. . . . Nobody gets that close unless someone betrayed Calandra. They have a traitor. De Rosa's looking for Lazarov on his own because he doesn't trust anyone else."

"How can you be sure?"

"He's on the warpath. He killed that Dutchman. That should tell you how important this is to him. Watch and see. He's coordinating with Calandra now. Just make sure you're far away when they pull the pin."

De Rosa returned several minutes later.

"I count eleven men," he said. "I don't see Lazarov."

"Patience," Federico advised.

Nikki checked her watch. It was 01:22.

At 01:46, two men came from the main house, strode across the courtyard, towards the hillside and into the woods. They returned a few minutes later, dragging a figure between them. Nikki's heart hammered and she strained to see.

He was dark with mud and blood, boots and clothes caked in it. It painted his face and hands, obscuring his features.

"Is it him?" she asked Federico. "Is it Valerio?"

She wanted to race down the hill and . . . then what?

She took out her phone and started filming.

The mud-stained man was clearly injured badly. When the guards dumped him on the ground, he lay motionless for a few beats before struggling to sit. There was something about the way he moved, the curve of his back, and the shape of his body. . . . Nikki grew more and more certain that she was right.

It was Valerio.

THIRTY-ONE

Things moved so quickly, Nikki couldn't be sure of everything that happened, or why.

A man came from the house and questioned Valerio. Then, suddenly, viciously, began kicking and punching him.

Nikki was on her feet, terror and fury propelling her forward. But Federico's hands were on her, wrenching her back to the ground.

"That's Luca," he hissed in her ear. "He'll kill you—or worse."

She yielded, heart aching, hands trembling as she tried to hold the camera steady.

The white-haired Lazarov arrived in a sedan, and dragged someone from the boot—a large woman in medical scrubs with a mop of curly hair. She cried and struggled—and he punched her. Then, one of the guards wrestled her upright and held a gun to her head. The woman sobbed. Valerio and Lazarov were shouting at each other. Nikki strained to hear what they were saying—when a report rang out. For a terrible moment, she thought Valerio had been shot. But it was a guard who fell, clutching his stomach.

Nikki looked between the players, trying to understand what had happened. The captive woman now had a gun. She was yelling, gesturing—when Lazarov shot her.

The bullet slammed her backwards. She crumpled.

Lazarov strolled to her and, with visible disdain, nudged the motionless body with his boot. Then he aimed his weapon again.

The echoing gunshot was followed by a wailing howl.

Nikki recognized Valerio's voice, but had never guessed he could make such a terrible sound.

Evading Federico and ignoring his protests, Nikki launched from her position and skidded down the hill, keeping low and staying in the cover of shadows and trees.

The descent was steep, tough, long—a one-way trip. She tried not to think about what would happen when she arrived at the courtyard lights and the army of well-armed men. Instead, she focused on maneuvering the difficult terrain, pausing to verify her cover and check what was happening in the courtyard where some of the men were arguing.

Her attention was on Valerio. He'd stopped moving.

"Don't let him be dead," she murmured, panic and dread making her sick.

She needed help.

The signal on her phone was low—not enough to send the video she'd taken of the woman's murder. But hopefully enough for a text.

He's here, she wrote to Maurizio. **Injured. Errichiello's place. Caserta. They just killed a woman. Bring police.**

She shared her coordinates.

She was nearly level with the courtyard now—Valerio so close that, under other circumstances, she could have strolled into the stark lights and felt for a pulse.

She wasn't sure what to do next, yet she knew that if she didn't act soon, Lazarov would kill Valerio like he'd killed the woman. As she watched, two of the men grabbed Valerio, and dragged him from the courtyard and into the woods at the rear of the house. She kept pace as best she could, but her progress was hampered by the thick brush—and she had to stop when a guard came close to her position and lit a cigarette, staring into the trees. She held still, hardly daring to breathe as he finished and strolled away.

She was motionless for a long time after that—watching the courtyard. Two men collected the woman's body and left. Then the buzzing bright lights switched off.

A welcome darkness enveloped the world.

Nikki listened, waiting for the activity to die down before she began moving again, towards the area where the men had taken Valerio.

About two hundred meters from the house, in an overgrown thicket, she found a small square concrete building. She waited and then approached cautiously. The only entry was a heavy wooden door secured with a large padlock and chain. She tapped on the door, and whispered Valerio's name. No reply.

"Valerio," she said again, this time louder. "Are you there?"

She strained to listen. Silence.

She examined the padlock and chain, hopeful that someone had been sloppy in securing it—but it was locked tight.

She rapped her knuckles against the door again . . . and again.

Suddenly, there were strong arms around her, wrenching her back, a hand clamped over her mouth.

A voice in her ear murmured, "What the fuck are you doing?"

Grabbing with both hands and wrenching the fingers away, she shifted her center of gravity, preparing to twist his wrist and elbow, to fight her way out.

"Stop!" he hissed. "Stay quiet."

It was familiar: the breath on her cheek, the smell and shape of him. The voice of De Rosa.

"Let me go," she whispered.

He released, and she pivoted to face him, fury and fear choking her. "He's in there. Valerio's in there."

He drew close, eyes like black holes punched in the darkness. "You saw the condition he's in. He's not going to make it. Get out of here while you can."

The words were calm and practical, but Nikki felt the emotion beneath them. She thought she had the measure of De Rosa, but she didn't understand this.

"Why the fuck do you care?"

He stared a long moment, then raised his hands and took a step back.

"Your grave," he said. He glanced at the door behind her and pointed. "Don't make a sound. Don't fuck this up or I'll kill you myself."

Then he turned and sprinted silently through the trees.

Nikki returned to the door. This time, to her immense relief, her knock was answered by a return tap.

"Valerio!" she whispered.

"Nikki! Good god, Nikki! Is that you?"

He sounded weak.

"I'm going to get you out," she said. "How badly are you hurt?"

He didn't answer for a long moment. Nikki worried what this meant.

"Bad," he said at last. "Bleeding out . . . leg's shot . . . and my head . . . something's wrong . . . can't stay awake."

"Okay, okay," she said. Her mind was racing.

"Thirsty," he said. "Do you have water?"

"Not with me. . . . I'll get you water," she promised. "Just hang on, okay? I need to get something to open this lock."

She wasn't sure how. If she couldn't find a key, then she needed to break the lock. *One thing at a time*, she told herself.

"Don't do anything stupid," Valerio said.

"Don't *you* do anything stupid," she answered.

She moved quietly back the way she'd come—heading for the building closest to the house. At a door on the side, she tested the handle. Unlocked!

Carefully, she pulled it open and slipped quickly through the gap.

To her relief, she was alone. Yet there was no escape here and few places to hide if anyone else came in.

Two parked Mercedes SUVs were in the space—one with its hood up, grease pan beneath. A working garage, then. There must be tools somewhere.

She crossed to a workbench and opened cabinets and drawers. What she needed—what she desperately wanted to find—was bolt cutters. But there was nothing! Nothing she could use to free Valerio. She growled in frustration.

She'd been here too long and spent her luck. She needed to get out.

No sooner had she thought this than she heard a noise outside. Someone shouting.

Fuck. Fuck.

Stooping, she crept along the wall, prepared to drop to the floor and roll under a car or bench if someone opened the door. Then she saw it: a rack of keys behind the doorframe. She sprinted, and grabbed them all, shoving them into her bag.

Outside, she dashed for the trees.

She hadn't gone far when the night erupted with shouts and the crackle of gunfire. Nikki hit the ground, waited and listened. But the activity seemed to be directed at the front of the compound. So many guns—far more than De Rosa's alone. Had he called in his men—or had Maurizio and the police arrived? She hoped the latter.

She stood again, and raced for Valerio.

"Nikki, is that you?" Valerio said as she slammed against the door.

"I've found keys," she panted.

She dug into the bag and started sorting—pushing the car keys aside, and trying the others. It was painstaking, slow work. The sounds of a gunfight drew closer, and she was seized with terror. Her hands and body shook.

"Please, please," she whispered. Then, to Valerio, in a loudly cheerful voice: "How are you holding up?"

"Doing great," he answered. "Take it easy, little devil."

Key after key . . . none worked.

She swung around to the sounds of running feet and rustling in the trees. A figure burst from the woods. One of Lazarov's men. He hesitated, obviously surprised to see her. Their eyes locked, and he raised his weapon. He never got the chance to use it.

Federico was behind him, the hollow cheeks and blank glasses of the tall man visible above the head of the guard. With startling speed, the long bony hands of the butcher moved around the neck. A blade flashed silver in the dim light, and the guard reached up to grab his throat as fountains of dark blood gushed from the wound. He made a terrible gurgling sound, heaving as he struggled to breathe, and collapsed.

Nikki watched in horror as the man thrashed. It was a terrible death. The worst thing she'd ever seen. Federico watched with her, a rigid stillness to his posture.

Somewhere nearby, an automatic weapon fired on repeat. This was followed by an explosion in the direction of the house, and a bright orange light flashed through the trees, bringing heat.

"Take his gun," Federico told Nikki.

Crouching, she wrapped her fingers around the cold grip. Heavier than she expected.

The time for quiet caution had passed; the night was consumed by the chaos of the approaching fight.

It took three tries before the bullet shattered the lock. She pulled the sharp and twisted pieces away and gripped the door, pulling it wide.

The surging stench of the dark cavity was unbearable, the buzz of insects enveloping her. Nikki's stomach heaved as she rushed inside and bent to grab Valerio's feverish body.

"I've got you!" she said.

But he wasn't moving. She leaned in and listened. His breathing was shallow.

"Help!" Nikki shouted to Federico. "Help me get him out."

The old man joined her, and they half dragged, half carried Valerio outside.

But there was no safety here. The forest around them was alive with the echoing crack and thud of bullets.

"How do we get him out of here?" Nikki asked. Federico shook his head, then leaned over and slapped Valerio's cheek.

"Valerio," he said. "You gotta wake up. Wake up, Capo."

Valerio's eyelids rolled up.

"Can you stand?" Nikki asked. "We can put you between us if you can stand."

He nodded.

But he grimaced when they touched him. Gingerly, they sat him upright and leaned him against the wall. His body lolled.

"Fuck," Nikki said.

She turned to Federico. "What if I get one of those SUVs? I can probably drive it through here. I stole their keys—one of them has to work."

He shook his head. "You'll never make it. We should hide . . . wait it out."

"He won't last," said Nikki. "He needs help now."

She pressed the gun into Federico's hand.

"Protect yourself," she said. "Protect him."

"What about you?"

"It's too big. I can't handle it properly. Besides, I need speed, not firepower."

Nikki's body moved automatically, numbly crashing through the undergrowth, every instinct shouting for her to turn back as she raced towards the sounds of the fight. She smelled smoke and, through the trees, saw that the house was burning, orange and yellow flames licking out of the windows. Shadowy figures chased in the dark, men shouted, hot streaks of bullets pulsed through the air.

Keeping low, trying to stay out of sight, she shoved her hand into her bag and grabbed one of the key fobs, pressing at the buttons.

In the courtyard, the lights of an SUV flashed. Without breaking stride, she headed for it, opened the door, dove inside, and hit the ignition. Shifting into gear, she stomped the accelerator. The heavy vehicle shot back, into the fight. Racing away, towards the billowing flames of the burning house, she was chased by strafing bullets tearing into metal and shattering glass. At the last moment, she veered left, around the western side of the building, and into the trees.

The path was narrow, and Nikki had to slow and maneuver, bumping and scraping across the uneven ground. The rugged SUV handled the bushes and small trees—but the path narrowed and, at last, she could go no farther.

Switching off the engine, but leaving the headlights to mark the way, she raced down the path.

She was relieved to find Federico and Valerio where she'd left them, starkly illuminated by the headlamps.

Federico slapped Valerio's face. "Wake up. She's back. Wake up, Capo. Don't you dare leave, you fucker."

Federico struggled to his feet, and tucked the gun behind him, into his waistband. Then he bent and gripped Valerio with both hands in one of his armpits. Nikki squatted on the other side of Valerio and slid her shoulder beneath his arm.

"On three!" she said. Federico nodded. They counted and heaved Valerio to his feet.

It was clear Valerio was trying to help, but his muscles were loose. His right leg was no good and his left was weak, stumbling, unable to support his weight for longer than a beat.

He was in obvious pain, yet didn't make a sound as Nikki and Federico struggled to move him the ten meters to the rear of the SUV.

At last, they opened the tail door, and helped him climb in. Valerio accommodated the effort, tipping and rolling, until he lay flat, chest heaving. He gave a thumbs-up.

Nikki breathed more easily now. They'd solved one problem. Now, they just needed to get the fuck out of here. She was about to step back and close the door when she heard someone speak.

"I'm taking that," said a man's voice. "Step away from the vehicle and give me the key."

Nikki raised her hands and turned around slowly.

Luca Errichiello was silhouetted against the flames of the house, aiming a gun at them.

Beside her, Federico also turned. Luca seemed to recognize him and opened his mouth in a loud, joyless laugh.

"You!" he exclaimed.

"Hello, Luca," said Federico.

"My god, I never expected to see you here," said Luca.

"That's because you have no imagination," Federico replied dryly.

"You're a clever psychopath—but you're also shallow, and vain. That's why I could always outmaneuver you."

"I don't see you winning this one," countered Luca.

"I don't need to win." Federico gave an encompassing gesture to the fire behind Luca. "As long as you lose."

Luca shot his brother.

Federico ricocheted against the rear of the SUV and slid to the ground. Nikki ducked and rolled beneath the vehicle in time to hear another weapon discharge. But it was Luca who hit the ground this time, body juddering.

"Check him," Federico said to Nikki. "Make sure he's dead. Get his gun."

She did as she was told, dodging forward and grabbing the gun from Luca's limp fingers before checking for a pulse. It was a headshot that had killed him, she noted with a distant sense of unreality. Although not as neat as the bullets that had killed Mac. This one had blown off the side of Luca's face. She turned and saw that it was Valerio who had made the shot, snatching the gun from Federico's waistband during the confrontation. He was lying motionless now, gun still clutched in his fingers.

Federico lay on the ground, bleeding badly, hand gripping his chest where Luca's bullet had torn through.

"Is Luca dead?" he wheezed.

She nodded. "Yes."

"Good . . . good."

She wanted to move him, to get him out of here, but it was too late. As she watched, Federico's face slackened, eyes turning distant and dull. She felt for a pulse. He was gone.

It was only as Nikki shut the door to the SUV and crossed around to the driver's side that she realized the shooting had stopped. The roar of the fire still overwhelmed the night, but the percussive gunfire had stilled. She wasn't sure what this meant, and drove cautiously, stopping when she reached the courtyard.

In the orange light of the burning building, bodies were strewn throughout the space. The stone fountain in the center of the drive was in pieces, water pouring on the ground.

Lazarov and three of his men were kneeling on the gravel, hands bound behind them, surrounded by men with assault rifles.

It was not the police who had secured the scene. Instead, striding around the captive men, a bandage across his chest, and arm bound in a sling, was Tito Calandra. The big man walked slowly, deliberatively.

He raised his gun and shot the first man in the back of the head. An execution. He did the same to the next. And the next. When he came to Lazarov, he lowered his weapon, and nodded to De Rosa.

De Rosa indicated, and two men came forward with a black sack that they put on his head, securing this with tape. Lazarov struggled as they dragged him to a waiting car and put him in the boot.

Someone noticed Nikki. A man raised his rifle, pointing it at her and shouting. Nikki raised her hands, and looked to Tito.

Across the distance, their eyes met. He stared at her and she looked back into that dark heart.

Then he gestured, and De Rosa shouted at the man to stand down, waving Nikki on.

The world was getting lighter as she drove from Luca Errichiello's compound. She didn't look back.

THIRTY-TWO

Maurizio met Nikki at the emergency entrance to Sant'Anna and San Sebastiano Hospital, together with the medical staff who had prepared for her arrival. They moved Valerio from the rear of the SUV onto a gurney, then Maurizio and Nikki ran alongside as they raced him down the passageway. Nikki tried to tell them about his injuries—the gunshot wound and the beatings . . . the loss of consciousness . . . the dehydration. But she felt inadequate as they asked more questions.

"Blood type?"

"I don't know."

"Any allergies?"

"I don't know."

It felt somehow significant that she didn't have answers—like she'd let him down.

Her knowledge of Valerio was something Nikki had trouble measuring. She knew the shape of his hands when he tied a bowline. She knew the way he puffed out his breath as he dashed around *Calypso*, trimming the sails. She knew the way he liked to knock the cap off his beer, the irresistible sound of his belly laugh, and the pungent stink of him after a day of hard work together under a hot sun. But she didn't know his blood type.

Afterwards, Nikki stood with Maurizio in the waiting room.

"Sonia called," he said, handing her coffee in a thin plastic cup. "The whole department is out there. She says it's a massacre . . . dozens of men killed. Everything burning. Nikki, how the hell did you get him out?"

She was saved having to answer when an orderly in blue scrubs called her name.

"They're bringing him into surgery," he told her. "He wants to talk to you first."

In the harsh lights, Valerio's bloodied and swollen face put an ache in Nikki's chest—something like homesickness and panic.

She maneuvered past the tubes and equipment.

Valerio's words were slurred. "Lazarov—not in charge," he told her. "Just the sheepdog . . . keeping Luca in line."

"That's what Federico and De Rosa thought, too," she said quietly. "Lazarov tried to kill Tito."

"Should've killed me," he said. ". . . Told him I worked for his boss . . . bought me time. Obedient sheepdog."

His eyelids drooped.

Obedient. She remembered the passage from *The Brothers Karamazov*: "Having chosen an elder, you renounce your individual will and surrender it to him in complete obedience . . ."

"Got to find the shepherd," Valerio said, eyes suddenly wide, meeting her gaze. "Now. Before it's too late."

Nikki pushed back. "What do you mean?"

"Luca's gone," Valerio said. "There's a small window . . . now . . . got to find the shepherd. Understand? You. Everyone else is . . . compromised."

Nikki was suddenly cold. An icy current surged through her.

"I wouldn't know where to start," she said.

"The rats are running," he mumbled. "See where they run."

Nikki watched as they pushed Valerio out of sight, frigid juddering, heavy with the weight of his expectation. Why had he asked her? Why not Maurizio?

Everyone else is compromised, he'd said. Did he think this included his partner?

Federico had believed the police were corrupt, too—and he'd been right about everything.

If you own a man's secret, he'd told her, *you own the man.*

And hadn't that been the point of Errichiello's business? Powerful men invited by Paride Silvestri to abuse underage girls. Compromise and leverage—a ruthless blackmail machine. So where were Errichiello's files now that he was gone?

Luca was dead, but he'd only been one head of the hydra. His death didn't stop any of this.

It's never enough to just take a head, Adriano had once said. *To kill the beast, you need to understand it completely . . . you must watch and learn . . . find its beating heart.*

She needed to find that beating heart. The man Lazarov obeyed. The shepherd.

She strode down the corridor, and left the hospital.

Outside, the air was chilly and dry. Pale sunlight bleached the trees, chipped concrete, and asphalt—an unsettling contrast between light and shadow. The sounds of traffic filled the air, and nearby, a dog barked. Behind these noises, she imagined she still heard the choppy static of gunfire.

She shut her eyes, willing it to pass.

Then, she seemed to hear her mother's voice. Not words of comfort, but that guttural hiss: *If the devil doesn't exist, but man has created him, he has created him in his own image and likeness!*

Her mother—with those wild eyes and rigid hands. Spending the last years of her life hunting for the devil who had murdered her son.

She didn't trust the formal investigation, Raoul had told Nikki. *She thought it was corrupt. . . .*

Nikki had assumed her mother's obsession had been a distraction from reality—a place to put her grief. But what if Beatrice's devil had been real? Like Valerio's shepherd?

She thought of Adriano again, his voice clear in her thoughts: *You must see—must understand the players and how they fit together.*

The corruption was so deep, so hidden, the hunt felt impossible. Beatrice had tried, and failed, to find the devil in the darkness.

Was it possible her father had found a clue?

Nikki dialed Raoul's number.

"What's the news on the Patalano case?" she asked.

He sighed. "There's nothing there. We're shutting down the investigation."

"But what about the sophisticated system you told me about?" she demanded, striding across the car park. She was exhausted yet oddly animated, as if her body was a puppet, strings frenziedly twitching. "What about the code names—Damascus, Diogenes, Zosima?"

"Patalano's ledger is two decades old," he said irritably. "If I'd been able to ask him—or if we'd gotten to it earlier—I could have put the pieces together. It's just too late."

Fuck.

It was too late to ask Patalano. Too late to ask her mother. Adriano. Claire. Gaetano. Federico.

All too late. The dead took their secrets with them.

Even Signora Dorotea, with her cold dry hands and long nails, had seen more than she'd said. *You are a child of Napoli . . . full of light and darkness . . . the divine and infernal wrestling. . . .*

What had she known? What secrets had she hoarded?

Nikki seemed to see the sly black glance as Dorotea adjusted the charms on her rucksack, as she arranged the items in the votive shrine.

"What were you doing?" Nikki asked the dead woman.

The question was an itch—something important close to the surface.

She closed her eyes, and tried to remember. But all she could think about were the fluorescent lights of the hospital passageway flickering past, and Valerio's battered body on the gurney, and the doctor's questions: "Blood type? Allergies?"

Suddenly, Nikki's eyes flew open. She understood now—not anything she could speak aloud yet, but the larger picture was coming into focus: the reason for all the killings.

The dead took their secrets with them! That was the point, wasn't it? A cold, efficient way to bury the truth. It was all connected. *Everything!*

The rats are running. See where they run.

She knew where to look for the shepherd.

Nikki raced to the SUV. Bullets had torn through the doors and fenders, punching through the leather upholstery. Blood and glass on the seats.

Starting the engine, she dialed the number for Jayston Lake. She was directed to voicemail. She called Audrey's phone. Nothing.

As she sped towards Naples, she dialed Sonia, and then Maurizio. No answer.

In the city, along the waterfront, she passed cafés, maîtres in pressed white shirts and long aprons among thickets of tables and chairs. She pulled up illegally near the marina and jogged the rest of the way to the pier. The smells of coffee and fresh bread wrapped around her, the bracing sea air rushing against her.

The gate guard refused to listen. Refused to accept her Phoenix Seven ID card.

"It's urgent," she insisted. "I need to speak with Signor Lake immediately."

"No," he said firmly, staring with disdain at her bloodied and disheveled clothes, then speaking into his handheld radio.

She dodged around the barrier. He grabbed her arm.

"Don't fucking touch me!" she yelled. Twisting, she broke free and, ignoring his shouts, sprinted.

The Prophet was gone. She saw the gap before she was midway down the pier.

She was too late!

She thought about Audrey Lake, and was gripped by a sudden spasm of fear for the little girl.

"It departed about an hour ago," called a voice behind her.

Nikki turned to see Vincente Di Pavola, near the tail of his yacht. For a moment, she nearly mistook him for his son, Enzo.

He strode towards her. "What's this about?"

Nikki jogged to meet him.

"Can you track them?" she demanded. "How fast is your boat? Can you intercept?"

He seemed to consider.

"If their AIS is transmitting, I can track them," he said. "A superyacht like that will manage a maximum of twenty to twenty-five knots. The *Fidelis* is arguably the fastest of her class. If we leave now, we could rendezvous in under an hour."

He spoke these words with enthusiasm—then his expression shifted, shrewd businessman peering through his eyes.

"I can get you there," he said. "You know my price."

They sped out of the marina, passing enormous cargo and cruise ships navigating from the busy port. A white winter sun reflected off the water, sea spray flicking against the screen.

Nikki's thoughts refused to hold steady. Heavy with fatigue, not even the jostling slam of the boat or her own worry seemed able to keep her alert. Her mind drifted, and she dreamed that she was flying just above the waves, wings reaching down to brush the white crests below.

They were passing Capri when Vincente said, "We should be getting close."

Nikki spoke into the VHF: "Motor vessel *Prophet*, this is motor vessel *Fidelis*. Over."

She repeated. And again. No response.

Nikki's phone pinged. Texts from Audrey Lake.

- Nikki help

- I'm scared

Nikki called. There was no answer. She texted: **I'm on my way.**

No response.

Nikki scanned the horizon, spotting two cargo ships and a handful of sailboats. Then, in the distance, the white shape of the enormous yacht came into view. They approached, and she saw that something was wrong. The boat wasn't sailing—but it wasn't anchored either. It drifted, rocking with the waves. Sunlight gleamed off the surface and, from the top deck, she saw thin tendrils of smoke.

Their hails went unanswered.

Vincente radioed the Guardia Costiera for help.

"I'll see if anyone's gone in the water," Nikki said, bolting from her seat.

Outside, it stank of burning plastic and hot metal.

The *Fidelis* made the final turn, around the stern of *The Prophet*, where a metal ladder dangled from the aft deck into the water. Fiona Lake was clinging to this. She wore a thin dress and orange life vest. She waved frantically, screaming for help.

Nikki shouted, "Jump! Swim here!" but Fiona stayed where she was, tightly clasping the ladder.

Di Pavola saw the problem and pulled his yacht nearer—but they were still a hundred meters out, and it wasn't safe to get closer. The *Fidelis* was large, not a rescue craft, and *The Prophet* was unmoored, bobbing on the waves.

"That's it," he told Nikki. "She needs to swim to us, or wait for the Guardia Costiera."

But the flames in the topmost deck of *The Prophet* were reaching higher, the stink of smoke thick in the air. By the time the Guardia Costiera arrived, it might be too late.

Nikki's mind sought out the little girl waiting to be rescued. She couldn't afford to wait.

Nikki took off her bag and heavy leather jacket, and the chill wind cut through her shirt. She crouched and unlaced her boots.

"What are you doing?" demanded Vincente.

"There are people on board," she said. "There's a little girl."

"Wait for the professionals," he protested.

She met his gaze.

"There's nobody else. It's just us."

The cold water was bracing, the salt stinging cuts she hadn't realized were on her hands and face. Pain was good, she told herself. Pain kept her alert.

The sounds of the fire intensified as she swam closer to the yacht.

At last, she arrived at the ladder. Gripping the lowest rung, she called up to Fiona: "Come down!"

Sobbing, Fiona lowered herself into the water beside Nikki.

"My baby," she screamed. "My baby is in there. You have to save her."

"Audrey's inside?" Nikki confirmed.

Fiona nodded, teeth chattering. "Yes. Yes. With Jayston."

A wave slammed into them, washing over their heads.

"Where do I go?" Nikki shouted.

"The main salon."

Clambering up the ladder, Nikki pulled herself onto the aft deck, opened the hatch, and stepped inside.

The roar of the fire and the sounds of the waves were immediately silenced as she pulled the heavy door shut behind her.

Inside, the air was fresh and cool. It chilled her wet skin and gave no indication that, several decks above, fire was consuming the yacht.

She didn't know how quickly the flames would travel, but she'd seen Errichiello's house burn, and knew that *The Prophet* would soon become an inferno.

At the end of the long passageway, she stopped at a closed door, and placed a hand on it, checking the temperature.

Inside was a carpeted lounge with heavy leather furniture, the only sound the peaceful whir of the ventilation system. The ship's captain, Henry, lay on the floor. His face was bruised. Blood trailed from a head wound.

Nikki raced to his side, and checked for a pulse. He was alive, but his breathing was shallow. She squeezed his shoulder, shook him.

"Captain," she said. Then again, louder. He didn't wake. She needed to leave him for now—and return when she could.

Nikki crossed through the next compartment, and the next, and climbed a set of ladders. The temperature rose, and the acrid stink of smoke. She was shaking, body screaming at her to leave.

At last, she arrived at the main salon and the smell of the fire intensified, the air thickening. Nikki's throat was tight and raw. But the flames hadn't reached this compartment yet.

She coughed and shouted for Audrey. No response.

Jayston Lake was sitting on the sofa with his back to her.

"Mr. Lake," she shouted. "Are you injured?"

She circled the room, coming around to face him.

Audrey sat next to her father, his arm around her as if they were tucked in for an evening of television. Her eyes were closed, and her cheeks flushed an unnatural pink.

"The yacht's burning," Nikki choked out. "We need to abandon ship."

Jayston seemed unsurprised to see her. His rugged, handsome face was slack.

Nikki took in his split lip, bruised cheek, and bloodied knuckles. Then she saw the black handgun. He aimed it at her.

"Leave," he ordered.

"Not without Audrey," she said. Her heart raced, body rigid with fear. She stared at the little girl, searching for breath. "Is she . . . ?"

She couldn't finish the question.

"Asleep." He kissed the top of Audrey's head. "I'll make it quick. She won't feel a thing."

The tension and fatigue in Nikki's body erupted into fury.

"I can see why you have a death wish, but don't take her with you!"

His expression darkened.

"Don't pretend you know anything about me," he growled.

"I know you killed Claire Sexton," she said. "And I know you killed Signora Dorotea."

"What makes you say that?"

"They never found Claire's rucksack," Nikki said. "But I saw it with the fortune teller: a keychain with Audrey's allergy tag."

The small silver charm on Dorotea's large canvas sack. Nikki had assumed it was just another trinket. But it had the symbol of a medical caduceus—entwined snakes. She'd seen the same image at the hospital.

"Claire was going to meet you that night," Nikki continued. "She worried you would take her bag—so she hid it, or gave it to the fortune teller for safekeeping. That's how you found Signora Dorotea: You'd put an air tracker in Claire's bag. Like the one you used to track Audrey."

"Claire was a sweet kid." He sighed. "I thought I could . . . get her to see reason."

"She was blackmailing you."

"It wasn't her fault," he said. "Her brother put her up to it—wanted me to fund his bloody app!"

He set down the gun and grabbed a tumbler of whisky, and took a sip, before picking up the weapon again.

"You could have invested," Nikki said. "You have the money."

He gave a coughing laugh. "Smoke and mirrors! I lost a fortune after Matthew died. Needed time to recover. The good Henry Antonov had . . . other avenues."

"You used your investment firm to launder money," Nikki realized.

"The firm was legitimate. Once."

"But why kill Claire?"

"I had no choice!" he exploded, words thick with fury and guilt. "Had I refused, they'd have killed her all the same—Fiona and Audrey, as well."

"Why not go to the police?"

"Have you ever had a benefactor like mine? Someone to clear the path for you?"

"No," Nikki said, thinking grimly of Tito.

"Whenever we encountered a . . . complication: a regulator . . . a policeman making inquiries—my benefactor would see to it."

"Did you ever meet this benefactor?" Nikki pressed. "Do you know who he is?"

He shook his head, no. The lights flickered. Smoke curled in along the crown molding.

"Henry oversaw that aspect of the business. Foolish of him to leave his computer unattended. Claire copied his files."

"But Henry didn't kill her," Nikki said. "You did."

Her face burned, eyes streaming with the smoke.

He shuddered. "Henry's a violent man. If I hadn't done it, Claire would have suffered."

The temperature had been rising as they spoke, and now water on Nikki's clothing was beginning to steam.

"We have to get out of here," she urged.

"It's no longer my business." His words filled with despair and rage. "I own nothing. Not even my own soul."

An eerie moan of straining metal filled the room.

Next to him, Audrey coughed. He gazed at her, and the fury in his expression softened into pain.

Nikki stepped closer.

"You love Audrey," she said. "That's why you worry about her. . . . Love protects! That's what it does. It protects!"

"I can't protect her anymore." His voice broke.

Behind them, on the liquor shelf, a bottle burst, an explosion of glass and liquid. Then another one. Shards of glass struck the wall. A sudden incursion of smoke rolled along the ceiling.

Terror surged through Nikki, and she reached out as if she meant to lift the sleeping girl.

"Let me protect her!" she begged. "You asked me to look after Audrey. My answer is: yes. Yes! I'll protect her. Please! Help me save her."

He examined her a long moment. Then, wordlessly, he set down the gun and stood, lifting the sleeping Audrey in his arms. Her head lolled against his shoulder, eyes fluttering open. He kissed her cheek and murmured something in her ear, then strode from the room.

Nikki followed Lake through the door. Behind them, glass shattered, heat surged. They ran blindly down a smoke-choked passageway, the rumble and heat chasing them.

At the end of the corridor, they reached a hatch.

Lake set Audrey down on her feet. She wobbled unsteadily and reached for him. He kissed her, then handed her off to Nikki, who clutched the somnolent child beneath the arms.

Jayston opened the door.

They were met with the thunderous roar of the fire raging above, and the crash of waves.

They emerged onto a small deck, and a railing overlooking the sea below. A blast of wind in their faces, as the heat and flames sucked in the oxygen.

"Go!" he shouted.

Nikki lunged forward, propping Audrey up. She felt Jayston's hands helping them up and over the rail, before the heat and rush of an explosion burst out the way they'd come.

THIRTY-THREE

"You should really eat some vegetables," Penelope said, looking disapprovingly at the steamed broccoli Valerio had left behind on his plate. "You need vitamins if you want to recover properly."

"He's saving them for later," Gemma said with an impish grin. She smoothed down the blanket, tucking the edges around him. "Aren't you, Babbo?"

She'd scooted her chair close to where he lay on the sofa, and kept reaching out a hand to touch his shoulder, as if checking that he was still there.

"Your broccoli is disgusting, Penny," Orlanda contributed. "You'll never convert Valerio to eating plants if you feed him those."

Leonora plucked the drooping vegetable between her fingers. "We aren't rabbits. It needs butter and cheese."

Penny frowned, looking disappointed. She'd created the menu from her new diet, a decision that was not generally appreciated.

Everyone was eating dinner in the living room of his mother's apartment—plates balanced on their knees—in order to be with him. Valerio was stretched across the sagging brown sofa, swathed in bandages and ministered to by his sisters, mother, and daughter. Two of Penny's boys had come along, too, but they weren't the ministering type. They, along with Davide, tromped in and out of the apartment at random intervals, door banging behind them, letting in the chill December air.

The mood was good—almost festive, tiny lights on the Christmas tree reflecting back in their eyes. Even Giorgia, when she'd stopped by for a few minutes, behaved herself.

It had been more than a week since Nikki and Federico had dragged him out of Errichiello's compound. Days that passed alternately in moments of forgetfulness and discomfort due to multiple surgeries and the pills he took several times each day for the distracting pain.

Valerio was trying to wean himself off the pain medicines. They made him slow. They also induced a sense of timelessness and restless dreams, which felt too similar to the hours he'd spent in the dark and stinking prison.

He was still terrified of losing consciousness. He slept with the light on so that, in the disorienting moments after waking, he could rapidly identify where he was. Yet some part of him felt as though he'd never really escaped, that this return to normalcy was the illusion.

After his discharge from the hospital two days ago, Valerio had wanted to recover in his own apartment, but was overruled by everyone—with their clamor of reasons why this was a bad idea.

"You're crazy," Maurizio told him, joining his voice with Leonora's and his sisters'. "How are you going to get out of bed to piss?"

They'd brought him to his mother's apartment, and Leonora had insisted that he use her bedroom, while she slept on one of the bunks usually reserved for the kids. When he protested, she tutted and scolded and refused to hear any argument.

The duvet on his mother's bed was unfamiliar—a cheap IKEA cotton in blue and white that she'd no doubt gotten on discount. But the rest of the room was as it had always been: the place where, as a child, he'd come for comfort after nightmares. It smelled of baby powder and lilac perfume.

Across from the bed was his mother's dressing table, with framed pictures of her children and grandchildren. On the wall above, a crucifix, an icon of the haloed Immacolata in a blue robe, and, in an ornate gold frame, a photograph of Costanzo. Leonora used to tell Valerio how much he looked like his father. But the Costanzo in the faded photograph with the thickly knotted tie and oversize lapels was so young and hopeful—nothing like the weary man Valerio saw in the mirror.

Dinner was wrapping up when Davide slammed the front door open and announced, "Nikki's here!"

"Clear out," Orlanda shouted to everyone. "Let's give them some privacy. Who wants dessert?"

Then she reached over and, squeezing Valerio's toe, smiled.

Leonora greeted Nikki first, with tight embraces and kissing both cheeks. Then she kissed Nikki's hands.

"The angel who saved my son. Bless you, bella. Bless you! I will pray for you every day until my death, and in the afterworld will continue to pray for your soul. May the Virgin watch over you always and minister to you."

Penny, in tears, stepped in next.

Nikki, who Valerio knew didn't like to be touched, endured this with good grace. Only Orlanda seemed to sense Nikki's discomfort and avoided the ritual.

As everyone else filtered from the room, Sonia joined Nikki.

"Good to see you," Valerio said.

In the hospital, he'd felt irrationally comforted whenever he woke and found Nikki there.

Sonia's presence was less comforting. She and the other team members had been at the hospital for several interviews. They were still exhuming bodies from the mass graves on Errichiello's property.

"You're looking better," said Sonia.

"You're a good liar," he replied.

Surgeons had repaired the cheekbone, and the swelling and bruising were beginning to subside, but his face was still misshapen and painful.

"Well," Nikki said with a crooked smile, "just don't enter any beauty contests for a while."

"How was Federico's funeral?" he asked.

This small service was three days ago. The doctors stopped Valerio from attending. But he thought about the old man every day. Federico had wanted out. He'd fought his addiction and his own demons to escape that dark world. And he'd managed it, too, carving a clean life for himself. Then he'd traded all his success, the years of hard work, gone back into hell, to pull Valerio out.

Nikki had told Valerio every detail. And he'd made her tell him again. And again. He would ask again when his mind was clear, and commit Federico's bravery to memory.

"It was good," said Sonia. "Some of his neighbors were there, and your guys from the Falchi squad. They know what he did—that he was a hero."

Did they? How could they possibly understand?

Valerio seemed to smell the cigarette and coffee of the old man's breath, the eyes huge behind those glasses, as Federico smacked his face, shouting at him to stay awake. He felt Federico and Nikki dragging him, their bodies straining to heave him free of the pit. In a final act of trust, Federico had shown him the gun in his waistband.

Perhaps Federico could have killed his brother, but he'd allowed Valerio that privilege.

Valerio came suddenly to himself, to the warm lights of his mother's living room, to Sonia and Nikki looking at him with expressions of concern.

"How's the investigation?" he asked.

"We've identified nine victims so far," said Sonia. "But we're still trying to ID the remains of another seventy-three. This goes back decades. We're examining every missing-person case, trying to match up—but we're not having a lot of success. Of course, Errichiello had refugees from Africa and the Middle East, so we may need to broaden our search. The problem is, we don't know where to start. By all accounts, Luca Errichiello kept good records—but everything went up in smoke."

"Maybe Silvestri or Ines Mancusi has copies," Valerio suggested.

"You haven't heard?" Nikki asked, glancing at Sonia.

"Both of them are dead," Sonia said.

"Silvestri's death was on the news," said Nikki. "His manager found him hanging in the bedroom of his villa in Sorrento."

This should have been a relief, but Valerio felt hollow. He'd sent the cops to Silvestri's place to rescue the girl there. They'd never found her. With Silvestri dead, there was no chance now. Guilt and shame fused to Valerio's bones.

"How?" he asked.

"It looks like suicide," said Sonia. "But that just feels too tidy for me."

"And Ines?" he asked.

"Also apparent suicide. Again, no records."

"Fuck," said Valerio.

"Claire Sexton copied some files that link to Errichiello," said Nikki.

Sonia nodded. "They're incomplete, but they've given us good leads."

Valerio was surprised.

"Jayston Lake was involved with Luca?" he asked.

Nikki nodded. "Lake laundered money for Errichiello and was also a beneficiary of Silvestri and Errichiello's real business: blackmail. They generated a portfolio of corrupt politicians, cops, magistrates . . . every one of them with an incentive to do favors . . . to shut down investigations."

Luca had meant to use Valerio in the same way, but Valerio hadn't guessed that he was merely another cog in the enormous blackmail machine.

"That's why Lake killed her," Valerio said.

"She hadn't realized Lake was involved," Sonia said. "She'd found blackmail on Henry Antonov's computer—the ship's captain. She wanted Lake to take the files to the police. When he refused, she ran away."

"Why didn't she go to the police directly?" Valerio asked.

"Her brother had put her up to it," Nikki explained. "Teddy Sexton and his friend, Kevin Walker, wanted Lake to invest in their business—they were using Claire to find information to pressure him. They didn't understand the extent of what she'd uncovered about Lake and

Antonov. Teddy convinced her to wait. That was why Kevin Walker came to Naples. He was supposed to meet Claire in Chiesa del Gesù Nuovo—to talk to Lake with her. But he was late, and Claire met Lake on her own."

"Lake met her to retrieve the data," Valerio said.

Nikki nodded. "But Jayston didn't realize that Claire wasn't carrying the information with her. She'd stashed it before their meeting."

"Did you recover it?"

"Signora Dorotea had it," Nikki said. "She'd taken Claire's bag after Claire went into the cathedral. She stored Claire's thumb drive and Fiona Lake's jewelry in a votive shrine near Montesanto—where she kept her treasures. Lake didn't find it when he tracked her down and killed her. It wasn't with the bag."

"The electronics had some water damage," said Sonia. "But Claire made a backup—on her brother's encrypted MindCapsule service. Teddy Sexton is cooperating with police, so we've been able to get the files. They expose twelve corrupt cops and regulators and magistrates in Italy and the UK who aided Lake in his business. Arrest warrants were issued this morning."

Valerio rubbed a hand gently across his bruised face.

"Twelve? That's all?" He hesitated. "I mean, it's a lot—but it must be only a fraction of Errichiello's business."

"Antonov must have been given only the files he needed," Sonia said. "There are more out there . . . hundreds, maybe even thousands."

Valerio considered this. Luca had been operating for decades, building a formidable network of favors and blackmail. But if he wasn't the man in charge, Luca's death didn't stop the blackmail. The corruption in the police and with the politicians and judges would continue as invisibly as before.

The shepherd was still out there, still pushing the buttons.

Valerio didn't want to talk about it with any of his colleagues until he knew whom to trust.

"We have enough to keep us busy for years," Sonia said. "It will be good to have you back to help, Valerio."

He was getting tired, the pain worsening, but he didn't want Nikki or Sonia to leave just yet. And he had one more question.

"Have you found Ravenna's mother? Family?" he asked.

"She had a lot of friends," said Sonia. "But we can't find any family."

He didn't want to think about Ravenna. She seemed close—a breath away—her death prying open a desperation and violent ache that he didn't understand. He hadn't known her. Not really. Only for a few days. But there was a sense of knowing, of intimacy, that went deeper than he had any right to claim. She'd passed into his heart so effortlessly, building a home inside him. He hadn't even understood she was there until that bright light flickered out, leaving him in darkness.

He'd drifted again, Valerio realized, coming painfully back into the moment, Nikki and Sonia looking at him.

"We should let you rest," said Sonia.

They stood.

"Let's go sailing," said Nikki. "When you're feeling up to it again. *Calypso*'s waiting—ready when you are."

The thought seemed to comfort him.

"Yeah," he told her. "Sounds good. I need the break. Besides, I owe you a beer."

He tried to stay awake, but he was asleep before they left the room.

Orlanda woke Valerio when it was time for her to go, so she could help him get ready for bed.

Coming into the bedroom, he saw a brown cardboard box on the bed, wrapped in clear tape.

"What's that?" he asked.

"A courier dropped it off a couple of hours ago. It's for you."

The return address was for a law firm in Rome: Damiani Studio Legale e Tributario.

The box, when he opened it, was full of papers and photos and an old computer hard drive.

There was a handwritten note on top.

Valerio,

If you have this, it means I'm dead.

I took these from Luca. Everything you need to make sure he's in prison forever.

You're the only one I could think to give these to. The only cop I could ever trust. A good man.

Federico

THIRTY-FOUR

The sun was low in the sky, shadows lengthening, temperature dropping as Nikki entered Naples. It had been another long day of negotiations, but she'd managed to get her bike back from the police impound yard in Caserta. The police had seized it, along with everything else associated with the massacre at the Errichiello compound, and it had taken nearly a week to get the paperwork and approval to retrieve it.

Raoul had taken her to Caserta, a drive that was notable for its silence. Her father's recent bout of enthusiasm had subsided when he visited her in the hospital where she was treated for smoke inhalation. This shift towards melancholy made Nikki uncomfortable because it reminded her of the way he'd been after the death of Beatrice.

Outside the city, stopping for fuel, he cleaned the windscreen, then took a half-filled carton of cigarettes from the glove box and threw it in the trash.

"Nasty habit," he said.

"Massimo says you're heading back home tomorrow," Nikki said. "Does that mean the investigation is finished?"

"Sì."

"I'm sorry," she said.

He shrugged.

"There was no grand conspiracy," he said. "No hidden messages. Just the fantasies of a foolish old man who thought he could be important again."

He paused before starting the engine, and looked at her.

"I don't see the right things, bella," he said. "I never have. Even when they're clear . . . and precious. And right in front of me."

Gently, tenderly, he took her hand, and kissed it.

Little was said after that.

Nikki felt relieved when they reached the impound lot and could say goodbye.

The week after Valerio's rescue and the sinking of *The Prophet* was among the most difficult of Nikki's life. She spent most of her days at the hospital with Valerio, or at the police station, where her description of the battle at Errichiello's compound was the only eyewitness testimony. She believed in cooperating with the police, but it hadn't felt safe to tell what she knew—so she kept most of the details to herself, building high brick walls around them.

Sealed inside, the memories were like an explosive. Menacing. Volatile.

The routine of everyday life was disconcerting—as if she'd drifted into a dream while the nightmare events were still happening. She heard the shouts and screams of men struck down, smelled the gunpowder and smoke, and the horrendous stink of the small concrete prison where they'd kept Valerio. Her heart still juddered and raced, terror lodged in her muscles and mind. That horror was not her world. She'd brushed against it in the past, but before now she'd only ever been on the periphery of the war.

The day after she was released from the hospital, Vincente Di Pavola sent his lawyer to her house with the nondisclosure agreement, instructing her to never discuss her relationship with Enzo. As if it had never happened. She signed her name, feeling numb—a sense of walls erected, gates locking.

She hadn't returned to Phoenix Seven, but yesterday, Pasquale had called, asking after her.

"Angelo took down the posting for your job," he told her. "I think he's getting pressure from the Americans to bring you back. It's becoming an embarrassment that he fired you."

Nikki had seen the news footage of Kami and Monica released from jail, and the press conference with Ambassador Lissom, Angelo hovering in the corner of the screen.

She didn't want to return and work for Angelo. The relationship had run its course. Angelo needed her to be different than she was, and she couldn't maintain that dissonance any longer. She wasn't sure what to do next, and she needed money. But she simply didn't have the energy to maintain the facade.

At the gate to her building, Nikki stopped to grab the mail. She tromped up the stairs and through the door to her apartment. It smelled of disinfectant still—an aftermath of the stay by Valerio's mother and sister: the floors, kitchen, and bathroom scrubbed, the jumble of shoes by the door straightened, scattered papers and boxes arranged into neat stacks.

Her phone rang.

"Darling, you lied to me!" Ethan scolded when she answered. "You promised I would be the first to hear about Jayston Lake—and now I find out about this on the news?"

"I'm sorry," Nikki said.

"How are you doing, my dear?" he asked, voice softening. "What happened to that little girl?"

"She's back in England, with her mother," Nikki said.

Saying goodbye to Audrey had been unexpectedly difficult: the girl clinging to her and crying. Nikki had felt frozen and awkward, but something inside wanted to howl along with her.

Nikki took off her shoes and crossed to the living room, setting to work arranging and sorting everything back into boxes. She stacked these in the corner, and was pushing her sofa back where it belonged, when the leg caught on something.

She tugged it away from the wall, and saw that a large floor tile had come loose. It was tilted up. Wobbling. She crouched and moved it back and forth, shifting it back into place—when the edge caught, tipping suddenly into a hollow space beneath.

Surprised, Nikki gripped the tile with both hands and lifted it back.

There was a cavity in the floor. Nikki shone a light inside and saw that it was about thirty centimeters wide and sixty centimeters deep. It seemed empty at first—but there was something at the bottom.

She reached inside, and her fingers closed on the rough skin of a hardbound book.

It was a practical, rather than ornamental, edition—covered in faded green fabric, the only nod to artistry an embossed signature on the front cover. Black horizontal stripes on the spine provided perfunctory decoration, and a title in Cyrillic: Братья Карамазовы.

Nikki stopped breathing. The translation app confirmed what she'd already somehow guessed: *The Brothers Karamazov*, by Fyodor Dostoevsky. Publication year 1957.

The pages were yellowed and stiff, although clearly once well loved—penciled notes in the margins. It smelled of dust and old ink.

The book fell open to a postcard serving as a bookmark: sent to Beatrice at this address. There was no return address, but the stamp indicated it had been posted from Russia on 22 November 2006.

Nikki stared for a long time at those numbers, mind suddenly thrumming. She knew that date. It was seared into her, a brand that still burned when she brushed across it: the day Adriano had been shot and bled out in her arms.

The words written on the postcard in a neat, elegant script were the same as those underlined in the book: *Я думаю, что если дьявол не существует и, стало быть, создал его человек, то создал он его по своему образу и подобию.*

Nikki knew what she would see before the translation finished, hearing the words in her mother's voice: "'If the devil doesn't exist, but man has created him, he has created him in his own image and likeness!'"

Trembling, heart racing, she returned to the inside cover of the book. Two sets of notes—each with different handwriting.

The first, in faded ink: *For my beloved Beatrice. Love always, Mot'ka.*

Below this, the careful, clear handwriting of Beatrice Serafino. Three words:

Diogenes

Damascus

Zosima

ACKNOWLEDGMENTS

Bringing a second book into the world is both a continuation and a reimagining, and I'm deeply grateful to those who made this one possible.

To my extraordinary editor, Laura Tisdel. Thank you for your patience, clarity, and unwavering belief in the arc of this series. Your insights continue to shape and sharpen the story at every stage.

To my brilliant agent, Sharon Pelletier. Thank you for your fierce advocacy, your trust in my voice, and your generosity as this book found its rhythm.

Heartfelt thanks to the team at Penguin, especially Julia Rickard, Matie Argiropoulos, Carlos Zayas-Pons, David Litman, and Alicia Cooper, for your dedicated work and thoughtful care. To the production staff, thank you for your precision.

To Simon Vance. Thank you for your extraordinary narration of *May the Wolf Die*. Your performance gave the characters and story new dimensions. As I revised this book, I often imagined your voice speaking the words, and so shaped the prose with that cadence in mind.

To my parents, Will and Mary. Thank you for creating the space and care I needed to finish this manuscript. For the eggs, the coffee, the obsessive mornings on the back deck, and your patient forbearance of my unwashed mutterings and ramblings, I am endlessly grateful. But even more, thank you for loving this story. Your enthusiastic reading, your questions, and your joy met me at a time when I was struggling to meet the book myself. Mom, your devotion as a reader and listener is unmatched. Undoubtedly, you know the details better than I do. Thank you both for your faith in this series and in me.

To Sara Spiga, whose support extends far beyond consultation. Thank you for championing this book at launch, for arranging research visits in Naples, and for continuing to share your insight and spirit so freely.

To Attilio Palladino, whose foundational contributions to the world of this series remain deeply felt.

To Loftin Harvey. Thank you for handing me *The Brothers Karamazov* and showing me how deeply a book could reach. You were my first creative writing teacher, and your faith in my voice all those years ago helped lay the foundation for this one. It is an honor to dedicate this book to you.

To Floriaan van Prooijen. Thank you for your loving care and steady support throughout the writing of this book.

Deep thanks to Eve and Tim McAnallen for opening your home to me in Pozzuoli during a crucial phase of research and rewrites, and for your thoughtful, generous feedback as early readers. Your hospitality and care made more of a difference than I can say. Eve, thanks for the wonderful research trip to the UK and for letting me pick your brain about CTIs and the role of the JAG.

To Christine Hughes, whose reading of my work has been a rare and generous gift. Your unwavering honesty and deep sensitivity to language have helped bring clarity and depth to my work again and again. Thank you also for the research trip in London, which helped enormously.

Thanks to Jenny Jones, who delved into my questions about diplomatic immunity, and John Riemen, who shared his policing expertise.

To my circle of early readers. Thank you for your time, insight, and honesty: Stacey Jenson, Kelly Russ, Kirsten MacDonald, Emily Heider, Amy Heider, Melissa Heider, Amanda Finlayson, Sarah Dachos, Gustavo de la Fuente, and Ruthann Povinelli. Your attention and feedback helped shape the final form of this story.

To the American Book Center in Amsterdam. Thank you for hosting the launch of *May the Wolf Die* with such grace and generosity. To Hannah Huber. Thank you for your thoughtful and spirited interview.

To all the bookstores who welcomed me on tour. Your enthusiasm and warmth meant the world.

Doug and Lyssa High, thank you for your friendship, and for opening your home and inviting me onto your news program at ABC 36.

Thank you also to Olly Clark, Teresa Brock, Tom Williams, Ken Jones, Melisa Poulos, Janna Said, Thomas Braden, and Kirsty McLean, and all the readers, reviewers, reporters, radio hosts, and influencers who advocated for the first book. Your support helped carry it further than I could have imagined. With thanks to Michael R. Katz, whose 2023 translation of *The Brothers Karamazov* was a joy to read while writing this book. Thanks also to Marco Mengoni and Paolo Buonvino, whose music kept me company.

To my film agents, Ali Lefkowitz and Ryan Wilson. Thank you for championing this story in new forms and new mediums.

To Benjamin, who read the first book with such joy and curiosity. Thank you for reminding me why stories matter.

And to Natty, who wanted to read it, too. Your excitement is its own kind of magic. Soon, my love.

To the brilliant research team at Microsoft AI4Science. Thank you for welcoming me with such generosity and for celebrating every milestone along the way. It was a privilege to serve as your PM. I am grateful to have walked alongside such minds and hearts: Paris Perdikaris, Johannes Brandstetter, Richard Turner, Max Welling, Cristian Bodnar, Megan Stanley, Ana Lucic, Wessel Bruinsma, Patrick Garvan, and Maik Riechert.

Much of this book was shaped during a season of deep grief. I want to acknowledge with love the memory of Paul Mosteller, Peter Perla, and Gerry Cope, whose wisdom and kind friendship left lasting imprints. And Luca The—a brilliant, beautiful soul who left far too soon. The world is darker with you gone, but I count myself lucky to have known your light. This book carries traces of everything that was lost, and memories I hold close.

To everyone named here, thank you for helping me carry this book forward, through light and shadow.

ALSO AVAILABLE

May the Wolf Die

A Novel

In Naples, loyalty and survival are never clean. Nikki Serafino–disciplined and detached–has built her life on vigilant self-reliance. But when a body is found in the bay, she's dragged into a violent conspiracy spanning the US Navy, Italian police, and Naples's criminal underworld. As institutions fracture and allies betray her, Nikki learns that control is no shield against grief, corruption, or love. To survive, she must choose: Resist the wolves–or join them.